Praise for the Novels of Cindy Miles

MacGowan's Ghost

"Miles's latest paranormal gem is utterly charming. Her wonderful stories are the perfect antidote to everyday stress." —*Romantic Times*

Highland Knight

"Cindy Miles completely captivated me with *Highland Knight*. . . . I was glued to the story line and loved how the characters interacted with each other . . . downright sexy."
—Romance Junkies

"When it comes to delivering charming, funny, and tender romances, Miles is at the head of the class. Not only are the primary characters wonderful, the secondary characters are engaging and bring depth to the story. This warmhearted book is guaranteed to leave you with a satisfied smile!" —*Romantic Times* (top pick, 4½ stars)

"This is a book to fall in love with and to read over and over. Cindy Miles has written a surefire winner for . . . fans of Scottish heroes."
—*Affaire de Coeur* (reviewer's pick, 5 stars)

"Spunky Abigail and typically gruff but warmhearted Ethan (and his rough and tumble kin) are sweetly entertaining." —*Publishers Weekly*

continued . . .

"An enjoyable ride, start to finish."—*The Romance Reader*

Into Thin Air

"Another sweet paranormal featuring a sparkling lead couple and a supporting cast of ghostly charmers . . . this adorable, otherworldly romp is sure to leave readers feeling warm and fuzzy."
　　　　　　　　　　　　　　　　　—*Publishers Weekly*

"Filled with humor, romance, mystery, and a lot of ghosts, *Into Thin Air* is a book that is hard to put down."
　　　　　　　　　　　　　　　　　—Romance Junkies

Spirited Away

"Absolutely delightful! Cindy Miles outshines the genre's best, writing with charm and verve sure to captivate readers' hearts. *Spirited Away* is pure magic."
　　—*USA Today* bestselling author Sue-Ellen Welfonder

"A sparkling debut, reminiscent of favorites like *The Ghost and Mrs. Muir.*"
　　　　　—*USA Today* bestselling author Julie Kenner

Also by Cindy Miles

MacGowan's Ghost
Highland Knight
Into Thin Air
Spirited Away

Thirteen Chances

CINDY MILES

A SIGNET ECLIPSE BOOK

SIGNET ECLIPSE
Published by New American Library, a division of
Penguin Group (USA) Inc., 375 Hudson Street,
New York, New York 10014, USA
Penguin Group (Canada), 90 Eglinton Avenue East, Suite 700, Toronto,
Ontario M4P 2Y3, Canada (a division of Pearson Penguin Canada Inc.)
Penguin Books Ltd., 80 Strand, London WC2R 0RL, England
Penguin Ireland, 25 St. Stephen's Green, Dublin 2,
Ireland (a division of Penguin Books Ltd.)
Penguin Group (Australia), 250 Camberwell Road, Camberwell, Victoria 3124,
Australia (a division of Pearson Australia Group Pty. Ltd.)
Penguin Books India Pvt. Ltd., 11 Community Centre, Panchsheel Park,
New Delhi - 110 017, India
Penguin Group (NZ), 67 Apollo Drive, Rosedale, North Shore 0632,
New Zealand (a division of Pearson New Zealand Ltd.)
Penguin Books (South Africa) (Pty.) Ltd., 24 Sturdee Avenue,
Rosebank, Johannesburg 2196, South Africa

Penguin Books Ltd., Registered Offices:
80 Strand, London WC2R 0RL, England

First published by Signet Eclipse, an imprint of New American Library,
a division of Penguin Group (USA) Inc.

First Printing, September 2009
10 9 8 7 6 5 4 3 2 1

PUBLISHER'S NOTE
This is a work of fiction. Names, characters, places, and incidents either are the
product of the author's imagination or are used fictitiously, and any resemblance to
actual persons, living or dead, business establishments, events, or locales is entirely
coincidental.

The publisher does not have any control over and does not assume any responsibil-
ity for author or third-party Web sites or their content.

For my son Kyle,
whose modern-day chivalry makes me proud
and gives me inspiration—especially for a particular
young knight named Jason. I love you.

Dear Readers:

While all of my novels can stand alone, they're ultimately all linked by a common denominator: characters—mostly, characters from the past. Somewhere, somehow, and at some point, they've all bumped into one another during their ghostly journeys. Tristan de Barre (from *Spirited Away*) and Gawan of Conwyk (from *Into Thin Air*) have known each other for centuries—since before any curses deemed anyone a wandering spirit or an earthbound angel. The Munros (from *Highland Knight*) met Gabe MacGowan (from *MacGowan's Ghost*, and the only modern hero so far!) *after* the medieval Highland lot had been relieved of their centuries-old enchantment. In *Thirteen Chances*, you'll find Christian de Gaultiers of Arrick-by-the-Sea is the hero who brings them all together. His lifelong friendship with Gawan of Conwyk introduced him centuries before to the Dreadmoor lot, and Christian's friendship with a certain secondary character, Captain Justin Catesby, has brought them all together from *MacGowan's Ghost*. Here, in *Thirteen Chances*, they'll all have a chance to get to know one another, thus linking all of the books to date. I had so much fun bringing the entire cast of main and a few favorite secondary characters together. It's like bumping into an old friend you really hated saying good-bye to once before.

I hope you enjoy!

Cindy

Prologue

Northwestern Wales
The White Witches' Souls for Eternity Convention
All Hallows' Eve, 1865
Somewhere in the dead of night . . .

"All right, ladies, open your scrolls!"

Willoughby's fingers tightened on the parchment, and she glanced up at the headmistress, Mordova, who impatiently awaited the opening of the Souls' Scrolls. A breeze wafted through the copse of trees, and dead leaves flitted to the ground. Somewhere close by, a field of dried corn crackled as the brisk autumn wind slipped between the stalks. Above, a harvest moon, large, full, and bright, shone through the canopy of birch and oak, bathing everything it touched in glowing silver. Several bonfires flickered with orange flame.

"Willoughby!"

Willoughby jumped, startled, then glared at her sister. "Don't do that, Millicent."

"Well, then open the bloody scroll!" another sister, Agatha, said under her breath. "I'm dying to see our assignment!"

Four Ballaster sisters gathered round and leaned their heads close together as Willoughby, the eldest, slowly unrolled the scroll.

Four Ballaster sisters drew in sharp breaths.

The gathering of White Witches ceased looking at their own scrolls and turned to stare at Willoughby.

"It's *them*!" squealed Millicent, the third Ballaster sister, pointing at the scroll. "Oh, Willoughby! Do you know what this *means*?" She clapped her hands in excitement.

"Yes, Willoughby Ballaster," said Mordova, who'd come to stand before them. "*Do* you know what this means?"

Willoughby looked up, and before she could say a word, the headmistress continued.

"It means you and your sisters have the most difficult of assignments." She turned, her long, silvery hair gleaming in the moonlight, and addressed the rest of the witches. "For those of you new to the convention this year, Christian's and Emma's souls have longed to be together for centuries, and for centuries they've been denied"—she waved an elegant hand—"all because they inadvertently *cursed* themselves." She *tsk*ed and shook her head. "Poor Christian of Arrick-by-the-Sea. A gallant and fierce Crusader, he vowed in the throes of death that he would forever await his Intended's love. And faithful to his vow, he is here, earthbound, yet a spirit, in truth." She clasped her hands together and paced. "And Emma, upon Christian's departure for the Crusades, performed an ancient incantation the poor lamb had no business performing." She stopped and shook her head again. "Mortals. Always convinced they have the control to conjure magic."

Willoughby and the other Ballaster sisters stared on with the rest of the conventiongoers. Headmistress Mordova faced first the crowd, then the Ballasters—seeming to focus in particular on Willoughby.

"In an attempt to keep her true love safe in battle, Emma concocted a Welsh spell using an aged, outdated book of incantations. Sadly, she didn't pronounce the verse correctly and, for lack of a better word, it backfired."

"What happened?" said a quiet voice in the crowd.

Mordova gave a winsome smile, and firelight cast her face in shadows. "Every seventy-two years, Emma's reincarnated soul returns to Arrick-by-the-Sea. Drawn like a moth to light, she is—only she doesn't know why. Nor does she recognize her true love."

A resounding sigh echoed through the moonlit night.

Mordova continued. "Patiently, Christian awaits his true love, his Intended, his eternal soul mate. Eleven times thus far he has made Emma fall in love with him anew." The headmistress heaved a gusty breath. "And due to that discombobulated scrap of magic, something inevitably happens and Emma dies, only to be reborn, her soul forgetting everything. Meanwhile, poor Christian's heart is severely broken each time, and I fear 'tis nigh unto being irreparable if this continues much longer."

Silence filled the night air.

Willoughby met the gazes of her sisters, gave a nod, then cleared her tightened throat. "Headmistress, we, the Ballasters, proudly accept this assignment." She looked out over the expectant faces of the coven and raised her voice. "We'll see that Christian and Emma are reunited once and for bloody all!"

A thunder of clapping sounded through the wood, accompanied by laughter and whoops and whistles. Many of the other witches walked up to Willoughby and the other Ballaster sisters to offer wishes of good luck— and a few homespun spells if needed. When the crowd thinned, Mordova stood before the Ballasters, staring.

Willoughby lifted her chin. "Can the council not help?"

The headmistress shook her head. "We are administration. We oversee, but do not give aid."

Willoughby sighed. "Figures."

"I know you girls have pure hearts and good intentions," Mordova said, her amber eyes shiny in the firelight. "I say this not to intimidate, but to encourage. Take heed; I beg you. Not one of your predecessors has succeeded in reuniting Christian's and Emma's souls, and they with many more centuries of experience at spell-making than you young Ballasters. The undoing and redoing of such a discombobulated incantation is precarious at best. 'Twill not be an easy task, and can be rather heartbreaking—as well as dangerous. I warn you: beware of the magic you use. Be absolutely sure of each and every word chosen, in any spells you conduct. For one misspoken word could mean the end of their chances. *Forever*."

Northwestern Wales, 1937
Castle of Arrick-by-the-Sea
Once again in the dead of night . . .

"We simply weren't prepared!" Agatha cried. "Whatever did we do wrong?"

"Another chance gone!" said Millicent, fretting her hands. "Oh dear, Willoughby, what shall we do now?"

"Perhaps we should contact the headmistress?" said Maven.

Agatha snorted. "She cannot help, Sister. Remember? She's *administration*."

Willoughby rubbed her chin with an index finger and looked out at the castle ruins. Through the moonlit night, she saw Christian walking the battlements. He'd just lost Emma for the twelfth time.

Willoughby could feel his pain from where she stood.

Something needed to be done once and for all.

She thought hard, and paced.

"Just look at him, poor dove," whispered Maven. "I cannot bear to see his anguish again. We must do something!"

"Indeed—Willoughby, where did we go wrong?" said Agatha. "Our spell was perfectly orchestrated. We planned it for seventy-two years!"

"Aye, and we should be thankful there's no retribution from it." Willoughby shook her head. "We're approaching this whole thing a bit too timidly, I think, especially when working with as discombobulated an incantation as Emma's. And conjuring from afar simply won't do," said Willoughby. "We need to be closer, for one. More aggressive. None of this peering from behind the tree line and conjuring spells from the wood business." She nodded to herself. "We shall become the new owners of the manor house near the castle. 'Tis for sale and we've the funds to purchase and restore it." She met each sister's puzzled look. "I know what else needs to be done, but 'tis risky."

Maven lifted a brow. "How risky?"

Willoughby stroked her chin. "The riskiest."

The three other Ballasters gasped.

"You don't mean the—," started Millicent.

"*Whsst!*" Willoughby placed two fingers over her lips. "'Tis the dodgiest of incantations and mustn't ever be spoken aloud." She cast a stern look to the others. "You know the one I mean, aye?"

"Aye," the others said together in a hushed whisper.

"I'm uncertain and not at all comfortable about it, Willoughby. No one has ever, in the history of the White Witches, succeeded. Using this spell will mean Christian and Emma's very last chance," said Maven. "Their eternal love relies on this one scrap of magic. If it fails—if *we* fail—'tis over."

"Forever," whispered Agatha.

Willoughby again glanced out at the ruins and watched the silhouette of the fierce Crusader as he paced the battlements. He stopped, turned, and stared out toward the sea.

"Well then," Willoughby said with determination, and met her sisters' eyes. "We mustn't fail, aye? We'll waste not another second. Time's of the essence, girls. Thirteen is a lucky number, and we've seventy-two years left to conjure the chanciest of charms!" She inhaled with gusto and puffed it out slowly. Under her breath, she said on a sigh, "By Morticia's wand, let's not screw this up."

Chapter 1

Savannah, Georgia
Forevermore Photography
September, present day
Sometime late in the afternoon . . .

"Emma, these are absolutely amazing. I can't wait for you to do my wedding."

Perched on the brick window ledge that looked out over River Street and the Savannah River, Emma Calhoun smiled at Zoë Canady—soon to be Zoë Zanderfly—as she looked through the McAdams' portfolio. The girls had been friends since college, and Emma had promised to shoot her wedding in December. "Is Jay still threatening to have his groomsmen all wear Curly, Larry, and Moe T-shirts beneath their tuxes?"

Zoë laughed, and Emma saw that *glow*—the one that lights up a bride-to-be's face like the aurora borealis. It really was something of a phenomenon, in Emma's opinion.

She wondered briefly what it felt like.

"Of course," Zoë said. "And I told him my maids and I would all be wearing football cleats beneath our dresses."

"And that you'd kick him with one," Emma added.

"Or that I'd wear them on our wedding night." They both laughed.

Late-afternoon sun beamed in through the window, bathing the two-hundred-year-old brick-walled studio in straw-colored light and gray shadows. "Well," Emma said, pushing off the sill and tidying up her work space. She glanced at her watch. "You'd better go or you'll be late for your dinner date with your future hubby."

"Yeah, you're right, but I've got a few extra minutes," Zoë said. She sat down at Emma's desk, idly tapped the mouse, and the computer screen came to life. "Wow."

Emma set a tripod against the wall and walked to peer over Zoë's shoulder. The Arrick-by-the-Sea castle ruins she'd been looking at during lunch gave her chills all over again.

"Where is this?" Zoë asked.

Emma leaned a hip against the desk. "Wales."

"Do you know anyone in Wales?"

Staring at the stark gray stones of the castle, the crumbling wall surrounding it, and the sea beyond, Emma blinked and shook her head. "Not a soul."

Zoë turned in the chair, pushed a long strand of strawberry blond hair—which Emma had always secretly coveted—behind her ear, and raised her brow. "You've been dreaming again, haven't you?"

Emma sighed and rubbed her eyes. "If you want to call it that. I really don't *see* anything in my dreams." She looked at her friend. "I *feel* it."

"And then you obsess and stay up all night long for nights on end, surfing the Net until you find the *feeling*?" She pointed at her. "You've dark circles under your eyes, Emm. You look like a vamp. How long have you been dreaming this time?"

Emma glanced back at the computer screen, and the imposing walls of Arrick. "Months." She couldn't explain it—not at all. But somehow, when she'd finally come across the breathtaking photo of the twelfth-century fortress, she'd *known*.

What she'd known, exactly, she had no clue. But she knew she had to go there. *Needed* to go there.

"When are you leaving, and why haven't you told me before now?" Zoë said, frowning.

Emma looked at her friend and motioned at her with two fingers. "Put those mean eyebrows away, Zoë." She sighed. "I didn't want to burden you. You're in the throes of planning a wedding, silly. The last thing you need is a whiney pal."

Zoë placed a hand on Emma's shoulder. "You goofball. It's not a burden and you know it. You're my best friend. So much of a best friend that you're the only one I'd trust to photograph my wedding." The mean eyebrows returned, just briefly; then she smiled, her expression softening. Zoë cocked her head as she studied her. "You are a very weird woman, Emma Calhoun. You capture the most astounding pictures of people in love, and yet here you are, twenty-eight years old and still all alone. Good Lord, look at you." She pointed at her. "Porcelain skin, beautiful cinnamon hair—you've got *abs*, woman." Zoë lifted her shirt and poked her own softer belly. "I'd give anything for abs. Anyway, you're a gorgeous girl, and yet you'll go home tonight, order a pizza, and watch . . . let me see . . . *The Mummy*, followed by *The Mummy Returns*."

Emma shrugged. "I like mummies."

"No, you like the guy who kills the mummies."

Emma didn't dispute it. She peered at her friend. "Are you trying to make me feel better?"

Zoë smiled. "When do you leave for Wales? And while I'm being selfish, more important, will you be back in time to shoot my wedding?"

Emma walked to the window and glanced down at the tourists walking the cobblestones of River Street. A tugboat blasted its horn as it pulled away from the docks, and a tour group hunting Savannah's spirits ambled by.

Even with the window closed, the scent of freshly made pralines wafted up from the sweetshop below. When she turned back to Zoë, she noticed the tiny dust particles flittering like fairies in the waning light that streamed through the glass. It was all quite surreal, but not nearly as surreal as her dreams.

Something pulled her to Wales, and specifically to Arrick-by-the-Sea. It was weird, and yeah—Zoë was right. She *was* a weird woman, because the dreams plaguing her sleep each night had no real definition, no flashing neon sign that said HERE LIES YOUR DESTINY. And yet, after months of accumulated feelings of urgency to get to those crumbling twelfth-century ruins, Emma had booked a round-trip flight to Wales, made reservations at the charming manor house B and B located just up the way from the castle, and had taken the entire month of October off to travel across the Atlantic to satisfy whatever it was *inside her* that was all but driving her into lunacy.

"Well?" Zoë prodded, waving a hand. "Earth to Emma? Promise?"

With a gusty sigh, Emma grinned. "I leave in a week. And yes, of course I promise to be back to shoot your bridal shower, your rehearsal dinner, and your wedding." She made an X over her chest with her forefinger. "Cross my heart and hope to die."

Castle of Arrick-by-the-Sea
September, present day
Eveningish . . .

"Och, look at you, lad. A fierce wad of squirmin' nerves—that's what you are, walkin' back and forth, back and forth. You're all but makin' me head spin."

Christian of Arrick-by-the-Sea stopped and glanced

at his longtime friend. The older knight was a resident ghost at Castle Grimm, but he frequented Arrick. Christian had known him for centuries. "I can't help it, Godfrey." He shrugged, sighed, and glanced out across the shadowy sea. "I just . . . can't."

Sir Godfrey of Battersby scratched a place under his big, floppy hat. "Damn, boy, you should be used to this by now. 'Twill be the ninth time, aye?"

"Thirteenth."

Godfrey muttered under his breath.

The ebb and flow of the brisk Irish Sea against the base of Arrick did little to comfort Christian this particular eve. 'Twas the night before *she* was to arrive, and it had his stomach twisted in bloody knots. Emma *Calhoun* was her name this time. Strangely enough, 'twas always Emma. But her surname was always different—as was her appearance. What would she be like? Aye, her soul was the same, but characteristics often changed. Not all, but some. Her looks differed with each rebirth. 'Twas, in a way, like meeting someone for the verra first time all over again.

Except that he *knew* who she was.

And that he already loved her fiercely.

Christian ran a hand through his hair. 'Twas enough to make a man bloody daft.

"Pull your head out of your arse, lad, stop sulkin', and tell me your plan. Do you know much about her this time?" asked Godfrey. "What she looks like, that sort of thing?"

Christian glanced at Godfrey. "I think you enjoy this way too much, old man."

Godfrey stroked his chin. "I confess, 'tis most entertaining, even if it does occur only every seventy-two years." He chuckled. "I especially like when you show yourself to her for the very first time." He shook his head. "Huge sport, it is. Everyone's talkin' about it, you know. Even o'er at Grimm. Although I don't fancy the ending overmuch." He looked at Christian. "Think you this time will be different?"

Christian shrugged and blew out a hefty sigh. "I truly hope so." He glanced behind him, down the way toward the sisters' manor. "I think the old girls are up to something. They said this time will be of utmost import, and that I should take extreme care in my wooing."

"You always take extreme care in your wooing," said Godfrey. He glanced in the direction of the manor. "Passing odd, those old lasses."

Christian rubbed the back of his neck and stared out across the black water. Mayhap this time he wouldn't take such care in the bloody wooing. "Knowing how it will end nearly makes me want to not try at all," Christian said. And in truth, he'd given that a lot of thought. Mayhap the best thing would be to avoid her *completely* . . .

"You've lopped off many a heads in your day, lad. You're as lethal a warrior as they come. I've no doubt you can handle the meeting of your beloved again," said Godfrey. He smoothed the big plume poking out from the side of his hat. "When does the lass arrive?"

"Tomorrow."

A smile stretched across Godfrey's face. "We could go to the airport and take a wee look for ourselves?"

Christian shook his head. He'd confessed his situation to the Ballaster sisters years before, after he'd lost Emma the last time. "Willoughby has already asked that I remain here."

A loud, boisterous bellow erupted from Godfrey. "My God, boy." He shook his head. "My God, you indeed have it bad, aye? And I thought young Gawan's case was somethin' else." He shook his head. "Well, she didn't ask me to remain here. I shall leave first thing in the morn. Young Catesby said he'd go with me." He gave Christian a half-cocked smile. "I'm sure you'll be just fine here. Pacing. Scrubbing your neck and such. Worrying."

Christian grunted. Justin Catesby, another spirit—although one much more irritating—would no doubt soon join Godfrey in the sport of poking fun at Christian. Justin was a rogue and an arrogant pup. He'd also been, like Godfrey, a close friend for centuries.

"But until then," said Godfrey, "what say you to a game or two of Knucklebones?"

Christian thought about his days of warring. Spears, swords, arrows, blood—his hand tightly wrapped around the hilt of his blade. Familiar, sweaty, *manly* things. But when it came to his true love? Would he really have the strength to avoid her? *Christ, she'd be here on the morrow . . .*

Butterflies flapped mercilessly in his stomach, and his mouth went dry. He pushed his fingers through his hair.

Aye. He'd indeed turned into a spineless twit.

"Arrick! Knucklebones, boy!" hollered Battersby.

Christian took a deep breath and joined his old friend for an even older game that he really didn't feel much like playing at all. He blew out a sigh. Godfrey of Battersby laughed.

It'd be the longest bloody night of Christian's life.

The very next day . . .

Emma held her breath and dug her fingers deep into the old car's seat cushion, and her feet pushed heavily on imaginary brakes as the vehicle squeaked between an ancient stone wall and a big delivery truck. She couldn't stand it. She closed her eyes.

A giggle erupted from the driver.

Cracking open an eye, Emma peeked at the sweet old

thing driving. Millicent Ballaster, one of the owners of the manor house where she was booked. At least they'd offered her a ride. And the sweet old gal had nearly squeezed the life out of her with a fierce hug when she'd first met her at the luggage carriage. With a carefree grin plastered across her wrinkled cheeks, old Millie barely gripped the wheel with one hand.

"Open your eyes, girlie. No need to worry." She patted the car's dash with pride. "Quite reliable, this old heap."

It wasn't the old heap she was worried about. It was her *life*. Emma tightened her grip on the cushion and gave a slight laugh. "Oh, uh, I'm sure it is." *Oh my God! I'm not going to make it to Arrick-by-the-Sea in one piece!*

It was the longest two hours of her entire life.

Soon they turned off the single track road they'd been traveling on and onto an even narrower road. They made two corners, and then the *old heap* began to climb. Tall trees lined the path on either side, so it wasn't until the road leveled and the car stopped climbing that Arrick-by-the-Sea came into view.

Emma's breath hitched in her throat, and her heart slammed against her ribs.

"Quite the sight, eh love?" Millicent said.

The car had barely stopped when Emma opened the door and slowly climbed out. "Quite," she whispered.

Then she simply took in the view.

They'd parked in front of a lovely stone manor house, situated off to the right of the path leading to Arrick's castle ruins. Three stories high and the length of a football field, the manor was by no means a small estate. Bold red and pink geraniums overflowed stone containers on either side of the massive wooden double doors, and according to the Web site, it'd been built in the seventeenth century but had fallen into disrepair.

It was now lovingly renovated and absolutely beautiful. Behind the manor, a maze made of rowan bushes, at least as tall as Emma, sat in a big square. Millie had told her a big fountain sat in its center. She'd have to check that out later.

Emma's gaze then moved back to the narrow path that meandered up the sea cliff.

And to the castle ruins perched right at the edge.

Once again, her breath hitched.

Without really thinking, she began to walk in that direction. She'd made it only a few feet before the doors to the manor swung wide-open and three older women bustled out. They huddled around Millicent and simply stared at Emma. Finally one of the women, pleasantly plump with a sweet face and red hair, clapped her hands together and smiled.

"Welcome to the Ballaster House B and B! I'm Willoughby and, oh my! You are such a lovely thing! We are ever so happy to have you here!" she said. As one big huddle, the four women moved toward Emma, and Willoughby continued. "We are the Ballaster sisters. Millicent, you've met."

"And thankfully survived her atrocious driving," said the tall, willowy sister in the middle of the huddle. She grinned. "I'm Maven."

"And I am Agatha," said the shortest sister, wringing her hands and all but jumping up and down in place like a Jack Russell wanting to play fetch. "Indeed, we are so verra pleased you're here." That last sentence came out on a squeak.

Willoughby gave a wide smile. "We've been eager for your arrival, dear. Quite eager, indeed!"

Emma gave each sister a smile. "Thank you for such a wonderful welcome," she said, wondering just briefly why the heck they were so happy to see her. Perhaps business was slow this time of year?

Then Emma's gaze drifted back to the ruins. The weathered stone of the gatehouse stood stark against the gray-blue sea behind it. The cavernous mouth where a steely-toothed portcullis used to be housed yawned wide.

Emma paused. How did she know that?

"Och, there's plenty of time to explore yon fortress," said Willoughby. She moved to Emma and grasped her gently by the elbow, and tugged her to the back of the *old heap*. Emma lifted out her one suitcase and her camera equipment bag, slung it over her shoulder, and shut the trunk. Willoughby patted her arm. "Come, sweetling. Let's get you unpacked and settled in first. You must be exhausted from that dreadful plane ride. We've hot tea and cinnamon cakes ready for you."

Emma met the gazes of four expectant Ballasters. All four were as different as night and day, yet all four . . . similar. She decided right then that she liked them a lot. She smiled. "Yes, thank you. That sounds great." It did, too. She hoped she wouldn't make a pig of herself. She'd have to try to rein in her appetite. She shifted her load and allowed Willoughby to pull her toward the manor.

Just before she stepped over the threshold, Emma stopped and glanced over her shoulder, back at the ruins of Arrick. The brisk September breeze rolled off the Irish Sea and bit her cheeks, and she shivered.

As she watched, a figure stood rigid on the wall facing her, legs braced wide, arms folded.

At the same moment, the sun peeked from behind an ominous gray cloud and a bath of gold washed over the stone, across the grounds, and finally, right into Emma's eyes. She blinked, and squinted.

The figure on the wall was gone.

"Come, love," said Willoughby, giving her yet another tug. "Let me show you round the house."

After a few seconds more of blinking and squinting at the space that now stood empty, Emma shrugged and stepped into her home for the next month.

Briefly she wondered whether there might be a castle curator taking care of Arrick's grounds . . .

Chapter 2

The moment Emma stepped into the foyer of the manor, two things assaulted her. The first was the rich, decadent aromas of cinnamon, vanilla, and caramel. It literally made her stomach growl, and she'd soon start chewing on her own arm if she didn't get to those darn cakes soon. Good Lord, they smelled heavenly.

And then, the second thing: she felt as though *eyes* were on her, or as if someone watched her from the shadows. It wasn't the sort of feeling one would experience when in a creepy haunted house. Not threatening at all. Just that feeling you get when you have to keep looking over your shoulder, or the hairs rise on your neck and arms. Quickly, her gaze raked every nook and cranny in the foyer and main room. The ceilings were fourteen feet high; beautifully painted tiles lined the baseboards; thick burgundy drapes hung from ceiling to floor at each window; and the lush, deep mahogany of the wooden staircase rail shone in the lamplight. She saw nothing, yet the feeling someone watched her remained.

Weird.

Or, not so weird. The manor was more than two hundred and fifty years old. She was used to old, and haunted, for that matter. Savannah was renowned for its spooks and specters.

Not that she believed in any of it.

"Emma, dear," said Willoughby.

Emma jumped. Willoughby giggled.

"Och, love, there's no need to be edgy in this place. No evil spirits, I personally guarantee it." She smiled and winked. "Cast them out years ago." She inclined her red head toward the staircase. "Now follow me to your chamber. You've the entire third floor to yourself. My sisters and I occupy the second floor, so we're just below if you need us." She winked. "You're our only guest, you see."

Emma returned the smile. She probably looked and sounded like an idiot. If four old ladies could live in this place, then it had to be completely safe. She followed Willoughby up three flights of steps, then down a long corridor lit with low-light Victorian wall sconces. Here and there along the corridor, straight-backed wooden chairs, each with a plush burgundy cushion, sat against the wall. Finally, Willoughby stopped at a door that was partially open.

"Here we are, then," Willoughby said, and pushed the door all the way until it bumped the wall behind it. She walked in, and Emma followed. Willoughby waved a hand about the room. "Make yourself at home, dear. Your bureau is there, en-suite toilet there, and a tea service by your bedside. Oh, and the fireplace is at your disposal. No telly, I fear." She folded her hands and rested them against her belly. "Right. When you've finished unpacking, you can find us in the kitchen." She winked. "You'd best hurry, love. Agatha can eat her weight in cinnamon cakes."

With that, she swooshed out of the chamber and closed the door.

Emma stood in the center of the room. Suitcase in hand. Camera bag on shoulder.

Wow. I'm finally here.

Now what?

Her eyes clapped on to the floor-to-ceiling drapes at the far end of the immense room. She set her stuff down and crossed over. Grasping the thick material, she pulled the cloth aside. Emma's heart fluttered and she grinned as she looked out.

She had a perfectly unobstructed view of Arrick-by-the-Sea.

As fast as she could, Emma put her belongings away, washed her face, brushed her teeth, changed into a big, thick, cream-colored fisherman's sweater, combed her hair and twisted it into a knot, fastening it with a clip. She'd toss down a few cakes, slosh down some tea, and then head straight over to the ruins for a closer look. Good Lord, she had hours before it grew dark. Lots of photo-taking and exploring time.

She had no idea what she'd find amidst the ancient stone and ivy, but for some reason, she absolutely couldn't wait to find out. Quickly, she dug in her camera bag, pulled out her smaller digital, and headed out the door.

Christian leaned against the north wall, crossed his arms over his chest, and kept his eyes trained on the manor. He continued to scowl.

It made him feel somewhat better.

"Och, boy, don't be so bloody stodgy. You could have just as easily sneaked into the sisters' manor and had yourself a wee peek at the lass." Godfrey chuckled. "She never even knew we were there."

"Aye," said Justin Catesby, who'd joined them. "She knew all right. Kept lookin' o'er her shoulder, this way and that," he said, showing just how she'd done it. "A wily one, that wee maid." He punched Christian's arm. "Wise choice, to remain here whilst we crept about lookin' at her." He shook his head and whistled. "Damn me, but she's fetchin'."

The grand thing about being a spirit, to Christian's notion, was that although he couldn't put his hands on the living, he could indeed put them on another ghost.

He grabbed Justin's throat and squeezed. "Careful, boy. I'm in no mood for your jesting."

Justin Catesby, a good seven or eight years his junior and almost nose to nose with Christian, met his scowl, then burst out laughing. The idiot laughed so hard, tears trickled from his ghostly eyes. Christian looked away and let his friend go.

"Damn, Chris," said Justin. "Lighten your mood, man. You've cause to rejoice, not be angered." He walked up and draped an arm over Christian's shoulder. "Your woman is here again, laddie. You've no' seen her in how long? Seventy-two years?"

"Aye, seventy-two years," echoed Godfrey. "A bloody long time, indeed."

Christian continued to glare. "So . . . is she well?"

Justin Catesby grinned. "You mean, what does she look like this time?"

Christian growled.

Catesby rubbed his chin. "Verra well, since you've no spine to sneak over and see her yourself, nor the patience to await her arrival at your gatehouse." When he didn't get a reaction, he continued. "I've not seen her like this before," he said. "I mean, she's always lovely, but this?" He shook his head and looked directly at Christian. "My God, Chris, she's breathtaking."

"Aye, verra much the looker," added Godfrey. "Hair the color of allspice, cut to about just here," he made a sawing motion at his shoulder.

"Nay, more like cinnamon," Justin corrected. "Dunna you think so?"

Godfrey glanced at him. "Hmm. You may be right."

Christian rubbed his eyes with his knuckles.

Justin stood close. "Skin like porcelain, creamy

smooth without the first blemish. And the verra bluest of eyes."

Christian removed his knuckles from his eye sockets and glanced at his friend. He studied Justin's weathered, ghostly features. "Methinks you took too long of a look."

Justin Catesby and Godfrey of Battersby both burst into laughter.

"Well, laddie," said Godfrey, after catching his breath, "you now have your opportunity to view the lass yourself." He inclined his head. "Here she comes."

Christian's stomach plummeted. He suddenly thought how much wiser it would have been to pay Gawan Conwyk of Castle Grimm a visit, instead of staying here and torturing himself. As though it had a mind of its own, his head turned in the direction of the manor; he swallowed hard and watched the small figure pick her way up the graveled path toward Arrick. He ran a hand through his hair. He scrubbed his jaw. He shuffled his feet. He sighed several times. Raggedly.

He cursed.

"I can honestly say that I never grow weary of watching you squirm when you see your Emma for the first time." Justin shook his head. " 'Tis vastly amusing. More so this time, for some reason."

"Apparently, since you make a special trip from Sealladh na Mara to Arrick just to watch," muttered Christian. "Go home."

Justin chuckled. "I'd rather die. Again."

Christian then decided to ignore both of his daft friends and instead concentrate on making sure his stupid half-witted self remained invisible while Emma made her way up the path. Mayhap just the smallest of looks would suffice. Then he'd leave Arrick.

It took what seemed like forever, the arrival of Emma off that narrow castle path. He paced, he swore a bit more, and as his patience had all but leaked out, he began to walk toward her. His stomach twisted into knots as she grew closer. His Emma. Here, again. Closer still . . .

"Steady, boy," said Godfrey, somewhere behind him.

Just inside the gatehouse, where Emma was out of view, Christian stopped, and waited. Even if he'd not made himself invisible, the shadows amidst the dark stone would have swallowed his form and completely hidden him.

Strangely, with the coming of death, he'd gained a few . . . *tricks*. He'd lost his life and earthly body, but had picked up a few choice talents in return. Compensation, he reckoned. Like the uncanny ability to hear the slightest of sounds at great distances. 'Twas most irritating at times, that. But he didn't have to use the ability now. The *crunch-crunch* of gravel beneath Emma's feet sounded all too close, and before Christian could form his next coherent thought, she rounded the corner and stepped into view, directly in front of him.

Emma froze and inhaled sharply.

So did Christian.

At first, he thought she'd seen him. But he vaguely registered the fact that she was staring at the structure of the gatehouse, not him.

He, on the other hand, had all but lost his own ghostly breath—as well as what little bit of bog for a brain he had. His knees turned soggy as she stopped directly beside where he stood, and he could do little else save drink in every inch of her with his eyes. She was no more than a foot or two away. Christian shamelessly ogled, not caring that it might be considered voyeurism by some, or that he was in fact causing himself more pain. He couldn't bloody help himself. With intensity he studied her, from her boot-covered feet, up the length of her jean-covered legs, farther up the too-big jumper, to the cinnamon color of her straight hair, streaked with lighter shades and presently fastened up in the back. The top of her head just reached his shoulder, and Christian's throat tightened as memories flooded his brain . . .

"I love how you rest your chin atop my head," Emma said. She slipped her arms around Christian's waist and laid her head against his chest. When he didn't immediately place his chin where she'd requested, Emma wiggled against him. With a smile, Christian did as she asked.

"There, that's better," she said, and snuggled closer.

Christian chuckled and wrapped his arms about his love. He drew in a deep breath, tasting the flowery scent of her skin on his tongue, and he kissed her hair. "Christ, woman, you make me daft . . ."

The image faded as Emma turned her face directly toward him, head cocked to the side, listening intently. Her chest rose and fell with weighty breaths, and Christian could hear the heavy beating of her heart.

Just then, Emma moved, the slightest of shifts, and the light from the gatehouse entrance illuminated her features clearly. Christian's mouth went dry as a bone as he studied the inquisitive blue eyes, rimmed with long, dark lashes and the perfectly shaped brows the color of spice. The full lips, which he'd tasted before, could spread into the most brilliant of smiles, but they were now worried between straight white teeth, and he knew without looking that at the ridge of her chin lay a small silver scar. His insides turned ice-cold. All familiar things—things he held so tightly to memory. *Things he thought he'd never see again . . .*

Because for the very first time since they'd both died, Emma looked *exactly* like *herself.* Like the very same Emma who'd watched him ride off to the Crusades, wiping tears from her eyes and staring after him . . .

"Please, Chris! I beg you, dunna leave me!" Emma

*cried. She dragged her hand across her teary eyes. "I fear
I shall never see you again."*

*Christian squeezed his eyes tightly shut, then swung
a leg over his horse's neck and jumped to the ground. In
two strides he was at Emma's side. He cradled her face
with his hands and met her watery gaze. With his thumbs,
he wiped away the wetness from her cheeks. "I have to go,
love. But I will return to you." He pressed his lips to hers,
kissed each of her eyes, then pulled away. "I vow it, Emm.
Wait for me."*

*Emma nodded. More tears leaked out. "I will wait for-
ever," she whispered.*

And then, before Emma saw his own tears, he left.

Christ.

With a gusty sigh, Emma walked past him, bringing
him out of the past once again. She walked out of the
gatehouse and into the bailey. Christian's heart twisted
as he watched her. Aye, 'twas the very same—the way
she moved, the way she walked. He fought not to in-
hale deeply in her wake, knowing he couldn't actually
catch her scent. He knew it was there, though, and very
sweet . . .

Again, his insides knotted. He rubbed his eyes, hoping to push the memories aside. It did no good at all.
'Twould be much harder this time, the losing of her. He
could bloody feel it. Mayhap, though, 'twas a sign, her
looking the very same, and that it just might be different
this time around. The thirteenth time Emma had found
Christian. So many years he'd hoped . . .

Without thinking, Christian let his gaze turn hard.
Surely, he was setting himself and Emma up for a great
deal of pain by pursuing her as he had in the past. 'Twas
a mistake. He could feel it.

Twice, Emma stopped and slowly glanced over her
shoulder, seeming to stare directly at him.

With one last, hard look, Christian swore under his breath and completely disappeared.

Emma stopped once more, and this time she swung around.

She could have sworn she'd just heard a man's deep voice *curse*. Of course, there was no one else around. She looked skyward. Maybe it'd just been a seabird, or just the wind slipping through the cracks in the stone. Shrugging, she turned back and swept her gaze over the view before her. Her eyes absorbed every detail. Arrick was an astounding place, and the Web site hadn't done it one bit of true justice. After walking through the dark, yawning mouth of the gatehouse, where, sure enough, she could see just where the jaws of the portcullis used to retract, she stepped out into an open courtyard surrounded by an imposing, aged, gray stone wall. Much of the main building was intact—she'd have to get a flashlight to investigate that. A set of steps was at the far side, climbing to the top of the wall facing the sea. The ominous main building rose at least a hundred feet high. There were even some places where Emma saw the holes where wooden beams held floor planks, probably stretching across the entire structure. While there was some decay, it was surprising just how intact the castle was. It gave her a strange, funny feeling deep in the pit of her stomach.

Fishing her smaller digital out of her pocket, she took a few pictures: one of the gatehouse, from the inside of the courtyard, another over the wall facing the Irish Sea, and still another of the stone steps, covered in ivy. Looking out to sea, she captured the blue-gray water whitecapped with the force of the fierce wind, and the vast stretch of sky rolling endlessly with dark clouds. She paused and turned around once more, expecting to see one of the Ballaster sisters standing behind her. The wind had caught her hair and worked most of it out of the clip. It whipped fiercely about her face, and she pushed it out of her eyes.

Again, no one was there. But the hair rose at the back of her neck, and her skin prickled.

She had the distinct feeling someone stood inches away, staring at her . . .

After a moment, she blinked, then laughed at herself. Apparently, her imagination was getting the best of her. How Zoë would roll laughing at her and her jumpiness. With a shake of her head and a half smile, she stuffed her digital back in her pocket, wrapped her arms around herself, closed her eyes, and drew a deep, long breath. The tangy brine of the sea settled on her tongue, and the crisp, biting wind rolled off the ocean and washed over her. It smelled—*tasted*—incredible.

And it gave her that strange feeling in the pit of her stomach. She opened her eyes.

What *was* that?

Then, her stomach growled—loudly. She certainly knew what that was from. *Starvation*. While she'd helped herself to tea and a cinnamon cake before heading out to the castle, it apparently hadn't been enough. The Ballasters had told her of a *chippy* just a few kilometers south of Arrick. After they explained that a *chippy* was a fish-and-chips-to-go shop, she'd gotten a craving for some. Maybe she'd walk into the village and check it out.

Just then, it grew a bit darker, and Emma glanced at the sky. The clouds looked angry. A few scattered drops of rain started to fall. The chip shop trip would have to wait.

Shoving her hands deep into her pockets, Emma glanced around at the courtyard once more before heading back to the manor. She had plenty of time for photographing, she supposed.

Just as she ducked into the gatehouse, that strange

feeling came over her again, stronger this time. She stopped, glanced around, and absently reached out and touched the wall. An odd tingle went through her hand, and she noticed how the damp stone felt cool beneath her fingertips and the flat of her palm. With a final glance behind her, she pushed her hands back into her pockets and hurried down the lane.

Tonight she'd take a long hot bath, rest, and snitch some more tea and cake from the kitchen. Then she'd settle in with a good book, and get up super early.

She planned on taking a few sunrise pictures from the castle. Maybe something would stir within her— something might just possibly happen that would justify her desperate dash across the Atlantic to visit Arrick-by-the-Sea.

Her heart light, Emma all but jogged back to the manor.   •

Chapter 3

Emma sank into the plush cushion of the sitting room's overstuffed chair. Agatha had stoked the fire in the hearth and it now roared to life, the flames spreading warmth across the entire room. After a filling supper of chicken stew and hard rolls, Emma's belly was stuffed. *Finally*. And all four Ballaster sisters sat side by side on the sofa, facing Emma. Smiling. Funny little gleams of . . . something in their eyes.

They simply sat, staring. Grinning. *Waiting*.

Emma cleared her throat. "You have an amazing place," she said. "I'd love to know some of the history."

The sisters beamed. Agatha all but bounced up and down. Maven smothered a squeal and wrung her hands. Millicent patted Willoughby on the knee. "You go ahead, Sister. You're so verra good at telling the tale."

Emma could have sworn she saw Willoughby scowl at Millicent. But as fast as the expression was there, it was gone. Willoughby leaned forward, just a bit, and smiled even more broadly. "Well. I must say, 'tis an exciting, romantic history we have here at Arrick. The manor itself was built in the seventeenth century by a young lord named Garrick. But he grew bored with landowning and took to the seas." She lowered her voice and leaned even farther toward Emma. She lifted a red brow. " 'Tis rumored he became a ferocious pirate."

"Aye, 'tis true, indeed," said Millicent. "Why, there are secret passageways and hidden rooms all throughout the manor."

"And don't forget the tunnels," said Agatha. "Tell her about the tunnels!"

"The tunnels?" Emma said.

"Oh, aye," replied Willoughby. "A labyrinth of tunnels just here, beneath the manor. Most connect with more tunnels beneath the castle and run straight to the sea."

"We think Garrick used to secret his booty away via the tunnels," said Millicent.

Willoughby sighed. "True, indeed. But the entrances have been sealed for more than a century. Dangerous, you know."

Emma smiled. "I imagine so."

"Tell her about *them*," said Millicent.

Willoughby glanced at Emma.

Emma smiled. "Who?"

"Well," Willoughby began, " 'tis really just a legend, if you will. But supposedly, a fierce Welsh warrior was the one who built the castle centuries ago. A big lad, he was, and 'tis said he could lop a man's head off his shoulders with one swipe of his sword."

"Clean as a dandelion's head," added Millicent happily.

Willoughby frowned at her sister, then continued. "Aye, he indeed was quite fierce. But then, 'tis said he met his true love, and she healed his verra gruff and lonely heart. 'Twas his Intended, you see, and they fell fast and hard in love. They'd planned to wed." Willoughby's face grew grim.

A slight sob escaped Agatha.

"His Intended?" Emma asked, completely fascinated. Now she leaned forward.

Willoughby nodded. "Aye. His eternal soul mate."

Emma's stomach did that funny little flip. "What happened?"

Willoughby sighed. "No one knows for sure, you see, but 'tis said the young warrior went off to fight in the Crusades." She sniffed. "And never returned."

A lump formed in Emma's throat. "And what of his Intended?"

All four Ballasters met one another's gaze; then all four turned to Emma. "She died of a broken heart."

All was quiet in the warm sitting room. For some strange reason, Emma felt a ping of grief. Stronger than a ping, actually. "How very sad."

Again, Willoughby cleared her throat. "'Tis said that the fierce warrior, so in love with his woman, has remained on this earth." She slid a glance at Emma. "Unable to leave without his Intended." She continued to stare expectantly at Emma.

Emma thought about that, and then, her eyes widened as she remembered seeing the silhouette on the castle wall, just as she'd turned in the doorway ...

No way ...

Just then, a hardwood snapped in the fire. Emma jumped and stifled a squeal.

"Is there something wrong, dear?" asked Willoughby, her eyes wide.

Emma met her inquisitive gaze, blinked, then gave the older woman a winsome smile. "No. Nothing at all wrong. It's ... like you said. Very romantic." She looked at them.

"Why don't you tell us a bit about yourself, love?" asked Maven. "You have such an adorable little accent. Where are you from in the States, exactly?"

"Well—," Emma began, only to be interrupted by Willoughby.

"Let the lamb get some rest, Maven," the eldest Ballaster said. "Look there, her eyes are drooping as we speak." She smiled warmly at Emma. "Why don't you retire to your room and get a good night's rest, eh? No doubt all that plane riding has worn you out. I'll have you a nice Welsh breakfast at the ready, first thing in the morn. How's that sound?"

Emma smiled, grateful for the escape. She very much enjoyed talking to the sisters, but exhaustion had caught up with her and her eyes felt as though they had sand beneath the lids. "That sounds fantastic, actually. Thank you." She rose, and the sisters followed suit. She smiled at each sister. "Good night."

"Night," they all replied in unison.

Millicent gave a little wave.

Emma waved back and made her way to the staircase. How funny the sisters were. They so wholeheartedly believed in their romantic tales. Still, they were sweet and very attentive. She looked forward to chatting more with them in the morning.

At the stairs, Emma glanced back, only to find all four sisters still staring after her. Grinning. She shook her head, unable to help another smile pulling at her own mouth, and began the climb to the third floor.

All was quiet as she hit the landing and started down the long corridor leading to her room. Again, she noticed just how dim the lighting was, the burgundy shades on the lamps casting a soft, pink glow. Once at her door, she let herself in, grabbed a pair of boxers, a T-shirt, and girlie stuff from her still-unpacked suitcase, and headed straight for the *en-suite toilet*. That seriously cracked her up.

The bathroom was larger than she'd expected, with an oversized claw-foot bathtub perched upon a stone dais. A large, arched window was just above it. No curtains, just a beautiful view of Arrick, and the Irish Sea beyond.

Emma plopped her stuff down on the toilet seat, plugged the drain in the tub, and started the water. She noticed a big bath fizz ball sitting in a small iron rack attached to the lip of the tub. Unwrapping it, she sniffed the heady scent of lavender and vanilla, then dropped the ball into the running water. It began to fizz immediately, white fluffy bubbles rising to the top.

While the tub filled, Emma fixed herself a cup of tea, set her toiletries on the edge of the bath, and then shucked out of her clothes. She eased into the steaming water, teacup in hand, and relaxed. The lavender and vanilla aroma nearly put her to sleep, but instead, her thoughts drifted first to the strange feelings she'd experienced at the castle ruins, then to the story of Arrick's ill-fated couple.

How sad, she thought. To find the one soul meant especially for you and only you, then to lose that soul . . . *forever*. She couldn't imagine how overwrought with grief the poor girl must have felt at losing her warrior.

"It'd be better never to find your Intended at all," she said sadly.

Just then, a draft of air grazed the wet skin on her neck, making her shiver. And just as suddenly, that odd feeling returned to the pit of her stomach.

That feeling was beginning to get on her last nerve.

Quickly, Emma pulled the drain plug, rose from the water, and stepped out, then grabbed a towel off the heating rack and wrapped it around her. She took another and turban-wrapped her hair. After drying off and rubbing lotion on her legs, she pulled on her nightclothes, dried and wound her hair in a knot and secured it with a band, brushed her teeth, and climbed beneath the heavy down duvet thrown over her bed. With just the table lamp on, she picked up the book she'd brought and began to read. But no sooner had she turned the first page than her eyelids grew heavy, drooped, and the book slowly lowered to her chest as she fell into a deep sleep . . .

*   *   *

"What in the bloody hell are you thinkin', lad?" asked Godfrey. "Have you lost what little wits ye've had all along? Ye canna go anywhere. She only just arrived!"

Christian rubbed his eyes with his thumb and forefinger. He didn't answer.

"Nay, Godfrey, mayhap we have it all wrong," said Justin Catesby. "Mayhap that's *exactly* what needs to happen. Christian should leave Arrick. Go hang out with yon ghosties at Castle Grimm. Aye. Definitely so."

Christian glanced at Justin, and he sorely wished he hadn't. The jackass had a smirk on his face that stretched from ear to ear, and that he'd be more than happy to wipe off. Instead, he glared.

The smirk turned into a full-blown grin. With teeth.

Christian growled, but didn't engage. "You two leave her alone. Mayhap what she needs is *none* of us." Aye, he'd given that much thought. Could it be that each time he interacted with Emma, he in turn caused her fate to carry itself out? What if he simply ... left her alone?

The thought made him feel ill.

"Bloody stupid idea, if you ask me," mumbled Godfrey.

"I didn't ask you," Christian said flatly. Then, quieter, "I just can't do this again."

Justin lost his wolfish grin and replaced it with a frown. "So, 'tis like that now, eh?"

Christian frowned back. "Like what?"

"All about you."

He didn't really know why, but that just made him boil even more inside. He looked at Justin and spoke low. "That's the last thing it's about."

Justin said nothing in return.

That made Christian even *angrier*. So before he smashed his friend's nose in, he drew a deep breath, avoided both of their expectant looks, and strode past them.

He made it all the way to the gatehouse before either spoke.

"So where are you headed off to, then?" asked Godfrey.

Christian ignored the question and continued on his way. He felt both pairs of ghostly eyes boring into his back as he retreated. He didn't care.

In his invisible state, Christian walked with long strides round the back of the manor's kitchen entrance. He waited there, listening. When he heard only the sisters' voices, he sifted through the door. Once he saw 'twas only the Ballasters, he materialized. Just as he suspected, Millicent jumped as soon as he was visible.

"Och! Young Christian! You scared the devil out of me!" she said, her hand clutching her throat. Then she batted her eyes.

Christian gave a nod, then found Willoughby. He drew a deep breath. "I'm leaving."

All of a sudden, the four sisters began talking at once.

He, of course, couldn't decipher a thing any of them was saying, so high-pitched and frantic were their voices. So he held up his hand. They stared at him, quieted, and blinked. Waiting.

"Why?" asked Willoughby. "She only just arrived."

He nodded, but looked at her directly. "I cannot go through this again, lady. I feel 'tis in ... *her* best interest if she never encounters me." He shrugged. "Mayhap 'twill set her free."

The Ballasters stared at him in horror. Willoughby, though, spoke up. Her voice sounded calm. Soothing. "You cannot mean it, lad. 'Tis finding you that saves her, each and every time. 'Tis what makes her life—no matter the length—complete. Dunna you understand that?"

The other sisters nodded with vigor.

Christian studied them. What he did know was that each time he lost Emma, another hole ripped through his chest. She at least died and moved on without the first memory of him, becoming reborn. Living a different life every seventy-two years. She endured very little pain in the few short months she remembered him.

He'd endured one long, torturous lifetime of pain.

If one called roaming the world as a spirit a life.

Christ. It was *all about him* . . .

Selfish bastard . . .

"Now, there, boy," said Willoughby. "I can see your pain, love. But do you really—*can* you really leave, without at least seeing her?"

"I did see her. Earlier."

Willoughby rubbed her chin. "She's upstairs now. Sleeping, I think. Perhaps you should at least say good-bye?"

Christian met Willoughby's questioning gaze. Her eyes widened innocently.

His narrowed.

"That's not playing fair, madam," he said.

Willoughby shrugged. " 'Tis your choice, of course. But if you're going to leave, you should perhaps take one last look at her. 'Twill be nearly a century before she shows up again."

Something flickered in Willoughby's eyes, but it vanished before Christian could figure out what it meant.

With a scowl, he gave a low short bow, turned, and headed for the stairs. At the base, he stopped. And waited.

"Third floor, last room on the right," offered Willoughby.

Without a word, Christian disappeared, mentally directing himself to the third-floor apartments, and then materialized in the corridor.

He knew he made not a sound as he strode to the

last room on the right. Once there, he stopped and listened. Just the sound of her deep, even breaths made his own catch in his throat. He squeezed his eyes shut for a brief moment, unsure if seeing her in slumber was the best thing to do. 'Twas bad enough, her returning as her original self. After the last time he'd lost Emma, he thought nothing could hurt worse. He was wrong. But he'd made his mind up to leave her in peace. Seeing her so vulnerable might very well compromise his strength to turn and walk back out the door.

Twice, he stomped back up the corridor. His movement was still soundless, but the motion of stomping made him feel somewhat better. But twice he returned to stand in front of the door. The damn bloody door that led straight to *her* . . .

Unable to stop himself, Christian sifted through six inches of solid oak. He knew every design of every chamber in the manor, knew exactly where she slumbered, and walked directly to her. He found it odd that, even after having been no more than a foot from her earlier, it was difficult to gaze at her in this vulnerable state of sleep.

Finally, though, he did.

And the pressure in his chest nearly made him gasp.

The low light of the table lamp fell upon her face, the book she'd been reading discarded against her chest. Her lips were slightly parted as she breathed, and dark lashes brushed her cheeks where they rested. Her face was painfully beautiful, her skin creamy white and flawless. Just as he'd remembered from the very first time he laid eyes upon her.

"Chris!" hollered Gawan.

Christian jumped back, Gawan's blade missing his stomach by less than a hand's breadth. His gaze remained on the thing that had wrested his attention from the swordplay. Without a word, he jammed his blade into the ground and wiped his brow with the back of his arm.

"What is wrong with you, man?" asked Gawan.

Christian didn't answer. Nay, he couldn't answer. How could he whilst his bloody tongue was wrapped around itself? His stare followed the three horses passing through the gatehouse. More so on the gel whose gaze peeked out of a garnet cloak and stared back.

"Och, ne'er mind," muttered Gawan. He walked over, shoved his own blade into the ground, and leaned on the hilt. He waved a hand before Christian's eyes. " 'Tis a good bloody thing the lass didn't happen upon you whilst on the battlefield. You'd be a dead lad for sure."

Christian vaguely heard his friend's jesting words. "She's astounding," he said, mostly to himself. The gel's pale, flawless face stood stark against the deep color of the cloak, and a pair of blue eyes held his with such intensity, Christian had to struggle to keep his wobbly knees from giving way. Just as they passed through the stone arch, a flash of white as she smiled made Christian's stomach tighten. He followed her until she disappeared; then he yanked free his sword, pushed it into the hilt over his shoulder, and started in the direction of the gel.

"Where are you going?" asked Gawan with a chuckle.

"To find out who she is . . ."

Emma sighed in her sleep, and Christian pulled himself from the long-ago memory. He blinked, and for a moment, he allowed himself a small amount of pleasure and drank in the sight of her. His Emma, fast asleep, so close that, had he substance, he could extend his fingers and brush her arm that casually rested against her stomach. Christ, how he wished he could smell her . . .

Swallowing hard, Christian drew a deep breath, leaned over, and studied her closely. He willed himself to maintain his strength and not go back on his word to leave her alone. But being this close to her . . .

He brought his lips close to hers, nearly touching, then

moved to her ear. "Christ, Emma," he whispered. He squeezed his eyes tightly shut as a myriad of emotions grasped him by the throat. "How I've missed you."

Just then, several things happened at once. First, Emma's large blue eyes flew open and, God help him, focused on *him*. Second, she pushed to her elbows, bringing her face incredibly closer than it had been, and her luscious mouth began to work fervently, although nothing lucid came out. Third, and this he'd remember forever, she drew in a deep breath, held it, and then screamed a cry worthy of any mêlée he'd fought.

Christian of Arrick-by-the-Sea closed his eyes, swore, and disappeared.

Chapter 4

Emma's scream bounced off every wall in the cavernous room, and she literally crawled up the headboard backward, like a crab, standing on the pillows her head had just been peacefully resting upon. She stared, eyes stretched wide, her gaze raking the room swiftly for signs of the face she'd been mere inches from only moments ago.

She saw ... *nothing*. No one. She was all alone.

But there'd just been a face staring at her!

After catching her breath, Emma eased off the bed. The cool wood floor chilled her bare feet as she tiptoed across the room. Eyeing the bathroom door, she started for it, stopped when she realized she had no weapon, and searched the immediate area. The blow-dryer she'd left on the chair beside the bed caught her eye, so she unplugged it, looped the cord, grabbed it by the handle, and crept back to the bathroom.

Someone could be hiding in there, she thought. *Someone could have sneaked in through a window, or maybe even through one of the secret tunnels*. Her heart beat double time as she placed her free palm against the wood, gave it a hard shove, and dashed into the bathroom, blow-dryer raised.

Again, no one was there.

Suddenly, she spun around. The hair on her neck rose.

She'd just heard a ... *chuckle*. A man's deep, amused chuckle. She was sure of it.

Emma eyed the bed. The bed had a good three feet of clearance from the floor. She'd never go back to sleep if she didn't look, so, quietly, blow-dryer gripped tightly, she eased down to her knees and hands, bent her head, and looked under the bed.

Nothing.

A long breath of relief escaped Emma's lungs. She pushed back, resting her backside against her heels, glanced at the blow-dryer, and thought just how silly she must look—fanny in the air, weapon in hand. Shaking her head, she rose, put away her bludgeon, and sat on the side of the bed.

The image of the face flashed before her, and she thought long and hard about it. Her first reaction—especially after scouring the room and finding nothing—was to conclude she'd imagined the whole thing. After all, she'd been reading Jane Austen's *Northanger Abbey*. While not particular spooky, the novel had gothic-y elements that may have caused her to dream something spooky.

No. That was not it at all.

Emma lay back atop the duvet and looked up at the ceiling.

What bothered her was that the face somehow seemed ... *familiar*. Sure, it'd scared the holy ho-ho out of her, but still. *Familiar*. How could that be? She certainly would have remembered a face like that in her past. She didn't think there was one single male in all of Savannah who could measure up to *that* face.

She could only describe it as painfully beautiful.

A square jaw, wide mouth with full lips, and nice brows—not too bushy, not too thin. A straight nose, hair the color of dark mahogany hung tousled in the front, nearly to his jawline and almost in his eyes.

Blue, amazing eyes that also seemed so very familiar to her. At first wide and surprised, they quickly narrowed and turned angry.

Just before the face disappeared.

Frustrated, Emma decided the excitement was over. She didn't know what had happened, but she felt certain no one had entered her room. She'd simply imagined it. Final answer.

Crawling across the bed, she pulled the duvet up to her neck, reached over, and flicked the lamp off.

And just as her eyes drifted shut, one more thought assaulted her.

That painfully beautiful face had had a deep voice, strangely accented, and it had known her name . . .

Just outside Emma's door, Christian leaned against the wall, arms crossed over his chest, head lowered. He stared at his boots.

What an idiot he'd been. Seeing her, being in such close proximity with her, only made him *want* her all the more. It made what he had to do all the more difficult.

Why couldn't he have just followed his instinct and *left*?

Because he couldn't help himself, that's bloody why. He'd only wanted to be closer, just to get a longer look at the face he'd given his heart to so many centuries before. Christ, she was just as beautiful. Nay, mayhap even more so.

The aura that made up Emma's soul had surrounded him, trapped him hovering close to her face—even after her eyes had flown open. He'd been powerless to move, until that hair-raising scream had torn from her lips.

He hated that he'd caused such a sound.

Closing his eyes, Christian went through the motion of bashing the back of his head against the stone wall.

He felt nothing, of course, but he thought it made him feel somewhat better.

It didn't.

Then his eyes flew open. It hit him. He knew exactly what had to be done.

"Look at ye, boy. Cowerin' out here in the passageway instead of in yon chamber with your mate. What's wrong with ye?" asked Godfrey in a foul whisper as he materialized from the opposite wall. "I could bloody well hear the lass' hollering all the way to the bailey. Sounded like ye were murderin' her." He narrowed his eyes to slits. "What'd ye do to her, then?"

Christian stared hard at his old friend, that ridiculous plume on his hat bouncing with each bob of his irritated head. He drew a deep breath, placed a finger over his lips, and inclined his head. "Come on, before you wake her."

Godfrey shrugged and followed Christian away from Emma's door. They materialized on the fifth floor—actually a large attic. And the chamber the Ballasters had graciously given to Christian. Once inside, Christian noted Justin Catesby reclined in the chair, his big boots crossed at the ankles. He grinned and threw up a hand in greeting.

"She's got superb lungs," Justin said cheerfully. He rose from the chair and strode to stand next to Godfrey.

"I thought ye were leavin', boy," Godfrey asked Christian with a frown. "Why'd ye go in and scare her?"

Christian rubbed his brow. "I didn't *mean* to scare her." He scrubbed the back of his neck. "I didn't mean for her to see me at all. 'Twas a bloody accident."

Godfrey and Justin exchanged a look.

Then they both broke out into laughter.

Christian glowered at them both. It didn't shut them up like he'd hoped.

Finally, *blessedly*, they ceased.

"So then, boy," said Godfrey, wiping his teary eyes,

"what is your grand plan now, eh? Are ye still goin' to run away?"

Christian waited. He knew what was coming. He didn't care.

'Twas *his* Intended. He could do with her as he damn well wanted.

Striding to the far end of the room, Christian stopped at the window facing the sea. "I'm going to scare her off. Make her leave Arrick."

Silence filled the chamber, but only for a moment, maybe two. When they could hold their tongues no longer, Godfrey and Justin again burst out laughing.

Christian closed his eyes, and pinched the bridge of his nose. How easily amused they were of late. He waited.

Justin bent over at the waist, gripping his knees while he caught his breath.

Christian shook his head.

"Okay," said Godfrey, finally. "So what's yer reasoning for wanting to scare the lass away? Why, after all this time, do you no' want to woo her?"

Christian glanced at Justin, who covered his mouth with his hand.

"It's not that I don't want to. I cannot go on like this, Godfrey. Every seventy-two years *I know* what's in store for Emma. I woo her, she finally falls in love with me again, only to . . ." He didn't finish the rest. The thought was beyond unbearable. He shook his head and looked at both his friends. "Mayhap if she doesn't go through all that again, if she merely . . . exists, carries on with her life without my becoming involved, the cycle will end for her. She won't have to suffer anymore."

Justin, his grin vanished, crossed his arms over his chest and met Christian's gaze. "Do you sincerely believe you have the upper hand with fate, Chris?" he asked. He rubbed his chin. "I dunna think so, lad. I think you're tempting fate in ways you cannot undo."

"Aye," agreed Godfrey. "I'm with young Catesby here. You should allow things to happen as they may. You cannot change her path, boy, just as you cannot change yours." He grimaced. "Unfortunate as it is."

Christian considered that. He thought, paced, scrubbed the back of his neck, and thought some more. Mayhap his old mates were right. Then again, mayhap they were not. Finally, he stopped and met his friends' gazes. "I've still got to try."

Both Godfrey and Justin groaned.

With a glowering gaze, Christian pinned them where they stood. "I don't expect either of you to understand or agree, but I *do* expect you not to interfere. 'Tis my own decision to try to change Emma's fate, and if I fail, I'll fail on my own." He gave them a hard look. "If you cannot tolerate that, you can leave."

Justin gaped long at Christian. Godfrey did the same. In the end, Justin spoke. "We willna interfere. But I am curious to see just how you're goin' to attempt to scare the wee lass." He cocked his head. "Certainly not with insignificant little ghostly tricks, aye?"

Knowing better than to engage in that sort of conversation with Justin Catesby, Christian shrugged. "I'll let you know when I decipher it myself." He rubbed his chin. "Why don't you two head over to Castle Grimm. You know they're gearing up for their annual tournament, aye?"

A long, slow grin came over Justin's face. "Maybe so, but 'tis much more interesting round here, just yet." He nodded. "I'll stay awhile. How about you, Godfrey?"

Godfrey's grin irritated Christian. "Aye. I've a mind to stay, as well." His eyes looked innocent. "We willna get into anything. We promise, right Catesby?"

Justin's smile didn't fade. "Absolutely."

Christian considered his two friends, then dismissed their unspoken intimidation. 'Twouldn't work on him and they damn well knew it. Furthermore, he'd not engage in the topic because they'd only drag it out, just to irritate him. He needed to be alone, walk, plan his strategy.

He rubbed both eyes with the heels of his hands. He didn't like frightening Emma. Not at all. What he sincerely wanted to do was spend hours just gazing at her face.

No, what he'd give anything for was the chance to touch her skin, hold her close, and taste her lips . . .

A frown fixed itself upon his mouth. He knew better than anyone that would never happen. But if he could find a way to let Emma find eternal happiness—even if it meant giving up his chance to see her every seventy-two years—then he would.

With a slight nod, Christian disappeared from the chamber. He had to plan.

And the sooner Emma left, the sooner he could start trying to forget . . .

Chapter 5

"Well, what do we do now?" cried Maven, wringing her hands together and pacing before the small hearth in their spell-making chamber. The Ballasters had gathered after hours. "Young Christian's going to leave!"

The other sisters moaned.

Willoughby drew in a deep breath. "No, he's not leaving."

Three pairs of eyes flashed to her, expectantly.

"Truly?" asked Millicent. "He's changed his mind?"

Willoughby nodded slowly. "Aye, he has, indeed." She looked at her sisters. "He's decided to scare Emma away instead."

The others gasped.

"No!" cried Agatha. "Why, by Morticia's wand, would he do *that*?"

"It makes no sense at all," muttered Maven. "What is that boy thinking?"

With a shrug, Willoughby walked to the hearth, picked up the poker, and stirred the ashes. She added another log. "The lad seems much more distressed at Emma's arrival this time, 'tis true enough. I can't imagine why."

"But we cannot just let him scare her away," wailed Millicent. "All will be lost if he succeeds!"

Willoughby turned to Millicent with a smile. "You've very little faith in our Emma, so it seems, Sister."

Millicent furiously blushed.

"Think you she'll hold up against his trickery?" asked Agatha.

Willoughby smiled. "I think so, yes. Indeed I do. She's much stronger than she looks, I think."

The other Ballasters sighed with apparent relief.

With a clap of her hands, Willoughby moved to a large, oval table in the middle of the chamber. Beside a large tome sat several small items, nestled together in one small pile. A candle log burned, giving off its cinnamon scent. Gingerly, she lifted a strand of hair from the pile, pulled it close for inspection, then set it back down. "There's much to be done before All Hallows' Eve, girls. Conditions of the spell-that-must-not-be-spoken-aloud need to be orchestrated just so, and in a small amount of time. Let's keep an eye on our sweet Emma, just to make sure she doesn't founder. She doesn't know it, but her battle has just begun, and her quick acceptance of Christian's existence is an absolute must. Not her memory, mind you. Just her acceptance of his spirited existence. We shall help coax her, if need be." She smiled. "Now! Let's get busy. The lass will be down for breakfast in just a bit. With that ravenous appetite she has, I'm sure she'll be starved."

With a round of ayes, they all gathered at the great table, huddled close, and planned their next step . . .

Emma cracked open an eye. The *tick-tick-tick* of a nearby clock sounded in the darkness surrounding her, and the air outside the covers felt cool and crisp against her cheeks. The distinct aroma of cinnamon filled her nostrils. Confusion muddled her brain, but only for a moment. It took her only a few seconds longer to register where she was. *Oh yeah. Wales. Arrick-by-the-Sea.*

She threw the covers back and sat straight up. The memory of an agonizingly sexy face staring at her flooded her brain. Reflexively, she scanned the room. She didn't merely find herself to be utterly alone, but was surprised to be slightly disappointed.

More than slightly, truth be told.

Pushing her hair out of her eyes, she pulled a pillow up, settled it behind her back, and leaned into it. In the darkness, the vision of that handsome face came immediately. The intensity of those eyes, and the way he'd said her name—

No. That voice hadn't merely said her name.

Emma squeezed her eyes shut, and the sound immediately came inside her head.

Christ, Emma. How I've missed you . . .

Her eyes flew open.

Holy ho-ho . . .

"I must be losing it," she said out loud. Giving her head a good, hard shake, Emma climbed from the covers and switched on the lamp. She'd better hurry if she planned on taking sunrise pictures at the ruins. She flung open her suitcase, her teeth chattering as she dug out a pair of worn, faded jeans, her white long-sleeved SCAD—Savannah College of Art and Design—T-shirt, a brown sweater, and a pair of thick socks. Hurriedly dressing, she freshened up in the bathroom, brushed her hair, snugged a multicolored knit hat down to her ears, pulled on her waterproof boots, and grabbed her camera case and tripod. Flicking off the lamp, she eased out of the room.

In the corridor, just beside her door, stood a small, folding table containing a thermos and a covered dish. Emma smiled. The Ballasters really were sweet ladies. Lifting the dish, she grabbed the two slices of cinnamon cake wrapped in clear plastic, and the thermos, and then headed quietly downstairs.

The only sound throughout the manor was the heavy *ticktock* of the tall grandfather clock in the foyer. As Emma passed it, she guessed it had to be all of six feet tall. Ornately carved and beyond gorgeous, the clock must have weighed a ton. She considered how the late-afternoon light would fall on it, and thought it'd be a great shot.

As Emma stepped out into the early morning, the brisk September air, tinged with smells of the sea and a sweetness—clover, maybe?—whipped against her face. She drew in a lungful, her insides feeling as though she'd just swallowed ice, juggled her camera bag and thermos, and started up the gravel path toward Arrick's ruins. In the predawn light she could barely see the path in front of her. Ahead, the castle rose out of a blanket of heavy white mist, and it drifted like a live thing in wispy sheets toward her. Emma thought it eerily beautiful. Stopping, she set her bag down, along with the thermos and cake, on a nearby rock. Quickly, before she lost the shot, she set up the tripod.

Once she had the digital locked in place, she chose her lens, her settings, and then stared into the camera at the scene before her. Lifting her head, she angled the tripod a bit more, then bent again to check the shot.

In the next second, she felt something tug on her hair.

Emma turned. No one was there.

A chill ran up her spine. The wind?

She shook her head and looked through the lens.

The shot was beautiful. To her, it screamed mystical, legendary, and ghostly. She snapped off a few shots. No doubt the tales Willoughby had told her had something to do with it.

"Leave this place."

Emma snapped her head up. She looked around. Of course, she found no one.

But she sure had heard someone whisper in her ear.

The wind excuse could seriously only last so long.

Deciding to ignore it, *whatever* it was, Emma lowered her head to the lens. She snapped off another shot.

"I . . . said . . . leave!"

Emma froze. The blood drained from her face—she could feel it. And as white as she already was, she probably could now pass for a vampire.

That voice was not friendly at all. And it was loud. *Very* loud. Fear made her body so stiff, she couldn't even turn her head. Whoever had whispered to her before was apparently now standing right beside her. Who on earth would be out so early, on the Ballasters' land, and even care if she was at Arrick or not?

"Don't just stand and ignore me, wench!"

Emma's eyes grew wide. Suddenly, she blinked.

Wench?

Turning her head, ever so slightly toward the voice, she braced herself for the brute that must be standing beside her.

Again, she found herself completely alone.

Turning in a circle, slowly at first, Emma studied her surroundings. The manor was at least fifty yards behind her, Arrick's gatehouse at least a few hundred. The only things close to her on the gravel path were a few trees, a few scattered rocks, and some clumps of sea grass. Farther up the lane, grass lay on either side. Wide open.

Nowhere to hide.

Was she hallucinating? Maybe she was being drugged? Perhaps the Ballasters were spiking the tea. Poisoning the cakes. *Was that really cinnamon?*

Another glance around proved to Emma she was indeed all alone. She bumped her forehead with the heel of her hand. Of *course* she was all alone.

Drawing a deep breath, she continued with her pictures. She knew nothing better to do. Running and screaming was out of the question. What would she say when the Ballasters finally asked her, *What's wrong, dear?* They'd think she was a complete dodo. Unless the wily old gals were orchestrating the voice themselves, as an added ambience to their haunted castle tales? That had to be it.

It was her only explanation.

After several minutes, with no threatening voices to interrupt, Emma decided to gather her courage and head into the ruins. She wanted to get a certain shot as the sun rose and by God, she'd get it. Quickly, she gathered her stuff and headed up the lane. She couldn't help the constant looking-over-the-shoulder thing she kept doing.

As Emma passed through the gaping black hole of the gatehouse, she shivered. Strangely enough, nothing happened. Somewhat relieved, she crossed the courtyard to the ivy-covered stairs, climbed them cautiously, then set her stuff down on the wall, waiting for the light to be just right. Unwrapping one of the cakes, she twisted the lid off the thermos and sipped the cocoa the sisters had made her. Still pretty warm, the smooth chocolate heated her insides.

Just as Emma's mouth closed over the cinnamon cake, the voice returned.

"Remove yourself from my wall!"

Emma inhaled sharply, drawing cake crumbs into her lungs, and nearly choked. While she worked on swallowing the cake, her eyes darted all over but could, as usual, find nothing. Eyes watering, she managed to clear her throat. Now she was mad.

"I don't know who you are, but I've had enough!" she said loudly. "Either leave me alone or . . . go away!" After a few moments with no response, Emma glared, lifted the thermos, and drank.

"Do not think to make demands on my land, wench. I said leave!"

"Oh!" Emma cried as she jumped at the voice, the thermos slipping from her hand. As she made a grab for it, she overreached. Her boot slipped on the wet stone of the step, and suddenly, Emma felt herself tumbling over the edge. With a frightened yelp, she grabbed on to the outer ridge of the step. She dangled, twenty feet off the ground. Fear crept into her throat, squeezing her vocal cords so tight she couldn't scream. She squeezed her eyes shut. "Help," she mouthed, trying to make herself heard, but the word barely coming out like a whispered croak. "Help. Please?"

"*Open your eyes, gel,*" the voice said gruffly.

"No," she whispered, and wouldn't do it. Why should she listen to *that* voice? "Leave me alone."

"Open them now," it said, much more clearly, and much more angry.

She didn't care. "No." She tightened her grip on the step. Her fingers were getting numb.

"Emma, open your eyes before you bloody fall!" the voice shouted.

The voice *knew* her *name*?

That got her attention. Slowly, she opened her eyes.

And stared straight into *the face*—the same face that had scared her the night before. And the face was now attached to a body.

A big body.

It crouched on the step, barely a foot away.

Too frightened to speak, Emma simply stared into the blue eyes looking down at her.

"Slide your hand toward me. You'll find a lip on the edge of the step." He frowned when she didn't move. "Move your left foot up about an inch. You'll find a toe-hold. Do it now."

"My fingers are numb," she answered.

"Do it anyway." His voice sounded steady. Even. Not so angry.

That encouraged her. Although falling wouldn't kill her, Emma didn't exactly feel like breaking any bones in a foreign country.

Slowly, Emma moved her left foot up an inch. Sure enough, she found a small toehold. That inspired her to slide her hand closer to . . . him. She found the lip.

"Now push with your foot, and pull," the man said.

She did. Her body shifted, just enough to gain leverage.

"Now pull yourself up."

Emma met the man's steady gaze. Never before had a pair of eyes been able to talk her into something the way this pair did. Without further hesitation, she did exactly what he instructed her to do. Within seconds, she was safe on the step. On her stomach, but safe all the same. After several seconds of regaining her composure—not to mention pulling her shirt and sweater down over her exposed midriff from all that squirming in her hipsters—she turned over, relief making her body feel faint. "Thanks . . ."

Emma's spine went cold. She glanced around, but found nothing save the empty, centuries-old courtyard. A gust of wind blew from the sea and washed over her. A gull screeched overhead.

The man was gone.

Oddly enough, Emma continued her sunrise photo shoot. Even odder was that she did it with disappointment.

Chapter 6

After several days without the first sign of a face, body, voice, or combination of any of the above, Emma felt compelled to make an attempt at sounding not half as ridiculous to the Ballaster sisters as she did to her own silly self by asking about the neighbors of Arrick-by-the-Sea. It was embarrassing.

She was fully convinced the Ballasters had nothing to do with trying to scare her. No wacky little parlor tricks to lure and keep guests, no promotional B and B gimmicks. Perhaps, though, they *did* have a crazy neighbor or something? Had she not been so frightened—then freaked out—by the appearance and swift disappearance of the man on the ivy-covered steps the day she slipped, she would have leaped up to the seawall and glanced over it. There, she probably would have found that guy shimmying down the same rope he'd shimmied up.

Or, and she liked this alternative better, that guy had found and used one of the pirate Garrick's secret tunnels. *That* definitely could be a possibility. The guy who'd helped her certainly was from the area. He had the strangest of accents.

Mesmerizing, truth be told. Smooth and deep, she couldn't believe she'd taken the time to notice it at all.

Hurriedly finishing her hair, which she'd quickly

worked into a loose French braid, she pulled on a black turtleneck, another pair of her favorite, worn-out jeans, and her boots, she jogged downstairs and entered the guests' breakfast room. There, the sisters all waited for her, and just like the past two days, they had a mouthwatering breakfast waiting.

Emma could get used to this. She patted her tummy in anticipation.

"Good morn to you, love!" cried the ever-excited Millicent. "Have a seat, just there," she said, pointing to the place she wished Emma to sit. "The cream scones are nearly done!"

The breakfast room was an add-on, one of those glass-enclosed scenery rooms used by many B and B owners to serve spectacular breakfasts in. It had a beautiful view of the castle, with several daintily set tables hugging the windows, with lovely lace tablecloths and white place settings. Emma's table had a vase with a handful of fresh flowers poking out of it. It made everything look colorful and inviting.

A tea service had been set for her to use, so she poured a cup and stirred in a heaping spoonful of brown sugar, and fresh cream. The sweet liquid warmed her throat.

No sooner had she finished her tea than all four sisters came out of the kitchen, each with a plate of scrumptious foods for her to select from. After choosing a fresh hot scone, scrambled eggs, thick slices of lean bacon, and a small portion of porridge, she gave the sisters a wide smile. "Thank you so much, although you really don't have to go to so much trouble for just me." *They probably think I'm a bottomless pit!*

"Och, no trouble at all, lass," said Willoughby. The other sisters hurried back into the kitchen with their platters. Willoughby, who'd been carrying the scones, remained.

Emma cocked her head. "I have a question, and I hope it doesn't sound too odd," she said.

Willoughby's eyes lit up. "Anything, love. What's troubling you this fine morn?"

Emma smiled. She loved the Ballasters' lilting Welsh accents. "Well," she began, rubbing her chin, "I was wondering, do you have any neighbors?"

Now Willoughby cocked her head. "Neighbors?"

Emma nodded.

"Why, yes, we do, although they're several kilometers away," Willoughby said. "Lovely old couple. Just celebrated their sixtieth anniversary a month back."

Emma sighed. "No, that couldn't be it." She thought about it some more. "Maybe someone from the village?"

A ghost of a smile touched Willoughby's weathered cheeks. "Just what are you after, girl?" she said.

Biting the tip of her index fingernail, she gave a slight smile. "Well," she said with a half laugh, "it's sort of silly." Especially when she hadn't told the sisters that she'd dangled from their seawall steps. "But I've . . . seen a man. Sort of."

Just then, the other three Ballasters joined them.

"A man?" asked Agatha. "What man?"

"Maybe if you can describe him?" asked Maven.

Millicent and Willoughby both nodded enthusiastically.

Emma met the expectant gazes of the older ladies. "Well, okay." She cleared her throat. "He's actually pretty cute, with big blue eyes, dark brown hair with sort of long bangs that hang to here." She did a sawing motion at the level between her jaw and cheekbone. "A square jaw and really, err"—she coughed—"he's very big. And handsome." She wasn't about to tell the Ballasters that the man she'd run into had really juicy lips. She found herself intrigued that she hadn't even noticed what the guy was wearing. She'd been too scared—and too busy staring into those eyes.

All four sisters had slight smirks on their faces.

"What?" asked Emma, smiling. "What's so funny?"

Willoughby, who, Emma now understood, spoke for the foursome as a group, smiled broadly. "Well, you see, we've had guests in the past claim to see that very same young man." Her eyes sparkled. "Quite the dish."

Emma grinned at the flirt in Willoughby's eyes. "Does he live around here?"

Millicent giggled.

"I would say yes, he's a resident of the area," said Willoughby, nodding.

Emma considered. The sisters were being strangely vague about him. "What's his name?"

A hesitant look flashed across Willoughby's face. "Err, well . . . right. We can't exactly say." She smiled. "Sorry."

"Why can't you say?" asked Emma.

Willoughby leaned forward, and whispered in a quiet voice, "You see, he walks amongst the living, but isn't one himself, I fear. And we're not allowed to tell you his name."

Emma blinked. "Excuse me?" Certainly she wasn't hearing Willoughby correctly. "Did you say—"

"I'm afraid I did, dear," said Willoughby, without even hearing all of Emma's question. "And no, I cannot tell you his name." She smiled. "But I will tell you that in the days of old, folks referred to the castle owners by the name of the castle itself."

Emma gawked, dumbfounded. Speechless, even. Then, she grinned. "Oh, come on. You're making all that up."

Agatha shook her head. "Nay, 'tis absolutely true. Often, in the old days, one referred to another by which castle they owned."

"Try it, lass," said Willoughby, with a wink. "Try calling out the name and see what happens."

With that, all four Ballasters bustled out of the dining room.

Emma just stared after them. Sweet, but very, very odd.

Stirring her food around on her plate, she dug in, mumbling to herself. "Basically, they're telling me that cute guy I've seen more than once is . . . is a . . . *ghost*?"

She snorted, nearly inhaling a large chunk of scone.

Working in downtown Savannah and surrounded by so many ghost tours she couldn't count them, Emma, while loving a good ghost tale just as much as the next person, hardly actually *believed* in them. The Gray Lady. The White Lady. The Lady in Black. That was . . .

She took several bites of egg.

Crazy. That's what it was. Cuckoo. Just fun stuff made up and passed along from generation to generation, merely to entertain. She confessed she loved them herself—even if for nostalgic purposes. But to actually *believe* in them?

After she'd eaten everything the sisters had prepared, Emma ran back to her room, brushed her teeth, gathered her camera bag and rain poncho, and headed out. The Ballasters waved good-bye at the door.

Shaking her head, Emma stepped out into the crisp morning. No sun, but a little less mist, she noticed as she made her way to the ruins. If the rain held off, she planned to head into the village of Arrick after taking a few more pictures there.

After Emma had set up in the courtyard, a thought crossed her mind. She felt like an idiot. She glanced around to make sure no one saw or heard her.

"Um, Mr. Arrick?" she said, hesitantly at first. "Hello?"

She waited. Nothing happened.

With a laugh, Emma shook her head and continued her shoot. Whoever the cute guy was, he apparently had decided to leave her alone. Maybe her dangling off the twenty-foot steps scared him a little? Just maybe he wasn't such an ogre as to see her get hurt.

The lighting gave a haunting, surreal look to the stark gray of the castle stone, and she took several photos of the wall, the steps, and the gatehouse. Next, she walked into the main building. The *keep*, she'd been told. Very medieval. And *perfect*. Funny, she'd never been drawn to the medieval period before. The era fascinated her now.

The keep actually was in great condition. An enormous hearth large enough to put a car in stood against one wall. Instead of one large set of steps, there were four sets of narrow spiral stone steps leading to the upper floors—one in each corner of the keep. Slinging her bag over her shoulder, Emma headed toward the steps closest to the hearth. She wasn't sure she should test the dark and shadowy steps. The sisters had told her they were safe enough, and would take her to the very top. They'd claimed a gorgeous view from that particular area of the keep, so with a gusty sigh, Emma started the climb.

"I thought I told you to leave."

Foot in air, hovering over the first step, Emma froze. It was the same voice—she'd never forget a buttery voice like that. Instinctively, and less frightened this time, she turned her head.

She wasn't the least surprised to find nothing there.

An absurd thought crossed her mind.

Could there actually be truth to the sisters' tale?

Emma cleared her throat. "Are, uh, you Mr. Arrick?"

Silence at first, then the deep voice deepened even more. "This place is dangerous. You should leave at once."

Hairs rose on Emma's neck and arms. *A voice was speaking, but no one was around!*

Could it be anything *but* a ghost? The ghost of whom? The word itself sounded ridiculous. But ... what else could it be?

Again, she cleared her throat and half turned, facing the keep's main floor. "I should leave Arrick-by-the-Sea?"

Silence stretched out again. "Nay. Wales."

He wanted her to leave the country? Surprised by her lack of actual fear, despite the absurdity of her talking to the empty air, Emma shifted her camera bag and quirked her head. "Why won't you show yourself again?"

She stood there for several minutes before realizing her ghost had said all he'd planned on saying. For the time being, anyway.

Placing her foot on the first step, Emma immediately stopped her ascent. An eerie sound came from the entrance of the keep. She turned, and her mouth dropped open. Her eyes stretched wide and her knees turned rubbery.

In what used to be the doorway stood an enormous helmeted figure. She blinked, unbelieving. A massive man—she guessed it was a man, anyway—dressed in ... some sort of medieval wear, with dark pants that had laces crisscrossing all the way up a pair of thick, muscular thighs, dark boots that came to roughly just between the shin and knee, some sort of shoulder and breast plate with a silver cross in the center, and armbands that looked like fingerless gloves, secured with leather, that went up to his elbows. Bare biceps—*huge* biceps—looked marked, or tattooed.

Just then, the figure began to move toward her, long, powerful strides that seemed to eat the space up between them in seconds. Those two enormous arms reached over his shoulders and grasped the biggest pair of swords Emma had ever seen. A hissing sound accompanied the movement. He stopped, no more than a few feet from where Emma stood, swords completely free of their sheaths. She could do little more than hold her breath. She couldn't even blink.

A pair of slits in the silver helmet, at the level of the eyes, seemed to glare furiously at her.

Then what happened next, happened all at once.

"*I . . . said . . . leave!*" the warrior's deep voice thundered. Then he lifted both swords above his head, and with a vicious yell, thrust them into Emma's body.

With a scream that would curdle anyone's blood and make a B movie queen hang her head in shame, Emma hollered until she ran out of breath. She grabbed her stomach and stared, her mouth dry, fear squeezing her throat closed.

Then, in the blink of an eye, the figure vanished.

Right before Emma's wide-stretched eyes.

The next thing she remembered was her breath leaving her in a long *whoosh*, and then the cold, hard dirt and gravel floor beneath her not-so-pliable body as she slumped down . . .

Chapter 7

Emma's eyes flicked open. The cold, damp floor seeped into her sweater, and she shivered.

Then everything rushed back. Surprisingly, she was *angry*.

So, there really was a ghost.

And he was a *jackass*!

Hurriedly, she pushed herself from the floor and checked her camera bag. She growled as she gently pulled out the contents and checked the lens and moving parts. "You'd better be glad nothing's broken," she mumbled. Satisfied that nothing had been damaged, she stood.

It made her even angrier when she glanced around and found herself alone.

"Hell-*ooo*!" she hollered. "Hey! Angry guy with swords! Come back here!" She walked to the center of the keep, looked in every corner, the roof, and turned in a circle. "Ex-*cuse* me? What's your problem?" She waited, but, as she expected, nothing happened.

So this is what her months-long obsession and night-filled dreams sent her packing to Wales for? To be bullied by a dead guy in need of an anger management class?

Precious.

She cupped her hands and shouted into the air. "I'm

not leaving, Mr. Arrick. Do you hear me? I'm not scared of you or your stupid fake swords!" She glared at the ceiling, since there really wasn't anything left to glare at, shouldered her camera bag, and stomped out of the keep. Mumbling naughty words. Honestly, she couldn't help it. She was furious.

In the courtyard, Emma stopped, her mind flashing ideas of just what to do next. Should she really leave? Sure, she shouted at the sword-ghost that she wouldn't, but why would she stay? What little scenery she'd witnessed in the last few days was in fact gorgeous—and she'd barely scratched the surface with her photography. Or should she tell the sisters? They obviously knew the brute existed. In their defense, they *did* try to tell her. Maybe they had pull with the bully-ghost and could at least tell him to back off while she salvaged something of her insane overseas trip.

Why was she so mad? Was it because she'd had some ridiculous idea about finding something . . . life-altering at Arrick-by-the-Sea? Well, she had—she discovered that ghosts really did exist. But in all honesty, that was sort of a letdown.

She'd expected . . . more.

Then, those treacherous, ivy-covered steps caught Emma's eye. Not really so treacherous—only when you slipped and dangled could they pose a slight threat . . .

As if a light had switched on in her brain, Emma thought of exactly what she needed to do. Hurrying over to a bench that sat with its back against the wall, she set her camera bag down, pulled her sweater down over her hips, and marched over to the ivy-covered steps.

Glancing up, Emma noticed just how gray and dark it'd grown outside. Willoughby had warned her of a storm brewing, but she figured when it started raining, she'd just head back to the manor until the rain cleared up.

She never imagined she'd be busy getting PO'ed at a spirit.

Reaching the steps, Emma drew a deep breath and recklessly took them two at a time. When she reached the top, she quickly said a prayer of thanks for not having a fear of heights, then turned and hollered over the courtyard. "You can show yourself at any time now, Arrick. Seriously. I've got all day. I'll just be right here."

And with that, Emma eased over the edge of the steps, fingers digging into the stone ridge, just as she'd inadvertently done before when the thermos had fallen. *Dangling,* twenty feet above the hard ground.

She didn't have to dangle long.

"*Are you witless? Pull yourself over!*" the voice thundered.

Emma smiled.

"I'm not moving until you show yourself," she said. She swung her feet a bit, and she could have sworn she heard a sharp intake of breath.

"Not doing it," she said again, wiggling. She closed her eyes.

She was awarded with a growl.

"*Are you daft? Get your stubborn arse back over here!*"

Emma's eyes cracked open, the voice closer, clearer. Sure enough, there knelt the helmeted warrior guy, not two feet away. His stare was fixed on her face.

Arse?

"I'll pull myself up once you take off that ridiculous helmet," she said.

No sooner had the words left her mouth than the helmet disappeared. A pair of brilliant blue eyes glowered at her through a fall of tousled, long bangs. "Now get up here."

Emma pondered. Her arms were starting to ache and her fingers had grown numb. She narrowed her eyes at the ghost. "If you disappear, I'll go back over and dangle some more." She really *did* want to get back up now.

"Just get up here."

With ease—only because she knew where the foot-holds were this time—Emma grasped on to the damp rock and pulled herself back to the steps. Quickly rolling to her backside, she sat. The ghost had kept his promise. He'd not disappeared.

He stood a few feet away, staring down at her. He was . . . massive. Perhaps not bulky-massive, like those World's Strongest Man guys who have trouble walking with their thighs reasonably close. This guy—*ghost*—just looked like he could kick the phooey out of anyone he wanted. With his eyes glaring and his face drawn tight, he looked so . . . furious.

Why did he seem so angry at her? She couldn't possibly have done anything to make him so mad. She'd been here a week, not nearly long enough to tick someone off. During high season dozens and dozens of tourists crawled around Arrick's ruins. What was it about her that bothered him so much?

Suddenly, he muttered something under his breath, then turned and headed down the steps.

And just as suddenly, it hit Emma square in the nose: she was interacting with a spirit, the ghost of someone *dead*. That guy with the chiseled face and gorgeous eyes had lived, and had *died*. And he was muttering, angry at her.

Why?

Quickly, she followed.

"Hey, wait," she called, trotting after him. When he didn't stop, she hollered, "*Please!*"

The warrior froze, and waited.

Emma, her heart pounding a bit faster now, cleared her throat. "Please turn around."

Several seconds passed as the warrior-ghost considered her request. Emma stared at his back while she waited. His hair, a deep mahogany color, had been cut, no, *shorn* short in the back, and she already knew it was a bit longer in the front. As she studied him, she noticed a tattoo on the back of his neck—a symbol of some kind. And through the straps of his leather forearm protector thing, she noticed another symbol—larger and more prominent, a band, maybe—she really couldn't tell what it was beneath all that leather.

The warrior then exhaled and slowly turned.

Emma stood frozen still as their eyes locked. Never had she been weighed and measured so ... thoroughly. He had to be all of six feet and three, maybe four inches, and it was a little bit perplexing to have something that large irate at her. His brows slashed down angrily, and those blue eyes blazed furiously through that tangled mahogany hair. The mouth that had such lush lips pulled into a tight, angry frown. The muscle at the hinge of his jaw flinched, and the thick tendons on either side of his neck tightened. Yet his eyes never lifted from hers. She fought not to squirm.

She sincerely hoped he wouldn't explode.

God, he looked so real ...

"Do you have another name besides Arrick?" she asked. Her voice didn't sound quite as confident as it had when she was dangling.

A flash of ... something crossed his face. Sorrow? Pain, maybe? It had happened so fast, Emma couldn't tell. The mean face was back now, though.

"Christian," he ground out.

She nodded, noticing how his r's rolled. She liked it. Funny name, though, for someone with such violence pent up inside. She crossed her arms over her chest. "Why are you so mad at me?"

"Because," he said, nearly in a growl, "you've no fear."

Emma's eyes left his long enough to glance at the

sword hilts poking up over each of his shoulders. She drew her gaze back. "Sort of hard to be scared of something that can't actually hurt you."

Christian's brows drew even closer together, and he took a step toward Emma. He lowered his head and stared profoundly into her eyes. She fought the urge not to retreat.

"You believe I cannot hurt you, aye?" he said, his voice dangerously low and smooth. He pulled closer still, his lips curved into a cynical smile. He glared a bit longer, eyes flashing. "Don't be so sure."

And with that, he disappeared. Just . . . evaporated, like smoke clearing.

It was only then that Emma drew in a decent breath. She blinked, staring into the space Christian had occupied seconds before. No trace of him remained now.

Wow.

It took a moment, really, to gain her composure. That, and the ability to walk on legs not made of rubber. It was as though he'd sapped the strength right out of her body, just by giving her the Stink Eye.

Emma turned, and walked across the courtyard to the bench where she'd left her camera equipment. Slowly, she shrugged the bag over her shoulder. Then she looked—really looked—at the ruins in which she stood. She turned in a circle, staring at the walls, the buildings, the tall, imposing keep, the dark, yawning mouth of the menacing gatehouse. A fierce sea breeze washed over the wall and blew against Emma, tousling her braid and making her draw in a deep breath. Brine. Clover. Clean.

Familiar . . .

No, not familiar. That would be impossible. It probably felt familiar because she, too, lived close to the ocean. The pungent bite of the sea was a scent one rarely forgot. Some thought it to be stinky. She loved it.

As she continued to inspect Arrick, a thousand

thoughts ripped through her mind. Christian of Arrick-by-the-Sea had once lived within the castle walls. He'd eaten, drunk, slept—and she could imagine, as she stared at the open apartments, wondering which one might have been his, that he'd had a fight or two, probably something *else*, as well, She glanced around, trying to envision what it may have looked like in his day, complete, no holes, no decay.

Whenever that was . . .

A heavy drop of rain splatted against her cheek, and Emma just then noticed the furious clouds swirling overhead. The air had grown colder, and the drops were coming a bit faster. She started for the gatehouse, her walk brisk. She was on a mission now, and it included having a little chat with four sweet, seemingly innocent B and B owners. They knew a lot more than they'd let on; she was willing to bet money on it. And Emma wanted to know a lot more about the ghost roaming the lands of Arrick other than that he was incredibly grumpy, an incredible bully, and . . . incredibly sexy.

Once inside the gatehouse, she turned to look at the courtyard. Gray and bleak, yet somehow . . . utterly striking.

Sort of like the original owner, she imagined.

"Meanie," she said out loud as she left the gatehouse and made for the manor.

As soon as Emma was out of sight, Christian emerged in the courtyard.

Things were not working out as planned.

"Well," said Godfrey, who materialized beside him, " 'twas rather interesting."

Christian grunted.

"I," said Justin, appearing between them, "especially liked the sword-stabbing part." He elbowed Christian in the ribs. "Quite effective ghost trickery, aye? You big meanie."

"I must say, 'twas a first, indeed," added Godfrey, chuckling. "I flinched."

Justin laughed, placing his hands on his hips. "Damn me, but did you see how she dangled purposely from the steps?" He shook his head. "Clever girl, if you ask me."

Christian glared at both of them. "If I weren't already dead, I'd throw myself off the seawall, just to escape you." He moved from between them before he clunked their heads together.

Godfrey and Justin merely laughed.

Christian shook his head and began to walk.

"Where are you going now?" asked Godfrey. "You're not going to try and strangle her, are you?"

" 'Tis plain to see she's no' goin' to frighten, Chris," called Justin.

Christian stopped, staring straight ahead. "Suggestions?"

Godfrey and Justin caught up to him. Justin slung an arm over his shoulder. "Aye. Stop harassin' the poor lass. You canna change fate's design, boy." He gave Christian a shake. "You just can't."

Godfrey approached. "You've only a fortnight, lad, and some of those days have already passed. Use the rest of your time together wisely." He gave a grim smile. "Enjoy her."

Christian sighed. "I thought you'd say that." He turned and met his friends' gaze. "But I fear I'm compelled to try it my way." With that, he continued to walk.

"Well, dunna try pokin' her with your blades again, lad," said Justin. "She'll only laugh next time."

Christian continued to walk until he could no longer hear his idiotic friends' laughter.

And as he disappeared into the mist gathered at the gatehouse, he knew without a shred of doubt that they were absolutely right.

Chapter 8

Just as Emma laid her stuff down by the bench in the foyer, Willoughby's melodic voice rang out.

"In here, love!" she called from the kitchen. "Just in time for tea and a fresh batch of cakes!"

Emma scowled at the kitchen door. She knew all the little tea-brewing, cake-baking conspirators would be in there.

Conspiring.

But before Emma could approach and interrogate, the phone rang. One of the sisters answered, then called, "Emma, dear! 'Tis for you!"

Just then, Millicent came bustling out of the kitchen, waving the cordless in front of her. "Here you go!" she said happily.

Emma took the phone and grinned through her teeth. "Thank you."

"Right!" she said, r's rolling, and then darted back into the kitchen.

Emma lifted the phone to her ear. "Hello?"

"So. How is it?"

"Zoë! What are you doing calling here?"

"I don't know. I have a few minutes before I meet with the cake lady and thought I'd check in on you." She lowered her voice. "Find anything interesting there?"

Emma couldn't help it. She snorted, then choked.

"Are you okay?" asked Zoë.

"Absolutely," said Emma. "Lots of . . . lore and legend around here. Very romantic. The B and B owners are very sweet and they've shared a few stories with me."

"That's nice. But what I meant was have you *met* anyone?"

If there was one thing Emma hated with a passion, it was lying. She'd gotten into many a predicament because of telling the truth, but she'd much rather face that than lie.

She could hold back on information, though.

"Emma?"

"Well, sort of," Emma said, not lying.

Zoë gasped. "Really? Tell me. Purge. Let it all go, baby. What's his name?"

Emma slipped a glance around the room and lowered her voice to a whisper. "Christian."

"Oh! Sexy. Why are you whispering? Is he around?"

"Probably," said Emma, again, not lying.

"Oh, okay. You can tell me later, then. I've got to go, anyway. I see the cake lady coming up the sidewalk. My God, she can tease that beehive hairdo high."

Ah, relief. "Lots of Aqua Net, I imagine. Good luck with the cake stuff."

"Um," hemmed Zoë, "you're still coming back in time for everything, right?"

Emma frowned. "Of course I am. Stop worrying so much, future Mrs. Zanderfly."

Zoë giggled. "I like the sound of that. I'll call ya later."

And with that, they hung up.

Emma eyeballed the kitchen door. *Interrogation time.*

When she entered, all four Ballasters stopped, turned, and looked at her. The smell of sharp spices, sugar, and vanilla hit Emma square in the nose. Her stomach growled.

"Are you ready for more cinnamon cake, love?" asked Willoughby. She inclined her head. "Just took it out of the oven."

"This time we added semisweet chocolate chips to the batter," said Maven.

Emma smiled. "Yes, thank you very much." She paused, twirling the end of her braid. "I met someone today. Very interesting guy."

The Ballasters gave her an innocent look.

"Really?" said Willoughby.

Emma sighed. "Oh, come on. I know you all know him." She waited, but the sisters didn't confess to anything. "Gorgeous guy by the name of Christian? Huge? Tats all over? Great blue eyes?" She gave them a frown. "*Dead?* Ring a bell?"

Willoughby met her sisters' glances, then simply grinned at Emma. "So he told you his given name, eh?" She giggled. "That didn't take long."

Emma leaned against the counter and crossed her arms over her chest. "Only after he tried to scare me by poking both of his swords into my belly." She glared at all of them. "I want information."

A smile crossed Willoughby's face as she came to stand beside Emma. "Well, let's go have some tea then, shall we? I'll tell you a bit, but I fear you'll have to coax the rest out of the lad yourself. 'Tis only right." She put her hand on Emma's elbow and tugged. "Come, love. Let's go sit down."

Emma resisted, and instead looked her host straight in the eye. "He's *dead.*"

Willoughby blinked, then nodded. "Why yes, of course he is."

Emma shook her head and allowed Willoughby to lead her into the dining room. Leave it to her *not* to have a normal ghostly encounter with the Gray Lady, or the Green Lady, or even the Lady in White.

No, no. *She* had to have an encounter with *He Who Pokes Swords in Belly*.

And of course he had to be brutally handsome.

Precious.

Close to one hour, two cinnamon cakes, and two cups of hot tea later, and Emma once more stood in the foyer of the manor, camera bag on shoulder. There wasn't much she knew now about the ghost of Arrick-by-the-Sea that she didn't know before she left him back in the courtyard.

Other than he wasn't normally so grumpy. Apparently, that was a trait Emma brought out in him. *Great.*

According to the sisters, he'd have to tell her whatever it was she wanted to know himself.

So it looked like she was in for another jaunt to the ruins. Not that she minded. The castle was beautiful, the seascape breathtaking, and, well, she just loved it. Plain and simple.

That it came equipped with a phenomenally sexy dead guy was something else to consider.

Zoë would think she'd lost her silly little mind.

Maybe she had.

"Off you go, then," said Willoughby, with Millicent, Agatha, and Maven all surrounding her. They looked as if they wanted to go, too. "You try to have a nice chat with young Christian. He really can be most charming."

Emma feared she'd have to see it to believe it.

She smiled. "Thanks. I'll see ya'll later."

The sisters giggled in unison. Emma smiled as she walked out into the cold. At least it'd stopped raining.

"Just call his name, love," reminded Maven. "Never fear. He'll hear you."

"Okay," Emma said, waved, and headed up the lane. She walked through the gatehouse, into the courtyard, and stopped.

It was empty.

What'd she expected? Him to be just standing around, waiting on her?

She made for the keep and took the set of steps Christian had stopped her from going up before. Willoughby had assured her they were safe enough. Tourists climbed them all the time.

Once at the top, Emma's breath caught. She indeed found herself in a vast room that once was probably absolutely gorgeous. A large hearth took up the expanse of one entire wall. *An entire wall.* That was one huge fireplace. Almost as huge as the enormous open space, sunk into a large alcove, that Emma could only surmise once used to be a big picture window.

It looked right out over the ocean.

A pair of narrow stone benches faced each other in the alcove, far enough apart that even with her backside on the edge and her feet stretched out, she couldn't reach the other one. She sat on the left one, and the wind blew in from the gaping hole in the wall, tossing the loose hair that had escaped her braid from her face. The scent of brine washed in, and Emma breathed deeply. The sun had failed to show itself, but somehow, that didn't exactly bother her.

She looked around. Shadowy corners lurked all throughout the chamber, but she didn't see anything resembling a hiding warrior. Finally, she took a few deep breaths to calm her nerves, and cleared her throat.

"Christian?" she said, her voice softer than she'd meant.

She waited, but the warrior didn't show himself.

Maybe he hadn't heard?

"Mr. Arrick!" she said, this time louder than she'd meant. "I'd, uh . . . like to talk. To you, I mean." She sighed. "Please?"

At first, the chamber's only sound came from the wind tearing in through the holes in the window. It whistled

eerily through various cracks and crannies of the ancient stone, somehow making the cold, damp stone that
much colder, damper. Outside, the Irish Sea beat mercilessly against the base of Arrick. A lone gull screamed
overhead.

Emma thought she'd never felt so alone. She drew in
a deep breath.

"You're still here."

Emma jumped, startled, and turned in the direction
of the voice. Across the chamber, within the depths of
the shadows, Christian's tall form emerged. He didn't
move.

"Well," started Emma, "of course I am. Why wouldn't
I be?"

He remained in the back of the chamber. "Because I
told you to leave."

Emma narrowed her eyes. "Perhaps I'll leave when
you give me one good reason why you want me to so
badly." She craned her neck. "Could you please come
over here? I can barely see you."

" 'Tis the point."

"Ugh," Emma muttered. She grasped the bridge of
her nose, massaged, then turned her back to him and
stared out to the sea. "Whatever."

"You have a dreadful temper."

Emma jumped in spite of her preparation not to. She
picked at the distressed hole in the knee of her jeans and
glanced over her shoulder. Christian stood just behind
her. She turned back to the window. "Can you sit?"

Silently, he slid onto the bench across from her. As
enormous as the alcove was, Christian's big self crowded
it.

Emma suddenly realized she didn't mind that at all.

"Anything else?" Christian asked.

Pulling her legs up, Emma secured them with her
arms and studied the ghostly form before her. He looked

so real sitting across from her, legs sprawled in a very guylike manner, hands resting casually on his thighs, head back, blue eyes staring out of that crazy, tousled hair. Even the thick veins snaking across the back of his hands looked real enough to have blood pumping through them.

She knew otherwise.

"Are you finished yet?"

Emma blinked, then blushed. "Sorry." She met his gaze. "It's not every day that I'm in such close proximity with a dead guy."

The slightest of movement broke the stone stillness in the corner of his mouth. "I imagine not." His eyes never strayed from hers.

Emma shifted under his intense scrutiny, and clutched her camera bag. "The sisters told me a little about you."

One mahogany eyebrow lifted. "Is that so?"

With a nod, Emma continued. "I couldn't squeeze much information from them, though." She gave him a slight grin. "They told me I had to get it from you personally."

He leaned forward, ever so slightly. The movement again made the space of the alcove feel tiny. "If I tell you what you want to know, will you leave?"

Emma met his fierce gaze with one of her own. "Absolutely." And that wasn't a lie. Not at all. She had a return ticket in her suitcase at the manor, just to prove it. Of course she'd leave. Her business and life were an ocean away.

Christian gave a slight nod. "Verra well. What do you wish to know?"

Emma studied the warrior before her. It hardly made sense at all—any of it, actually. Here she was, sitting in an ancient fortress, sharing space with a mouthwatering ghost, and she had the floor. She could ask the questions that had been burning her brain ever since she realized just what she was dealing with.

She'd barely come to terms with that, actually.

A *ghost*? It sounded absurd.

Emma brought her legs down and sat cross-legged, hands folded in her lap. She thought about her first question, and then smiled. "Why did it take my dangling for a second time off those steps to get you to reappear?"

The frown was back on Christian's face.

Emma could hardly wait for his answer.

Chapter 9

Why, oh bloody why, did the gel have to ask that?

He looked at Emma hard. Hell, he couldn't keep his eyes off her.

"Because," he started, "I didn't want you to fall and break your scrawny neck."

She cocked her head. "Why is it that hordes of tourists can venture onto Arrick's lands, climb all through the ruins, and yet when I arrive, you want nothing more than for me to leave?" She leaned forward. "How many tourists have you scared the wits out of by poking those swords through their gut?"

He frowned. "Dozens."

She frowned back. "Why are you so cranky?"

Christian studied her. His strength to remain angry at her was fading fast. She was infectious to be around—more so now than ever before. And by the saints, he really didn't want her to leave. Memories of past wooing assaulted him, so much that he thought twice about trying to force her to go—even if it was for her own good.

He was an idiot.

"Okay," Emma said, her tone lightened. She relaxed, and she smiled.

He nearly fell off the bloody bench at the beauty of it.

"Let's try a new approach," she suggested. "All

this grumpiness is very out of character for me. Not natural."

"You seem to be holding your own."

She rolled her eyes. "Let's start over, okay? Let's forget about all that dangling from the steps, hollering, and sword swinging." She stuck her hand out. "I'm Emma Calhoun."

Christian stared at her hand; then he couldn't help it. He grinned. "I know."

"Oops," she said, withdrawing her hand and using it to push a stray strand of hair behind her ear. "Sorry." Then she quirked a brow. "How did you know? My name, I mean." She stared at him with those fathomless eyes. He couldn't help but drop his gaze to her mouth. Christ, the memory of his first taste of Emma's lips hadn't faded . . .

"Emma?" Christian said in a low voice.

"Aye?" she replied.

Christian pushed a long strand of hair from Emma's cheek. Her skin felt soft against his roughened knuckle. He looked at her then, his heart in his throat. "Can I kiss you?"

Emma said nothing, but a smile began and stretched across her cheeks. She simply nodded. Slowly, he ducked his head and pressed his lips to hers . . .

"Christian? My name?"

He shook his head as the memory faded. It was like a punch in the gut that she remembered nothing.

Christian cleared his throat and leaned back. "I know everything that goes on around my lands, Ms. Calhoun."

"Emma," she said, smiling.

Her gaze dropped to his mouth. 'Twas no mistaking, she'd done so. That familiar clout to his heart nearly knocked him backward. He didn't know whether to rejoice, or beg her to leave at once.

Christian had a feeling no amount of begging would

make her leave any sooner than when she wanted to leave.

"This is so unbelievable," she muttered, looking now at her hands. She looked up. "It's unfathomable, to be sitting here with you, like this, and you like . . . that." She rubbed her chin. "Did I really fall from those steps and am lying somewhere, dazed and dreaming?" She didn't wait for him to answer. She got up from the bench and started walking around the chamber.

"I mean," she said, inspecting each corner, "who would have ever thought this was possible? Who *really* believes in ghosts?" She shook her head and bent to retrieve something off the floor. She looked at it, tossed it a few times, then closed her fingers over it, and continued her pacing. "People get feelings that others exist on another plane. They don't really sit down and have a chat—*oh*!" In the next instant, she stumbled and fell hard to the floor. Quickly, she pushed to her backside and sat. Something dropped from her hand and clattered against the stone.

Christian was up and by her side. He squatted down, peering closely. She held one hand with the other, eyes wide. "What's wrong with you?" he asked.

Emma glanced down, at her clasped hands, and Christian did the same.

She looked up, her face pale. "Oops."

Bending over to get a better look, Christian noticed the steady stream of red oozing from her hand. Blood. He looked at the object that she'd dropped. It appeared to be a shard of glass. Probably dropped by a tourist. He frowned. "Dammit, Emma. Why would you pick that up? 'Tis sharp as a blade."

"I . . . wasn't thinking. It's not that bad, really."

He shook his head. "Let's get you back to the manor." He looked at her white face. "Can you make it without falling?"

"Yes." Slowly, she stood up.

Blood drops splattered against the stone floor, and Christian's mind scrambled. "Take your jumper off and wrap it about your hand first. To staunch the blood."

Emma nodded, lifted her arms above her head, and pulled off her jumper, leaving a thinner white shirt beneath it. He saw a flash of her stomach and looked hastily away.

He thought it exceedingly rude to gawk whilst one was bleeding.

"Good. Now wrap it about your hand," he ordered. When she did, he nodded. "Let's go, and be careful going down the steps. God knows I can't catch you if you fall."

"I know," she said, her voice not exactly weak, but not strong, either.

"Willoughby can help," he assured her.

She didn't answer. She was busy making her way down the steps.

Blessedly, they made it down without her falling. "Does seeing blood make you weak?" he asked.

"Not really," Emma said a bit faintly. "But I'm a bit opposed to losing too much of it."

It was then Christian glanced down at the jumper. It was black, so difficult to see the color change. It was not difficult, however, to see they were leaving a trail of blood splatters all the way from the keep.

"Oh God, that looks like a lot."

Christian. " 'Twill be fine, Emma. Just hurry, aye? And don't look down." He didn't want to leave her side, else he'd hurry ahead and tell the sisters.

"Okay, aye," she answered.

They did hurry, with Christian gaining ground, stopping and waiting for Emma, then starting back again at a fast pace. He couldn't help it. He wanted the damn thing sewed up so she'd stop bleeding everywhere. Why on earth would she pick up a bloody piece of glass in the first place? He'd shout at her later for that. Right now, he wanted her in the manor where Willoughby could stitch her hand.

No sooner had they gained the front entrance than Emma swayed a bit. "I think I'm going to be sick," she said. She leaned her head against the wall.

"Steady, lass," Christian said, then disappeared through the wall. He went straight to the kitchen, where he knew he'd find at least one Ballaster. He did, and thank the saints, 'twas Willoughby. "She's bleeding," he said. "The front door."

Christian didn't wait for Willoughby. He knew she'd be right along. He materialized back through the front door to stand beside Emma. She still held her hand tightly, a small puddle of blood building beneath her on the stone walk.

She looked at him, her eyes bleak. "I'm mortified."

Ducking his head so his face was close to hers, he locked on to her gaze. "Be mortified later, Emma. For now, just concentrate on staying upright."

"Okay. I'm all right. Really."

Just then, the door flew open and Willoughby, flanked by Maven, Agatha, and Millicent, bustled out and grasped Emma by the elbows. They led her into the kitchen. Christian followed.

First, they took Emma to the sink. Willoughby unwrapped the hand and gave Maven the blood-soaked jumper. She hustled out of the room with it.

"I'm sorry," Emma said weakly. "Honestly, I don't expect you to help me—"

"Nonsense, child," said Willoughby. "Just you be still there. Millicent, hold on to her."

"Is Christian still here?" Emma asked.

"Aye," he answered, and moved to stand behind her. "I'm here."

"Good."

The word came out with such relief, Christian had to step back. He wanted nothing more than to push his way next to Emma and take care of her wound himself.

Something that would never happen . . .

"Okay, girls, let's move her to the table for the stitching. Move, Christian, love."

"Stitching?" asked Emma as the sisters sat her down.

Christian sat across the table from her.

"Pah, not to worry, dear," said Maven. "Willoughby here was a fine nurse in her day. She'll have you stitched in a jiff."

Christian thought Emma turned an alarming shade of green at the prospect.

Agatha mopped Emma's forehead with a wet cloth while Willoughby rested her hand atop a clean towel. Slowly, she opened Emma's hand, exposing the wound. 'Twas an inch or so long, straight between the thumb and forefinger. It still oozed blood.

"Oh," said Emma, and she swayed in the chair. "Shouldn't I go to the emergency room for that?"

"Look at me," said Christian. When she didn't right away, he said it again. "Emma. Look at me."

She did. "Yes?"

"Willoughby here can stitch just as fine as any doctor at the infirmary, if not better. Let her do her work. Why don't you tell me a bit about yourself? Mayhap I won't be so inclined to boot you out if I find you interesting enough."

Willoughby nodded her approval at his distraction tactics, and started the task of stitching Emma's hand.

"Just a sting, love," Willoughby said.

Emma flinched, but didn't pass out, either. 'Twas a good thing, indeed.

"Look at me," he repeated. When she did, he nodded. "Good. Keep your eyes on mine, aye?"

A slight smile touched her lips. "Aye."

"Where do you come from?" he asked.

"The south. On the coast, like here."

Christian gave her a nod. "Very good. And what do you do to make your coin?"

She took a quick peek at her hand.

"Ah-ah," he warned.

She looked back at him with a sheepish grin. "I take pictures. I . . . have a studio."

He nodded. "What sort of pictures?"

She cocked her head. "How do you know what pictures are?"

With a grin, Christian shrugged. "I've been around, lass. Now, what sort of pictures?"

With a slight laugh, she, too, shrugged. "I'm a wedding photographer."

"Oh, that's lovely, dear," said Millicent, listening. "How romantic!"

"Millie, scissors!" said Willoughby.

Emma's eyes grew wide. "Scissors?"

Christian pointed his finger at first her eyes, then his own. "Gaze right here, Emma."

She did.

Christian fought to stay upright.

Then, suddenly, her eyes widened again, except this time, they were fixed behind Christian. He turned to see Justin and Godfrey, looking on with interest.

"There are more of you?" she asked incredulously.

Godfrey had the good grace to blush, just before he gave a low bow. "Good eve'n, lass. Godfrey of Battersby. This young rogue is Justin Catesby."

Justin simply grinned. "Lass," he said with a slight nod.

"Oh boy," she said. She fixed her gaze back on Christian. "If you think I'm leaving anytime soon, you're crazy."

Justin Catesby burst out laughing.

"There! Good as new!" exclaimed Willoughby. "You're a wonderful patient, dear. You didn't squirm even once!"

Maven plopped a glass full of liquid in front of Emma. "Here, love, drink up. 'Twill make you feel much better."

"Let me see," said Christian. Emma held her hand out to him, and he leaned over it, inspecting the bandages Willoughby had placed. He nodded. "Well done, lass. Now drink your potion."

Willoughby looked at him over Emma's head and lifted an amused brow.

Emma sipped at the drink, then drained the glass. She looked at Willoughby and smiled. "Thank you so much." She flexed her hand gently. "I've never had stitches before. This wasn't nearly as bad as I thought it would be."

Willoughby smiled. "You will be feeling good as new verra soon, I promise. Now, why don't you lie down for a bit? Supper won't be ready for a few hours."

Emma nodded. "That'll be great. Thanks." She glanced at Justin and Godfrey, then back to Christian. "Will you stay with me?"

Christian blinked. "Stay with you?" Christ, he had a hard enough time sitting across the table from her and trying not to look pained.

She again nodded. "I never got to finish my interrogation." She smiled.

Little did she know, he'd do just about anything to coax that smile from her lips.

He cleared his throat. "If you wish."

She beamed. "I wish."

He looked at her wistfully. *As do I . . .*

Chapter 10

"You rest now, sweetling. If you need anything, young Christian can let us know." Willoughby smiled and closed the door.

Leaving her alone with Christian.

Emma wondered briefly what he thought about that. She peered at him, sitting against the far wall in a straight-backed chair. The dim light from the bedside lamp cast a hazy glow over the room, making Christian look even more surreal than usual. Like earlier in the keep, his legs were sprawled, forearms resting against his thighs, hands dangling between his legs.

Swords poked up above his shoulders.

She sighed, coming out of the duvet Willoughby had so neatly tucked her into. "I feel ridiculous, being put to bed." She looked at her bandaged hand. "It's just a little cut."

Christian looked at her and frowned. "That little cut bled all over my solar, and then my courtyard. You left a trail from the castle to the manor. You can stay put for now."

Emma considered that. "I am sorry for bleeding all over your castle." She glanced down at her hand.

"Does it hurt much?"

Emma shook her head. "Just when I flex it."

"Don't flex it."

She grinned at him. "Very funny." Then, she studied him. "I feel as though when I leave here, I'll look back on this like a big, weird dream." She shook her head. "It hardly seems real. *You* hardly seem real."

Christian raised his head, his hair falling boyishly over his eyes. "I can assure you, I'm real."

She nodded. "Can I ask you some questions now?"

Slowly, he nodded.

"Okay." She sat up, adjusted the pillow behind her, and sat, watching him. The harsh beauty of his face nearly made her nervous. But something about him made her feel at ease instead. "When were you born?"

"In 1110."

Emma gaped. "You're kidding me?"

Christian simply stared at her.

"How old were you when you died?" she asked.

He seemed to think about it. "Thirty-five."

Emma nodded. "Do you remember? Dying, I mean?"

Silence stretched for seconds. "Aye."

As much as Emma wanted to know how, she didn't push. For some reason, she felt as though it still pained him. She wondered what it'd been like. Maybe she'd find out later. She cleared her throat. "Wow. And you've been at Arrick ever since?"

His eyes never left hers. Even across the expanse of the room, she could see that. Bright blue and brilliant, they nearly glowed behind that fall of hair. "Nay. I can move about."

"Oh. I hadn't considered that." She picked at a piece of lint on the duvet with her good hand. "I suppose, since you've two ghostly friends out there," she inclined toward the door with her head, referring to Justin and Godfrey, "that there are more out there. Like you."

"More than you might imagine."

Wow. If he would just keep talking, she'd be the most

content, happiest person alive. His voice, tinged with a Medieval Welsh accent, and something else unidentifiable, came out buttery smooth and deep. Unfortunately, every answer he had was short and sweet. Man of few words, she supposed.

Suddenly, her eyelids grew heavy. Emma fought to keep them open. Her tongue felt heavy in her mouth, too. "So Cwistian. Do you have a . . . girlfriend?" Boy, that'd been hard to get out. She knew she'd said it wrong, but couldn't correct it. Maybe she should rest after all.

She thought she heard a chuckle, but couldn't be sure.

In the next instant, he was standing over her. Blue eyes studied her, and she froze. She struggled to keep her eyes focused on his chiseled jaw, but they kept slipping over to check out the full lips. She didn't think she'd ever seen a man with such sensual lips. *She wondered what it would feel like to kiss them . . .*

Now the room turned hazy, and she couldn't see Christian's outline clearly. She thought she saw him smile.

"Are you leaving?" she heard herself ask, even as her eyes were closing.

"Do you want me to?"

Emma scooted down into the duvet and gave in to sleep. She vaguely felt the sting in her cut hand. "Stay," she managed in a whisper. "Stay."

Christian swallowed hard. He knew his heart had beaten its last beat centuries before, but it slammed into his ribs now, so much so he could clearly feel the pounding. Christ, he could barely take it.

He was in love with Emma already, whilst she didn't even know him. He'd been in love with her all this time, and could still feel her lips tentatively pressing against his.

It pained him now not to lean down and try it himself.

All she saw was an anomaly, some strange new thing she never thought existed. *Ghost*. He'd never hated the word more than right now.

"Stop glaring at me," she mumbled in her sleep.

That almost brought a smile to his face. There was indeed something different about Emma this time. He couldn't put a finger on the change, but 'twas there all the same. Mayhap she was bolder, or more outspoken. Still sweet, he could tell that much, but in all the other times he'd encountered Emma's soul before, not one of them would have considered dangling off the parapet steps the way *this* Emma had done.

Something about that characteristic intrigued him.

Moving closer, he bent over at the waist and watched her face in slumber. Before he'd left for the Crusades, he'd memorized every single line, every single mark, the curve of her lips, the way her lashes rested against her cheeks, the line of her jaw. *Everything*.

Even now, in between the years when he didn't encounter Emma's soul, he banked those mental images to memory and thought about them often.

"Christian?" she mumbled.

He blinked. Was she truly asleep? "Aye," he whispered back.

"I think you have the most luscious lips I've ever seen," she said.

Something lodged in his throat. Something *large*. Something he couldn't swallow past. His heart pounded.

"Did you hear me?" she said.

"Err, aye," he answered. Christ, he felt like an idiot. He knew she talked nonsense in her sleep, but . . . he hoped she didn't stop anytime soon.

"If you weren't dead, would you like me?"

Christ. Mayhap he should leave . . .

"Would you?"

"Aye, Emma," he said quietly. "Indeed I would."

She seemed to have settled down. Christian moved to return to his chair.

"I mean, *like me*, like me."

He swallowed hard. "Yes."

"Good," she said, then promptly began to snore.

Christian blinked. He wondered if she'd recall any of it when she awoke.

He wasn't positive he wanted her to.

Settling back into the chair—or at least going through the motions of it, since he wasn't *actually* sitting in a chair, he waited, and watched Emma sleep.

Subconsciously he'd already started counting the days he had left with her.

"Whist!" hissed Willoughby. "Honestly, the *older* you two get, the *louder* you get. Keep it down! If either one figures out what we're up to, all will be lost! You are fully aware that part of the success of this spell is keeping both parties from knowing what's being orchestrated. Now shush!" She leaned over the Ballaster transcript of *The White Witches' Guidebook and Regulations*. Running her finger down the page, she found what she was looking for. "See? There it is. I knew it!" she said in a very low voice.

The other three Ballasters gathered round. Agatha leaned over, peering at the spot Willoughby's finger pointed to. "What is it, Sister?"

Willoughby smiled smugly. "By obtaining a drop of Emma's blood, we're able to bypass steps three and four of *the spell-that-must-not-be-spoken-aloud*." She propped her hands upon her hips. "See? We're further along now!"

Millicent shook her head. "I'm uncomfortable with this whole thing, anyway," she said. "What we have to do to her in order to make the bloody spell work—"

"Zerp! Shh!" cried Willoughby, Maven, and Agatha in unison.

Willoughby patted her sister's shoulder. "Steady, Sister. You know the actual tasks of the spell must not be spoken, either. Refer to them as *steps*. Now, we can only hope for the verra best, and we all knew that going into this. 'Tis what's best for them both in the end."

"*If* it works at all," said Agatha, ever the pessimist. "I will be crushed if it does not."

Willoughby stared at the small stone dish in the center of their potion table. So far they'd not had trouble collecting the ingredients. Emma's blood came as a surprise, although she wouldn't have been opposed to getting it by another means. It did save steps, after all, not to mention she'd already had all the required doses of cardipherous amphibicus phosphate.

"Our Emma has completed step one, aye?" asked Millicent.

"Aye, indeed she has," answered Willoughby. "The girl can certainly eat, and the ingredients hide quite nicely in the cinnamon cakes." She shook her head. "I don't know where that wee girl packs all the food. She's narrow as a reed but eats like a horse."

"Methinks the whole thing is taking a harsh toll on young Christian," said Agatha. "Did you notice his sorrowful features?" She sniffed. "Makes me want to burst into tears at the way he looks so longingly at her."

"It's got to be the worst sort of pain," said Millicent. "Such a shame."

Willoughby's expressions tightened. "That's why this will work, sisters. It *must*." She clapped. "Now come along. This has to ferment whilst we prepare for step two."

They flipped off the lights and hustled out . . .

Emma's eyes slowly opened. She blinked several times, her vision focusing in the dimmed light of her room. As she lifted her hand, it looked as though she had on a boxing glove. *The cut* . . .

Her eyes flashed to the far wall. Christian was there, leaning casually back with his legs stretched out and crossed at the ankles, his eyes fixed on her. She grinned. "You stayed." Somehow, the fact that he'd stayed made her feel happier than it probably should have.

"How do you feel?" he asked.

Emma thought about it. She flexed her hand a time or two, and blinked. "The grogginess is gone, and my hand stings only a little bit." She looked at him and grinned. "I'm sorry I passed out on you." She looked down at her bandaged hand, and she remembered what she'd said to Christian before she passed out. She hadn't meant to, really. It had just ... slipped out. Easing her gaze, she smiled sheepishly. "Err, sorry about before. I'm not usually so bold."

"Is that so?" Christian rose from the chair he'd so patiently sat in while she rested. He walked slowly over, and when he reached the bed where she now sat propped up, he bent over at the waist, studying her fiercely. His eyes peered out from behind the disheveled hang of bangs, and a slow grin started that nearly knocked Emma from the bed. Not a big grin, mind you—she hadn't witnessed that yet. But this grin? It gave her butterflies in her stomach.

That or the way his eyes seemed to stare all the way to her bones.

"You, lady, are vastly amusing whilst you slumber." His eyes suddenly dropped to her lips, and Emma's breath caught. When he looked back at her, the usual bright blue seemed ... stormier. Then he rose. "And that's all I shall say about that."

Emma closed her eyes and bonked herself against the forehead with her good fist. "Ugh, that means I spilled the beans." She looked at him. She wondered briefly if she'd said something else. "What were the beans? What'd I say?"

Christian simply turned around and walked toward the door. "I shall forever keep that"—he glanced over his big, sword-toting shoulder—"happily to myself. I'll wait downstairs for you."

"Wait!" Emma cried.

His chuckle sounded in the room even after he'd disappeared through the door.

"Ooh!" she said, and slapped the mattress with her uninjured hand. "There's no telling what else I said. I'm mortified."

Christian's laugh sounded even louder.

Perhaps, Emma thought, she shouldn't say so many things out loud . . .

With that she eased out from beneath the duvet, fished for a fresh change of clothes, and headed to the bathroom. A smile touched her lips.

Ghosts. Who would have *ever* thought ghosts were responsible for her mad dash across the Atlantic? Or that you could interact with them on a somewhat normal plane?

And to think she still had more than three weeks before she had to return home . . .

Chapter 11

By now the sun had dropped completely, and the sisters had turned on just about every lamp on the bottom floor of the manor. The enticing scent of beef and baked bread filled the air, and Emma's stomach rumbled as soon as she inhaled. But she found that more than to eating, she looked forward to her table company.

She couldn't wait to see Christian again.

So many questions tumbled around in her brain. She wanted to know all about him, his life before he died, what had occupied his time all these years.

He was born in 1110 . . .

Holy ho-ho.

Emma found herself hurrying through the manor.

The high-pitched peals of the Ballasters' laughter, along with more than one male's deep pitch, trailed through the manor, leading Emma to the glassed-in dining room. Gently, she pushed the door open and peeked in.

The Ballasters were seated at two tables pulled together, and the other two ghosts, Justin and Godfrey, sat with them. Christian sat across from one empty chair.

He was looking at her.

Suddenly, those wacky butterflies were back, wreaking havoc in her belly. What was that all about, anyway? A dead guy caused her stomach to flip? She couldn't even remember the last time a live man turned her head.

Insane.

Emma started into the room. The intensity of his thoughtful gaze unnerved her, but she remembered to keep breathing and smiled.

"Oh, there you are, love," said Willoughby. "How's the hand feeling?"

"Much better, thank you," Emma answered. She glanced at Justin and Godfrey. Godfrey blushed.

Justin stroked his roguish goatee and grinned as if he'd planned on having her for dinner.

She gave a tentative smile in return, then slid into the seat across from Christian. His eyes hadn't left her since she'd poked her head in the door.

"Hi," she said.

"Hi," he said in return. No smile, just that weighty stare.

She squirmed.

His lip twitched.

"Here you are, then," said Maven, plopping a large bowl of beef stew before her. Millicent followed with a covered basket of hot bread.

"Um, smells great," Emma said, and smiled. "Thanks."

"There's more, of course," said Willoughby, and pointed to a large silver pot at the far end of the table. "Just there."

She smiled again. "Thanks."

"Right! Let's get the kitchen cleaned up, sisters, and let these young folk have a chat," said Willoughby.

All four bustled out of the room, giggling and waving.

Leaving Emma alone with three ghosts.

"I'll make them leave if you wish it," said Christian.

Emma glanced at Justin and Godfrey and smiled. "I don't mind if they stay." She considered Justin Catesby. He definitely looked like a pirate, what with his long leather coat, his high leather boots, and the pistols hanging off both hips. Not to mention the cutlass. His sun-streaked hair was pulled back into a ponytail. When she looked up, his grin became even more wolfish. She smiled and shook her head.

Godfrey, on the other hand . . . she couldn't figure him out. Just a nice old guy, she thought, with a big, funny hat. A large ostrich plume, or some sort of feather, bounced off one side. He grinned, too.

"Chris tells us you're from America," said Justin.

Emma took a sip of iced tea. "That's right."

Justin nodded. "I know a few lads there, from Charleston."

She smiled. She was sure *lads* meant *spirits*. "Is that so?"

Justin grinned. "You've a charming accent. Reminds me of another lass I know."

"Enough. You two leave now," said Christian.

Justin gave Christian an irritated look. "We've only just started here."

Christian's look didn't falter. "Perhaps the lass won't mind your visiting tomorrow? 'Tis late and you're keeping her from eating."

Justin flashed a grin at her. "My pardon, lass. On the morrow, then?"

Godfrey nodded.

Emma smiled. "Absolutely."

Justin rose then, and came to stand beside her. He lowered his head to her ear. "You know you can ask him anything and he'll have to tell you the truth."

She glanced up at the pirate.

"He's a knight. He won't lie."

Godfrey chuckled.

Christian growled.

And with that, the pair disappeared.

She calculated the space they'd just occupied, blinking. "That's . . . interesting." She shook her head. "It's still so unbelievable."

"Eat."

"Yes sir." She grinned, absolutely loving her new tidbit of information, and dug in. The savory beef stew had chunks of carrot, potato, celery, and onion, and made her mouth water before the first spoonful even hit her taste buds.

"I see you're not one of those fickle gels who get embarrassed eating in front of people."

She wiped her mouth. "Nothing stands between me and my food."

"So I see."

Spooning in a few more bites, Emma studied Christian just as intently as he continued to study her. Not an easy task, simply because she had to struggle to keep her stare fixed on his. Never had anyone affected her like he did. Again, she wiped her mouth and cocked her head. "You're a knight."

Christian gave a single nod.

Finished, she pushed the empty bowl aside and sat back. "That would explain the big swords."

His mouth twitched. "It would."

Folding her hands, Emma leaned forward. "What else did I say in my sleep?"

Now Christian grinned. "I refuse to say."

"But you cannot lie."

He shrugged. "I am not lying. I'm refusing to tell you the information you ask."

Emma shook her head. "No, I'm not asking. I'm *begging*. Please tell me what I said." She batted her lashes. "Purty please?"

Then, he did something she thought she would never in her life forget. Prayed she'd never forget.

He *laughed*. Out loud, white teeth showing, head thrown back—the works.

It was beyond beautiful; it made her breath catch.

However, instead of showing him how much he affected her, she scowled. "Well, I'm thrilled you find it so amusing. I suppose I've learned my lesson by asking you to stay in my room and then falling asleep."

He continued to smile, and the stare was back. She decided to give up trying to force the info out of him. He was tight-lipped and wasn't giving it up.

Instead, she changed directions in the conversation. "So, I'm assuming that since you're sitting with me here while I eat dinner, you've introduced me to your friends, and you sat with me while I slept after getting my hand stitched up, that you've given up on the idea of trying to make me leave?"

Christian studied Emma without answering. Christ, he couldn't imagine the girl getting more breathtaking, but he could barely keep his eyes off her. The indigo jumper she wore brought out the very bluest hues in her eyes, and her cinnamon-spiced hair was swept up into a clasp at the back of her head, making several wisps poke up here and there and bounce with each step and movement. 'Twas the first time he'd known her as a modern lass and the casual, worn-out, and faded jeans she chose looked indeed most comfortable—even with the small tears at the knees. They slung low on her hips and hugged her backside in ways that made his mouth go dry.

Damn.

"Mr. Arrick?"

Focusing his gaze back on his beloved, he gave a short nod. "Aye, it seems for now I've given up trying to oust you from Arrick." What other choice did he have? He couldn't force her to leave, and damn—she was just too infectious for his weak self to refuse. He still had hopes that she could escape the fate that always awaited her at Arrick and live out the rest of her life in peace. Mayhap she'd just remain curious this time, and he would refrain from wooing her. Finally, she'd leave, go home convinced her mission to Wales had been to discover spirits actually walk the very same plane of existence as the living and nothing more. Her heart would remain intact and safe. He leaned forward and pasted a false scowl to his face. "And stop calling me Mr. Arrick. 'Tis silly."

She smiled. "Really? I'm not getting ousted?"

He kept his eyes on hers. "Really."

They watched each other silently. Emma bit her lip, mayhap out of nerves, and his eyes were drawn to the small mark in the corner of her mouth, the ever-so-slight curve that was a fierce reminder that no matter what year, what lifetime, she was his alone. 'Twas a mark only he could see. 'Twas the mark of his heart's Intended, his soul mate, and that she belonged exclusively to him.

Belonged to him, yet would remain out of his grasp for eternity.

Every seventy-two years, she came back to him. He'd woo her, and just as her memory of their original love rushed back, she'd—something would happen to take Emma from him. An accident of sorts. Once, she'd fallen from a horse. Another, she'd fallen down the steps. The very last time, she'd been in Wales as a nurse during the War. He pushed those painful memories away. Just as hurtful was that he hadn't touched her, physically touched her, since the day he rode off to the cursed Crusades.

He had indeed dreamed of touching her aplenty. Craved it.

"Hey," she said. "What's next?"

He cleared his throat, grateful for the interruption of his thoughts. "Are you overly tired?"

"Not a bit," she said.

He inclined his head. "And the hand?"

Emma held the wrapped and injured hand up and gave it a wave. "I barely know the cut is even there."

Christian rose from his chair and nodded in the direction of the door. "Would you care for a walk, then? The moon is high this eve."

Emma's eyes sparkled. "Absolutely. Let me run upstairs and get my coat."

And with that she hurried out of the dining hall.

No sooner had she disappeared through the door than Justin Catesby appeared. He leaned casually against the wall.

Christian glanced at him. "What?"

"So, she's staying?" Justin said.

With a gusty sigh, Christian gave a nod. "Aye. It appears so." He looked at his friend. "Now that the amusing part of her arrival and subsequent fright of finding me a specter has passed, why don't you run along back to Sealladh na Mara? I am fairly sure young Gabe MacGowan is wondering where his friend is of late."

Justin shook his head, and an uncharacteristic dark look flashed over his usually jubilant features. "Nay, he's too busy with his new bride."

Christian remembered that Justin had sort of fancied young MacGowan's American, whom MacGowan had hired to oust Justin and his lot of ghosts from Odin's Thumb Pub and Inn. A lovely, energetic lass with a head full of blond curls had strolled into the seaside village and stolen everyone's heart—including Gabe's. The lad had thought to leave Sealladh na Mara, but instead had found himself a wife. From what Justin had told him, things had turned out rather well. But he didn't wish to ponder that, so he moved on. "What of Godfrey? Where'd he carry himself off to?"

"Grimm." Justin pushed off the wall. "I think I shall join him there. If you need me—"

Christian thumped his old friend on the back. "Aye, I'll know where to fetch you." He looked in the direction Emma had gone. "Tell Gawan and Ellie I just may bring a friend over."

Justin grinned. "Indeed."

Christian nodded. "At least that would keep her occupied. I'm trying not to woo her, you know."

With a gleam in his eye that had won him many a fist against the jaw, Justin Catesby gave a short nod. "Good luck with that, Arrick."

And then he disappeared.

Christian made his way to the stairs. He could hear Emma thumping down them two at a time.

Aye, he thought grimly. He'd certainly need luck.

Luck, indeed.

Chapter 12

Emma hurried down the steps, coat in hand, camera bag on shoulder. This time, she'd remember to take a few photos. She'd been sort of preoccupied before, what with having her first official meeting with a spirit. She thought of what was waiting for her at the bottom.

Rather, *who*.

She shook her head as she took the second-floor steps two at a time. It was beyond ridiculous to get all giddyup over the spirit of a man—knight, rather—who'd died more than eight hundred and fifty years before. The time difference nearly made her gasp.

More than eight hundred and fifty years . . .

Okay—plenty of reason to be all giddy. But why the butterflies?

Because he's freaking hot, that's why. Dreamy-sexy hot. Der.

As Emma pounded down the last flight of steps, she gave herself a mental shake. Certainly she wasn't so shallow that, after meeting an actual ghost, someone from *the other side*, the one thing she couldn't get over was his hotness?

At the bottom of the steps, Christian of Arrick-by-the-Sea stood in the pale light of the lamp, casually leaning against the wall, arms crossed over his chest, that perpetual look fixed and boring into hers. It was as though he knew the exact moment and the exact place she'd emerge.

Emma gulped. Her heart pumped harder. *Yep*. She indeed was that shallow.

How very strange for her . . .

Flashing a wide grin in hopes he couldn't read minds, Emma hurried to Christian's side and looked up at him. "Hi."

The corner of his mouth pulled. "Hi back." He inclined his head toward her shoulder. "Do you plan on photographing at night?"

"Absolutely."

"You're ready, then?"

The intense blue gaze and buttery, deep voice nearly made her run back up the steps. She'd been around good-looking guys before, but they were all relatively safe. They were the bridegrooms of the weddings she photographed. Other than that, she'd really not dated much at all. Nothing serious, really, and nothing runway model good-looking.

Then, she stopped and looked at Christian. *Really* looked at him.

Sure, he was by far the most absolutely gorgeous guy she'd ever seen in her entire life. Talk about *safe*? How much safer could one get than an eight-hundred-plus-year-old ghost?

Her smile, along with her confidence, grew. "Ready!"

Emma continued to stand there, jubilant, waiting. Smiling.

Christian just continued to watch her. Finally, he cocked his head toward the door.

"Oh!" cried Emma. "Sorry." She quickly opened the door and bounded outside. Christian followed, chuckling.

The crisp night air stung her cheeks and reminded her that it was the first of October already. She thought she liked the breathless feeling the chill air brought. Together, she and Christian walked up the lane. A crescent moon hung behind them, having risen to just above the tree line in the craggy forest of Arrick. It threw a silvery blanket over the ground, making Arrick's stones nearly shimmer with moonshine. Slipping her camera out, she adjusted the settings and took a few photos. When she slipped a glance at the impossibly tall warrior beside her, she was surprised to find him just a little bit less tangible than during the day. She wanted badly to reach her hand out and brush his. She knew it'd go straight through, but she wanted to *feel* it go straight through.

Emma refrained, in case that was considered bad manners in the ghost world.

Still, she wondered what it would feel like ...

"Deep in thoughts tonight?"

She laughed. "It's all still just a bit much to take in," she said. She gave him a quick glance. "You in particular." She shook her head. "Very, very weird."

Christian chuckled. "I'm weird then, aye?"

"No! Not you, exactly," Emma explained. "Your ... ghostiness."

That made him laugh. She thought she'd do and say more silly things to make him do it more often.

As they passed through the darkened gatehouse, Emma shivered.

"You're not scared, are you?" asked Christian.

Emma chuckled. "Not hardly. Even though it is incredibly dark in here."

"It used to not be," he said. "Just there, at the foot of those small spiraling steps, a torch was continuously lit." He nodded to the opposite side. "And there, as well. If you look closely in the daytime, you can still see where the stone was charred. 'Twould be the gatehouse sentry's duty to keep the torches well coated and replaced when they no longer burned properly."

"That is so interesting," Emma murmured, peering at the places Christian pointed out. How fascinating it was to hear of how life carried on at Arrick more than eight hundred years ago.

The courtyard looked surreal bathed in moonlight, and Emma's critical photographer's eye scanned the area, looking for the best place to shoot it from. She grinned when she found it. "Let's head over there," she said.

"Whatever you wish," Christian said, his voice washing over her just as smoothly as the light of the moon.

Emma gave a light laugh. "That's a dangerous suggestion to give a woman, you know."

"Mayhap. I'm bold that way."

Emma laughed harder. "Here we go," she said as they reached the ivy-covered steps. "Let's go up there." She pointed to the top. When she glanced up at Christian, his blue gaze locked on to hers. It was strange how much more ghostly he looked at night—almost as though an eerie light, or aura, vaguely surrounded him. She had no difficulty seeing his features clearly.

A single mahogany brow rose and disappeared into the windswept bangs hanging in his face. One corner of his mouth lifted into a boyish grin. "No dangling?"

Emma's heart skipped a beat. Christian was so substantial standing there. She could hardly believe he wasn't alive.

She smiled in spite of her pounding heart. "No dangling." She held up her injured hand. "I can't dangle with only one hand." She winked. "Not for long, anyway."

Christian shook his head and chuckled. "I'll go up first, and you step where I step, aye?" He looked down and gave her a fierce glare. "And for the saints' sake, be careful. I cannot save you if you fall."

"I promise to be careful," she answered. How strange it felt, she thought, to have not only a total stranger but a *dead* total stranger actually care whether or not she fell.

She found she liked it. As a matter of fact, she found she liked a *lot* of things about Christian of Arrick-by-the-Sea.

She smothered a sigh as she watched his backside climb the steps in front of her.

A man who'd once lived, long ago. A knight. A warrior. He was charming, handsome, and he completely fascinated her. It made her heart ache that they'd never be anything more than acquaintances . . .

Christian reached the top and stepped onto the parapet. He could have just materialized there, but he wanted to try to maintain what small scrap of normalcy there was between him and Emma. He glanced down at her now. True to her word, she was being very careful. Her good hand clung to the wall as she climbed the steps.

Once she stepped onto the parapet, she stood without hesitation and glanced out across the silvery sea. "Wow. This is truly amazing."

He looked at her and his insides twisted. "Truly."

Thank the bloody saints, Emma had kept her attention trained to the sea. He was an idiot, in truth. How could he maintain a mere friendship if he continued to allow such ridiculous things to fall from his mouth?

So they spent the next hour making conversation while Emma took photographs. 'Twas vastly astounding. After she took the picture, she'd press a button and turn the camera toward him. He could see the image right away.

They were sitting on the parapet now, he with his legs over the edge, Emma with her legs folded crosswise over each other. She'd just finished snapping several shots.

She leaned toward him. "How's this?" she asked.

Christian knew Emma didn't realize how close they were sitting. He, on the other hand, was painfully aware.

He tried to ignore it—that feeling in the pit of his gut, the feeling that he wanted to lean closer still, and put his lips as close to hers as possible.

Instead, he leaned away from her. He peered at the small screen on the camera, then looked at Emma. "You have a gift, lass."

Her lovely mouth stretched into a wide smile. "Thanks. I mostly take photos of people, though." And before he knew it, she'd lifted her camera, faced it directly at him, and snapped a shot. With a shrug, she glanced out over the courtyard. "You never know what may end up on the picture."

Christian was sure she'd find it fairly void of him, anyway.

The wind had picked up—not that he could feel it, but he noticed Emma's hair had begun to toss about. He clinched his hands into fists to keep from trying to push a long strand out of her eyes.

Thankfully, she did it herself.

"I was thinking something," she said.

"And what is that?" Christian answered. Her voice sounded hesitant.

Emma gave a light laugh, shook her head, and continued to stare down at his hand. "You're going to think I'm a complete weirdo, but . . ." She shook her head again. "Never mind."

"Go ahead, ask," Christian encouraged. He suddenly discovered he wanted to know everything there was to know about *this* Emma. Emma Calhoun. She seemed to have so many fascinating sides of her personality that, well, the others had somehow lacked. Mayhap it had to do with the century?

"I'm embarrassed," she said, looking down at her hands.

Christian swallowed, cursed himself for tempting himself the way he was about to tempt himself, and leaned closer to her. "Do not be, Emma."

Slowly, she turned her face toward his. They weren't so very close—not nearly as close as Christian would have liked. But closer than they had been. Emma's eyes widened as she locked on to his gaze, and a brief smile touched her lips.

Then her gaze dropped to his mouth.

Quickly, she brought it back to his eyes. She smiled. "I, err . . . want to touch you."

Christian all but choked. On what, he hadn't a clue. He had no spit, air couldn't get caught, and God knows he hadn't had food in more than eight centuries.

'Twas fear, he realized. He was bloody choking on *fear*.

Emma suddenly chuckled. "You perv. I want to touch your *hand*." She shook her head. "Jeesh. I'm not that kind of girl."

Christian steadied his gaze onto her blue ones, which seemed glassy in the darkness. "Too bad." He held out his hand. "Go ahead."

Emma narrowed her eyes at Christian, then turned her full attention to his outstretched hand. It hovered between them, and she inspected it mightily before moving.

She hesitated and looked up. "Are you sure?"

"Aye." He wasn't. Not really. This would only make it tougher on him. But if she wanted to, he'd not deny her.

Moving her hand closer to his, Emma suddenly stopped. She again looked up at him, their faces not all too much apart. "Will it hurt?"

Christian couldn't take his eyes off her. "Nay. It will not hurt, Emma."

"Okay." With a quick smile, she glanced back down at their hands. With painful slowness, she brushed hers through his. He hid his reaction well, he thought. But he'd braced himself for it.

She gasped, then yanked her hand back at the sensation Christian knew she immediately felt.

Then Emma slowly swiped her hand through his once more. With wide eyes, she searched his. "*What* is *that*?" she asked in a whisper.

What he wanted to tell her was that the feeling only occurred between two souls destined to belong to one another. Intendeds. He couldn't. He could not bring himself to tell her. Not now. Not *ever*. He'd done it twelve times in the past. And twelve times she'd grown to love him.

Twelve times he'd lost her.

He'd not lose her again.

As long as he knew Emma was alive and happy, living somewhere in her world with a husband, mayhap several children, he'd be satisfied. He'd deal with his pain, his loss, and he'd do it his bloody way.

So he did the one thing that went against all things he'd vowed so long ago, to a king who'd convinced him that war in the Holy Land was the right thing—the Christian thing to do.

He *lied*.

" 'Tis merely the sensation of your bodily matter passing through what little remains of mine," he said, then shrugged. "Nothing more."

Her face immediately fell. "Oh."

Quickly, he removed his hand and stood. "Are you ready to head back, then?"

Emma stood, too, and swung down to the steps. "Sure."

Inside, Christian cringed. Her mood had changed from light to hurtful, and 'twas because of his stupid, flippant remark that it was so.

As he watched Emma clamor down the stone steps, he briefly applauded himself.

He'd not lied fully. He hadn't completely broken his knightly vow not to lie.

'Twas in fact a tingle caused by the passing of their

bodily matters that Emma had felt. She simply didn't realize the impact it'd had on him.

Or that he was saving her from the same wretched heartache he'd now endure.

As they walked back to the manor in silence, Christian silently cursed fate.

Chapter 13

Emma all but stomped back to the manor. She had no idea why, but, well, dang it—she felt like stomping.

She glanced to her left. Christian kept up with her. Silently, but he kept up.

Why had she felt so hurt all of a sudden, when he'd brushed the feeling of their hands passing off as nothing out of the ordinary? She'd thought it was extraordinary.

Perhaps he'd felt it many times before?

Ooh. She hadn't thought of that. Then another thought bonked her on the brain. Man, she must be full of herself for not thinking of this before.

Maybe, just maybe, Christian had experienced that tingly, phenomenal, electric feeling with . . . *someone else*?

Sheesh.

She was an idiot. He'd lived on the earthly plane for more than eight centuries. How had she not thought it possible that he'd . . . encountered someone, another *female* someone—one he might have possibly had feelings for?

Okay—had someone openly discussed this with her a week ago, she would have immediately urged them to see a doctor. A shrink. A voodoo priestess. *Anything.* She would have thought it completely and utterly insane. But now she was experiencing it herself, it didn't sound so insane.

Emma knew ghosts existed now.

Her life was changed forever. She glanced at Christian and sighed.

She'd just acted like a horse's ass.

Pouting. *Pouting* of all things!

Time to reevaluate her attitude. In the time it took them to finish walking up the lane, she'd given herself an attitude adjustment.

At the manor, Emma turned to Christian, looked up at him, and smiled. "Thank you." She meant it, too.

The expression on his face looked puzzled. He cocked his head. "For what?"

"For . . . I don't know," she stammered. "For opening my eyes, for one. You've shown me a whole new world I never believed existed." She looked down. "And for not making me leave after all."

Christian was quiet for so long, Emma finally looked up at him. His eyes flashed in the moonlight, and bored profoundly into hers.

"You're welcome," was all he said.

It made her shudder in her boots.

Pretending he didn't affect her, she grinned. "How obvious would it look if you went into the village with me tomorrow?"

The corners of his mouth twitched. "Why do you want to go there?"

His smile was infectious. "To photograph, of course, and to go to the chippy. The sisters told me how fabulous it was."

"Ahh," he began, and leaned against the stone wall beside the door frame. " 'Tis your belly you seek to satisfy." He shrugged. "We can make it look . . . not so obvious, if you wish."

Emma narrowed her eyes playfully. "What do you mean by that?"

His grin widened. It actually looked more . . . devious. "You'll see," he said. He stared at her for several seconds. Then he pushed off the wall. "Now off to bed with you. You'll get dark circles beneath your eyes if you don't get enough rest."

Emma smiled. "Okay." Gosh, she almost felt as though this were a date. She immediately envisioned Willoughby flickering the porch lights on and off as a warning. She stifled a giggle at that thought. "Will you be at breakfast?"

He grinned. "I will if you wish me there."

"I do wish it." She opened the door and stepped inside. "Good night."

Christian's gaze lingered on hers for some time. Then he gave her a short bow. "Until."

And then he disappeared.

Emma fought the urge to throw her back against the door and heave a heavy, hearty sigh. Obviously, she'd watched too many movies. She refrained and kept the excitement of spending time with the most gorgeous creature she'd ever met all to herself.

She wouldn't let anyone—including the gorgeous creature himself—know just how he made her feel. It'd do no one the first bit of good.

In less than a month, she'd be gone.

As she crept up the three flights of stairs to her chamber, Emma considered just how much that seemed to bother her. The leaving, anyway. Of course, she had to leave. Her life, her job—her business was back in Savannah. She loved her work. It's what she lived for, really.

At her door, she let herself inside, dropped the camera bag onto the bed, and kicked off her boots. Gently, so she wouldn't jostle her sore hand, she pulled her sweater over her head and laid it across the back of the chair.

The same chair Christian had sat in the entire time she rested . . .

"Okay!" she grumbled at herself. "Seriously, Calhoun." She growled low in her throat, much like Christian did. "Seriously."

Now that she had a plan in motion (she wouldn't call it a date out loud), excitement made her steps a bit quicker, her mood much lighter, her attitude thoroughly adjusted. Quickly, she jumped in the shower, washed and shaved as fast as she could without skinning herself alive, towel-dried her hair, lotioned her legs, brushed her teeth, and yanked on her pajamas. Wrapping her hair into a knot, she secured it with a scrunchie, flicked off the lights, and dove into bed.

Reaching over, she turned off the lamp, then settled back into the fluffy comfort of the down mattress topper, pillows, and duvet. It felt as though she were floating on a cloud.

Her thoughts strayed to the twelfth-century warrior who was now her friend.

How she'd give anything to have him as more than just a friend.

Emma resisted the urge to slap herself against the forehead.

She sounded like a dorky ole greeting card.

Her eyelids grew heavy, and the lines between conscious and awake blurred, and Emma heard her own voice whisper out loud. "Christian, are you there?"

Just as she slipped into slumber, she heard him reply. "Aye. Now go to sleep."

Smiling, she did.

At seven a.m. the alarm on Emma's watch sent out a series of shrill beeps, dragging her from sleep. When her eyes fluttered open, she was surprised to find the palest of light streaming in through the picture window in her room. Kicking out from beneath the duvet, she flew to the window and peered out.

While a far cry from sunny, it wasn't overcast and rainy, either. The mist had risen, as well, and Emma could clearly see Arrick's ruins, and the Irish Sea beyond. The treetops bent ever so slightly, so she figured the wind wasn't too bad. Leaning her face against the glass, she was surprised to find it cool, but not freezing as it had been.

She smiled. It was going to be a perfect day. If the light remained as it was, photography conditions would be her most favorite—light, with no shadows, no flash needed. Perfecto.

At the bureau—she'd finally managed to put all of her clothes in a somewhat organized manner out of her suitcase—Emma chose a favorite pair of faded jeans, a long-sleeved tie-dyed tee, and another long-sleeved tee, this one in black. On the sleeve of her right arm and left chest was her business' logo: two Celtic knots entwined, with FOREVERMORE PHOTOGRAPHY in a fine scrawl over and beneath the knots, in cream and emerald green. She'd created the design herself. Digging through the drawers, she fished out a comfy bra and a pair of socks.

Just as she had her pajama top lifted halfway up her stomach, she froze, yanked her top back down, and cleared her throat. "Christian?"

A few seconds passed, and she grasped the hem of her top again.

"Aye?"

Heat flooded Emma's face. "Please tell me you're not in here watching me skin out of my jammies."

Christian's voice chuckled. It did sound a bit . . . muffled.

"Nay, girl," he said. "I'm in the dining hall, waiting for you."

Emma glanced around the room. "Then why can I hear you?"

Another chuckle. " 'Tis one of the few tricks I possess. Now hurry up. Your porridge is looking a bit . . . dodgy."

"Okay." Shaking her head, Emma threw on her clothes, all the while thinking how completely insane the entire ghost experience was. She wondered briefly whether, once home, she would look back on her trip and think it all a crazy dream. Would it still seem real to her?

Would Christian?

She laughed. Of course he'd still seem real to her. Why wouldn't he?

Hurrying to the bathroom, Emma pulled her hair into a fast pair of braids, brushed her teeth, applied all the girlie stuff she normally applied, a teensy bit of makeup, and decided on footwear. Since they weren't hiking today, and it seemed relatively dry outside, she chose her favorite old pair of comfy Converse sneakers. Since she had to come back up and brush her teeth anyway, she left her camera bag and hat on the bed, and hurried downstairs.

As soon as she stepped into the first sitting room off the stairs, Willoughby greeted her. She wore a pair of navy blue sweatpants and a matching sweatshirt. Her red hair matched her lipstick.

Emma thought she was absolutely delightful.

"Good morning, love! How was your sleep?" Willoughby glanced down. "And your hand? How's it feeling this morn?"

Emma smiled, then wiggled her fingers. "It feels a little stiff, but okay. Thanks."

"Well," Willoughby said, "after breakfast I'll check the wound, clean it up a bit, and re-dress it before you and Christian head out, aye?"

Emma nodded. "Sounds good."

"Well, run along." Willoughby shooed her toward the dining room. "Your breakfast and . . . your handsome escort for the day await you."

With a giggle, Willoughby Ballaster hurried off.

Emma watched her go, shook her head, and then continued on to breakfast. The air in the manor carried the pungent scent of citrus, and she couldn't help but hope the sisters had cooked up something else tasty and very . . . Welshy. Oooh, boy, maybe they'd made a lemon tart. She thought she could eat a whole one.

A handful of seconds later Emma reached the dining room. She opened the door and poked her head inside. Her eyes found Christian right away, seated at the same little table she'd sat at each morning. It had a perfect view of the castle.

Smiling, Emma stepped in and started across the room. Christian stood.

"Good morn to you," he said.

Emma stopped in midstride. Her breath caught in her throat and she blinked, resisting rubbing her eyes. Somehow, her feet continued to carry her to the table.

She swallowed once, then once more. She cleared her throat as she took in the sight of him, head to toe. She blinked again. "How . . . did you manage to do *that*?" she asked.

A grin slowly slashed across Christian's face. He gave a casual shrug. "You wanted inconspicuous, aye?"

Emma thought she nodded. She could have possibly said aye. Her mouth went dry.

Good Lord, give me strength . . .

Chapter 14

At the table in the Ballasters' glass dining room, amidst the sea cliffs, crags, and forests of northern Wales, stood Christian of Arrick-by-the-Sea. A twelfth-century warrior who'd lost his life at the age of thirty-five—although he didn't exactly appear to be quite that—he'd been roaming the living plane of existence for more than eight hundred and fifty years. He wore a pair of lethal blades over each shoulder. He'd once hacked heads off with those blades, so she'd been told.

Pretty crazy, right?

Emma continued to study that ghost, Christian.

The same one who'd assured her he could be inconspicuous while they were walking around the village together.

The *very* same one who'd used one of his special *tricks* to change out of the lethal-wear of a twelfth-century warrior and into . . .

Spectacularly modern . . .

"Step from behind that table and let me see you," Emma commanded.

Without a word, Christian did as she asked.

Emma thought she'd start from the floor and go up.

A pair of worn, brown leather boots replaced the midcalf ones he normally wore. Comfy-looking, faded jeans clung loosely to his long legs, a white tee beneath a dark blue long-sleeved shirt, unbuttoned and untucked, covered his torso. His unruly long bangs were pulled back and secured at the nape of his neck with . . .

"Turn around," Emma instructed.

With a grin, Christian turned.

. . . a small silver clasp.

Wuh.

"Inconspicuous enough?" he asked, turning back around. Blue eyes were back on hers, flashing.

"That all depends," Emma said, moving to her seat.

"On what?"

She shrugged. "On how many girls with a pulse there are in the village."

Christian chuckled. "I take it you approve?"

Emma smiled and sat down. "Definitely." She eyed him again, stunned by just how incredibly gorgeous he was. "So, are you saying *anyone* can see you? And are you going to explain to me how this ghostly trickery of yours works?"

He gave a nod and pointed at her bowl. "Nay, only those who are sensitive, and that I wish to see me, can see me. And aye, I shall explain whilst you eat."

"No problem there." Emma dumped three spoons of brown sugar into her porridge, followed by a big, plopping spoonful of butter. She eyed the cream and poured some of that in as well. As she stirred, she felt Christian's gaze on her. She looked up, his features tight. "What's wrong?"

He inclined his head toward her bowl. "How does that taste after you've added so many more ingredients?"

Lifting a spoonful, Emma took a bite. Steaming hot, creamy porridge with all the good stuff added in. She chewed and licked her lips. "Like heaven."

It was then she noticed how Christian's eyes had followed the path of her spoon.

She cleared her throat. "Trickery?" she prompted, and continued to eat.

A fraction of a second later, he looked up. " 'Tis nothing more than my mind conjuring an image around my form. Does that make sense?"

Emma looked at him, spoon in mouth, and studied him. Finally, she removed the spoon and shook her head. "Not at all."

Christian tried hiding his smile behind his hand.

"So," Emma started, "am I . . . sensitive? Or am I one of those folks you wish to see you?"

He leaned forward, moved his hands to the table, and looked at her. "Aye on both accounts."

"Interesting." Emma noticed that his hands were very close to her teacup, just resting there, casually. How real they looked, with fine, line variations in the skin, the roughened cuticles, the thick veins. One hand even had a tattoo, atop the hand, in the space between his thumb and forefinger. She leaned closer. "What's that?" It looked like initials, but in another language.

Christian glanced down, then met her questioning gaze with a slight smile. "A reminder."

Emma set her bowl aside, drained her teacup, and wiped her mouth. "Of what?"

"Oh, good! You've finished," said Willoughby, bustling into the dining room. Agatha and Millicent trailed her. They quickly, before Emma could protest, gathered her dishes.

"Follow us into the kitchen, love," said Willoughby. "I'd like to look at that hand before you two leave." She winked at Emma as Christian stood up, and leaned over to whisper in her ear. "Quite a dish, eh?"

Emma grinned as she snuck another peek. "Quite."

In the kitchen, Willoughby swiftly unwrapped Emma's injured hand and inspected the stitches. At the sink, she poured something over the cut—peroxide, Emma thought, since it bubbled—patted it dry with a disc of cotton, and dabbed ointment onto it. Then, she wrapped it with a fresh length of gauze and secured it with tape.

"There," exclaimed Willoughby. "Good as new. Now, you two run along and have a lovely day."

Emma flexed her hand and smiled. "Thanks, Willoughby. You've really gone way beyond the duty of a B and B host, you know."

Willoughby, sweet thing that she was, blushed as red as her hair. "Go on with you now, lass. Shoo." She glanced at Christian. "As for you—try not to walk through anyone, aye?"

"Yes, ma'am," he answered, with that odd, sexy accent. He gave Emma a smile.

She nearly tripped from the impact of both.

Instead, she took a breath. "I'll be right back."

And before Christian could answer, she dashed up the stairs to brush her teeth and retrieve her camera bag and a light jacket.

This day, she thought as she made it to the second floor, *will be one I'll want to remember for the rest of my life . . .*

Willoughby pulled the curtain back, watched the unlikely pair amble down the lane, and turned to her sisters.

"Well, at least he's being more cordial. I thought for a minute there he'd remain a brute," she said in a voice barely above a whisper. She knew Christian could hear the lightest of noises and he certainly didn't need to hear any of their goings-on.

Maven, Millicent, and Agatha all nodded in agreement.

"Everything seems to be going accordingly," whispered Maven. "Don't you think?"

"Aye," whispered Willoughby in return. "I see no recognition on her part yet, which is just what we want." She glanced back out the window. They were out of sight. "And whilst the lad seems to be having difficulties remaining ... platonic, he's holding his own. I'm most proud of him."

"Aye, especially since he's clueless of our plan," said Agatha.

"As it should be," added Millicent. "We mustn't slip up this time."

"We've six hundred and seventy-two hours to make sure everything happens as it should," said Willoughby. "Step two should begin kicking in rather soon."

Millicent wrung her hands together. "But what if the poor lamb falls, or truly hurts herself—"

"It won't happen, Millie!" said Willoughby with determination. "It just ... can't." She glanced at her sisters. "We've already drastically altered their normal seventy-two-year path by initiating the *you know what.* If we succeed, things will indeed not be as either would have ever hoped. But loads better than if they'd just continued ... existing." She glanced at them. "Aye?"

The Ballasters all nodded in agreement.

"They must continue on the path they're on now—as friends. And then build from there. The longer they both fight their urges, the better. They mustn't admit their ... feelings too soon. And she mustn't discover who she ever was in the past. Not now, anyway. Very tricky business, but 'tis the rules. Agreed?"

Maven tilted her head, rubbing her chin with a forefinger. "What if, by chance, they *do* admit their ... feelings too soon?"

The sisters all waited.

"Well," started Willoughby, "we'll just have to make sure that doesn't happen. The balance here is precarious, indeed. We want them together, but not ... like that. Not yet." She eyed her sisters. "We shall take shifts to keep an eye out, if needs be. Agreed?"

"Agreed," they all said at once.

"Splendid. Now let's get started on dessert. That lass has a monstrous sweet tooth. I daresay 'tis most convenient for our . . . ingredients . . ." Willoughby grinned.

Christian walked beside Emma, keeping a safe distance from her side. Not that he didn't want to be close. That part of him would never subside. But he didn't want to *merge* into her.

He shoved his hands in his jeans pockets and glanced down at her. She had a knitted hat of a myriad of colors pulled down over her head, and two braids poked out, one on each side, resting on her shoulders. She carried a perpetual smile on her lips, and every several handfuls of steps, he noticed her drawing in a deep breath.

She liked it at Arrick.

She always had . . .

"I don't ever want to leave here," Emma said on a sigh. *"The way it smells, the scenery . . . I love everything about it." She smiled at him. "Especially you."*

Christian's heart pounded. Yet at the same time, that same heart sank. "You deserve more than a spirit, Emm. I can never give you what a live man could."

She looked at him then, those large, blue eyes round and soft. She lifted a hand, close to his jaw, and smiled. "You give me more, Christian. So much more . . ."

"Hello? Earth to Christian?" Emma said, snapping her fingers.

Christian blinked and looked at her. When she smiled up at him, like she was doing now, it all but wrenched his heart out, knowing she remembered nothing of their past.

At least she seemed to like him.

The path from the manor wound nearly two miles down the craggy hill, and every so often Emma would stop, point her camera at some bit of flowering weed, or a clump of rock, or an old tree. She always asked what the names of things were, and he'd tell her. She'd nod thoughtfully as if banking it to memory. Very curious, his Emma.

His Emma. He'd always thought of her as that, but this time had to be different. If he was going to allow her to stay on at Arrick, so that she'd go back to the home she'd made in America, they'd have to just remain ... Christ, saying the word in such context nearly made him ill. But he said it anyway. At least, to himself.

Simply friends.

Surviving it would be his second death.

"You're awfully quiet," Emma said beside him. "Are you sure you want to come along?"

His eyes moved to hers. "Aye. Just enjoying the day. It's been a while since I took such a leisurely walk about with a, er, company."

"Hmm." She looked down at her feet while they walked. "Can I ask you a question?"

Christian eyed her. No good could ever come from a woman speaking that handful of words. "Just one?" he said with a slight grin.

Emma laughed and kicked a stone with her funny little shoe. "Probably not. I'm curious about too many things to stop at just one question."

"No doubt." He laughed, too. "Ask away." Hopefully her questioning would be safe enough. Too much jostling of her memory may cause her to remember. And as much as he selfishly wanted that, he knew 'twas not what was best for Emma.

As they carried on down the lane, toward the one-track road that would lead to the village, Emma began her onslaught of questions.

The first, he should have known, was one left over from breakfast.

"That mark on your hand," she said, pointing at it. "You said it was a reminder." She looked up at him. "What did you mean by that?"

Christian glanced at first his mark, then to her.

He hastily reminded himself they should simply remain friends.

He drew a breath. "The man who slew me gave it to me as I lay dying," he began. "As a reminder throughout my eternal existence that he bested me, that he was the victor, the better warrior."

Emma stared at his hand for several moments. "I know it's been a long time, but . . . ," she said, giving him a look that he'd remember for the rest of his roaming. "I'm sorry."

Christian cleared his throat. "Aye, 'tis been a long enough time, lass. Don't worry so."

They walked the lane in silence, but only for a handful of moments.

"I've another one," she said.

He waited.

"Were you ever married?"

He looked at her then, and her face was turned up, waiting an answer.

He gave it.

"Nay," he said quietly. "I've always been alone."

Chapter 15

Emma looked both ways before crossing the road. But not before Christian had stepped ahead of her and done it first.

It amazed her that even after nearly nine centuries, the chivalry instilled in him as a knight was still so strong.

Emma found she liked that.

Thinking herself sneaky, she chanced another peek at Christian as they walked. He still completely fascinated her. He lumbered beside her in a totally guy fashion, with long, casual strides, hands shoved deep into his jeans pockets, bent over just the slightest to make up for his height compared to hers, she figured. He'd duck his head to look at her when she spoke. Those ancient blue eyes, always studying her.

Had he not been dead, she'd have been slightly intimidated. She didn't have a complex about her looks or anything; she accepted herself for what she was. Ordinary. She was fine with that, really. Flashy just wasn't her style. But her looks were ordinary, her features ordinary, and Christian? She snuck another glance. Had he been alive in the present, looking like he did now? No way would he ever give her the time of day. Guys like that preferred girls with tans and big boobs, manicured nails, salon-styled hair, and high-fashion clothes. There was absolutely nothing wrong with that look, of course. She was just happiest in jeans, T-shirts—she was simply . . . Emma.

"No more questions?" he asked, ducking his head to catch her gaze.

Emma smiled. "Oh, loads of them. I'm just pacing myself."

Christian chuckled.

Emma absently glanced up at him. Her gaze was drawn to his hair. He wore it parted roughly in the middle, and the tousled bangs hung loose and longer. Now those bangs were pulled around to the back and secured with a silver clasp. Pretty sexy, but a thought struck her. She cocked her head, suddenly intrigued. "I thought the guys in your century wore their hair long." She reached her arm around her back and touched the middle. "About here. Why is yours short?"

Christian looked down at her, grinned, and shrugged. Again, in such a guy fashion, it made Emma smile. " 'Twas something I did before going off to war so it wouldn't get tangled . . . in . . . my . . . helm. Emma?" He stopped and looked back at her. "What's wrong?"

Emma had stopped. A strange feeling in the pit of her stomach had struck her—much like it had when she'd first arrived at Arrick-by-the-Sea. She continued to stare at Christian, even as he drew closer. He bent his head to hers, their eyes locked.

"Emma? Are you ill?"

Emma rubbed her temples with the pads of her forefingers. Something . . . weird was happening. A flash, like a frame from a movie.

It was so quick; she barely even knew it'd happened.

"Emma?"

That fast, the feeling faded, and she met Christian's worried gaze. "I'm fine, I'm fine." She laughed, and shook her head. "But I think I just had a mixture of movie flashback and my own creative imagination."

His brows drew closer, worried. "What do you mean?"

She shook her head again. "This is going to sound weird, but for a split second I saw you, sitting on a hacked-off tree stump, cutting off your long hair with a knife." She peered at him. "Funny, huh? I must have seen something similar in a movie."

A muscle flinched at his jaw. "Aye, mayhap so." He inclined his head. "Ready?"

She smiled. "Absolutely."

They walked, they talked, but Emma could tell something was bothering Christian. His mood wasn't quite as light as when they'd left the manor. She wondered why that was. Maybe he was getting tired of all her questions? Maybe she'd said something offensive.

As they continued down the narrow, one-track lane, a few whitewashed cottages began to appear. They'd passed a sign printed in Welsh, with a roaring red dragon painted on it—the country's symbol, Christian had told her.

They rounded a turn, and then suddenly, there it was. The village of Arrick-by-the-Sea. Emma stopped and took in the view. She'd noticed remnants of an aged stone wall, sometimes stretching for quite a ways, other times not there at all. It now stood prominent, completely encircling the small, medieval village. A walled village. How cool.

A small row of brightly colored storefronts faced the sea, so Emma could really only see it from the side. A few buildings, made of stone, stood taller than the storefronts. It made a nice contrast, she thought.

"Let's stop right here for a minute," she said. "I'd like to get a few shots from this angle."

"Whatever you wish, Emm."

Emma froze, and she turned her gaze to Christian. A current of . . . *something* shot through her, and she stared. He stood there, staring right back. *Emm . . .*

Just that fast, the weird feeling was gone again.

She shook her head. "I think I must be needing food soon," she said.

Christian laughed. "I'm not surprised at all."

Fishing out her digital and lens, Emma made the lighting adjustments, then took several shots of the quaint medieval town from the lane. She heaved a sigh.

The rest of the afternoon went just as perfectly.

As they walked the cobbled paths of Arrick, Christian pointed out various landmarks that had been there in his day. Most of the buildings were much newer, he'd said, but the somewhat taller, narrow stone building at the point of the crescent used to be and still was Arrick's kirk—a church, he'd explained.

Not many people were out and about, Emma noticed. That was a good thing. Twice she witnessed firsthand just how quick a six-foot-three-inch warrior could be. Once, an older man and his wife were strolling by, and they thought to stop and ask for directions to a certain set of ancient standing stones. Christian whispered the directions to Emma, and she obliged the older couple. But when they made to leave, they darted straight toward Christian. He had to jump out of the way—out of everyone's way—to avoid the older couple from passing through him.

If they only knew.

All in all, Emma found Christian to be the perfect tour guide, the perfect gentleman, and the perfect companion. He'd stopped for every photo opportunity she'd wanted, including pictures of several of the villagers. People were her best subject.

Although the female population was scarce, what little was there, young and old alike, couldn't help but gawk at Christian as he sauntered by. Heads literally poked out of storefronts as they passed. Emma knew. She'd turned around to see.

Christian had seemed completely oblivious to it. Strangely enough, all his attention seemed to be focused on *her*.

She'd caught him several times, simply staring.

The big knight's attention made her a little nervous, but it was impossible not to feel special when Christian turned his sights to her. She simply wasn't used to being the subject of one's close scrutiny. It pleased her, though she'd never admit it.

The only thing he'd seemed hesitant about was visiting the church. She'd been able to tell from his expression that he didn't want to go there. Perhaps it'd held a bad memory for him. She didn't know, but as wonderful as he'd been the whole of the day, she wasn't about to pout about not going to the church.

The last stop of the afternoon was at the chippy. Emma's stomach growled at the delicious aroma of fish-and-chips rolling out of the open doorway. Three stone benches sat just outside. She turned to Christian, smiling.

"I'm going to bring some back for the sisters," she said. "They've been so kind to me." She held up her injured hand and wiggled it.

Christian inclined his head to the benches out front. "I'll wait just here." He glanced inside. "The fit is too tight in there for me, I believe."

Emma gave a nod. "Okay. I'll be right back. Try not to get into trouble." She wiggled her brows. With that, she strode into the shop.

A tall, lanky, friendly man with a shock of black hair and green eyes stood behind the counter. He grinned as she walked through the door. "Hallo, there, miss. What can I help you with?"

Emma smiled. "Five orders of fish-and-chips, please."

The man cocked his head. "All for you?"

Emma laughed. "Tempting, but no. I'm taking some home."

He laughed and shook his head, and started on frying the fish. Emma watched, occasionally peeking out of the door to watch Christian.

"From the sound of it, you're a wee bit far from home, aye?" he asked. "Here on holiday from America, are you?"

Emma nodded. "For a month. I'm staying up at the Ballasters' B and B."

He chuckled. "Och, you run into any ghosties of late, then?"

Emma's eyes darted to Christian, now standing and leaning against the lamppost just outside the shop. She smothered a smile. "Why do you ask?"

The sizzle of frying fish-and-chips in hot oil nearly drowned out his laugh. "The old girls didn't tell you about the legend?"

They'd told her about a couple, but after meeting Christian, it was sort of hard to concentrate of myths and legends anymore. She smiled. "A few. Why, do you know any?"

He chuckled, shaking the fish, then settled the basket back into the oil. "Oh, aye, for a certainty. Everyone round here knows of the Saracen's Dread."

Emma blinked. She'd not heard that one, but it sounded interesting. "Saracen's Dread?"

The man nodded, wiped his hands on his white apron, and leaned on the counter, facing Emma. His eyes gleamed. "Long ago, a twelfth-century Crusader cut a path of destruction through the Holy Land. So fierce was he that even the knights fighting with him feared his fury."

"Wow," Emma said.

He turned, dumped the fried fish out onto a paper-towel-lined flat pan to drain, then lowered a basket of chips into the oil, which sizzled loudly. He turned back to Emma.

"Aye, wow indeed. 'Twas said to be a mighty lad, nearly six and a half feet tall and could hack a man's head off with one swipe of his blade."

"Umm," Emma said, trying not to envision the scene too realistically. "Appetizing."

The man laughed. " 'Tis said the warrior carried a lethal pair of swords—one over each shoulder, and could use his right just as well as his left. But simultaneously? Lethal. 'Tis said that's how he acquired the name Saracen's Dread. The Saracen warriors even feared him." He inclined his head to the right. "Up the way a bit you'll notice the pub, Saracen's Dread. Named after him, it was."

Emma watched him, unblinking. "And why should I have heard that at the B and B?" She already knew the answer.

The man lifted the basket of chips out of the oil and dumped them to drain. He turned back, smiling. "Because, lass, 'tis said his restless spirit roams the ruins, looking for heads to hack off."

Emma glanced out the door where Christian waited for her. She thought she saw his mouth lift in the corner.

"Here you go, then," the man said, setting a large bag atop the counter. "There's another tale—this one the lasses seem to like better."

Emma handed him payment and took the bag. "What is it?"

As the man turned to put the money in the cash register, he started. " 'Tis said the same warrior lost his true love when he went to the Holy Land. 'Tis rumored that he still haunts, not because of the Holy Wars that took his life, but because he refuses to pass into the next life without his love."

"That's," she started, meeting the man's gaze, "really something else."

He nodded, satisfied. "I knew you'd like that one." He nodded toward her. "Enjoy the fish, and make sure to grab yourself plenty of sauce and vinegar."

She smiled. "Thanks."

Gosh, she had been so caught up in accepting being ushered around by a ghost that she'd forgotten the story of the warrior who'd lost his soul mate. *It was Christian . . .*

Then, before she had time to ponder that thought, several things happened at once.

First, she glanced out the door. When her eyes landed on Christian, who was leaning casually against the post, his hands shoved into his pockets, that crazy, weird feeling gripped her again. So powerful was the feeling that it nearly made her drop the bag.

Next, she heard a high-pitched voice—that of a girl— outside the chippy. She heard her holler a name, a man's name.

After that, Christian turned, presumably looking in the direction of the hollering girl.

And then, before Emma's eyes, she watched as that same girl hurled her excited self right at Christian. Of course, she fell right through him.

The proceeding blood-curdling scream echoed off every surface in the chippy.

Emma couldn't reach Christian fast enough.

Chapter 16

Christ's saints alive, the girl had thrown herself at him faster than he'd expected. She must be powerfully sensitive, he thought. And he'd had his mind so intently on Emma that he'd not paid attention. He'd allowed himself to appear.

He stood, dumbfounded. The girl was sprawled on the ground, her face white.

Shrieking.

"Excuse me," said Emma, out of nowhere, stomping right up to the girl, who looked to be in her mid to late twenties. She helped the girl up. "You should think twice before launching yourself at another woman's man," Emma said, her voice sharp. "Some women might get a bit jealous."

"But," the girl started, her eyes darting back to him, "I fell—"

"Yes, you did," said Emma, scowling. "After throwing yourself at my man. Now, let's just part ways and forget it happened, okay?"

The girl looked befuddled, glancing between him and Emma. Finally, she shook her head and shrugged. "Sorry. Mistook him for someone else."

Emma gave the girl a short nod, then walked right up to him. "Bend your head toward mine," she whispered.

Christian lifted a brow. "What?"

"Just do it and then be very still," said Emma. "Now."

And so he did.

Emma then rose up on tiptoes, tilted her head just so, and brought her lips as close to his as she could without falling through his form.

She pretended to kiss him.

It nearly knocked him to his knees.

Slowly, she pulled back, her eyes wide, staring hard into his.

He couldn't take his off her.

Neither one noticed the young girl hastily walk away.

Embarrassment suddenly replaced the look of surprise on Emma's face, and she looked away. She cleared her throat, then glanced around. "Well, um, I guess my plan worked, huh?" She looked up at him then, suddenly shy. "Sorry about that."

Bleeding saints, what was he to say to that? What he wanted to say, nay, beg, was for her to do it again. Except make it longer.

Instead, he grinned like the dope he was and inclined his head to her bag of fish-and-chips. "Mayhap we should get those to the manor before I stumble through another soul, aye?"

Emma nodded, and gave a soft laugh. "Yeah, you're right. Let's go."

Christian often felt idiotic, but he felt more so now than ever. "I wish I could carry some of that for you," he said, inclining his head to the bags.

Emma's pace picked up as they climbed the path leading to the one-track lane, out of the village of Arrick. "No problem," she said. "I'm used to doing things on my own." She gave him a slight shrug. "It's the way of the twenty-first century. Not much chivalry left in my world." She glanced at him and gave him a half grin. "It's what women are used to these days."

Again, he hardly knew what to say to that.

Luckily, Emma knew how to change the topic.

"I heard something interesting from the fish guy," she said, staring straight ahead as they continued their climb to the road.

"Is that so?" Christian said. "Do tell."

Her laugh was lighter, as though she was glad to distance herself from their sort-of kiss.

He'd not forget it.

She cut her eyes at him. "Heard you had yourself a little nickname."

Christian laughed, then met her gaze. "I've many. Which one did you hear?"

"Saracen's Dread. Pretty frightening tale, I might add. I seem to remember not all that long ago being on the receiving end of those double swords." She grinned. "Although I'm pretty sure my experience was a lot less scary than the poor Saracens'."

Christian again laughed and shook his head. He shoved his hands deep into his pockets, walking as close to her as he could without their limbs falling into each other.

Not that he'd mind that all too much, either.

"Those Saracens could hold their own," he said. "What else did you hear?"

They'd just reached the road. No cars, so they crossed and started up the lane to the manor. He'd noticed Emma wasn't even the least bit out of breath. He liked that. Good, strong, healthy. . . he wanted her to stay that way. Forever.

"I did hear of another," she said, a bit more quiet. She looked at him. "The fish guy said that the Saracen's Dread still haunts Arrick-by-the-Sea because he lost his soul mate and won't pass on to the next life without her." Suddenly, Emma stopped, kicked a rock with her shoe, then looked up to him. "Is that true?"

The pain of his Emma asking such a question was akin to having the wind knocked out of his lungs. He couldn't help but want her to remember. He knew it was wrong, that in order for her to carry on with this life, he'd have to pretend her standing so close didn't affect him.

Christ, it *did* affect him—so much that it made him ache.

With a deep breath, he forced a smile. " 'Tis very romantic, Emma, but I can assure you if I'd had the chance to end centuries of roaming by now, I would have." There. That wasn't a lie. If he couldn't have Emma, he didn't want to continue on.

"Oh," was all she said, almost with disappointment. "I suppose that makes more sense."

"Indeed it does. Now, let's continue on so you can eat your food. I can hear your stomach rumble from here."

From there, it didn't take long to reach the manor. By the time they'd reached the front entranceway, Emma seemed to have put aside all thoughts of his losing his one true love. Her smile was wide and her laughter loud and genuine. Painful as it was, being her friend proved better than not having her at all.

He wondered how long he could bloody last.

What he needed was a distraction. A distraction without actually giving up his time with her. They had a handful of weeks before Emma would return home.

Smiling, Christian followed her inside. The perfect plan was beginning to form. He could interact with Emma, selfishly holding on to what precious time he had with her, yet keeping her safely at arm's length. He'd worried when, earlier, she'd had a flash of what he could only surmise to be old memories. He'd take her to Castle Grimm, where nothing could stir old memories. She'd never been there before—in any of her previous lives. He'd like Gawan of Conwyk to meet her, as well as his bride, Ellie. 'Twould certainly do him good. A bit of swordplay, a change of scenery, old friends. Aye. 'Twas a fine idea. He'd hie himself off to Grimm whilst Emma had her supper, and have a chat with Conwyk first—just to make sure they'd be home. Those two were prone to take their entire brood and travel about at any given time of the year. Unpredictable, the Conwyks.

He was positive Emma would love it. If she thought *him* an anomaly, she'd really fancy the inhabitants of Castle Grimm, although she'd met a handful of them—including Gawan—more than a handful of times in the past.

He could barely wait to proposition her . . .

Emma finished the fish-and-chips with a satisfied smile. Cod fillets batter-fried to a golden brown, they were, possibly, the absolute best she'd ever eaten. She didn't exactly know what the brown sauce was, but it was mouthwatering, along with a sprinkle of vinegar.

Had the sisters not cleaned their plates, she'd have begged for leftovers.

Then, the dessert. Warm, crusty butterscotch and walnut pie with vanilla ice cream. Emma thought she'd died and gone to heaven. When she stood up to help clear away the dishes, Willoughby shooed her aside.

"Love, go for a stroll, or read your book. We will have this cleaned up in no time," Willoughby said. "Now go."

"Okay. Thank you so much," she told Willoughby. "For everything." She glanced out at the ruins. "I think I will go for a walk before it gets too dark."

"Good, good," said Willoughby. "Just be careful, aye? Without young Christian here to protect you, you know."

"I'll watch my step," Emma promised, then realized that, even though he was a spirit and not a man of substance, she felt . . . safe with Christian.

She also realized she missed him in the few hours he'd been gone.

With that thought, she hurried upstairs, brushed her teeth, and grabbed her jacket and hat. She bounded back down the three flights of stairs, anxious to walk off some of the cod, potatoes, and pie she'd consumed. Zoë always told her that going to bed on such a full stomach would give her nightmares.

Emma knew it to be an absolutely true wives' tale.

Outside, the sky had turned an ethereal sort of lavender. Fitting, she thought, since she was, in fact, at a haunted castle. The wind had chilled and picked up a notch or two, and Emma zipped her jacket to the throat. Snuggling her hat down over her ears, she started for the ruins.

The trees—beech, sweet chestnut, walnut, and oak, according to Christian—had a myriad of autumn leaves. A good portion had been jostled down to the ground by the wind, making a scattered blanket of reds, browns, and yellows. Inhaling, Emma took in the mixed scent of sweet clover, the brine of the sea, and the wood burning in the Ballasters' fireplace. She didn't think she'd ever forget how it smelled at Arrick.

Or who resided at Arrick, for that matter.

Absently, she leaned over, picked a large yellow leaf from the ground, and continued on, twirling it in her fingers. How on earth had she come to be here? Why, out of the twenty-eight years she'd been walking the earth, did she *finally* find someone she really, truly liked, who was not only charming, chivalrous, funny, and heart-stoppingly handsome, but . . . *dead*.

Oh my God, he's actually dead.

As in not alive, a *ghost*, through and through.

Only she, Emma Calhoun, could manage such a feat.

Only Emma Calhoun could have the total hots for a spirit.

Figures.

She kicked a rock, watched it hop up the lane ahead

of her and roll to a stop, just before she reached the gatehouse.

The waning light outside had cast the inside of the gatehouse pitch-black in shadows. Still, Emma lingered. She ran her fingertips over the charred places where Christian had told her the torches used to be—

Emma gasped, closing her eyes against the dizziness that washed over her. She leaned against the cool, damp stone and drew in long, deep breaths. Another vision flashed before her, sudden, hazy, and then, suddenly . . . very, very clear.

Right in front of her, so close she had to back up, a man held and kissed a woman. His back was to Emma, and his body shielded whomever he kissed, but when he lifted his head, she saw his profile, just before the vision faded. A profile such as she'd never forget: square jaw, straight nose, full lips stretched into a wide smile, and that fall of tousled hair . . .

Her stomach knotted. The weird feeling washed over her. It was Christian, plain as day.

Moving forward, she ran her uninjured hand over the stone wall where she'd just witnessed the kiss. Nothing happened. It was just a blank, dark wall of stone.

Rubbing her eyes with her thumb and forefinger, she sighed; then she hurried out of the gatehouse and into the barely lit courtyard.

She laughed out loud. What in the world was wrong with her? Why was she seeing images of Christian, and why were those visions giving her such strange feelings in her gut?

More than that, why did it bother her to see him kissing someone?

With that, Emma nearly snorted out loud.

How much more ridiculous could she be? Of *course* he'd kissed women. Looking like he did, she was positive he did a lot more than that.

Shaking her head, Emma continued on across the courtyard, to the Dangling Steps, as she now referred to them, and climbed up. The waning lavender hues now looked gray, but she could still view a bit of the sea, and the sounds of it smashing into Arrick's base gave her a sense of peace. She found a good sitting spot on the ledge—*parapet*, Christian had corrected her—and sat down, back against a small section of higher wall that still remained. Pulling her legs up, she hooked her arms around her knees, careful with her injured hand, and stared out to sea. One thought occupied her mind. She groaned out loud.

She was falling for a twelfth-century ghost.

Chapter 17

"I'm surprised I didn't find you dangling again."

Emma jumped, and there stood Christian, just a few feet away, back in his twelfth-century lethal-wear, his pre-going-to-war shorn hair loose and disheveled, and looking exceptionally . . .

. . . *heart-stopping*.

His strange accent, smooth and exactly the right depth of pitch, washed over her, made her heart thump quicker.

Dang it.

Wrapping her arms more tightly around her pulled-up legs, Emma cocked her head and grinned—hoping he couldn't pick up on her newly discovered attraction. "I reserve dangling for the most serious and drastic of times."

Even in the near-darkness, Emma could see Christian's blue eyes studying her. She briefly wondered what he thought of her, staring at her as he did all the time.

Christian moved a bit closer, then eased down beside her, hands resting on his thighs, legs sprawled. "I'm beginning to wonder whether you have any fear at all. Do you know how dangerous it is for you to be up here?"

Emma peeked around her knees, right through the missing stones of a section of wall, and directly out to the sea. She glanced at him. "Only if I were running up and down the parapet and throwing my arms in the air, would it be dangerous, Christian." She threw him a wide smile. "But I'm all huddled up against the wall, nice and safe. See?"

His profound gaze remained on her for several moments. "I do indeed."

Emma wanted to squirm. Instead, she glanced back out to the sea. "It's beautiful out here. I would love to have my studio right here." She swept the area with her hand. "Gosh"—she looked back at him—"I don't think I'd ever want to leave the office."

In the fading light, the softest of expressions crossed his chiseled, surreal face.

"What?" she asked, unable to help herself, almost embarrassed. "Why do you look at me like that?"

He didn't even deny that he'd been staring. After a moment, Christian smiled. " 'Tis hard to look away, I suppose."

Emma didn't exactly know what to think of that. She gave a nervous laugh. "I bet you say that to all the mortal girls."

Christian merely smiled. "Hardly."

Emma's stomach did a funny little flip. They were silent for a few moments, then she cleared her throat. "I—"

At the very same time, Christian started. "I—"

They both stopped and chuckled.

Emma inclined her head. "You go first."

Christian nodded. "I thought, mayhap, you'd be interested in a small journey. To a friend's home."

In the twilight, Emma blinked. "Seriously?"

The corner of his mouth lifted. "Indeed."

She thought she could watch that devilish smile all night. She took in his profile, the muscles in his jaw, his Adam's apple and how it bobbed when he spoke.

"Why do you look at me like that?"

Heat flushed Emma's cheeks as he repeated her very question to him, and she was grateful for the waning light. "It's just really strange," she started. "You look so absolutely real." Her eyes went to his throat. "Just watching your body movements, gestures—you even look as though you're breathing." She lifted her eyes to his. "It's hard to grasp the fact that you were born centuries ago, and it's even harder for me to wrap my brain around the fact that actually you're not sitting here beside me."

She reached out tentatively, and ran her fingertips just above Christian's knuckles.

He lifted his opposite hand and lingered over hers. "I am sitting here beside you, Emma," he said quietly. "I'm just not as solid as I'd like to be."

Try as she might, Emma couldn't peel her eyes from his. So close was his voice, his . . . presence, that it made her shudder inside. The tension in the air was palpable, like the heavy, healthy thrum of a heartbeat in a silent room.

He didn't exactly look away, either.

Actually, his gaze dropped to her mouth and lingered there. He was so close, close enough to touch, and she was surprised to find herself wanting desperately to do just that. That fall of long, unruly bangs made him even sexier than he already was.

Suddenly, though, he gave a slight smile and glanced out over the sea.

They both drew deep breaths. It had to be the single most intense moment of Emma's entire life.

"So you're interested, then?" he asked.

Emma's eyes widened. *Certainly he wasn't asking . . .* "Excuse me?"

A very slow grin came across Christian's face. "The journey to my friend's home. Are you interested?"

If heat didn't stop rushing to her neck and face, she was sure to self-combust.

What a ding-dong she was.

"Oh," she said, giving an embarrassed laugh. She hoped he hadn't picked up on her accidental insinuation, but by the wolfish grin on his face, she doubted it. "Absolutely," she said. Then she cocked her head. "Are they . . . dead or alive?"

Christian studied her for a moment. Then, his shoulders began to shake. He threw back his head and laughed.

Emma couldn't help but laugh, too.

"I fear you'll find some of each at Grimm," he answered. "Quite a unique tale to be told there—several tales, in fact."

Her eyes widened. "Really?"

"Really."

Nodding her head, Emma smiled. "Sounds exciting. I'd love to go." A gust of wind blew off the ocean, and she tugged her hat down lower. "Where's Grimm?" Strange name, she thought.

Then again, what *wasn't* strange here?

" 'Tis on the northeastern side of England. A grand castle, much like Arrick but fully intact." He grinned. "I think you'll find it to your liking."

Emma looked at him. "How will we . . . travel? I could take the train and meet you there." It sounded strange to her ears. She was hooking up with the ghost of a medieval warrior and traveling over to the northeastern side of England to meet his friends.

Zoë would definitely have her committed.

Christian chuckled. "No need. Gawan is sending the helicopter. It'll be here tomorrow morning at ten."

Emma blinked. He spoke of sending helicopters as though it were an everyday thing. "You're very hip for a guy more than eight hundred and fifty years old."

He shrugged. "I get around." He winked. "And I watch the BBC every chance I get."

Emma laughed, and raised an eyebrow. "Pretty sure of yourself too, huh?" She narrowed her eyes. "What makes you so sure I'd say yes, anyway?"

He lifted one brow and said nothing.

"Your confidence is phenomenal," she said dryly.

They both laughed.

Christian then turned his stare to the sea for several seconds, as though pondering something heavy on his mind. "Why did you come here, Emma?" He turned to her. "Out of all the fortresses in Wales, why Arrick?"

Emma rested her chin against her up-pulled knees, her back pressed into the stone wall of the parapet. That multicolored hat barely covered her ears, and those ridiculous shoes—Converse, she'd claimed—were on her feet, which she had crossed at the ankles.

He'd known Emma through twelve previous lifetimes and incarnations. Each time he'd fallen in love with the woman she had been before and the woman she had become. But this Emma was a blend of all that she'd been, plus something new, something he'd seen glimpses of in the past but which was full and fresh in this Emma. Mayhap 'twas her boldness, or her determination? Her confidence? The modern Emma before him now had become . . . absolutely and breathtakingly perfect.

Christian watched her response. He *knew*, of course, what had driven her here. But each time, each century, led to a new response. He wanted more than anything to hear his modern Emma's method of finding Arrick.

Of finding *him*.

She shrugged. "You'll think I'm a lunatic."

Christian heaved a gusty sigh. "Aye, you're right. I'm sure anything you say will sound far crazier than anything I've ever encountered."

She looked at him. He grinned.

Emma laughed. "I guess you're right. I honestly can't

say how I chose Arrick. I'd started having these strange dreams. Not dreams, really, but more like ... feelings." She shook her head. "I've tried to explain it to my friend Zoë. She doesn't get it."

He indeed got it.

"It's weird, really. I've had these feelings before, just not as compelling as now. Lately, I've bordered on obsessive. I felt it was a place I was looking for, so I started just searching the Internet." She leaned forward. "You know the Internet?"

Christian laughed. "I do indeed."

She laughed lightly. "That's so strange. A twelfth-century warrior who knows the Internet. Anyway, the more my feelings solidified, the more clearly I knew what to look for. Months later, I ended up on a Web site for Welsh castles—was there for hours and hours until finally, I saw it." She smiled at him. "I saw the most stunning picture I'd ever seen. And it was of Arrick-by-the-Sea." Glancing up, she studied the sea. "I was immediately drawn to it, and ... I don't know, I felt I had to come." The corner of her mouth lifted in a smile when she looked at him. "Little did I know what I'd find here, though. Pretty kooky, huh?"

Christ, how he wanted to draw closer to her. Just sitting as they were now made his insides weak. He wondered what she smelled like. "Not so kooky, I'd warrant." He watched her. "What of your family? You've not mentioned them at all." He asked, so not to seem rude, although he knew fully well of her family. 'Twas the same each time her soul returned. Her parents would be dead, and she'd be on her own.

Emma sighed. "My mom has greater faith in me than my father does," she said. "He constantly worries about everything, and I've been on my own since college." She shook her head. "He nearly had a heart attack when he found out I was coming here, alone. Actually came over to my house and forcibly stashed three cans of pepper spray in my luggage. I had to wait for him to leave before removing them from the suitcase. Airport security would surely have busted me for having that."

Christian blinked, surprised. "Your parents are alive?"

"Of course," Emma said slowly. "Why?"

"No reason," he said. "I just assumed." He shrugged, then sighed. "The elderly didn't have a long life in my day."

"Oh."

He studied Emma's profile. She shivered, and Christian rose. "Come along, lass," he said. "Your lips are turning blue and your cheeks are going to be wind blistered if you don't seek warmth soon."

Although he had to admit he found her most adorable, pulled up into a ball as she was, perched upon his parapet, with that crazily-colored hat pulled down to her ears.

Quite adorable, indeed.

Without question, she stood, and moved toward the steps. "Christ, woman, will you please hold on to the wall?"

She grinned, and held lightly to the wall with her hand. "You're as bad as my dad."

Once on the ground, they walked side by side across the courtyard. After a moment, Emma looked up at him.

"I have a hard time believing you never had a wife. Aren't you sort of . . . old?"

He scowled.

She laughed. "I mean, old to be wifeless in the twelfth century. I thought you guys married off at age seventeen back then."

"Sixteen." His gaze moved to hers, and he couldn't help but stare a fraction lower, to her mouth. He wondered if it would taste as sweet as it had all those centuries ago. "And I suppose I never found anyone who suited me well enough to wed."

"I can see that," she muttered.

Christian lifted a brow. "Why do you say that?"

She shrugged. "Not to make your ego any larger than it probably already is, but I'm fairly sure a guy like you would have a difficult time finding a good . . . match."

They ducked into the gatehouse, and Christian stopped. Emma stopped with him.

"What does that mean?" he asked.

She grinned. "You're pretty dang hot, Mr. Arrick."

At first, Christian just stood there, shocked she'd just admitted such to him. But her features, brushed by moonlight streaming in through the mouth of the gatehouse, made him catch his breath. Her grin turned into a full-blown smile, and her eyes danced.

It all but turned him to mush.

Instead, he returned the grin. "You, Ms. Calhoun, have a bold way of blurting out what's on your mind." He eyed her, pleased that she found his person to her liking. "Not shy, are you?"

Her eyes met his, and he noticed how intently she studied his face. "One of my gleaming characteristics, I've been told."

"No doubt," he returned.

They continued on their way, and after a moment, while concealed in the cover of darkness between the manor and the castle, Christian leaned closer. "I find you rather fetching, as well." When she glanced at him, he grinned. "Scorching."

Even in the moonlight, Christian could see the blush stain her cheeks.

Chapter 18

Emma stood before the bureau, hair wrapped in a towel, another encasing her body, and stared at her choice of clothes. She wrinkled her nose.

There were several things she hadn't factored in for her trip to Wales. The first was the obvious: Christian of Arrick-by-the-Sea.

He thought her *scorching*.

That made her skin grow warm again, and a smile touched her lips at the memory of that strange accent of his, mingled with the speech of a modern-day man. The fall of disheveled, knife-shorn hair that always seemed to be in those wide blue eyes, and that square jaw . . .

She wouldn't go into detail again about the full lips.

Nope. She definitely hadn't factored in *that* guy.

Which meant she would have never factored in a side trip to the north of England via helicopter to visit one of Christian's mortal friends.

Emma shook her head. *How can all this be real?*

With a gusty sigh, she continued to dig through her very casual wardrobe. She imagined a modern-day lord, living in a renovated castle would be, well, stinking filthy rich. Would probably dress as such, too.

She eyed the contents of the bureau. Jeans. Sweaters. A couple of turtlenecks. A few T-shirts. Hiking boots. Converse sneakers.

She should have listened to Zoë and packed a nice dress, or a pair of slacks. She sighed again. At least she'd brought her black leather boots. That might dress up her jeans and sweaters a bit more than the Converse sneakers . . .

The north of England would just have to accept Emma Calhoun as she was.

Plain. Which, truth be told, was totally fine with her.

Grabbing clean understuff, a pair of dark hipsters that flared just a bit, a thin, black, ribbed turtleneck sweater, and black leather boots, Emma quickly dressed. After blow-drying her straight hair, she added a bit of makeup, lip gloss, and a dab of perfume. Neatly packing the clothes she'd chosen to take on the trip into a large canvas bag Willoughby had loaned her, she stuffed her sneakers in, along with her small case of makeup, and toiletries, and took a deep breath. She was ready to go.

And she was only a *teensy* bit nervous. For some reason, she wanted to make a good impression on Christian's friends.

How very, very strange it was to have a friendship with a ghost, a being she could easily pass her hand through, who'd died so long ago. He had friends, here on earth. Live ones. And, as she'd already encountered, not-so-live ones, as well.

What a whole new world Christian had shown her. One she would have never, ever believed really existed. She briefly wondered just how many more roamed the plane of the living.

"Emma?"

Christian's voice sent a thrill down her spine. She glanced around. "Where are you?" She couldn't help but wonder if he'd sneaked a peek while she dressed. He was, after all, whether dead or alive, still a man.

His low chuckle sounded from the other side of the door. "In the passageway. Are you ready?"

Emma almost hated the excitement she felt at hearing his voice. What was wrong with her? She hadn't acted like this in . . . well, never. She couldn't *ever* remember having such crazy reactions at hearing a man's voice. She crossed the floor, smoothed her sweater, and opened the door.

There Christian stood, once again in a pair of faded jeans, boots, and this time, a baggy, cream-colored sweater. It made that gorgeous mahogany hair, which again was pulled back, really stand out. She struggled to keep her jaw from sliding open. "Hi."

Christian leaned casually against the door frame, hands shoved into his pockets. His lopsided grin nearly made Emma's knees buckle.

But not nearly as much as his assessment of *her*.

The grin disappeared from Christian's face and was replaced by something Emma really couldn't define. He showed no shame whatsoever in starting at her head, then slowly moving his gaze down until it rested on her feet. He lingered there momentarily, then slowly moved back up to her eyes. His stare rocked her.

A slow grin crossed his face. "Aye. Scorching."

Emma felt her skin turn hot. That only made Christian laugh.

"You're crazy," she mumbled, then turned to grab the canvas bag and her camera equipment. "Okay," she said, smiling brightly, hoping he'd ignore her flaming blush. She walked back to the door and stopped a foot from him. "I'm ready."

Looking down at her, he studied her for a handful of seconds. "So you are." He pushed off the door frame—or at least it looked like he did—and inclined his head toward the stairs without taking his eyes off her. "After you."

Emma moved past him. "Thanks."

Christian fell in beside her. "I believe you'll have

many photo opportunities whilst at Grimm. 'Tis a beautiful place, situated much like Arrick, on the sea."

Emma nodded. "I can't imagine it being more spectacular than here." She glanced at him. "And your friends don't mind you bringing a guest?"

Christian laughed. "That's my second home, lass, and Gawan is like a brother to me. Don't worry. 'Twill be fine. I promise." His grin widened. "Actually, the whole castle is anxious to meet you." He leaned his head close to hers. "I can only imagine the fights that will break out."

They reached the stairs, and Emma started down. "Why will fights break out?"

His lumbering self chuckled. "Over you, of course."

Emma highly doubted that.

Once downstairs, all four Ballasters met them in the foyer. Willoughby rushed forward.

"Oh dear, you look absolutely stunning. Doesn't she, girls?" gushed Willoughby.

The sisters bobbed their heads enthusiastically.

"How's your hand feeling?" asked Maven.

Emma flexed her fingers. She'd left the bandage off once she saw how well it had healed. "Nearly good as new." She lifted it up and peered at her hand. "I didn't know you'd used dissolving stitches, Willoughby. I hardly even feel the tug of the wound anymore."

Willoughby beamed. " 'Tis my special ointment, love," she said. "And before I forget, here's a change of bandages, in case you need them, and more of the ointment. Just apply it before you go to bed." She tucked them into Emma's bag.

"Thank you," Emma said. She pushed her hair behind her ears, then gave the sisters a warm smile. "Is everyone as sweet as you four in Wales, or did I just get lucky?"

All four Ballasters giggled.

Just then, a loud rumble sounded outside.

"The Grimm chopper is headed to the courtyard," said Christian. He gave the sisters a slight nod. "Ladies, I promise to take care of your tenant whilst we are away." He winked.

Once more, they all giggled and waved good-bye.

Outside, Emma and Christian started for the courtyard. The sun had yet to make an appearance, although it was nearly ten in the morning. The ever-present bite of fall slipped through the air, and Emma inhaled the scents of brine from the ocean, and hardwood burning. She inhaled again, a long, deep breath, just for the sheer pleasure of it.

Out of the corner of her eye, she noticed Christian watching her closely. He didn't say a word.

Emma simply smiled.

In the courtyard, the helicopter had landed square in the center, scattering the fallen, multicolored leaves everywhere. A tall, broad-shouldered yet lanky young man, his auburn hair pulled neatly into a ponytail, climbed out. He was wearing a white T-shirt, a brown leather jacket, jeans, and brown hiking boots, and Emma thought him absolutely gorgeous. He looked to be around twenty. As she and Christian grew near, the young man waved enthusiastically.

"Chris!" he hollered, and jogged toward them. His wide smile showed white, even teeth.

"Pup," said Christian, hollering back. "You're looking well." He inclined his head. "This is Emma Calhoun."

The young man turned his full attention to Emma. With a low bow, he then rose and met her gaze with absolute, sincere honesty. His already dazzling smile widened. " 'Tis wondrous to meet you, lady. I've heard much about you. My name is Jason, presently of Dreadmoor. Here, let me take your bags." He had to yell over the whirring chopper blades as they walked closer to the open helicopter door.

Emma could barely do anything, save gawk. She glanced at Christian, who merely shrugged and grinned. Before she could respond, though, the handsome young man had relieved her of both bags, shouldered them, and grasped her by the elbow, his fingers warm and strong. "Allow me to give you aid in climbing into the chopper. 'Tis a bit of a step up, I fear."

Emma had no choice but to allow Jason, presently of Dreadmoor, to guide her up into the chopper. She'd been in many before, but she'd never tell him that.

He was so . . .

She glanced again at Christian.

Chivalrous.

Jason settled Emma into her seat—even strapped her in—then looked at her with a pair of mischievous, light green eyes. " 'Tis no doubt that yon ghost behind me wishes furiously he could do this himself. But since he cannot, I am more than happy to oblige."

Then he winked.

Christian chuckled.

Emma merely gulped. "Thank you for . . . obliging, then."

Jason smiled, slammed and locked the door, then strapped himself in beside her.

Christian appeared in the seat across from her.

She briefly wondered if the pilot thought any of it weird.

As the chopper lifted off, Jason reached over, placed a set of headphones on Emma's ears, and did the same to his own.

"How's that?" he asked.

She nodded. "Perfect."

He gave her another wink.

She was pretty darn sure she'd never, in all her twenty-eight years, encountered a young man Jason's age quite so well mannered. Oozing with charm and authentic politeness, he had just about as much chivalry as any of Arthur's knights, she supposed.

He was English, after all, if his thick accent meant anything. Perhaps that was it?

"How go things at Dreadmoor of late?" Christian asked Jason.

As the two settled into conversation about a place called Dreadmoor, Emma briefly wondered how it was that Christian could establish conversation with the deafening whir of the chopper blades. She guessed it to be one of his tricks, but she'd have to ask him later. She stared out the window and watched the scenery pass beneath her. Large patchworks of green and brown and lighter brown, indicating fields, looked like something out of a picture book. Tiny white dots—sheep, she supposed—flecked the countryside, and many times she noticed the crumbling stone remains of an ancient fortress, or a meandering wall. They passed over a lake or two, and then the chopper went higher, and Emma lost the ability to make out much else. Instead, she settled into her seat and listened to the two handsomest guys she'd ever seen in her life speak in a very similar, strange manner.

Well, Jason was handsome—charming, even.

She looked at Christian.

His gaze was directly on her.

She gulped. Handsome and charming just didn't seem to sum him up accurately enough. While he spoke to Jason, he kept that penetrating gaze on her, and Emma absently slipped her finger over the pulse in her wrist.

It thudded furiously.

Christian smiled, and it reminded Emma of a wolf who'd cornered its prey. It was almost as though he knew the effect he had on her.

And he seemed to enjoy it.

A *lot*.

Bravely, she met his gaze with hers. She refused to look away. No, charming definitely didn't sum up Christian of Arrick-by-the-Sea exactly right.

Painfully breathtaking, perhaps. Yes, it actually hurt to look at him for too long.

His smile widened.

Emma resisted the urge to bonk herself on the forehead.

He knew, all right.

"So, Lady Emma," started Jason, breaking the trance between Emma and Christian, "have you ever attended a medieval tournament?"

Emma looked at Jason. *Lady Emma?*

He lifted one auburn brow. His mouth twitched.

Christian's laugh filled the helicopter.

Chapter 19

"I suppose I've not once in my life attended a medieval tournament," Emma said. "What is it?"

Jason and Christian exchanged glances before Jason gave her a warm smile. "Oh, you're in for a vast surprise, lady. Just you wait."

She looked at Christian, who merely grinned. "A vast surprise, indeed," he said.

Emma wondered if he'd always be so full of surprises. She quirked a brow at Christian. "How is it you can communicate over the chopper blades?" she asked, still wondering.

"Oh, aye," Jason answered for him. "He just throws his voice into our heads. 'Tis an easy enough feat, right Chris?"

Christian simply grinned.

"There's Grimm now," said Jason, pointing.

Emma leaned over and glanced out the helicopter's window and her breath caught.

Wow.

"Marvelous, aye?" Christian asked.

"It's beautiful," she answered, and took in the view. An enormous, walled fortress sat right at the sea cliffs, just like Arrick. With tall, gray towers at each end, an intact parapet that encircled the whole of the castle, an enormous gatehouse—even a working drawbridge! Emma could easily envision what it might have been like back in Christian's day. As the helicopter swooped and began its descent, Emma noticed a small lane wound from a small village and up to the castle. Again, similar to Arrick.

And yet as breathtaking as it was, it didn't have the same impact on her as the ruins of Arrick-by-the-Sea. Nope, not by far. *Perhaps it had something to do with its owner* . . .

"I shall hold your hand if you fear the descent," offered Jason. He shot a glance at Christian—one that looked more than mischievous. "You wouldn't mind, would you, Chris?"

Christian kept his eyes on Emma. His mouth twitched. "Not at all."

Emma smiled, her cheeks warming. "Thanks, err, Jason, but I think I'll be okay."

Jason leaned toward her, his grin stretching across his handsome face. "I had to try, of course," he whispered. "'Tis vastly amusing to try to rile Chris' feathers, although 'tis not easily done, as you can see."

She narrowed her eyes. "I can indeed."

Christian barked out a laugh.

As the helicopter descended onto the launch pad below, Emma couldn't help but watch Christian and wonder—wonder what he'd be like, were he alive in the flesh. He seemed aloof and didn't let Jason's flirting bother him in the least. Was that because he didn't care one way or another? Or was it because Christian didn't feel Jason was any sort of a threat?

Or, she thought gloomily, was it because she really didn't matter all that much to Christian?

She blinked at her own inner thoughts. Now where had *that* come from? Sure, she knew *she'd* started falling for *him*, but other than friendly flirtation, Christian hadn't given the first indication that he thought of her in any other way except a . . . novelty, perhaps. And a safe one at that. She lived thousands of miles away, in another life, and would probably never return to Wales. *The safe mortal girl who would soon leave . . .*

Suddenly, Emma glanced up. Christian's gaze was fixed to hers, watching her closely. His ghostly blue eyes seemed to see straight through to her thoughts, and she shuddered.

How could a *ghost* have such an effect on her? It seemed ludicrous.

Emma peeked again. His eyes hadn't left hers, and then a slow, easy smile lifted the corner of his incredibly sexy mouth.

She suddenly wished she had a Big Gulp.

Perhaps, she entertained, he actually liked her, had he the substance to do anything about it. Unless he was one of those men who flirted with all women . . .

Emma mentally slapped herself across the face. *Get a grip, Calhoun! You're acting like an idiot! He's a ghost; you're a mortal. He lives here; you live somewhere else. Besides, it's not as if you could actually have a relationship with him. And that's that!*

Christian inclined his head. "Ready?"

Emma allowed a smiling Jason to help her out of the chopper, which had landed inside the walled area, and again, Christian simply showed up beside her as they walked across the landing pad and across an enormous courtyard. Wooden benches perched here and there against the wall, with a large grassy area in between. More tall trees with vivid leaves of oranges, reds, and browns lined the courtyard and beyond. The wind was ice-biting cold, and the gray skies lent a bleak, dreary, gloomy look to the place. It seemed . . . grim. *Grimm.*

"I cannot tell you how often I've wished for the uncanny ability to read minds instead of hearing," Christian whispered close to her ear. "I vow I'd give anything to read yours."

Emma flashed him a look, just as Jason grasped her elbow and pulled her along to the main entrance.

Christian merely smiled.

"Christian!"

A pretty, young woman with an infant strapped to her front in a carrier hollered and hurried toward them. By her side was a tall, handsome man, as well as a younger boy, perhaps age ten or so. They all had warm smiles on their faces.

"Saints, Chris," said the man, who was just a fraction shorter than Christian and just a fraction less gorgeous. He wore his brown hair pulled into a ponytail. He grinned. "You're rather fetchin' in that garb." He looked down, chocolate eyes warm and kind. "And this lovely creature must be Emma." He grasped her hand in a gentle shake. "Welcome to Castle Grimm. We are ever so glad to meet you. I'm Gawan."

"Yes, we are," said the woman, smiling. "Christian has told us so much about you."

Emma slipped Christian a glance. He merely shrugged.

Gawan placed an arm around the woman's shoulder and kissed the top of her head. "This is Ellie, my wife, and our wee girl, Ensley." He ruffled the young boy's hair, standing beside him. "And this strappin' lad is Davy."

Davy grinned and gave a low bow. "Nice to meet you, miss!"

Emma smiled at all of them, then turned to Gawan. "Thank you for inviting me."

He smiled down at her. "We'll see if you feel the same way by the time you leave here, aye? 'Tis a bloody madhouse, most of the time." He winked. "Wait until the rest of the lads get here."

"Gawan Conwyk, don't scare her," said Ellie. She gave Emma a warm grin. "Why don't you come with me, Emma? I'll show you to your room and you can put your stuff down. And then we can see what Nicklesby has cooking in the kitchen. I'm starved. Jason?"

"Coming, Lady Ellie," he said, still shouldering Emma's bags. He threw a grin over his shoulder. "See you later, Chris."

Emma, for the third time in just a few hours, allowed a charming Jason to lead her away from Christian. She turned and glanced over her shoulder.

Christian and Gawan both watched as she left. One a spirit, the other quite alive. Yet there was something definitely different about Gawan Conwyk.

Just as she turned, Christian's mouth tipped up into a heart-stopping smile.

She could hardly wait to see what the next handful of days would hold.

"She's stunning."

Christian watched Emma disappear into the great hall. "Indeed she is."

"She appears as she did when you first met."

Christian sighed and shoved his hands into the pockets of his jeans. How very perceptive his friend was. He looked at Gawan. "Aye. Yet she has changed."

Gawan inclined his head, and he and Christian began walking. "I know how difficult it is for you each time you find her, Chris. I wish there were something I could do to help."

Christian nodded and watched the path they took round the side of the entrance, to a smaller entrance that led up the height of the keep wall. He followed Gawan inside.

"So what's different this time?" Gawan asked, taking the steps leading to the top effortlessly as they'd done so many times when they were lads.

"For one, her parents aren't dead," Christian said. "All twelve times past, she's been completely alone. Unattached."

"Hmm. That is odd."

"And whilst she seems to have had a few flashes of old memory, they're not nearly what they usually are by this time. And she's not had the first dream," Christian continued.

"What about you?" asked Gawan.

Christian shook his head as they continued. "I remember everything, Gawan. And Christ, it hurts." He shrugged. "I supposed once I decided to stop hiding my feelings for her, the sadness sort of . . . went away."

"All o' it?"

Christian shook his head. "Nay, not all, I suppose. But this time, with this modern Emma?" He chuckled. " 'Tis as though all the wonderful qualities I've fallen in love with for centuries are bound up in this new woman. She's bolder. Confident. Funny."

Gawan laughed. "Modern women are all that, I reckon."

They reached the top and Gawan pushed open a small door. He ducked through it and stepped out onto the parapet. Christian followed.

"So," Gawan said, "her parents are still alive and active in her life, and she's not remembering you like she usually does. And this is the first time she's looked as she did when you first encountered her. Uncanny."

Christian rubbed a hand over his jaw and looked his friend in the eye. "Aye. She looks exactly as she did in the twelfth century. Mostly, anyway. Her hair is modern, of course. But her features are identical."

Gawan nodded. "That's never happened before."

"Not once."

They both leaned against the parapet wall and stared out over the North Sea. "What are you doing about it?" Gawan said without looking at him.

Several seconds passed before Christian answered. Somehow, it didn't sound as sturdy a play saying it to

Gawan. He said it anyway. "I'm doing my best to keep her from remembering this time."

Gawan stopped and turned his head. "For argument's sake, could you explain why?"

Christian glowered. "Because mayhap, if she goes on with her life instead of suddenly remembering the one we had together, and all the past times we've tried, then she might be able to simply live out her life happily." He frowned more. "Not be reborn to do the whole bloody thing over again. And all for naught."

Gawan studied him for some time. Finally, he scrubbed the back of his neck and sighed. "Chris, trust me when I say this—you canna trick fate. 'Tisn't possible." He gave an assuring smile. "I should know."

Christian considered his friend. "Aye, but your situation was vastly different, Gawan. Your station in life was different, as well."

"Aye," he argued, "you're right about that. I had a bit of a connection, did I no'?"

Christian sighed and rubbed his eyes.

"Listen, my friend. Whilst I cannot tell you exactly what's in store for you and Emma, I *can* tell you this: making an attempt to alter fate's design simply won't work. If the two of you are meant to be, eventually, you will be." Then he sighed. "If no', then 'tis something unfortunate, in truth, and I'll do my best to help you get through it."

Christian regarded Gawan of Conwyk. Not too long ago, Gawan had faced challenges no one—ghost and mortal alike—thought he could overcome. He'd won his immortality on a battlefield in 1145 and walked amongst the living as an earthbound angel for centuries. His retirement had finally arrived, his mortality just within his grasp, when Ellie, his Intended, showed up. *Sort of*. She'd had a wee problem of being *mostly* dead at the time. They overcame it. Fate led them to each other, in the end.

Would fate finally lead him and Emma to each other? Dare he even hope such?

"Besides," continued Gawan, as though he'd never finished speaking, "from those heated looks you cannot seem to keep yourself from throwing at poor Emma, you're not winning that battle of challenging fate after all." He waved a hand before his face. "A downright bloody inferno within a ten-foot radius of either of you, and it's far worse this time than the last." He grinned. "In other words, laddie, you're failing miserably at trying to dissuade Emma."

Christian knew it. Damn, he'd tried. His eyes always wandered back to Emma. And stayed. He was drawn to her like air to lungs, and he wanted nothing more than to get as close to her as his flimsy, spectered self could. He wanted to tell her how he felt, how much he loved her, how badly he wanted her. How he would beg her to spend whatever time they had left together, he as a spirit, she as a mortal. 'Twould never be enough, but better than nothing at all.

More than that, he wanted her to say the same things back to him.

"Have you told her about us?" asked Gawan. "Ellie and me, I mean."

Christian knew he referred to his and Ellie's struggle and triumph against fate. "Nay."

"Hmm. Does she remember any of us?" Gawan continued. "Dragonhawk and his knights? The Munros?"

Christian shook his head. "Nay. I told her nothing, and she's remembered nothing. She has met Justin Catesby and Godfrey. She didn't recognize them."

"Well," said Gawan, smiling and rubbing his hands together, then shoving them deep into his jacket pockets, "the lass will be in for a hearty surprise, eh?"

"No doubt."

Gawan laughed. "Why did you bring her here?"

Christian shrugged. "I thought 'twas the best place to keep her distracted. I wanted her to see more of my world, yet I didn't want to dislodge any memories." He glanced at his friend. "She doesn't remember any of you, and she's never in the past recalled coming to Grimm. I thought 'twas safer than at Arrick."

The smile on Gawan's face grew wide. "Well, we'll just see about that now, won't we, laddie?"

Chapter 20

Emma followed Ellie Conwyk through the massive oak double doors and into the main part of the castle, Jason close on her heels. It was the great hall, he had informed her. *Wow*.

She could certainly see why.

Dark wooden open rafters crisscrossed the ceiling from one end of the mammoth room to the other. Old-fashioned sconces decorated the walls in no apparent pattern—just wherever light was needed, she supposed. A massive fireplace, taking up almost the entire far wall, was ablaze with a nice, toasty fire. Two huge, black wrought-iron chandeliers hung from the ceiling on opposite ends. A sweeping staircase led upstairs. And hanging here and there on the stone walls were enormous tapestries, each depicting medieval battle scenes.

All in all, it was the most impressive place she'd ever encountered.

Except, of course, the Arrick ruins. She felt particular about that place.

"Well," said a smiling Ellie, who'd patiently allowed her to gander. "Welcome to Grimm." She winked. "Don't let the name fool you, though. This place is magical."

Emma had little difficulty believing it. "It's absolutely beautiful," she said. "Thank you again for inviting me."

"Are you kidding? As long as I've known Christian,

he's never brought a girl over," she said, giggling. "You're the first. Isn't that right, Jason?"

He grinned down at her. "Indeed, lady. You are the first, and I must say I'm vastly glad 'tis you."

That, too, was something to consider.

The wrapped bundle hanging from the carrier on Ellie's chest wiggled and grunted, and she pulled back the pink blanket to reveal a head covered in downy brown hair. Ellie stroked the baby's cheek. "Oh, sleepyhead is finally waking up—you want to follow me upstairs? It's changing time. Jason can see you to your room. Then I'll meet you there." She smiled. "Show you around a bit."

"Sure." Emma smiled wistfully at the little girl. Her poochy lips sucked an imaginary bottle, and her wide blue-green eyes seemed to stare right at her. "She's so sweet," she said.

Ellie laughed. "Wait until you hear her lungs. *Fabulous* lungs," she said. "So, Christian tells us you're a photographer?"

Emma nodded as she climbed the stairs beside Ellie. "I am. I mostly do weddings," she said. "But after arriving in Wales, I've decided landscapes are fast-becoming a favorite."

Ellie grinned at her. "It's gorgeous here, isn't it? America is beautiful, of course, but there's just something special about this place. Don't you think?"

"Absolutely." They reached the second-story landing and Ellie turned to her.

"Jason will take you the rest of the way up. I'll go change little Miss Stinky Pants here and then take you on a Grimm tour." Ellie smiled. "See ya in a few."

"Okay," Emma said.

"Right this way," said Jason, close to her ear. "You're on the fourth level."

Emma followed Jason, who continued to glance down at her and grin. Such an infectious personality, she couldn't ignore it if she tried. She smiled back. "Are you always this cheerful?"

Jason wagged his auburn brows. "Of course. What man wouldn't be, walking with a beautiful maid as yourself?" He nodded. "Aye, it in fact puts me in the sweetest of moods, indeed."

Emma laughed. "Not very shy, are you?"

His eyes twinkled. "Not in the least." He inclined his head. "One more flight to go."

Emma couldn't get a handle on Jason. In fact, all the men she'd met on this trip had been, oh, a little larger than life. Gawan and Jason were so unlike the men she knew in America—it was hard to chalk the difference entirely up to being British. She'd met Brits before who hadn't filled a room with their sheer size and charisma. These men reminded her in a way of Christian, though certainly they were more solid . . .

Down the corridor they walked, Jason chatting away. At the last door on the right, he stopped. "Here we go, lady," he said. He opened the door and gave it a push.

Emma walked into the room and held in a gasp. It was enormous, with a wide, picture window overlooking the North Sea. Before the window stood a big, plush sofa.

"Wow," she muttered, walking straight to the window.

"Aye, wow," said Jason cheerfully, joining her. "I've never grown weary of the sight." He set her bags on the floor, then leaned against the sill. He crossed his arms over his chest and gave her a warm smile. "If you like, once Ellie has given you the Grimm tour, I can give you the Grimm village tour." He winked. "Best chippy in the north of England."

Emma grinned. "You just discovered the way to my heart—food." She winked back. "You're on."

He gave an enthusiastic nod. "I like a girl who can hold her own at the supper table." He leaned closer.

"But I wouldn't put it past Sir Christian to want to tag along. He's powerfully protective, you know."

Emma blinked. "He is?"

"Oh, aye," Jason said. "Fiercely so."

She cocked her head. "Why?"

A soft expression settled on Jason's handsome features, and his smile was warm. " 'Tis how any knight reacts when his lady is around." He shook his head. "Lucky man, Sir Christian."

Emma gave a nervous laugh. "I don't exactly think Sir Christian has any reason to be so protective over me." She shrugged, and couldn't help but wish she were wrong. "We're just friends."

An all-too-wise look lit Jason's eyes. "Of course you are." He pushed off the sill. "So, are you ready for the tournament?"

Emma took in her room, complete with its own fireplace, an enormous four-poster bed, and a private bathroom. She looked at him. "I'm not exactly sure what the tournament is." She grinned. "What is it?"

Jason shoved his hands into the pockets of his leather jacket. A new smile touched his mouth—one that was purely male. " 'Tis the most extreme of sports, lady. Swords. The joust. Wrestling." He winked. "You'll fancy it, I'm sure."

"No doubt I will. When does it begin?" she asked.

"Two days from now, which is why I'm in a fierce hurry to take you into the village alone. Once the Dreadmoor knights and the Munros arrive, I'll be lucky to even catch a glimpse of you."

Emma smiled and shook her head. "What does that mean?"

Jason beamed. "Oh. You shall see, lady." He inclined his head. "Would you like to freshen up?"

"That would be great," Emma said. "I'll just be a minute."

Jason nodded. "Excellent. I'll just run to my chambers, and I'll meet you back here. We'll accompany Lady Ellie round the castle; then we shall make for the village." His grin stretched from ear to ear.

And with that, he hurried out the door.

Emma made quick use of the bathroom and gave herself a once-over in the mirror. She didn't look half bad for having spent the morning in a helicopter, but she was glad for a minute to smooth her hair and put on some lip balm.

She spent a minute admiring her room and trying to catch her breath from the whirlwind of her trip. How strange that her in-depth feelings had brought her to Wales, to Arrick-by-the-Sea, and ultimately, to Castle Grimm, where her hosts were more than welcoming, and the tournament . . .

Once again, she felt very lucky to have happened upon that Arrick Web site.

"Ready?" asked Jason, whose head appeared in the doorway.

"Ready," said Emma.

She wondered briefly what Christian was doing.

She wondered in depth if he really, sincerely thought of her as *his lady* . . .

As soon as she and Jason made it to the first floor, he was pulled away.

"Lady Emma," Gawan said, giving her a warm smile. "Would you mind letting me borrow young Jason for a score of minutes? I promise to return him, posthaste."

Emma couldn't help but return the smile. "As long as I get him back before the chippy closes."

Gawan smiled. "Indeed you shall." He threw Jason a look. "Come on, boy."

Jason winked at Emma, shrugged, and loped happily along beside Gawan as they left by the front entrance, leaving Emma completely alone in the enormous great hall.

Knowing Ellie would be down soon, she decided to take a quick look around. She'd never before been inside a renovated castle, and so far Grimm completely fascinated her. What drew her attention first was the largest tapestry hanging, so she made her way over and stood before it. It was indeed breathtaking.

In the tiniest of stitches, it depicted a battle scene. A woman in armor sat astride a powerful horse in the center, surrounded by a band of armored knights and farmers with pitchforks. One warrior, Emma noticed, wore no armor, and had numerous tattoos across his chest and back. She pulled closer, and stared hard at the fierce knight.

How strange that she thought he looked . . . *familiar*?

"There you are!" exclaimed Ellie.

Emma turned, and Ellie hurried across the hall, the baby bouncing in the carrier, and a toddler in each hand. Behind her, hurrying along, was a tall, lanky man with a kindly face and big ears. He sort of reminded Emma of—

"My lady! I'm ever so sorry not to have greeted you upon arrival!" the man said, stopping before her and giving her a short bow. "My name is Nicklesby, and I am ever at the ready for anything you need."

Nicklesby all but hopped from one foot to the other, he was so excited.

Emma smiled. "It's nice to meet you, Nicklesby, and thanks for the offer."

His grin seemed to lift his entire face. "You are most welcome, love." Then, he turned and took the toddlers from Ellie. "Seth, Jacob—come along, lads," he said, addressing Gawan and Ellie's young twin boys. "Come help me in the kitchen, won't you? I've a bowl and wooden spoons for you to play with whilst I make lunch."

With a shriek of delight, the brown-haired boys, who looked no more than two, began hopping up and down—much like Nicklesby had. Nicklesby smiled and allowed the tykes to drag him to the kitchen.

"Now," said Ellie, "let's take that tour I promised you. Now's the best time, because after tomorrow you won't hardly be able to move in here."

"What do you mean?" asked Emma, following her lead.

Ellie laughed. "Oh, you'll see. Four teams for the tournament, and trust me—they aren't little guys. Once they're all here, it'll be shoulder-to-shoulder testosterone in the great hall, and anywhere else you try to escape."

"Wow. That's a lot of testosterone."

Ellie shook her head. "You have no idea."

Emma followed the lady of Grimm and baby Ensley through the castle. It had the right combination of medieval versus modern, and she suddenly discovered she was very much drawn to the Dark Ages. They'd just left the armory when Emma hedged in a question.

She hadn't been too sure whether to ask it.

"How, um, long have you known Christian?" she asked nonchalantly.

Ellie sighed. "Nearly as long as I've known Gawan." She looked at her, a grin splitting her face in two. "Why do you ask?"

Emma shrugged. "I don't know. Just . . . curious about him, I guess."

Ellie smiled as they walked. "Well, I'll tell you this much. I rank him right up there with my husband. He might be a bit gruff at times, and more than annoying, but he's one of the most honest, caring, and straightforward men I know—dead or alive." She winked. "And he's drop-dead gorgeous."

Emma laughed. "He definitely is that." She looked at her host. "I feel like I belong to some strange sort of sorority where we see and interact with ghosts. How did you take it at first, meeting Christian?"

Ellie stopped midstep. Her pretty brow was creased. "Has he not told you?"

Emma stared. "Told me what?"

Ellie's wide, blue-green eyes narrowed to slits. "Ooh—I'm going to let him have it! Good Lord!"

"I shall relieve you of your guest before you, err, let me have it," said Christian out of nowhere. Suddenly, he appeared across the corridor, leaning casually against the wall. "Your temper has shortened considerably since having babes, Ellie," he said. The corner of his mouth lifted.

"Bite me, Arrick," said Ellie, then turned and gave Emma an apologetic smile. "Sorry about that. Living with ninety-eight percent men makes me a little quick to react at times. But make sure you ask Mr. Smarty Pants here all about how Gawan and I got together, okay?"

Then Ellie stepped forward and gave Emma a quick hug. She pulled back and smiled. "It's so nice to have a *female* here for a change." She jostled baby Ensley. "Isn't it, sweetie?" She shot Christian a mean look. "Don't you let her come to dinner tonight without *knowing things*, Christian de Gaultiers. At least a heads-up. And I mean it."

"Yes ma'am."

"Make him tell you, then help yourself to whatever Nicklesby has in the kitchen," she said to Emma, then disappeared down the corridor.

Emma stared after her. Make him tell her *what*? When she turned to face Christian, she found his gaze already on her. The sexy curve of his mouth lifted into an even sexier grin. Emma wondered at how fast her heart beat when he was around.

"What's so funny?" she asked, finally. "And DeGaultiers? That's your full name?" She thought it absolutely beautiful.

He gave a slight shake of his head and pushed off the

wall. "Aye, 'tis so. Come on, Lady Emma. I'll show you a place I'm certain Ellie forgot about."

Emma narrowed her gaze but nodded. "Okay."

As they walked, Christian glanced down. "Drop-dead gorgeous, eh?"

His chuckle grew louder the redder her face became.

Chapter 21

"Hold tightly to the rope, lass," instructed Christian. "If you fall, I vow I won't be able to stop you."

Emma grabbed the rope, hanging from the very high ceiling of the tight, circular staircase hidden within the wall. She grinned at Christian. "The perils of hanging out with a ghost, huh?"

He grinned back.

Her knees nearly buckled.

"Something like that," he said. "Now climb very slowly."

"Are you taking me somewhere so secluded that when you tell me whatever it is Ellie wanted you to tell me, my screams will not be heard?"

Christian chuckled—so close, she could almost feel it on her neck. She shivered.

"Just climb, woman. There will be time for talk once we're on solid footing."

The drafty stairwell felt cool and damp, and smelled a little musty, but the rope was sturdy and Emma kept a tight grasp on it as she climbed. She thought about the man climbing behind her. There, yet not really there.

She also thought about how much she'd missed him over the past couple of hours. More than what she'd care to admit. Strange, really.

"You're nearing the top now, Emma, so take care in

opening the door. The wind might very likely yank it from your hand—and you with it, if you've not a tight grip."

"Comforting."

"I know your penchant for heights and dangling."

Emma laughed softly. "I'll be careful."

Christian grunted.

At the door, Emma grasped the handle tightly, slid the bolt, and pushed the door open. The wind wasn't quite so fierce, and she stepped out onto the walk and closed the door behind her. Christian appeared by her side. Then Emma turned to take in the view.

It nearly robbed her breath.

The North Sea stretched as far as she could see, and tiny whitecaps flecked the surface as the wind tossed at the water. "It's beautiful," Emma said softly.

"Aye, very," said Christian.

Emma glanced at him. As usual, his direct gaze had settled right on her. Again, she felt her face grow warm.

"What did you want to tell me?" she asked, hurrying to cover up her blush. She noticed how well-suited his modern-day clothes were on him, and how it struck such contrast with the hair she knew had been shorn with a knife before a battle that had taken place more than eight hundred years in the past.

All very baffling, she thought. More baffling, though, was that she'd fallen for him. She briefly wondered what he'd think of that.

"The tournament will begin day after next," he said.

"Right."

He turned and faced her full-on. "Most of those you'll meet will have at one time been in almost the same predicament as I." He stared at her. "And are nearly the same age."

Emma blinked, then returned his stare as she tried to soak in what he'd just said. She looked out to the sea, then back to Christian. "What do you mean, exactly?" She had a suspicion, but she'd rather hear it from him.

His eyes studied her. "Gawan and I grew up together. Jason is one of fifteen knights who were murdered and cursed in the thirteenth century. You'll meet the Munros, who were enchanted for nearly seven centuries."

Emma felt her eyes widen. "They were all ... *dead*." She shook her head and looked at him. "But now they're not?"

Christian shook his head. "Nay, not quite. Gawan was killed on the battlefield but before his time," he began. "He served as an earthbound angel for centuries. He was close to retirement, mortality being his reward, when he met Ellie." He smiled. " 'Tis a long story, lass, and one you shall hear, I vow it. But later. Tonight. And when Dreadmoor and the rest of his knights arrive on the morrow, you'll hear their tale, as well." He smiled. "And how they love to tell it."

"But what about Jason?" she asked. "You're telling me Jason was once a ghost?"

Christian nodded slowly.

"And now he's not?" She rubbed her forehead. "I think that's harder to swallow than just accepting you're not standing there, alive."

"Looking drop-dead gorgeous?"

Emma frowned at him. "That was not meant for you to hear," she said.

He moved closer. "But I did hear it."

She studied him carefully. His expression didn't carry one ounce of humor. "If they can all overcome *death*, then why can't you?"

"My situation is different."

The wind picked up and whipped furiously at Emma's hair. She pushed it out of her eyes and behind her ears. "How is it so different? They were dead; you're dead."

The slightest of smiles tipped the corner of his mouth. "You act as though you care, Emma Calhoun."

She frowned. She wasn't about to lie. "Of . . . course I care," she said softly. "Why wouldn't I?"

For the first time since she had met him, Christian looked taken aback. He blinked. "In truth?"

She scowled at him and turned to leave. "Yeah, in truth."

She opened the door, but Christian was there, so close she nearly passed through him.

"Emma, wait."

She stopped and glared at him. And waited. She wasn't too happy about baring her feelings, only to be laughed at.

"Why are you angry?" he asked. He stood close, his height looming over her, but his head bent close.

"Because," she said, then sighed. "Flirting is one thing when it's reciprocated. When one changes from flirting to caring, but the other is still hung up on just flirting . . ." She shook her head. "Never mind. That doesn't even make sense to me and I'm the one who said it." She tried to move, and could have passed through Christian easily, but she didn't. He blocked her the best way he knew how, she supposed—by simply standing there. She closed her eyes, mortified she'd confessed anything at all to the handsome ghost. "Now I'm embarrassed."

For several seconds, the only sounds that reached Emma's ears were the sounds of the North Sea and the wind colliding. She stood there, allowing the chill October air to wash the heat from her skin, and she inhaled several times, long, cleansing breaths.

"Open your eyes, Emma."

His voice washed over her, deeper this time, more serious. It made her heart slam against her ribs. Her teeth began to chatter. "No."

"Please?"

At first, Emma enjoyed her rebellion and kept her eyes shut. She was embarrassed; dang it, she just all but admitted she liked the guy. The least he could do was let her wallow in mortification in peace.

"Now."

With a resigned sigh, because he'd just continue to bug her, she did.

Christian was no more than a few inches from her face. His eyes searched hers; then his gaze dropped to her lips where it lingered as he spoke. "I like it very much that you care about my fate, Emma Calhoun. And for the record," he continued, now lifting his gaze back to her eyes, "I never flirt. I mean every single thing I say."

"Oh," she said, unable to say anything else.

Somehow, he drew closer, crowding her into the tiny space the single door provided. He ducked his head lower. "And if I had substance, I'd be kissing you right now."

Her eyes widened and a lump formed in her throat.

"And when I finished," he said, his mouth drawing close to her ear, "you'd have to concentrate to draw your next breath."

Emma couldn't find one thing to say. Electricity pulsed through her, and she found it difficult to breathe even now, without him actually kissing her. Just the words alone, and his closeness, made her knees wobble.

"Look at me," he asked.

She lifted her gaze.

"Will you be my lady at tournament?" he asked, then smiled. "It may not sound like much to you, but to me it would mean . . . a lot."

Emma cleared her throat so her voice wouldn't sound like a croaking frog. "What does that mean?"

Christian grinned that heart-stopping grin. "It means I claim you, and you cheer only for me." He shrugged. "Quite a big deal in medieval times."

Emma swallowed her fear and embarrassment and gave Christian a nervous grin. "That sounds sort of like you're asking me to go steady."

"That's exactly what I'm doing."

She smiled, not nearly so nervously now. "Then I accept."

The return smile on Christian's face nearly knocked the wind from her lungs. "Then let me escort you to the kitchen so you can eat. You'll need to keep your strength up, you know." He inclined his head to the door.

Emma smiled. If Jason didn't show up soon, she'd have to scrounge in the Grimm pantry for a snack. She stepped into the cool, damp stairwell and started the descent, rope firmly in hand.

She felt as if she could swing on it, she was so thrilled. She hurried down the narrow steps, and before long, they reached the bottom. She looked at him and laughed. "And to think I once had to dangle to get your attention."

Christian looked down at her, eyes serious. "You had my attention from the moment you set foot on Arrick land."

Suddenly, the small space at the foot of the spiral steps shrunk even smaller, and while Christian might not have substance, he still dominated every spare inch. Emma smiled up at him. "Finding Arrick-by-the-Sea was the best thing that's ever happened to me," she said, her words coming out breathy and light. "I never expected to meet anyone—especially someone like you."

For a moment, they simply stared. The smile he gave her sank clear to her bones.

" 'Tisn't every day the lives of ghosts and mortals become entwined," he said, then grinned. "Here more than other places, I'd warrant."

Emma studied him. "It's just so astounding. How did the others go from being dead—a ghost—to finding life again? How do body organs go from not working, to working again? And why," she said, peering up at him, "has it not worked for you?"

Christian drew close. "I've explained somewhat of Gawan's experience. The Dreadmoor lot were cursed. With the help of a determined woman, that curse was undone. The same for the Munros."

Emma shook her head. "It seems so far-fetched."

"Are you sure this is something you can handle, Emma Calhoun? Is it something that you *want* to handle?"

Emma met his gaze and considered. Actually, she'd already been considering it. A lot. She couldn't pinpoint the exact moment she began falling—*really* falling for Christian of Arrick-by-the-Sea—but it had indeed happened.

Probably more so for her than for Christian. She'd simply never had any success with men—live ones, at least. She just wasn't *that* type of girl. The type that drew men's attentions, that caused their heads to turn. That simply wasn't her. She wasn't ugly—at least, she didn't *think* she was. But she was average, and that had always been A-OK with her. Average height, average weight, average eye color, average hair, etc.

Strange that, in the end, she'd end up with a far-from-average guy.

Not that she was *with* Christian. Not . . . *really*. They'd only just met. Sort of.

Gazing at the ghostly form of the twelfth-century warrior before her, Emma could hardly believe that someone like Christian of Arrick-by-the-Sea would even be interested in her. One day, when her courage reached a higher level, she just might ask him. For curiosity's sake, of course. She couldn't help but wonder what sort of miracle it would take to free him from death . . .

Christian's brows furrowed as he waited for her to answer.

"Of course I want to handle it," she stated. "I'm a lot tougher than I look, Arrick."

His smile blinded her. "I see that."

She placed her hand on the door, but before she could push it open, Christian stopped her.

"One more thing, Emma," he said, giving her another serious look. "Grimm is a haven for spirits, and the ones who reside here have been sort of . . . waiting on you to hear of them. But they're about to burst to meet you."

She swallowed. "More ghosts, huh?"

He smiled. "Scores of them."

Emma nodded. "Well, I think I'm certainly ready to meet any and every soul who inhabits Castle Grimm."

"Good. I'm sure they'll find you sooner than later."

Together they stepped out of the spiral stairwell.

Jason was waiting, a huge grin on his adorable face. Emma didn't think she'd ever look at him the same. He was once a ghost, she reminded herself. *Unfreakingbelievable.*

"Lady Emma, there you are," he said, looking pleased with himself. "Are you ready to head to the chippy? I vow, I'm near starved."

Christian frowned. "We were—"

"Oh, Chris," said Jason, his eager smile still at the ready, "Gawan and Justin Catesby are looking for you. They need you in the bailey, posthaste." He winked at Emma. "For training."

Christian met Emma's gaze. "Do you mind?"

"We won't be gone overly long," offered Jason.

Emma smiled. "I'll be right back."

Christian glowered at Jason, who returned that sour look with a victorious grin, then turned to Emma. The sour look turned smoldering. "Until."

Then he disappeared, his white teeth the last to vanish.

Chapter 22

Emma reached over with her forefinger and poked Jason in the chest. She shook her head and looked at him. "It's almost too much for my mind to wrap around. You were once *dead*. A ghost, just like Christian." She shook her head and studied the young knight. She knew something was different about him. "How can it be?"

Jason looked down at her and grinned. Then he inclined his head to the main entrance. They started toward it. "'Twas a miracle, lady. A blooming miracle. I cannot describe it any more than that." He opened the door for her and they stepped outside. "And the fact that it didn't simply affect me, but all of the Dragonhawk knights, as well, is something to consider."

Jason led Emma to a dark blue Rover. He held the door open for her as she climbed in, and they soon were driving over the wooden planks of the drawbridge and through the gatehouse. Turning left, they made their way down the crag and then took a winding, single-track lane that hugged the coastline. The day certainly had a grim look about it, with gray, swirling skies and the bleak, brownish grass. Clumps of faded heather dotted the area, as well as a few sheep, all on one side of the lane. On the other side was the coastline, with a pebbly beach and choppy North Sea water.

"What was it like?" she asked, glancing over at Jason.

He tossed her a look, then a grin. "Being a ghost, you mean?" He shrugged. "Saints, I was one for so long, it just sort of became my way of existence. There are actually many things I miss dreadfully, like slipping through walls, or just ... making myself be one place, then another." He laughed. "My master, Lord Tristan—he'd get so bloody irritated at me. He'd holler, 'Jason!' and I'd just pop up behind him." He chuckled. "Used to drive him nuts. I don't think I ever grew weary of it."

His expression turned solemn, then. "You crave the human touch, though. Not just the touch of a woman, mind you—*any* touch at all." He shook his head. "Nay, I'd not trade slipping through walls for my life now for anything."

Emma watched him closely. He couldn't be more than twenty. So young, yet so ... old and wise at the same time. Sad, and yet ... overjoyed that he'd overcome fate.

"I'm awfully glad your miracle happened," she said. "You're too young and way too handsome to remain a ghost for eternity." She eyed him. "I bet you have all the girls in a one-hundred-mile radius just drooling over you."

He threw her a sideways grin. "Mayhap." He pointed. "Look there; that's the village. I can smell the bakery from here."

Emma did look, and found a quaint little seaside village, with small, whitewashed buildings and stone establishments nestled at the bottom of the hill and hugging the water's edge. They made their way toward it.

As Jason crept through the tiny streets, he pointed out several B and B's, a post office, a fishmonger, and a bakery. Finally he pulled alongside the curb in front of the chip shop and cut the engine. He turned to face her. "As much as I jest with Sir Christian, I want you to know that I uphold the highest respect for him as a knight and a man," he said. With his big hand, he reached over to lay it over hers. He squeezed. "Do not give up hope," he said, his eyes wide and earnest. "I understand the difficulties of mortals and ghosts being together. I watched Sir Tristan with his wife, Andi. 'Twasn't easy for them, but their love was—*is*—so strong, I believe it would have withstood all things had he not regained his mortality."

Emma considered his words. The extent of what he was saying struck her right square in the gut. Another mortal woman had apparently fallen deeply in love with a ghost. She'd traded the warmth of a live human touch, just to be with that ghost. That was the thing that got Emma the most. How she'd once envisioned ghosts and specters was completely wrong. So very, very wrong. They didn't exist beneath white gauzy sheets, with little holes poked out for eyes. They didn't float around like a gray lady or a green lady. They were souls. They were themselves, as they had been in life.

Just *dead*.

Emma met Jason's intent gaze, and she smiled. It was a weak smile—she felt it.

His return smile was steady, stable. Strong. "Just keep in mind his feelings, lady," Jason said. "Whilst a spirit in truth, he is still a man. 'Tisn't often a ghost finds a mortal who believes as fiercely as you do." He chuckled. "More here than elsewhere, I imagine."

Emma laughed. "That's the same thing Christian said." She grabbed his hand and squeezed. "Thank you. For your ghostly insight, I mean." She glanced out over the village. "It's very weird. Before today, rather, before I came here, I never would have thought any of this possible." She returned her gaze to Jason's. "And had someone come to me with these notions, I would have thought them a lunatic. I'm so glad I was . . . enlightened."

"As am I." He quirked a brow. "I imagine he's already asked you to cheer for him at tournament, aye?"

"He did," said Emma. She smiled. "But I will quietly cheer for you, too."

Jason winked. "Good. Now let's eat. I'm starved."

After ordering two fried cod-and-chips, plus Cokes, Jason led Emma down to the wharf at the foot of the hill, where they sat on a stone bench not three feet from the water's edge. The sun still hadn't shown itself, but the turtleneck sweater she had on kept her warm enough. The fried batter crunched as she bit into the cod, and the chips steamed in a cluster, crispy on the outside, soft on the inside.

She'd squirted lots of brown sauce and vinegar all over both.

Emma wiped her mouth, took a pull on her Coke, and turned to Jason, who'd just crammed the last of the fish into his mouth.

"Do you think a miracle could ever happen to Christian?" she asked.

Jason regarded her while he chewed. He finished and wiped his mouth. "I truly believe anything is possible," he admitted. "With us, 'twas a matter of breaking a curse, righting a terrible wrong. But with Chris"—he glanced away—" 'tis a bit more . . . complex."

Emma blinked. "More complex than a curse?"

With a smile, Jason nodded. "Aye. And I fear you'll have to pry the rest out of Sir Christian yourself." He winked. "Even I know what boundaries not to cross with him."

Emma understood that. The next time she and Christian were alone, she'd ask him about . . . *things*.

"So this tournament," she began. "Ghosts and mortals are able to compete with one another?"

Jason popped a handful of chips into his mouth, chewed, and shook his head. "Gawan and Chris are somehow able to accomplish it, but we think 'tis due to their attachment prior to Gawan's retirement. None of us understand how they do it, but 'tis miraculous to watch. They don't compete in tournament, though.

"The ghosts separate into teams and compete with one another"—he winked at her—"and there will be scores of ghosts from all over England, Scotland, and Wales—possibly even Ireland—showing up on the morrow. Events are judged and points awarded. There are ultimately two victors—one from the mortal team, one from the ghostly team." He smiled. "Is that why you're here? For the tournament?"

"No, although I'm awfully glad that I am now. It sounds fascinating." Emma continued to explain to Jason her weird feelings, and what drove her to Arrick in the first place.

He listened attentively, then smiled. "Sounds to me that you weren't searching for Arrick, but for the lord of Arrick instead."

Emma wadded up her empty, white fish-and-chips paper and grinned. "You may be right, Jason." Perhaps that *was* what drew her to Arrick. She didn't know it at the time, though.

After that, they walked around the small village a bit. Emma purchased a few postcards from the general store, then stopped by the post office and sent one to Zoë and another to her parents, and then she and Jason climbed back into the Rover and headed to Grimm.

One thing was for certain: the view approaching Castle Grimm on land was vastly different than approaching by air. The castle loomed ahead on the cliffs, massive and dominating the coastline. She could easily imagine what it must have been like, centuries before, riding up to Grimm on horseback and seeing such an intimidating and foreboding structure.

Suddenly, Emma's skin grew cold, and her vision blurred. She continued to stare straight ahead, and the more she looked, the more the vision changed. The scenery shifted, trees disappeared and reappeared in a different location, and people surrounded her. She was on horseback, and when Emma looked down, she saw her own tiny legs and feet sticking out on either side of the horse. She was riding behind someone . . .

"Emma? Is there aught amiss?" Jason's voice interrupted her, seemingly from far away.

Emma blinked. The vision completely disappeared.

"Emma?"

She glanced at Jason, whose face was drawn with concern. "Yes?"

He'd stopped the Rover just outside the gatehouse. "You were staring off into space. Is something troubling you?"

"I, um," she started. "Very strange, actually. I . . . thought I was riding on the back of a horse, but I wasn't me," she said. "I was a little girl." She shook her head. "Weird, huh?"

Jason's light green eyes studied her. Satisfied that she was okay, he nodded. "Weird, indeed, lady." He pulled through the gatehouse, then slowly clamored over the drawbridge. The wooden planks *clack-clack*ed as they passed over, and then Jason parked in the small gravel lot, close to the main entrance.

When Emma stepped out, she immediately heard a strange and unique noise. It sounded like . . . metal against metal. It rang out over the courtyard.

Before she could ask Jason what it was, he grinned and grasped her by the arm. "You're in for a treat, lady," he said, pulling her along. "Come on. You won't ever see this anywhere else, save Grimm, I'd warrant."

Jason led—no, *dragged*—Emma through the courtyard, then out a small iron gate that led to a large, grassed-in area.

It was more like an arena, she thought.

In the distance, Emma could make out a small gathering of people, who all seemed to be watching something of interest a bit farther away. The closer she and Jason drew to the small crowd, the more Emma could make out who was watching, and what was being watched.

Her jaw slid open, and she stopped, efficiently yanking Jason to a halt, too. He grinned at her, then gave her a gentle tug.

"Come on, girl," he said, chuckling. "You've got to get closer than that."

Emma walked, grateful that Jason led the way, making sure she didn't trip and fall on her face.

Emma's eyes widened as they locked on to the pair of shirtless men circling one another, several feet from where she stood: Gawan and Christian, hair loose and wild, fierce scowls upon their faces, and each holding a very sharp and lethal-looking sword.

Well, Christian held *two*.

Gawan, though, held one that had to be nearly as tall as Emma.

They looked like they were trying to kill each other.

"Oh, my dear, look! We've a seat for you!"

Emma slowly peeled her gaze from the sword fight to the voice she'd just heard. Her eyes enlarged again as she took in the small crowd of sword-fight watchers.

Ellie sat with all three children, plus Davy. Next to Davy, Justin Catesby. On the other side of Ellie, Godfrey. And in front of them, perched in two folding chairs, sat two ladies Emma hadn't met yet. One she was drawn to immediately. Her hair had been fixed in the shape of a swan. The other, well, she looked sopping wet. Both wore period clothing, although Emma had no clue as to which period.

The lady with the bird on her head waved and patted the seat next to her.

"Come along, dear, and have a seat," she said, smiling.

The sopping-wet lady waved.

"Emma, come on!" hollered Ellie. Her boys were bouncing in their seats.

Justin Catesby simply stared. And grinned.

Jason pulled on her arm. "Come on or you'll miss it."

Emma allowed him to pull her to her seat, next to the swan lady. Ellie quickly introduced them to Emma.

"These are Ladies Follywolle and Beauchamp," Ellie said. "They couldn't wait to meet you."

Emma greeted them with a smile. "Nice to meet you, too."

Then a string of harsh words in a language Emma didn't understand flew from the fighters, and her attention was immediately drawn to them. She'd not seen Christian, or Gawan, for that matter, with their shirts off, and the sight of it now nearly made her break out in a sweat. Both men had multiple black tattoos, but they were different. Gawan's were small, all down his back, across his chest, and down his arms to his wrists.

Christian's, though, were larger, more intricate, and he had one on the right side of his chest, a large one on his back, and a wide band encircling each bicep. She couldn't tell from where she sat what the designs were, but she'd be certain to find that out as soon as possible.

She sincerely hoped that would be sooner rather than later.

Chapter 23

Christian and Gawan circled one another, legs clad in leather boots and pants that had straps crossing up their thighs. They crouched, swords raised menacingly, the muscles in their backs, stomachs, shoulders, and arms pulled taut. Their biceps bulged from the weight of their weapons, and Emma noticed veins on both of Christian's arms that traveled upward and fanned out over his chest. He looked so *real*.

And those *had* to be foul words coming from their mouths. Neither of their faces looked friendly at all.

"How is this possible?" she asked, mostly to herself.

Jason leaned closely. "They used to train all the time when Gawan was still earthbound. Trained for centuries. It's really just a play of illusion, sound included. For whatever reason, they maintained the ability, even after Gawan's retirement."

The strike of steel against steel filled the bailey as Gawan and Christian came at each other, Christian swinging dual swords, Gawan swinging his one giant one. Sweat plastered their hair to their skulls, and they both looked ferocious enough to hack the other's head off in the blink of an eye.

Emma shuddered at the thought.

The pair suddenly called a halt, and both men stabbed

the ground with their swords and leaned their weight against the hilts, breathing heavily.

As she stared, her vision blurred, colors became more vivid, and it made her head feel light. That familiar feeling in her stomach twinged, and she gasped.

"Emma, are you unwell?" asked Jason.

Emma blinked, and her vision cleared. What *was* that? She smiled. "No, I'm perfectly fine." Again, her eyes lighted on the warriors. They leaned over their swords, breathing hard. She was positive Christian's was for show. Could he get winded? She didn't see how.

There was so much of his world she didn't understand.

But she found herself wanting to more and more.

Actually, as her eyes locked with Christian's, and he yanked the one sword out of the ground and started walking toward her, she discovered she wanted to know *everything* about him . . .

Christian couldn't take his bloody eyes off Emma. She sat, eyes wide as they stared back at him, her mouth slightly open. Her reddish brown hair hung straight to her shoulders, parted slightly off to one side and tucked neatly behind each ear. Her hair stood out in stark contrast to the black, form-fitting jumper she wore, and her faded, holed-at-the-knees jeans hung low on her hips, snug in just the right places. Her skin, pale and flawless as alabaster, set off her wide blue eyes.

She was the most beautiful creature he'd ever laid eyes on.

Once again he found this time, this thirteenth chance, vastly different from their previous lives together. 'Twas the same loving soul—he recognized that much—but many of the characteristics that carried from one life to the next were absent, replaced by this modern Emma's own uniqueness, which Christian found intriguing. The Emma he'd met long ago had been painfully shy. This modern version could blush furiously, yet still be bold enough to say exactly what was on her mind. He rather fancied it. And he dared to hope things might end up favorably this time round . . .

As he drew closer, a smile lifted each corner of Emma's lush mouth, making his lifeless self shudder on the inside like a lad of ten and three meeting his first girl.

Bloody hell, he was suddenly *nervous*.

Finally, Christian reached her. She'd stood and was staring, a look of wonder etched in her lovely face.

Slowly, she shook her head. "You . . . are amazing." Her breathy voice washed over him, and he couldn't help but smile with pride.

" 'Twas nothing, lass. Just a bit of knightly sword-play." He gave her a slight nod. "But I am enormously glad you enjoyed it."

A giggle erupted beside her. Christian shot Lady Follywolle a mock glare, but it hushed her up, so that made him happy.

Lady Follywolle stuck her tongue out.

"Chris, you old smooth talker," said Ellie, suddenly beside them. Ensley lay asleep in the little pouch swing against Ellie's chest. "You know, watching that entire sword fighting stuff—especially for the first time—can make a girl swoon."

Ellie winked at Emma, who tried to smother a grin.

Ellie and Gawan's twins ran up then, jumping all around, smiles stretched across their little faces. "Unc Cwiss! Unc Cwiss!" they yelled. "Me! Me!"

He found he never grew weary of hearing it.

"Boys, get back," said Ellie sweetly. They hugged her, one on each leg, and continued to grin at him.

He'd always wanted a score of babes. Good thing Gawan and Ellie were of the same mind-set. At least he got to be Uncle Chris.

Gawan joined them, along with Davy, Gawan's arm draped over the lad's shoulder. The others stood, Justin, Godfrey, and the ladies, and that ever-present, smug Jason, lately forever at Emma's side.

Not that he could blame the pup.

"Well," Ellie said, patting little Ensley's bottom through the carrier, "I'm headed in to start baths and feedings." She looked at Emma. "Will Chris' company be okay while I get the kids all ready for bed?"

Emma's cheeks turned red.

"Would you like me to help?" Emma asked.

Ellie's gaze flashed to Christian, and for an instant he thought she'd take Emma up on her offer. Gawan's wife lifted one mischievous brow, then shook her head.

"From the look on Christian's face, Emma, you'd best appease him and hang out until supper." She grinned. "Besides, I have a junior warlord who is very good at handling the twins in their bath."

Lady Follywolle giggled. "Come, come, ladies, gentlemen. Let's convene in my solar for a game of Knucklebones whilst the young ones have their time." She batted her lashes at Christian. "Behave, Lord Arrick."

Justin Catesby grinned; then he, along with the ladies, disappeared.

Godfrey looked at young Davy. "You comin', boy?"

"Oh, aye!" hollered Davy, who in turn looked at Jason. "And you, sir?" he asked.

Jason shot a glance at Emma, who gave him a tender smile. Jason shrugged, and both lads took off running toward the side entrance of the hall.

Gawan gave him a look, grinned, then stared at Emma. "Lass, are you sure this whoreson's company is worthy?"

Emma blinked, and glanced from Christian to Gawan. "Um, yes. Perfectly."

He gave a short nod. "Well done. We shall see you two at supper, then." He placed an arm around his wife's shoulder, then corralled the twins in one arm and lifted them, squealing.

Ellie turned and grinned over her shoulder, and mouthed the word *Bye* to Emma.

Efficiently leaving him and Emma completely alone.

Christian knew that wouldn't last for long.

Then, he looked down, and noticed Emma had eased closer, and was now intently studying him, or more specifically, his markings. He stood still, allowing her perusal, until finally, she stopped and looked at him. She said nothing.

He squirmed.

A smile tipped her mouth. "Got any more interesting things to show me?"

Christian gaped.

Emma rolled her eyes. "Around Grimm, you perv."

He grinned. "Mayhap." They started walking, and he sheathed both swords. He noticed Emma kept slipping a glance at him. Somehow, that made him walk a bit taller.

They crossed the bailey, then went through the iron gate and into the courtyard. Her head barely reached his shoulder. Small though she was, he knew she could hold her own in most any situation and certainly with the crowd coming tomorrow. Modern lasses had more . . . reserves than medieval ones. It fascinated him, yet made him desire nothing more than to hold open an iron gate whilst she passed through it.

Something he'd never be able to do.

A brief thought struck him, and struck him hard. What if Emma did know just how long he'd known her? Would she be angry? 'Twas a mighty secret, in truth. Only God knew how things would turn out this time. Mayhap, since so many things were different, the ending would be as well?

He could only hope.

Absently, Christian led Emma to the cliff side, where Gawan had installed several stone alcoves for sitting and viewing the sea—at Ellie's insistence, of course. There wasn't a thing Ellie wished for that Gawan didn't try to make happen.

"I know I sound like a groupie, but"—she looked up at him briefly—"I just can't seem to get over . . . everything. Mainly, you, I suppose." She shook her head. "To know you fought in wars centuries ago, and with *those*," she said, gesturing toward his blades. "It's really, really hard to take in." She smiled up at him. "It fascinates me. Actually, you fascinate me, Christian."

He'd die three more times, just to hear her say his name like that.

The wind whipped fiercely off the sea, tossing Emma's hair about her. She seemed not to mind overmuch, turning her face to it and closing her eyes. She smiled, then looked at him.

"The sun doesn't seem to show itself here much," she said. "Funny—I live where the sun shines constantly; it's hot, humid, sticky. I don't mind this so much."

He smiled at that. "How do you keep your skin from becoming scorched?" he asked, just as they reached the man-made alcove.

Emma slid into the stone retreat and shrugged. "Lots of sunscreen, I imagine." She looked at him as he moved in beside her. "Do your markings have a meaning?"

Christian glanced down at his chest and his arms. Embedded in the one on his chest was Emma's name, in Pictish symbols. He couldn't very bloody well tell her *that*. A long time ago, she knew . . .

Emma's soft fingertip traced the Pictish marking scorched into his chest. The sensation of her skin against his nearly drove him daft. She rose up on her toes to study the symbols more closely. Then she grinned. "What does this one mean, Chris?"

Christian wrapped his arms about her tightly, reveling in the feel of her soft body pressed against his. He lowered his head and brushed his lips against hers. " 'Tis your name, love." He kissed her.

"That means I shall always be with you," she murmured against his mouth.

"Aye, it does indeed," he said. "I shall love you forever . . ."

"Christian?"

Back in the present, he smiled. " 'Tis markings of a Pictish warrior." He pointed to several symbols on his arms. "This is a bolt of lightning, meaning speed. This here," he said, pointing to a sickle, "represents the swiftness of my blade, and a blessing to use it viciously against my rival."

She tentatively reached a hand out, her finger directly pointing to the symbols of her name. "And this?"

Bloody hell.

" 'Tis a symbol that means close to my heart," he said. And 'twasn't a lie.

"Oh," she said softly, and leaned her head against the back of the alcove. She looked at him, studying him closely. They were quiet for several moments, and finally, she sighed. "I believe you're the reason I came to Arrick-by-the-Sea," she said. "It's so very strange, but I can't think of any other good, logical reason." She gave a soft laugh, and pushed her fallen hair behind her ear. "I worry my confidence comes from your state of unliving," she said shyly, "but I'm going with it." Her gaze was direct, earnest, profound. "Why me?"

He stared at her. Had she lost her mind? Even had she not been the soul he'd been in love with for nearly nine hundred years, he'd still have fallen for her. Everything that made up her character appealed to him.

With his forefinger, he gently grazed the line of her cheek, keeping just enough space between his essence and hers to keep from passing through. Her eyes widened at the sensation he knew she felt.

He felt it, too. It made his stomach do funny things.

Leaning forward, he drew his face close to hers. "You have no idea just how beautiful you are, do you, Emma Calhoun?" he asked. He simply drank her features in, from the arch of her brows, to the roundness of her eyes, to the small, straight angle of her nose, and to the curve of her lush lips.

And, especially that unique mark, just at the corner.

So close, they were naught but a whisper apart. Emma's lips were slightly parted, and for once, she was speechless. Christ, he'd never wanted to kiss her so badly in all the centuries he'd experienced time with her.

This thirteenth chance was proving to be the most challenging.

"What would it feel like?" she asked, her voice barely above a whisper. "If you tried to kiss me, I mean?"

Christian looked at her, long, hard, and thorough. She stared up at him, her head still resting back. He leaned closer still, placing his hand beside her head against the wall.

"You tell me," he said. "Close your eyes."

Slowly, she exhaled, then did.

And then he lowered his head.

Chapter 24

Emma's heart pounded hard against its cage, so hard she felt as though it jolted her with each thud. She kept her eyes closed, just as Christian had asked.

She wanted to open them. Badly.

She didn't dare.

Then, a tingling started at her mouth, first on her lower lip, then the corner, then the top. The sensation was so distinguishing, it made her gasp, and while she tried not to, she couldn't help it. Slowly, she opened her eyes.

Christian's head was bent to hers, ever so slightly turned to one side, so very close that she knew without being able to see that their lines of definition blurred. His eyes were closed, and he was all but melded to her, his lips gently parted and resting against hers. The air lodged in her lungs, she was so fearful that, if she breathed, she'd lose the sensation altogether. Finally, on an exhale that she could not help, she said his name.

"Christian," she said softly, lifting her hands to rest idly by his jaw.

Christian pulled back, just a fraction, and the sensation lingered a moment, then disappeared. The intensity of his gaze burned through her.

"You've no idea the strength I muster to keep from trying to touch you," he said, his gaze dropping to her mouth once more, then back to her eyes. The very corner of his mouth tipped upward. "I can hear your heartbeat."

Emma gave a nervous smile. "It's kind of fast at the moment."

"So I see."

He still leaned close to her, and she couldn't resist lifting a finger and tracing the square of his jaw. She noticed an intake of air, or at least the sound of it.

He'd felt that, too.

Just then, a gust of wind brought with it several droplets of rain. Emma didn't even turn her face away. She welcomed the tiny barrage of water. Hopefully, it would douse her desire.

She didn't want to be accused of jumping a ghost in broad daylight.

Instead of jumping Christian, Emma pulled her legs up and huddled against the back of the alcove. Luckily, it was built deep enough to provide shelter, as long as the wind didn't whip the rain in. She scooched into the corner, legs up, chin on knees, and simply stared at her warrior.

Her warrior.

Wow.

Christian's eyes narrowed as he watched her. "I'd love to know what exactly is going through that brain of yours, Ms. Calhoun," he said.

She smiled. "You couldn't pay me enough to tell you what's going through my brain right now."

"Interesting."

The sexy look on Christian's face made her heart accelerate. Then, his expression grew serious.

"A large lot of healthy, viable knights will start flooding Grimm's gates on the morrow," he said. "I, well . . ." He glanced away.

"What?" Emma urged.

After a moment, he turned back and gave her a look that made her squirm in her seat. " 'Tisn't fair of me to force you into a relationship where the other half isn't ... tangible. If you decide to choose another—"

Emma frowned. "Don't tell me you're dead *and* crazy," she said. "First, let me assure you that I'm the last person on earth who can be forced into doing something I don't want to do. Second ..." She took in his grave features, the perfect square cut of his jaw, and those full, inviting lips. She started again. "Second, I didn't come here to play the *Dating Game* or *The Bachelor*—or whatever." She huffed out a breath. "Something did bring me here, Christian. But it wasn't to find just any old knight, viable, healthy, or anything else in between." She smiled. "I was sent here to find *you*. I know it now just as I sit here and breathe. You're a miracle in itself, mister, and although I know our relationship is way too young to confess any sort of....long-standing feelings, I do know what my heart is telling me."

The very corner of his mouth tipped up. Not a smile, really. But something *else*.

"And what is it telling you?"

Emma's breath came faster, mad, but not mad, her heart pounding quicker. "It's telling me that you're the kind of man I'd desire no matter what form you're in." She gently swiped her hand through his tattooed arm. "Ghost. Not a ghost." She shrugged. "Makes no matter to me. I like you just the way you are."

"Is that so?"

She gave a single, firm nod. "It is."

Christian seemed to ponder that. Ponder it, albeit with a satisfied grin on his face.

"You realize, though," he said, looking grim once more, "that I cannot protect you. Not physically, that is. I'm rather worthless in that category."

Emma narrowed her eyes. "In case you haven't noticed, this isn't the Dark Ages anymore. There's really not a need for protection, you know." She held her arm up and flexed it in a show of muscle. "Besides, I took a self-defense class." She squeezed her puny bicep. "I can take care of myself, Arrick. I always carry pepper spray. And," she continued, "I haven't had an enemy since, oh, second grade."

He chuckled. "I cannot fathom what sort of mischief you could have combined in the second grade to acquire an enemy."

"Let's just say I'm not one to be trifled with," she answered.

"I can barely wait to hear."

Emma sat back and wrapped her arms around her legs. "Big Marjorie stole my lunch every day for a solid week. My mom made the best chicken salad sandwiches—you know, with little chopped-up pieces of celery? God, they were good. Anyway, Big Marjorie kept on stealing my sandwiches. So one day, I decided to get her back." She grinned. "She outweighed me by, I don't know—I was always kind of scrawny—but by a lot. Taller than me, too, and she could beat up most boys in my class. But I'd had enough, and I didn't want to be a tattletale."

Christian rubbed his jaw, then wiped his hand across his mouth, no doubt trying to hold in a laugh. "What did you do?"

Emma grinned. "You know, in the South, where I live, we have an abundance of these teeny-tiny marsh snails—no bigger than my pinky nail"—she held out her nail to show—"and I peeled a bunch of them off the marsh grass and stuck them all in my sandwich." She grinned.

"Crunchy?" Christian asked.

"Very. When she discovered they were in there, after she'd eaten a good three-quarters, she barfed all over the cafeteria." Emma sat back and smiled smugly. "Big Marjorie didn't bother me or my sandwiches ever again."

Christian chuckled, his blue eyes gleaming. "You are indeed a force to be reckoned with, Ms. Calhoun."

"Don't you forget it."

They sat in silence for a few minutes, simply being in each other's company. The gray skies began shifting, turning darker. That familiar time of day settled in, that space of time that was neither daylight nor darkness.

"I love this time of evening," Emma said, staring at the sky. "It's . . . magical." She looked at him. "You're proof of that."

Christian gave a soft laugh. " 'Tis the gloaming hour," he said, and returned her stare. "Indeed, 'tis a magical time of day." He shrugged. "If you believe in that sort of thing."

"I would say there's something to it," said Emma. "There's two men in the castle whose lives were very different at one time, and another pack of them showing up tomorrow." She leaned closer to him. "If something magical—something miraculous can happen to them, Christian, it can happen to you, too."

He looked at her, his gaze fixed and penetrating.

"It can. You have to believe," she said, then shook her head. "I know I keep saying this, but a couple of weeks ago I wouldn't have believed any of this," she said, making a sweep of her hand toward the castle. "You, Jason, Gawan, Justin, Godfrey, the ladies—I would not have believed a single soul, had they approached me to say you existed." She gave him a warm, hopeful smile. "I believe now." She rubbed her forehead. "I can't say for sure why you chose *me*, but the rest I totally get."

Christian slowly shook his head. "Mayhap I'm better off with you not realizing how breathtaking you are. Surely, if you knew, you'd pick someone else—mayhap a live someone else—over me."

Emma stretched and climbed out of the alcove, where she stretched again. The rain had subsided, and the sky had grown dark. She threw him a grin. "*Live schmive.* It's highly overrated, methinks."

Christian threw back his head and laughed.

Together, they walked back to the great hall, allowing the gloaming to surround them. They didn't speak; they just . . . existed. It felt comfortable, relaxed.

And somehow, familiar.

Emma wondered about that.

She also couldn't help but wonder how sudden it all seemed. She'd not been in Wales long, yet it felt as though she'd known Christian her entire life.

Weird.

She slipped a glance at the tall, lumbering warrior beside her. His legs, clad in those medieval britches with medieval boots, were nearly as long as she was tall. Leather straps crossed his chest and back, holding in place the double swords over each shoulder.

He was still shirtless.

Emma's mouth suddenly went dry.

He ducked his head—something she noticed him doing more than once when with her, probably to accommodate for her lack of height—and grinned. "Will you take photographs of the tournament?" he asked, innocent in that he obviously had no idea what his presence did to her.

Fine with her. For now.

"Absolutely," she answered. She noticed how his crazy hair swung forward, yet remained shorter in the back. She loved it.

"I fear I won't show up in any of them," he added.

"Don't worry," Emma said. "When I get home I'm going to see a friend of mine—an artist. She'll certainly be able to paint a portrait based on my description." She smiled, happy about that.

Christian, though, now wore a solemn expression. "Indeed," he said, then coughed and cleared his throat. "Those bloody Dreadmoor knights will no doubt be quite the photo hogs once they realize you're taking pictures," he said. "Not to mention you'll get to hear the story of their *return to the living* at least a score of times before the tournament's over." He grinned. "Arrogant lot, they are."

Emma smiled. "I'm beginning to think that was the norm for the medieval era."

Together, they laughed.

As they grew closer to the hall, the shadows stretched and swallowed everything in their path. Emma's senses soared with the newness of the budding relationship with Christian. As they neared the west wall, she stopped. Christian followed suit.

Together, without words, they simply stared.

"I was wondering," Emma said, suddenly embarrassed. "I mean, it is still so new—"

Christian must have read her mind, because suddenly, he was there, crowding her against the cool stone wall of Castle Grimm, completely engulfed by shadows. A crisp autumn wind caressed Emma, cooling her skin that she knew was several degrees warmer because of the man who stood so very close, so very intimately. She backed into the wall until she felt both of her shoulder blades cool from the damp stone, and Christian loomed over her, nearly just as real and tangible looking as any man.

The tension between them snapped in the air, and Christian placed his large hands on either side of Emma's head, and studied her, eyes boring into hers, head tilted. Her heart raced and her breath came faster, and she noticed his chest rose and fell a bit quicker, too. How that was possible, she hadn't a clue.

She didn't really care.

Then, his mouth hovered close to hers, and his whisper,

so sensual in that deep, sexy, strange Welsh accent, engulfed her just as thoroughly as the shadows. He moved his mouth to her ear, and the tingling sensation began, first at the outer shell, then down to her lobe. Emma closed her eyes as the sensation washed over her.

"Christian," she murmured, not knowing what else to say.

"I swear I can smell your scent," he said, his voice ragged as it moved from her ear to her jaw. "Christ, how badly I wish I could touch you in truth."

He moved his mouth to hers, just like before, thought better of the angle, and tilted his head a bit more, settling his ghostly, sexy lips against hers. Their essence mingled, the lines once more blurred, and there, in the shadows of a twelfth-century castle, Emma experienced absolutely the most *sensual* kiss of her life.

Without her realizing, she pushed her hands against the wall to hold herself upward, for at any minute her rubbery knees would surely give way and she'd fall to the ground.

Then, just when she thought she'd die, Christian pulled away. He smiled, and it was the sweetest, sexiest smile Emma had ever seen.

"Do you think you can walk?" he asked.

"Not hardly," she answered, her voice just as shaky as her legs.

"In a moment, then," he said, and she fully agreed.

Chapter 25

"Do you think it's working, Willoughby?" asked Maven, wringing her hands. "With them gone and out of sight, I'm so nervous!"

"I'm positive everything's all right, Sister," said Willoughby. "The lamb has no memories of Castle Grimm, and what recessed memories she does have of the others are insignificant at this point, so she's in the safest of places to keep from remembering her original self." She patted Maven's arm. " 'Twill be all right, love. You'll see."

"There's nothing we can do besides wait?" cried Agatha.

"Aye, 'tis such a helpless act, waiting," agreed Millicent. "At least when we were performing the steps of the spell, we were useful."

Willoughby nodded once. "We've had the past seventy-two years to prepare and follow all the steps accordingly. We have done so."

"What if the smallest of things mishappens? What if Emma discovers a way to avoid All Hallows' Eve? Her return flight back to America is two days before!" wailed Agatha.

Willoughby grinned. "You've little faith in your older sister, eh? That's already been taken care of, Sister."

All the sisters looked her way. "Truly?"

Willoughby nodded. "Truly. I cancelled the original return date and booked a new flight, returning three days later."

"And what if she's resistant to staying?" probed Millicent. "What if something happens and she wants to go home early?"

Willoughby met each of her sisters' gazes. "Now you three listen to me. This is going to work. Those two belong together, and young Christian deserves . . . well, you know what he deserves. The spell forbids me to say it aloud." She sighed. "I've complete confidence that Emma will be exactly where she needs to be, at exactly the required time she needs to be there, and on the correct date."

The younger Ballasters looked at her.

"Now pull yourselves together. We've more than two weeks left. You'll frazzle yourselves if you don't stop all this worrying."

"All right," they said in unison.

Willoughby smiled. "That's it, girls. Now let's get to work."

And with that, they did.

"Have you decided to tell her?"

Christian blew out a frustrated breath. "Nay."

Gawan glanced at him. "Nay, you've not decided, or nay, you aren't going to tell her?"

"I've not decided anything yet. We've only just admitted our attraction to one another." He kicked at a rock. His foot went straight through it, of course, but the action of it made him feel somewhat better. "Christ, Gawan," he said, glancing at his friend. "She's . . . far different this time. Harder to resist. Funny." He shook his head. "I was actually bloody nervous about kissing her."

"You've already done that?" Gawan asked. He whistled low. "Always has baffled me how you do it, exactly."

"Well, I bloody well won't show you."

Gawan laughed. "Thank God."

They continued walking the parapet along the north wall. They'd done it in life, and now, centuries later, they continued.

Gawan stopped, gripped the wall, and stared out across the wood. "Mayhap all these changes mean something," he said. "A sign of sorts? Mayhap 'twas fate's will to bring you to the present before something miraculous happens?"

Christian nodded, and leaned a hip against the wall. "You may be right. But how fair would it be of me to allow her feelings to grow, only to latch herself with a bloody spirit for the whole of her life?" He shook his head. "Bloody selfish of me, I'd say."

Gawan smiled. "You cannot be the judge of her feelings, Chris, no more than you can be the judge of yours. 'Tis a woman you've loved for nearly nine hundred years, man, and fate keeps sending her back to you. She's fallen in love with you, what? Thirteen times now? There's something to that, don't you think?"

He looked at his friend. "I dare to hope it."

Gawan pushed from the wall and stood, staring directly at Christian. "You're not asking for my advice, but I'm giving it all the same. Tell her. Eventually. Mayhap not right now, but eventually. If she doesn't remember, that is. Don't keep it from her, Chris. She deserves to know."

Christ, he knew it. Knew it all too well. In the past, he didn't have to tell her. She remembered on her own. But in the past, she remembered a lot faster than now.

As it was, she didn't even give an inkling that she remembered.

He looked at Gawan. "Because you had connections from the higher-ups, I'll listen to your advice. But I'll give her a bit of time. Now is too soon."

"Don't wait," Gawan said. "Not too long, anyway. Remember how I tried to not tell Ellie everything?" He visibly shuddered. " 'Twas a grave mistake—one that nearly turned disastrous. I don't want my best friend making the same error."

Christian grinned. "That almost sounds as though you love me, Conwyk."

Gawan smiled. "God knows I do, brother. Now, let's get to supper. I'm starved."

Me, too, he thought. Starved to see his Emma again.

The great hall was thumping with activity. Emma thought she'd never seen anything like it—and probably wouldn't ever see anything to compare. Between Nicklesby, that charming . . . she couldn't figure out what he was. More than a nanny, more than a butler—she couldn't put her finger on it. The Conwyks adored the wiry, funny man with enormous ears, regardless.

Nicklesby was running around, chasing after the twins. Godfrey and Davy were playing some sort of game in one corner, with Godfrey bursting out with a hearty *Bloody good move, lad!* every five minutes or so. And the ladies Follywolle and Beauchamp leaned over little Ensley's playpen, close to the hearth, goo-gooing and gah-gahing at each sweet little noise the infant made.

Lady Follywolle and that bird hair—it had to be the most hilarious thing Emma had ever seen. Every time she moved, nodded, shook her head, her hair looked as if it were about to take flight.

Stepping off the final stair, Emma caught sight of Lady Conwyk, rushing in and out of the kitchen. She made a beeline for her, to help with the meal. Just as she managed to cross halfway to the kitchen doors, she was intercepted by a young knight.

"Emma!" said Jason, rushing to walk with her. He grinned down at her. "How are you?"

Emma laughed. "You mean since the last time you saw me, oh, about a couple of hours ago?" She patted his arm. "I'm fine. Finer than fine, actually."

His eyes lit up, and a soft expression touched his face. "As I said before, that Christian is a lucky whoreson."

Emma shook her head. "I think you must have lost a few screws in your transformation from ghostism to mortalism," she said. With her forefinger, she made a swirly motion next to her temple.

He chuckled. "And why do you say that?"

She gave him a sideways glance. "Because. You consider him so darn lucky and I don't understand why."

Suddenly, Emma noticed she was walking alone. She stopped, and turned around. Jason had stopped in the center of the hall, a look of bafflement on his face. For some reason, it made Emma laugh. "What's wrong?" she asked.

Jason slowly walked up to her. He looked down, his light green eyes soft. "Are you daft, girl?" He slowly shook his head. "You have no idea how fetching you are, do you?"

Heat rose to Emma's cheeks. "That's silly. Very kind of you, but silly."

Jason's grin spread from ear to ear. "See? That makes you just that more fetching." He shook his head. "Lucky, lucky whoreson, indeed."

Emma rolled her eyes and grabbed Jason by the arm and tugged. "Come on, smooth talker. Escort me to the kitchen, handsome, so I can give Ellie a hand."

"Anytime," he answered with a laugh.

They entered the kitchen and Ellie turned, a smile splitting her face. "Hey guys!"

Emma smiled in return. "Need some help?"

"I'd love some. Nicklesby and I changed jobs today, and he's so much better at cooking than I am. He usually does the supper and I chase the twins." She grinned.

"But they love their uncle Nicklesby so much that they wanted him instead of me tonight." She blew a strand of hair from her eyes.

Emma could do nothing but laugh. "Well, I'm not sure how good I am at cooking, but I love to eat." She pushed up the sleeves to her turtleneck. "Point me in the right direction and tell me what to do."

Jason cleared his throat. "I think I shall go help Nicklesby chase the twins."

"Bye," Emma and Ellie said in unison.

Jason chuckled as he left the kitchen.

"Okay, so what are we making?" asked Emma, glancing around the kitchen. There were double sinks by a small window, a hearth, a pantry, and a long wooden table off to one side. A long, red-tiled island sat in the center, complete with a sink and stove top. Pots and pans hung from a rack above. A large oven had been installed above the hearth, and a monstrous, double-sided stainless steel refrigerator stood against the opposite wall.

Impressive appliances for a twelfth-century castle.

"I have two thawed-out chickens, a bag of potatoes, and a bunch of other stuff," Ellie said. "I've Americanized the pantry a bit. Any ideas?"

Emma looked through the pantry, the refrigerator, then turned to Ellie and grinned. "I've got it. Let's get that bird cut up."

They worked together cutting the chicken, laying it into two large casserole pans, and covering the pieces with cream of chicken soup. Once that was baking, they started peeling the potatoes.

"So. What's it like being in love with a ghost?"

Emma turned to see Ellie steadily chopping up a potato. A grin lifted her mouth.

"Well," Emma answered, feeling her cheeks grow warm, "I can't say for a fact that I'm in love with him yet. I've only just met him."

Ellie glanced sideways at her. "Really?"

Emma smiled. "I . . . seriously am crazy about him."

"I see." Ellie continued her chopping. "Have you thought yourself crazy yet?"

Emma laughed. "I thought I was crazy right off the bat. At first I felt eyes on me while I walked around Arrick's ruins. Creeped me out at first, and then . . . he appeared." She lifted a brow. "Not so nice at first, though. I think he was trying to scare me off."

Ellie smiled. "Good thing it didn't work, huh?" She shook her head and began peeling another potato. "I'd have to say that medieval men are pigheaded when they want to be." She winked. "Until, that is, they meet one of us modern girls head-on." She held up her pinky and wiggled it. "After that, we got 'em wrapped."

"Wrapped, eh?"

Both girls squealed at Gawan's raspy voice in the doorway.

Christian stood, leaning against the opposite frame.

Both warriors had smirks on their faces.

Oh God! How long have they been standing there?

"Emma, I pray you're a better cook than my beloved," Gawan said.

The look in his eyes did not match the words. Never had Emma seen so much love in a man's eyes.

She shyly shifted her gaze to Christian.

His looked the same, with that reflective stare, and something . . . different in the depth of his eyes.

Holy ho-ho.

"Oh, you two get out if you're going to make fun," teased Ellie. "You're going to love this dish. And if you don't? Err, it was Emma's idea. Pulled it right out of a Betty Crocker cookbook."

Emma grinned at Gawan and shrugged.

They all erupted into laughter.

"I am jesting," said Gawan, giving Emma a short nod.

"It smells heavenly." He moved to his wife, slipped his arm around her waist, and pulled her close. He leaned his head to her ear, obviously whispering something sweet, because Ellie's almond-shaped blue-green eyes turned soft. He kissed her cheek, she pulled his hair that he'd secured in the back of his neck with a silver clip, and then she swatted his backside.

Emma nearly blushed again, being witness to such intimate play between Gawan and Ellie.

She chanced a peek at Christian.

His grin was absolutely predatory.

He made his way to her, and dropped his head to her ear. "I'll see you at supper," he said, the sensation of his ghostly mouth close to her neck causing her to shudder. "After, though, you're all mine."

Emma gulped.

Christian laughed.

She could hardly wait.

Chapter 26

The buzz all around the supper table revolved around the big Grimm Tournament.

Apparently, it was a pretty big deal amongst the dead, the previously dead but recently revived, and all that falls in between.

Christian's focus, though, seemed not to be on the tournament. You'd think a medieval guy would be all hyped up about competing in an extreme sporting event, with sharp blades and horses and fighting and pointy poles to jab and poke at one another.

Nope, not so much.

That weighty, sexy stare of his stayed glued on *her* nearly the entire meal.

Emma did a lot of squirming at the dinner table.

Only a few times did someone steal his attention, and half the time he'd answer whoever was speaking to him without removing his gaze from her. It was unnerving, yet . . . strangely erotic. Sensual.

She wasn't positive she could handle that one-hundred-percent, hot-blooded medieval male, were he alive.

She could barely handle him *now*.

"Emma?"

Jumping at the voice interrupting her thoughts, Emma turned to Ellie. "I'm sorry?"

A few chuckles rounded the table, and she felt her face heat up. Christian, of course, simply grinned that mischievous grin.

She'd come to realize how naughty he really was.

Ellie hid a smile with her hand. "Tell us about your profession. I've always been interested in photography. What's the name of your studio?"

Emma smiled nervously, not only feeling Christian's gaze but now that of everyone in the room. She cleared her throat. "Forevermore Photography. It's a small studio on the riverfront, and I mostly shoot engagements and weddings. Also a few private sessions, like for families, college grads, high school grads, that sort of thing." She smiled with genuine excitement. "I thought it'd be fun to shoot the tournament." She glanced at the sweet little girl in the swing next to Ellie, and the crazy little twins on either side of Gawan. "And the kids, families. If you don't mind?"

Ellie beamed. "Are you kidding? That'd be bleeping fantastic!"

Emma grinned.

Gawan gave her a warm smile. "Your talents will greatly be appreciated, lady," he said with a half nod. Then his grin turned mischievous. "I'm sure you'll have your hands full with the Dreadmoor lot. Isn't that right, Jason?"

Jason nodded; he finished chewing a mouthful of chicken, then wiped his mouth. He looked at Emma. "You've no idea. Mayhap your most challenging subjects."

Emma sipped her tea. "The more challenging, the more fun."

"Aye, but there's a daft lot coming in from Ireland," said Godfrey. "Ghosties, all of them, but I wouldn't put it past them to try to get in a few of your pictures."

Everyone laughed.

Just then, a barking started up. Far away at first, it quickly grew louder and louder. Everyone casually looked up, and Nicklesby groaned. "Cotswold! Good heavens, here he comes!"

Suddenly a big, shaggy, *ghostly* dog ran straight through a wall and skidded up to the table, wagging his big tail and lolling his big tongue.

Emma felt her jaw drop.

Davy scooted from his chair, grinning, then stopped and looked at Ellie. "May I be excused?"

Ellie smiled. "Yes, and take Cotswold with you. He needs a good run."

With that, Davy ran from the table. "Cotswold! Come on, boy!"

The pair ran up the stairs and out of sight.

Emma simply blinked. "I guess I'd never considered a ghost dog before."

Everyone laughed.

Ellie quickly explained a rather difficult-to-grasp tale of how she'd once been in-betwixt, not quite dead but not quite alive, either. She'd slipped in and out of a coma, crossing the boundaries of the living and the dead. She also explained how Gawan, who'd once been a nearly thousand-year-old angel close to retirement, had given up that retirement by sacrificing his life force to save Ellie. The Fates had been kind, had seen to the pair reuniting in what Emma thought to be the most absolutely romantic thing *ever*. Then, Ellie explained about how Davy, who'd been a ghost himself when she first met him, was actually her *great-uncle*.

That story had Emma's mouth hanging open.

Apparently, the young boy had been given a second chance at life after his first chance had been so horribly taken away, after witnessing his brother's—Ellie's grandfather's—murder. Little Davy's chance came after Ellie, a genealogist, had solved the case. Emma couldn't help but consider all the ghosts she'd met—Justin Catesby, Godfrey, the ladies—why hadn't they been given a second chance, yet the others had? Was it because Gawan had had an in with the higher-ups? Or was it because it simply wasn't their turn yet?

Emma looked at Christian, who sat across from her and kept that sexy gaze directed at her. She wondered briefly what sort of sacrifice it would take to get *his* life back.

And in that quick second, she knew for a certainty she'd be willing to make that sacrifice. She was only slightly surprised to find herself *not* surprised at that revelation.

"Well," Gawan said, "our guests will indeed start crossing the drawbridge on the morrow, and knowing those Dreadmoors, fairly early. Thank goodness Lady Andi is accompanying them this time. She always seems to have a way of keeping them in check. I, for one, am turning in. I suggest the same for all of you."

"Telling us when to go nighty-night now, eh, Conwyk?" said Justin Catesby, in his heavy Scottish brogue.

Everyone chuckled.

Gawan grinned. "I'm just saying—those lads will come roaring up on their motorcycles before the dawn breaks, I'd warrant. And once here, they'll want to begin training right away." He flashed a grin at Christian. "As do I."

Everyone rose, and Emma gathered dishes to help with the dinner mess. Quickly, she and Ellie, accompanied by Nicklesby and Jason, had everything cleared and cleaned, the dishwasher loaded and washing. When they all left the kitchen, they found Gawan and Christian sitting by the hearth. Ensley was fast asleep in her swing next to Christian, and Gawan had a twin in the crook of each big, tattooed arm.

It was a precious sight, indeed.

When Emma and Ellie walked up, Christian stood.

He gave a low bow to Ellie. "Lady, whilst frustrating not to have the capability to eat your fine food, the company was, as always, the very best." He grinned and winked. "But I shall now relieve you of your guest."

He looked at Emma and inclined his head, that wicked smile tipping his mouth up into something more sensual than devious.

Emma gulped and hoped it wasn't too noticeable.

"Err, lady?" said Jason. He cleared his throat. "Mayhap you need me to guard your door whilst you sleep?" He gave Christian a humorous look. "To keep out unwanted guests, you see? Not to mention maintaining your honor, of course."

Christian gave Jason a murderous look. "She needs no guarding of doors, lad, nor of her virtue. Understood?"

Everyone roared.

Jason tried to hide his grin with his hand. "Err, right. What was I thinking? Christian of Arrick-by-the-Sea is indeed one of the most virtuous knights I know, next to myself." He gave Emma a low bow. "Should you need me, though, I am but three doors down from your chamber."

More snickers erupted from the crowd.

"Come on," growled Christian in her ear.

Emma turned to hurry away with him. She smiled at Jason and waved. "Bye."

Jason merely chuckled and shook his head.

Emma had no doubt in her mind that, had Christian had substance, he'd have dragged her from the great hall.

As it was, he fell in behind her, *right* behind her. So close, she could feel the ghostly electricity that radiated from him. It made her shudder.

Christian noticed, and chuckled. "I've been waiting all eve to get you alone, Ms. Calhoun," he said, a whisper against her ear. "Move faster. One more flight up, then all the way to the end."

"Will I need my coat?" she asked, hurrying up the steps. She didn't want to freeze her patootey off.

"Nay."

"Oh." She could barely stand it, the waiting and not knowing. She wasn't used to surprises, and it seemed Christian of Arrick-by-the-Sea was full of them. She wasn't used to being the center of attention, and although a little uncomfortable—especially in a room full of near strangers—she seemed to be getting used to it. Used to the ghosts, used to the Conwyks, used to Jason.

And very used to the ghostly warrior hurrying her up the steps.

They reached the top floor and Emma started for the end of the corridor. Christian stepped up beside her, and lowered his head. "The door at the very end. 'Tis unlocked."

"Okay," Emma said, and glanced up at him. In the dim light, his features took on a slightly illuminated radiance. Not much—he wasn't glowing like a sixty-watt bulb or anything. Just . . . surreal. She didn't think she'd ever seen anything so fascinating.

At the end, they stopped before the narrow, single door. Emma looked at Christian, he inclined his head with a grin, and she opened it.

Emma slowly stepped inside, and blinked in surprise. It was the tiniest of turreted chambers, barely big enough for the comfy-looking sofa facing the floor-length bay window, and the hearth. A fire blazed and crackled, making the room toasty warm. Candles sat perched on a small coffee table, and on the lamp tables flanking the sofa. The walls were, like the rest of the castle, made of stone and mortar, and it fascinated Emma to know just how old they were, and of the hands who put them there. And that one of those pair of hands stood right next to her.

Unbelievable.

"What are you thinking?"

Emma looked at Christian. Really looked at him. He'd changed from his bare-chested, tattooed, double-bladed warrior lethal-wear, and back into sexy, casual, modern-day clothes. It amazed her how both suited him perfectly. With a white cotton button-up long-sleeved shirt, tails loose and out, a pair of worn jeans, and brown leather hikers, he looked more like a guy on the cover of *Outdoor Magazine* than a twelfth-century warrior.

All but the hair. For some reason, Emma really loved that crazy, long and tousled-in-the-front, short-in-the-back hair

It just looked *good* on him.

"Um, Emma?"

Emma blinked. Christian was waving his hand in front of her face.

He grinned. "Are you finished? Or would you like me to turn?"

She narrowed her eyes. "Turn."

With a mischievous glint in his ghostly eyes, he did. Slowly. And in such a casual, guy manner, like everything else he did.

It nearly buckled Emma's knees.

"Okay, enough turning," she said, smiling. "This room is fantastic."

"You didn't answer my question," he said, inclining his head toward the sofa.

"Oh," she answered, and walked over and sat down. Christian sat beside her. She settled back against the plush cushions and looked at him. "I was thinking how incredible all of this is," she said, waving her hand. "This place, Arrick-by-the-Sea." She felt her face heat up. "Especially you." She shrugged. "It's almost incomprehensible. Ellie told me you helped Gawan build Grimm." She shook her head and smiled at him. "And here you are, hundreds of years later, flirting and talking with me."

A serious expression crossed Christian's features. He studied her closely, and turned to face her. He was quiet for several seconds, his gaze examining her with such intimacy, it made Emma's heart race. The muscles in his jaws tensed. The deep breath he took was barely noticeable.

"Keep very still," he said quietly, that Medieval Welsh accent growing heavier, washing over her. He leaned close, placing one hand on the armrest next to her, the other on the seat between them, and his eyes boring into hers. The very slightest lift tipped one corner of his mouth up. His body crowded her in a good way. An arousing way.

In a painfully slow, utterly pleasing way . . .

"Now," he said, bringing his mouth close to hers, and a hank of that crazy hair falling across his eye, "let me show you the difference between flirting and wooing."

Emma's heart nearly stopped as he settled his mouth over hers, as close as possible without falling through her. She slowly drew in a breath through her parted lips, and sighed against Christian's mouth as he seemingly tasted first her bottom lip, then her top. Her skin tingled at the sensation. He didn't move, simply lingered, then pulled his head back, lifted his hand, and traced her jaw with his finger. He stared. It made her shudder.

"What I would give to taste you in truth," he said, his voice coarse, regretful.

Emma lifted her hand and traced the curve of his lips. "I know," she said quietly. "But I'll take you this way." She sighed. "Gladly."

Chapter 27

Christian watched Emma sleep. Christ, she was so beautiful.

So much, it nearly hurt.

After his bit of wooing, he and Emma had sat before the fire, as close as possible, and talked. He'd learned things about her that he'd never known before, even with his twelve previous encounters. She was ticklish on her sides. He'd merely jabbed at her, jokingly, and she'd nearly leaped off the sofa. In anticipation, she'd said, of the tickle. Of course, he couldn't really tickle her, but her instinct had made her jump all the same.

He'd found it a fascinating detail.

They'd talked for hours, and he'd learned all about her life as a photographer, the school she'd attended, and the studio she now owned. Quite successful, it seemed, and she truly loved taking pictures. They'd crept downstairs to Gawan's study, and Emma had pulled up her Web site on the computer. Christian had thought her work astounding. She'd somehow captured the absolute truest emotions of love in each couple's faces, and in their eyes. And the brides were, even to him, blushing beauties. Their faces all but glowed with bliss, and the photos she'd taken of families and children showed the very same. He'd never seen anything like it. Emma was an artist, and she was most proud of her work.

He rather admired that.

After that, he'd walked her to her room, and they'd said good night. He'd nearly lost control kissing her at her door. 'Twas nigh unto impossible, kissing but not *really* kissing. He'd almost fallen through her twice. He'd almost told her how much he loved her. Thankfully, he'd bit his own tongue. 'Twas too soon for that. He felt it.

And yet he didn't think he'd ever wanted her—*craved* her—as badly as he did now.

This thirteenth time.

I'll take you this way, Emma had said.

His heart had dropped at the words.

Strange, how the twelve previous times he'd encountered Emma's soul, she'd begged him to find a way to change. Come to life. But this time? This Emma?

I'll take you this way . . .

Just then, a low rumble met his ears. Christian rose and looked through the window. Far down the lane, eight motorcycles growled toward Grimm, followed by a blue Rover, a big red Jeep, and a silver Porsche.

Saint's blood, that arrogant Dreadmoor lot had arrived.

His eyes narrowed. What he wouldn't give to be a live warrior for the tournament.

"You're here."

He turned and met Emma's sleepy gaze. She'd pushed herself up and rested her weight on one elbow, her hair standing on end, her face flushed. Wide blue eyes stared at him, a slight tilt to her sexy mouth.

"*Ach fel 'n arddun*," he murmured, without really thinking about it.

She pushed all the way up to a sitting position and scrubbed her eyes. She yawned and stretched, and he felt his stomach tighten at the sight. "What's that mean?" she asked.

He hadn't realized he'd spoken in Welsh. She used to speak it, as well.

In three strides, he was at her side. He sat on the edge of the bed, and traced a long strand of hair. "You are so beautiful," he said.

Emma's cheeks blushed. "Oh," she said, her voice breathy. "You've . . . been in here all night?"

He grinned. "What was left of it, aye."

She glanced toward the window. He'd never known a maid to blush so much. He found it utterly adorable. "What's that noise?" she said.

Christian sighed and glanced at the window. "The most arrogant lot of lads you'll ever encounter."

She grinned, then slipped from beneath the covers, hurried to the window, and looked out. "More arrogant than you, even?" she said, staring outside.

His mouth went dry. Bloody dog-bone dry.

The reaction of a young, inexperienced lad seeing his first pair of bared, female legs, he supposed. He was not young. He was far from inexperienced.

But, *Christ*. Emma stood at the window, with the palest of light shining through her nearly transparent and slightly snug white T-shirt and, he gulped, shorts that hung at her hips with a goodly amount of stomach showing. The sight almost made his knees buckle. And, she was apparently cold.

He tried not to wheeze.

"What's wrong?" she asked. Then, she must have followed his eyes, which were latched on to her breasts, because her face flamed and she crossed her arms over herself. "Oh. Sorry."

Sorry?

"I'm not," he muttered, his eyes transfixed, unmoving.

"Christian, get out!" she squealed. She covered herself tighter. "I mean it! I'll call Jason!"

"Call him," he said, his lips twitching at her modesty. "It will take his slow mortal self several minutes to get here—"

A pillow flew through him and hit the wall.

"Ouch," he said.

Her face immediately paled. "Oh! I'm sorry! Did I hurt you?"

It took him several seconds to ponder his response. It was one second too many. She scowled.

"I mean it, Christian of Arrick-by-the-Sea. Get out of my room right now and let me get changed," she said, her voice low, menacing. If possible, her arms tightened even more about herself.

He looked at her then, his gaze meeting hers.

Her lips twitched.

He laughed. "All right, my little modest modern maid. I shall meet you in yon passageway when you've finished." His lecherous gaze dropped to her scantily clad body once more; then he gave her a low bow. "Until."

With reluctance, he disappeared.

Emma heaved a sigh as she watched Christian disappear.

The look he'd had on his face—prior to her covering up—was that of pure hunger.

It'd made her mouth go dry.

Then he'd given her that quirky smile, and combined with the mischievous gleam in his eye and that crazy hair, she'd found she couldn't stay mad, or terribly embarrassed.

Hastily, she threw on her typical outfit of jeans, double-layered long-sleeved T-shirt, and a cotton hoodie. She tied her Converses, freshéned up in the bathroom, and pulled her hair into a ponytail. When she stepped out into the passageway, Christian was leaning against the wall, waiting. Assessing. He must have found what he saw pleasing because he grinned from ear to ear.

Then the roar of motorcycles in the bailey met her ears.

Christian glanced down at her, one corner of his mouth lifting. "Come on. And stay close."

They hurried to the first floor, and just as they took the last step, the double doors of the great hall flew open, and what looked like no less than a football team piled in, grumbling, laughing, and hollering.

"Oh for God's sake, will you boys stop all that pushing and yelling?" said a small, auburn-haired woman with a ponytail, much like Emma's. She squirmed in between them and turned to scold. "Your big mouths are going to wake up the whole household. Now be quieter."

Emma could have sworn she saw the men's heads droop in quiet submission.

A few more men came through the door. One carried a toddler of about one year on his shoulder. The little tyke had two fistfuls of the man's sandy-colored hair and was yanking it hard, and drooling in it, too. The man winced, but didn't say a word, nor did he relieve the kid of his hair.

"Be nice to Uncle Richard, Calen," the woman said. Then she looked around. "Tristan? Do you have the diaper bags?"

Then another man walked in. "Aye, love, right here," he answered—grumbled, actually.

A chuckle ran through the men.

Emma felt her eyes widen.

She thought she heard a growl from Christian.

The man was absolutely the biggest she'd ever seen. No, scratch that. Another had just walked in behind him, even bigger. But the one with the bags? A bit larger than Christian, even. Gorgeous, he had long, dark hair pulled back at the nape, and muscles like an iron man competitor. He had two bulging diaper bags gripped in one hand, and a kid on his shoulders. This one looked to be a bit older, maybe three, and he had a death grip on the man's ears. With a thatch of dark hair, there was no mistaking whom the toddler belonged to.

It was then that Emma noticed something odd.

Every man in the hall wore jeans.

And a sword.

Just then, Gawan and Ellie, accompanied by Jason and all the Conwyk children and ghosts, joined in the great hall. The two women met and embraced. Nicklesby scurried about, shouting orders to keep the floors clean and blades out of the woodwork. The Conwyk twins were right on his heels.

Christian leaned toward Emma, his whisper brushing her ear. "That's Tristan de Barre and his wife, Andi, and their two little ones. The other lads are his knights."

"Jason!" hollered Tristan de Barre. "Stop standing about gawking and come relieve me of these diaper bags, man, before my son rips my ears from my bloody head."

Jason trotted up to Tristan. "Aye, hand me those bags, sir. I'll take them to the nursery." He took them, then winked at Emma as he trotted past.

And then Tristan de Barre moved toward her. He stopped just a few feet from her and looked down. "Arrick, who is this lovely maid you have beside you? Introduce us, man."

Emma jumped at Tristan's big, booming voice. With another strange, medieval accent, he had his gaze directed *directly* at her. She peeked around him. All other medieval eyes were on her, as well. She felt the heat beneath her skin rise from her neck to her cheeks in a millisecond as fifteen pairs of knightly eyes, plus everyone else congregated in the Grimm great hall, stared at Emma.

"My God, man, she's fetching, Chris," he said in a low voice.

She wanted to melt into the stairs.

Then she noted the slow grins spreading on all the knightly faces. Friendly grins. Assessing grins.

Christian took a slight step forward.

"Oh honestly, Tristan!" said his little wife. "Leave her alone, and the rest of you, shoo!" She swatted her husband's backside as she ran over to stand in front of Emma. "Hi, I'm Andi," she said. Ellie had followed, and Andi glanced at her. "We're so relieved to have another girl join our Hall of Testosterone," she said, grinning.

Ladies Follywolle and Beauchamp had sifted through the wall and joined them. All nodded with enthusiasm.

"Thanks," Emma said.

"Well, come on," Andi said, pulling on her arm. "Give her up for a while, Chris," she said. "Tristan's been dying to start training right away, and we girls need to get to know one another." She winked at Christian. "Nice modern duds, fella. Lookin' good."

Christian chuckled.

The other men roared.

Then Andi and Ellie gathered their children, then pulled Emma, along with the ladies Follywolle and Beauchamp, along to the nursery.

Emma glanced over her shoulder at Christian.

He merely stood, staring, before being swallowed by a sea of big, strapping medieval bodies as the Dreadmoor knights gathered around him.

And so it was that Emma, along with new friends Andi de Barre and Ellie Conwyk, as well as their children, and the ghostly ladies of Grimm, headed off to the nursery.

Funny, Emma thought as she made her way down the corridor. Before, she'd had one good best friend in Zoë. Now she had several more good friends.

And the funnier thing was, it felt *right*.

Just like Christian de Gaultiers of Arrick-by-the-Sea felt right.

Amidst the kids hollering and Andi and Ellie chatting away, and the Grimm ladies giggling, Emma thought how much her life had changed in such a short time.

She could barely wait to see what the rest of her visit held.

And as they entered the expanse of the nursery, a thought crossed Emma's mind that hadn't really crossed it in quite a few days.

Eventually, she'd have to go home.

Chapter 28

Over the course of the rest of the afternoon, Castle Grimm had been transformed into a big, giant, tournament ground. After all the Dreadmoor folks had arrived, another group of ridiculously large and handsome guys had shown up: the Munros, from the Highlands of Scotland. Loud, boisterous, and mouth-wateringly gorgeous, they had delicious accents. In a relatively short time, Ellie and Andi had updated her on how the Munros had been enchanted, and had lived for centuries as spirits—save the gloaming hour, or twilight, when they'd gain substance for just an hour or so. Lucky for them, fate had smiled upon them, as well. Ethan, the laird, had married an American named Amelia Landry, a best-selling mystery novelist from Charleston. Emma had read several of her books and adored them. It was beyond cool to meet her—especially knowing she'd saved them from an eternity of enchantment after solving a centuries-old crime and breaking a spell. It was . . . almost beyond Emma's comprehension. *Almost.* Not quite, though.

She'd discovered too many oddities since arriving in the UK. She wasn't so easily stunned anymore.

She soon found Amelia was just as lively as Andi and Ellie.

One more couple had arrived later in the day, and

surprisingly, they were normal. Well, sort of, anyway. They were both from the present century. That counted for something, although they lived amongst spirits as if doing so were simply part of everyday life.

She supposed it was.

Gabe and Allie MacGowan had driven from a small Scottish seaside village called Sealladh na Mara, where they owned and operated a pub and inn. It happened to be the haunted residence of not only one naughty spirit in the form of Captain Justin Catesby, but a few others. They'd all come for the big tournament, including Jake, Gabe's and Allie's young son. Jake and Davy ran around with Cotswold, the dog, and had a huge, fun time. Emma hung out with the girls, played with the kids, took loads of photos, and, well, gossiped.

They caught her up to speed on just about everything.

By nightfall, Castle Grimm was wall-to-wall with tournament-seeking spirits. They had come from all over: Wales, Scotland, England, Ireland—plus a few from Germany, as well as France. Ellie had called it a Grimm Fiasco.

Emma fully believed it.

In the great hall, warriors from nearly every century lined the walls, inside and out. Some camped on the tournament field. Ellie assured her that, unless invited, the ghosts wouldn't just pop into her room.

Jason had graciously offered once more to guard her door.

Given the looks of some of the fierce warriors, Emma nearly agreed to let him.

Christian reminded her that whereas Jason might be better equipped at handling a mortal, *he* certainly could more aptly take care of a few arrogant spirits. And boy, he wasn't kidding. Embarrassingly, more than a few warriors had approached her. One look from Christian had sent them scampering.

Currently, the ghost in question sat on the arm of the sofa, right beside her. Jason sat to her other side. Tristan was busy retelling the tale of how Andi had saved him and his knights—he'd told it twice already. Emma could see the love shining in his eyes for his wife, and the same light shone in Andi's. The other warriors, alive and not so alive, sat and listened, entranced.

It was more than fascinating, she had to admit.

"Let's go."

Emma turned at Christian's whisper. His eyes, unreadable, locked on to hers. No way could she refuse his request.

She leaned toward Jason. "I'll see you later, okay?" she whispered.

Jason gave Christian a look that Emma could easily read. *Mind your manners.* With a grin, Jason gave a short nod.

Emma rose and, with Christian by her side, picked her way through the hordes of souls gathered in the Grimm great hall. She'd never seen more swords in her life. When they were close to the stairs, Christian stopped her.

"Let's get your coat. I don't want you freezing to death," he said. His mouth tipped up. "We might be a while."

Emma gulped.

Minutes later, they were back downstairs and headed out into the crisp autumn night. A briny wind stung Emma's cheeks, and she felt tiny crystals of ice in the air. There were more warriors loitering outside, huddled against the keep, lounging against the bailey wall, probably looking a whole lot like they did in their own times. A few let out whistles and catcalls. At first, Christian handled it good-naturedly. After several, he was clearly irritated.

"No bloody manners," he mumbled, leading her away from the keep.

"Where are we going?" Emma asked. She pulled her multicolored hat down over her ears and shoved her hands deep into the pockets of her black peacoat.

"To the seawall," Christian said. "Hopefully a place we can be alone." He stared down at her. "I've grown bloody weary of sharing you."

Emma's heart did a flip, and Christian walked closer. His height and mass, although ghostly and nonsubstantial, still had the capability of making Emma feel protected.

Around the bailey they walked, and Emma glanced over at the drawbridge, and down to the double-towered gatehouse.

"What are you thinking?"

Emma gave Christian a smile as she picked her footing along the spongy ground. "I don't know. I guess I just can't get over how amazing all of this is." She shook her head. "I've never really given medieval times, castles, and people from times past a second thought." She met his intense gaze with one of her own. They reached the cliff overlooking the North Sea, and stopped at the wall. She shrugged. "Almost familiar, in a way. Almost as though I was meant to be here, now."

Christian grew very still. Emma could feel his tension in the air. Quite a strange thing to feel from a spirit, but she *had*. And internally, she cringed.

She looked up at him. "Ugh," she groaned. "I'm sorry."

Christian fought for control. Every ounce of his soul wanted to reach out and pull Emma tightly against him, press his mouth to hers, and kiss her until she lost her breath. He wanted to feel her body against his, and it hurt to think of it and not be able to do a bloody thing about it. So instead, he clenched his fists and tensed his muscles.

He drew a silent, deep, calming breath. "Why are you sorry?"

He almost didn't want to hear her answer.

Emma turned directly toward him, tilted her head back, and stared. Her warm breath turned into white puffs of frosty air. Finally, she shrugged again and gave him a crooked smile.

"Because," she said, "guys are guys, no matter what century they're from. They get uncomfortable hearing a woman's innermost thoughts. Her *feelings*." She looked away, out over the sea. The palest light from the moon shone onto the dark water, and the sound of waves crashing filled the air.

Yet Christian was more acutely aware of every single sigh Emma made.

She made one now.

He studied her profile, so very beautiful, so very dear to him.

"Christ, woman, I am so in love with you," he murmured against her temple. "I cannot believe you're all mine."

Emma slipped her hands about his neck and pulled his mouth to hers. "I've waited for you all my life." She kissed him, her lips warm, soft. "My warrior . . ."

The memory nearly pained him. Aye. He indeed needed to tell Emma just how much she meant to him. *And how long he'd felt that way.* But first, he needed to be sure of her feelings.

"Emma," he said, "look at me."

Slowly, she turned, eyes wide, the moonlight turning the blue color black and glassy. She waited.

"You've no idea how it pains me to keep my hands off you—to not be able to physically touch you," Christian said, as quiet and in control as his will could possibly muster. "Ever since you set foot on Arrick's land, you've invaded my thoughts, enough that I thought I was daft." He gave a short laugh. "Mayhap I am anyhow."

"Why?" she asked, the frost making her dark lashes spiky.

He shook his head in amazement. "You don't see the effect you have on me, do you?"

She blinked. "I . . . don't know."

Emotions Christian had kept in check boiled to the surface. He swallowed, drew a breath or two, then closed his eyes tightly shut. After a moment, he opened them and looked at her. "Back up."

Emma glanced behind her, toward the sea. "What?"

"Move back," he said, as gently as he could, "toward the seawall."

A puzzled look crossed her face, but she took a step back. "Like this?"

"No." He moved closer. "Put your back against the stone."

"Oh." Then, she did.

Christian took one more step, and it was literally as close as he could get to her without blending his essence into hers. He looked down at her, where she stared straight ahead at his chest. "Look at me, Emma."

Very slowly, she did.

Her breathing came faster, little white streams of chilled air rising between them with each ragged breath. She said nothing, simply breathed.

Placing a hand on the seawall behind her, Christian ducked his head, so that he looked her square in the eye. "When you first came to Arrick, I was determined to drive you away. Once I lost that battle, I was determined to hold you at arm's length. To keep myself from needing you so badly." He drew a deep breath, lifted his hand, and traced her lips with his knuckles. The barest of tingles coursed through him, and he could hear how it affected Emma. He could hear her heartbeat quicken.

"I lost that battle, too," he said. He stared at every single inch of her face, every line he'd grown to love centuries before, yet found himself astounded that he loved them even more now, even without Emma's soul remembering him. "I haven't the strength not to be in your life, Emma Calhoun." He grazed her jaw. "I need you too much."

They stared at each other, and tears welled up in Emma's eyes. The wind caught a strand of her hair and blew it across her cheek, where it caught on her lip. With a forefinger, Christian absently moved to brush it back.

His finger went right through it, and Emma let out a small gasp.

Christian's insides winced. Bloody hell, what was he thinking? He couldn't touch her. Not now. Not ever.

And it simply wasn't fair to ever ask her to accept it.

"What ... do you mean?" asked Emma, her voice barely above a whisper. She shivered now, her heartbeat quickened even more, and her breathing came faster. She looked at him. "I see in your face you've changed your mind already. Don't." She pushed closer to him, then pulled a hand from her coat pocket and traced his cheek. "Please, tell me."

Christian couldn't help but study her face beneath the autumn moon. So beautiful, so honest and caring a soul she was, it hurt to watch her and not touch. It bloody *hurt.* "Did you mean what you said a moment ago? That you feel as though this is your life now?" He swept a hand toward the sea, half turned, and did another sweep toward Castle Grimm. "All of this? Things you can touch, feel, taste, and things"—he dipped his head and moved his mouth to hers—"you cannot?" He slowly dragged his lips as close to Emma's skin as he could, to the corner of her mouth, across her cheek, then to her jaw, just below the ear covered by that crazy hat she wore. He hovered one hand close to her hand clutching the stone behind her. He traced each knuckle until she gasped. "Truly, can you stand to not fully taste? Could you be satisfied with just closeness, and not true intimacy?" He ducked his head and kissed her throat.

"Could you stand to never feel my hands, my mouth, my tongue on you?"

Christian pulled back and stared at Emma. Her chest rose and fell with each ragged breath, and her eyes had drifted shut. She'd caught her bottom lip between her teeth and now bit down, and a tear trickled from her pinched lids.

Then, without opening her eyes, she whispered the most common of words in the most sensual of ways.

He'd never hear it the same, ever again.

"Truly," she said, her voice breathy and slight. She opened her eyes. "As long as it's you, yes. Truly."

They stared at each other for several seconds, and Christian's heart cracked.

Then they both smiled.

And lost themselves in the only intimacy they could conjure . . .

Chapter 29

After two days of training, including a gargantuan amount of grunting, sweating, swearing, hollering, ugly hand gestures, fistfights, and ringing of steel against steel, not to mention the pounding of horses' hooves in the jousting arena, Emma's whole sense of the medieval era had changed completely. So many males. So much testosterone. So much *blood*.

Even the horses were boys. Studs, at that. And *they* fought.

The Dark Ages had been vicious.

Everyone had now separated into teams. On the mortal side, Team Grimm, Team Dreadmoor, Team Munro. On the ghostly side, there were so many that the teams had to be broken down into three groups and the warriors then had to choose teams. Team Arrick, Team Donovan, and Team Le Maurant. The Irish were so plentiful that they made up Team Donovan alone. Many of the Welsh spirits had joined Team Arrick, as well as several Scots and English. A few drifted in from Romania, and they'd joined the Germans and the French for Team Le Maurant.

She couldn't deny how incredibly fascinating those medieval warriors were to watch. The ghosts and the mortals took turns training—all except Christian, who could actually, somehow train with Gawan. Emma had stopped asking *how* a long time ago. The Dreadmoors and the Munros were . . . fascinating. All brawn and muscle and fierceness, and Tristan? God Almighty. When he and Ethan Munro had faced off with the swords, it was Ultimate Fighting at its very best. Well, almost.

There were two others who, in her opinion, rose just a fraction above the rest.

Christian and Gawan. *Wow.* They were a true sight to see. All tattooed and wild-eyed, with their hair loose and their bodies bare, they seriously looked like they would kill each other, if given the chance.

She watched them now, as did no fewer than a hundred mortals and ghosts combined.

Bared to the waist and crouched like lethal cats ready to spring, they moved in graceful, calculated, predatory circles around one another, Gawan with his one large sword, Christian with his deadly double blades. Emma's eyes fastened on Christian's markings, black, ancient, and menacing, the one on his back flinched with each muscle movement, as did the ones on his arms.

Had she been a warrior, she'd have never had the guts to pick up a sword and face either one of them. Their look alone would have made her surrender.

"Fascinating, dunna you think?"

Emma turned to the man standing beside her. Just as gorgeous as the rest of the warriors, he was not one of the participants. Gabe MacGowan along with his wife, Allie, stood close. They were friends of Justin Catesby, so she'd been told, and proprietors of the most haunted pub and inn in Scotland, she recalled. She smiled up at MacGowan. "Absolutely. I still can't get over it."

His wife peered around her big husband and grinned at her. "I bet you've never attended a sporting event like this one, have you?"

Emma sighed and turned back to the fighters. "Hardly."

"I see you're rootin' for the wrong team, lass," a deep, heavily accented voice said on the other side of her.

Emma turned and looked up. The man, dark haired and sexy as all get-out, he wore a flirty grin and reeked of arrogance.

Much like Christian, she thought.

He lifted her hand and raised it to his lips, and brushed the lightest of kisses across her knuckles. "Aiden Munro, lady." He inclined his head to her shirt. "Team Arrick, aye? I've a Team Munro shirt I could give you, should you choose to change teams."

Gabe MacGowan snorted.

Emma smiled. Last month she'd have melted on the spot at such a gorgeous man's charm.

But after being wooed by Christian of Arrick-by-the-Sea, she found that everyone else paled in comparison.

"I'll keep that in mind," she said, retrieving her hand from his.

Aiden Munro simply smiled.

"Canna leave a lass alone for a second, aye?" said another deep, brogued voice. Ethan Munro, accompanied by Tristan and several of his knights, pushed in beside him to lean against the fence. They all chuckled.

Emma slid her gaze over all of them. Big and powerfully built, they were dangerous with one another, yet gentle as kittens when it came to women.

"And what lad in his right mind would leave a lass such as Emma at the fence alone?" asked Aiden. He winked at her.

"Lad, I'd give a month's wages to hear you say that, were Arrick in the flesh and blood," said Tristan. He, too, leaned forward and gave Emma a wink. "Now leave the girl alone. I've a powerful mind to defend her in Arrick's honor."

A round of *ayes* sounded through the men, and Aiden Munro beamed. "Och, you're on, Dreadmoor." He glanced down at her, bent his head, and kissed her cheek. "Be right back," he said. The arrogance followed him like a heavy mist.

Just then, swearing from the arena pulled Emma's attention back to Christian and Gawan. Both of Christian's blades were on the ground. Gawan stood, the tip of that big, sharp sword pointed directly at Christian's throat.

Christian stared hard at Aiden Munro.

Aiden merely threw his head back and laughed . . . then promptly took off running, his sword slapping his thigh.

Tristan de Barre, followed by a growing crowd of warriors, fell in behind him.

"I suddenly feel rowing and making little marble chess pieces isn't quite so . . . manly anymore," mumbled Gabe MacGowan, beside her.

She looked at him, and his expression made Emma laugh. She looked at his wife, Allie, who stared up at Gabe with so much love and adoration, it all but sent an electric wave through the air. "Oh, I think you're doing just fine," Emma said.

Gabe pulled Allie close and kissed her on the top of her head. "Thank God."

Christian strode to the fence, placed a booted foot on the bottom rung, and propped his arms on the top. He stared down at Emma. "I see you've picked up a few admirers," he said.

"That big lad Tristan took off to defend her in your honor," offered Gabe. "My money's on Dreadmoor."

Christian laughed and gave a nod. "I'm counting on it. Arrogant pup, that Munro."

"I think he's cute," offered Allie.

Emma bit back a laugh.

"Well," Gawan said, walking up to join them, " 'tis nearly dark, and the tournament begins in the morn, promptly at nine." His eyes gleamed. "I for one cannot wait."

Emma noticed Christian had the same gleam.

Allie leaned over her husband. "Let's go find Ellie,

Amelia, and Andi. I'm starved." She paused. "Have you noticed all of our names start with A or E? I'll be stumbling all over the alphabet now."

"Me, too," said Emma, and gave Christian a long stare. "See ya."

Christian's eyes met hers in a way that made her want to squirm. "Aye. See ya."

And with that, Emma and Allie left Christian, Gabe, and Gawan at the fence, and headed off to the great hall to find a bit more estrogen, and to get a bite to eat.

The rest of the evening was spent in the great hall, where Emma heard stories of days gone by, of yesteryear, of once-warriors and the battles they fought, the women they'd loved, their homes and their families. Many of the spirits were lost, had no memory of how they'd become ghosts at all. Gabe's wife, Allie, had pulled several aside, listening intently to what they did remember, taking notes, and promising to help them.

Emma also saw, with her own eyes, a total of twenty-two men, all from another place in time, another century, living their lives in the present.

Some of their old selves still existed. How could they not? They were medieval men, born hundreds of years in the past. While they'd certainly adapted to modern times—heck, half of the Dreadmoor guys drove Harleys—they'd maintained a greater portion of their old lives. Sometimes, the two centuries—the one they'd lived in the first time, and the one they lived in now—converged.

How they wore their swords and 501s at the same time was a perfect example of this convergence.

Emma leaned back against the stone wall of the hearth, and pulled her knees up. Christian sat on one side, Jason on the other.

That darn flirty Aiden Munro sat directly across from her.

She thought for sure Christian would beat him to a pulp.

Amelia, Ethan Munro's wife and Aiden's newest cousin, who was sitting on the other side of him, reached over and bopped him on the head. Then she winked at Emma.

Christian of Arrick-by-the-Sea simply smiled at Aiden Munro, and Aiden smiled back. They understood each other, so it seemed.

Jason leaned toward her. "I vow 'tis wondrous to see you reject yon Munro. Quite the conceited lad, aye?"

"Cocksure," mumbled Tristan, who sat not far away, his wife, Andi, leaning back against him. She nodded enthusiastically with her husband's comment. "Cute, but cocksure," she added.

Aiden's smile grew wider.

Then, the tall tales and legends began. One by one, the warriors recalled myths of their lands, their time. One warrior—a Welsh Pict from the ninth century—spoke in an ancient language. The room became quiet, and Gawan translated.

Gawan nodded. "Oy, aye," he murmured. "He speaks of the eternal well of magic water, farther up the northern coast of Wales," he said. "Farther north than Arrick, even." He nodded, listening to the warrior's words. "St. Beuno's Well, it's called. 'Tis only a myth, aye Chris? How many times did we look for it?"

"Scores," Christian said. "We looked our entire teenage years, did we not?"

Gawan laughed. "Methinks you're right."

"So," Emma said softly, "what sort of magic powers does it have?"

Gawan shrugged. "'Tis said that one soul, pure of heart, must risk death to obtain water from the well." He winked. "'Tis said to have mystical healing powers."

"That would have come in bloody handy," said a ghostly soul.

Everyone roared.

Emma's heart leaped.

Gawan shook his head. "If only 'twas so simple."

"Let's quit this hall, aye? I've a mind to get you alone once more this day," whispered Christian.

Emma shivered at the suggestion.

She stood and smiled at the crowd. "Good night."

Many responses sounded through the hall. Some were in English; some in Old English; some in a language completely unknown to Emma.

"Bright and early, right Emma?" said Ellie, grinning from her cozy spot next to Gawan. "We'll have to get a head start on feeding this crowd in the morning."

"Absolutely," Emma agreed. "See ya then."

As she let Christian lead her from the hall, they passed a giant of a man, standing against one of the largest tapestries in the room.

"His name is Sir Brian," said Christian, as they approached. "A big enough German knight, aye?"

"Aye, indeed," whispered Emma. They stopped at the tapestry, and while he and the German knight spoke, she studied the artwork.

She'd glimpsed the tapestry a few times before, but hadn't *really* looked.

She looked now. At the bottom of the piece, Eleanor of Aquitaine was stitched in old script. So Queen Eleanor was the woman in the center, sitting on a horse and wearing battle gear. The warriors surrounding her were all different—some with pitchforks, some with swords, some with axes. Then there was that one in particular without gear—bare-chested and with no helmet. Hefted above his head was an enormous sword.

His body was covered in strange, black tattoos.

Emma's eyes widened. "Holy ho-ho," she muttered.

"What is it?" said Christian quietly.

She looked up, then pointed to the bare warrior. "That's *Gawan*."

Christian and the German knight looked, and Christian nodded. "So it is. Ready?"

She was, and they left.

And like each night before, Christian walked Emma to her room.

At the door, they stopped, and Emma looked up.

Christian's gaze had the ability to knock the breath from her, and she'd bet he knew it. He stared at her a *lot*.

" 'Tis a ritual during the tournament that the warriors remain secluded from their women," he said. With a thumb, he grazed her cheek. "To keep our minds void of anything, save winning. I vow it bothers me more now than ever."

"Well," she said, smiling, "it can't be all that bad, can it? I mean, we can still see each other in the evening, when it's time to break for the day. Right?"

He gave her a grim smile. "Whilst appealing to those who have maids awaiting, aye, 'tis tempting to break the rules." He heaved a heavy sigh. "But there are those who do not have maids, myself included until recently, who find it . . . distracting. So aye. Our knightly oaths kick in and we stick to the rules."

"Oh," she said, disappointed. "So all I get to do is wave a white hanky at you and cheer from the sidelines?"

Christian moved closer, and ducked his head. "For three solid days, aye."

Emma met his gaze. "Gosh, I'll miss you. Who will walk me to my room?"

"Nicklesby?"

They both laughed.

She gave him another long look. "About St. Beuno's Well—"

" 'Tis a legend only, girl," Christian said quietly, then chuckled. "Don't you think we would have all dragged ourselves down there, were there truths to the legend?"

Emma sighed. "I suppose so."

"That's my girl. Now, I'll see you in the morn, maid, when you see me off," he said quietly.

And then he kissed her.

Chapter 30

Willoughby flipped through the Ballasters' copy of *The White Witches' Guidebook*. She'd done so several hundred times before over the last seventy-two years, but the closer it grew to All Hallows' Eve, the more anxious she became.

Morticia's wand, she hoped they'd done everything right.

"Ah-hah!" she said, and pointed to the page. "I knew it! Page four thousand and twenty-three, paragraph six."

The other Ballasters gathered round, peered over her shoulder, and listened as Willoughby read aloud the passage.

" 'Once a spell has been conjured and 'set into motion, it cannot be undone. Once the coordinates of such spell have been chosen, they, too, cannot be undone. Not a minute too soon. Not a minute too late.' " She looked at her sisters. "So no matter what the circumstances, Emma Calhoun *must* be at the designated place before the last stroke of the bewitching hour for her soul to survive, and to counteract that atrocious spell she concocted all those centuries ago. The rest," she sighed, and met her sisters' anxious gazes, "is in fate's hands."

"She's not recovered her memory yet, so our potions obviously are working. That's a good sign, don't you think?" asked Maven. "Think you we'll hear news soon?"

"Indeed, I do," said Willoughby. "Now shush. You know we mustn't speak of it aloud."

They all nodded, and continued their perusal of the guidebook. They'd nearly two weeks left. Willoughby knew the spell was the chanciest—had known it ever since she'd suggested using it. Spells truly did only work into fate's design if fate so destined it. But she'd not depress her sisters by telling them so. She had to have faith. Hope.

So far, so good . . .

Emma stared out of the window. She pressed her cheek against the glass, and her warm breath fogged the cold pane. Outside, the darkness had slipped away as morning approached, but left in its wake a heavy blanket of mist, wisps and tendrils of white fog reaching out and wafting over the tournament field below. Colorful flags waved from poles, indicating teams, and she easily found Team Arrick.

A lone man emerged from the mist, and he stopped, glanced her way, and held up a hand. There was no mistaking the muscular build, the arrogant stance, and that wild hair, even from the height of her window.

Emma smiled. "Christian," she whispered, and gave a wave back. He stood for a moment, then turned and joined several others who'd walked up. "God, why can't you be real," she whispered.

Christian's head turned toward her then, almost as if he'd heard. He stared in her direction for a moment, then joined the others as they left for the stables.

She'd dreamed of St. Beuno's Well the entire night. *If only it were true . . .*

Emma pushed off the windowsill and dug through her clothes. Pulling on a pair of jeans and a long-sleeved, black T-shirt, she yanked on her Team Arrick tee over that, made a trip to the bathroom to freshen up, double-knotted her Converses, and left the room.

She, Ellie, Andi, Amelia, and Allie had an enormous breakfast to prepare.

And then they had to do an official *fare-thee-well* to their champions.

Gabe and Nicklesby had child-care duty while the cooking went on, while Davy and Jake were preparing for their first tasks as squires. Nicklesby ran in and out of the kitchen, chasing one, if not both, of the Conwyk twins. Meanwhile, Gabe had *all* the babies.

Emma had her camera.

Luckily, he'd been very good-natured about having his picture taken.

An hour later, the great hall had been transformed into a feasting hall. While there were some spirits who preferred to train, since they couldn't eat, some piled in with the living for breakfast. The hall was packed. Team Donovan, the Irish, stood off to one side, taunting those still eating, saying they'd stuffed their bellies so full they'd not be able to heft their own blades.

Emma had to agree with that one. She'd glimpsed the Dreadmoor and Munro table. Good Lord, they could pack away the food. She couldn't imagine their grocery bills. They'd just eaten enough scrambled eggs, bacon, sausage, and toast to feed a small army.

Well, she supposed, that was *exactly* what they were.

Christian, who sat with Gawan, Godfrey, and Justin Catesby, hadn't taken his eyes off Emma since walking into the great hall. The thought of it made her cheeks heat up.

Soon, though, breakfast was over. The men all cleared out, leaving Emma, Amelia, Ellie, Andi, and Allie to the mess.

"I think I want to compete next year so I can simply

walk away from all this," mumbled Ellie. She grinned. "Good thing we used paper plates!"

It didn't take them long to get everything cleaned up. And while they cleaned, Emma glanced at all four women. Ellie, who never missed a thing, caught her.

"What are you thinking about?" Ellie asked. "You all but have smoke pouring out of your ears."

Emma twisted the dish towel in her hand. "It's funny, I guess. All of you have experienced nearly the same sort of thing." She smiled. "The same thing I'm experiencing now." She shook her head. "How did you stand it?"

"You mean," Andi said, grinning, "being crazy in love with someone who was not only dead and untouchable, but who lived centuries before you were born?"

Emma shook her head. "No, not that. That's actually been the easy part for me." She looked at all of them. "I'm talking about that space of time when all you could think about was *what if*? What if I could change things? What if I did change things, and he disappeared?"

All four women nodded their heads.

"We all experienced it, Emma," said Amelia. "Ethan and his men weren't dead, but there was always a fear that they'd disappear forever."

"And even though Allie wasn't in love with a ghost, she still feared some of the same things," said Ellie. "One wrong step and he'd be gone forever."

Emma sighed. "Not a great feeling," she said.

"What would you do if you knew you could change Christian's fate, despite the outcome?" asked Allie. "Would you sacrifice your time together for his salvation?"

Emma didn't hesitate. "In the blink of an eye." Her response didn't even surprise herself. She'd known Christian for such a short time, yet she felt she'd known him all her life. She'd do anything for him.

Not that she wouldn't hurt for the rest of her days; she'd miss him so very much. But would she give up their time together if it meant saving him from an eternity of roaming? Not that he'd really complained much about it. But still . . .

Amelia walked up and put her arm around Emma's shoulders. "Don't worry. It will all work out in the end." She smiled. "It always does."

Emma wanted badly to believe it.

"That's right," Ellie said. "You're an official member of the Girls and Ghouls Club." She grinned. "I just made that up."

They all laughed.

Just then, Gabe walked into the kitchen. His face was pasty white, his blue-green eyes wide. He carried an infant in each arm.

He had baby barf down the front of his shirt.

"Help," he said.

They all laughed again.

After Amelia and Ellie had retrieved their little ones, Allie took Gabe to the kitchen sink to help him clean up.

"I think I shall squire next tournament," he mumbled.

Just then, a trumpet sounded from outside.

"Oh," said Ellie. "First warning. We'd better hurry if we want to see our guys off."

By the time all the babies were cleaned and changed, and the girls had reached the great hall, another blast from the trumpet sounded through the bailey. Ladies Follywolle and Beauchamp joined them.

"We look great," said Allie, smoothing down her Team Arrick shirt. "What a cute idea, these shirts."

"I agree. Oh, let's go," said Ellie, adjusting her little Ensley into her baby sling. "I love this part."

They all filed outside, and for once, the sun barely

peeked from behind the clouds. The temperature still registered colder than it ever did in Savannah in October, but for England, it was tolerably pleasant. The barest of chilly winds came from the North Sea, and the frost from the night before that had gathered on the ground had already melted. It smelled of brine and clover, leather and . . . horses.

The trumpet blasted for a third time.

Emma looked; then she gasped.

Each team had separated, forming two long, giant lines of horse and riders. On one side were Team Dreadmoor, Team Grimm, and Team Munro. On the other were Team Arrick, Team Donovan, and Team Le Maurant. One side mortal; one side ghostly.

Both impressive as hell.

The trumpeter sounded his horn, and Emma was surprised to find he, too, was a spirit, and wearing a large, floppy hat with a big feather in it.

Similar to Sir Godfrey's.

Once he finished, he became the tournament crier, as well.

"Here ye! Here ye!" he shouted. "Welcome to the second annual Grimm Tournament! Warriors, ghostly and not so ghostly, begin the official procession!"

Allie grabbed Emma's hand and leaned close. "This is so exciting! I wish my pal Dauber were here to see it. He's off visiting friends in Ireland."

"It really is exciting," Emma whispered back. And it honestly was. Warriors from as far back as the ninth century had arrived in their best battle gear. Some in complete armor, some in chain mail, like what the Dreadmoors, Christian, and Gawan wore. Some wore barely anything at all, like the twin Pict brothers who wore little more than blue war paint. Some were on foot; some were mounted on . . . *ghost horses*?

She supposed that could be so.

No matter the century, or the gear, they all marched their procession with their heads held high, and confidence so thick, Emma thought she could slice it with a knife.

Finally, four warriors remained. All on horseback. All looking lethal.

First, Gawan—probably because he was host of the tournament. With his hair pulled back, his leather gear, chain mail, and a helmet on—for a change—he walked his horse toward Emma's little group. Ellie stepped forward as he neared, reached her hand out, and handed him something. Gawan flipped his visor, opened his hand, grinned, and bent down to place a kiss on his wife's lips. Then he retreated.

Tristan de Barre was next. That was one big joker. Wearing head-to-toe chain mail, and a black tunic with a mystical creature sewn into the center, he followed the same pattern as Gawan—except when Andi and her little one reached his horse, he swept one big arm down, pulled her off her feet, and kissed her hard. The crowd roared, and Andi handed him something, as well.

Next came Ethan. Those Scots were something else. Wearing a mixture of plaid kilts and armor, Ethan, with his long dark hair and wide smile, was something to place in her memory book—and in Amelia's too, if the grin on her face meant anything. He kissed her, and she handed him something.

What in the world?

In her fascination with the ritual, Emma hadn't noticed the one remaining knight until Amelia had passed her with a wink. Christian, mounted on a majestic black horse, wore full battle regalia. He nudged his horse with his knees, moving closer. Ellie gave her a push, and Emma started to walk. They met, no more than a foot away, and Christian pushed his visor up. Double swords jutted over each shoulder—even his mail creaked, as did the leather of his saddle. *So very real.* Wide, sexy blue eyes watched her; muscles flinched at his jaws. All signs of joking had vanished.

They simply stared at each other.

"*Cara 'ch hwchwaneg awron na 'r 'n flaen amsera Adfeiliasis i mewn cara chennych,*" he said, barely above a whisper.

Emma felt her knees weaken. "What does that mean?"

He stared at her for quite some time. Then he smiled.

"Wait for me," he said quietly. "I shall return soon."

At once, a thousand shards of broken light pierced Emma's eyes, and everything, like an out-of-control kaleidoscope, flickered behind her lids.

For the briefest of moments, she saw Christian in another time, another place, saying those same exact words.

She saw *herself.*

Just as fast, the vision disappeared.

"Emma?" said Christian, frowning. "Are you ill?"

Emma smiled. "Nah, I'm fine. Probably didn't eat enough." She waved a hand. "Shoo, so I can cheer you on." She put on a fake scowl. "Win, okay?"

Christian stared hard at her for several seconds; then he gave a single nod. "For you."

Then he turned his horse and galloped off.

Emma stared after him, her heart in her throat.

She could have sworn she'd seen him do that very thing before.

That'd be impossible, she thought, and started for the bleachers.

Chapter 31

She had to hand it to Tristan de Barre. That guy seriously *owned* the joust. By far the most fast-paced, cutthroat of all the tournament events, the joust was like no spectator sport she'd ever seen. She'd watched him take nine opponents out after the first pass. The thundering of hooves and the splintering wood of the lance gave her shudders.

It made for some kick-patootey pictures, too.

Then, the hand-to-hand sword fighting. She'd watched Jason, presently of Dreadmoor, take on at least three of the guys from Team Grimm—most of whom were warriors Gawan had personally trained for battle. When on earth had sweet, charming Jason become so ... *ferocious*? She'd gotten some good shots of him, as well as all the other mortals.

The ghostly competitors she'd have to bank to memory.

All except Christian of Arrick-by-the-Sea.

While the spirited competitors couldn't really hurt one another, it still looked and sounded fierce. Big, muscular, and determined, Christian took on and won every event he entered. Hand-to-hand sword fighting was his best event—even against the crazy Team Donovan. She'd watched, her breath held, as Christian advanced on a big, brawling Irish warrior named Aderigg.

The brute topped Christian's height by at least three inches, and had biceps the size of bowling balls. Christian didn't seem to care much. With a look that made a shudder run through Emma's body, he took graceful, powerful, calculated steps, taunting the big Irishman with the swiftly moving double blades. Christian waved them as if they were as light as a Victorian lady's fan, yet his muscles pulled and strained with each movement, so much so that Emma could see the tattoos flinch. But when he attacked full force? Emma had never seen such fearsome strength and determination. It simply astounded her.

But there wasn't a single ghostly soul who could oust him from his saddle at the joust. He sat so majestically on his mount, those big, muscular thighs clamped down against the horse's sides. Staring down his opponent, Christian would flip his helmet visor closed with a snap, and holler a yell that gave Emma chills down her spine. Then he'd charge the warrior crazy enough to face him. The sound of impact as wood smashed into either more wood or steel, and the shattering of the lance, rattled her insides. And it sounded so dang *real*.

She briefly wondered who would win, should Christian and Tristan ever face off.

If only . . .

Just then, a holler rang out, and she looked up, out of her thoughts. Christian was once again saddled and ready. He glanced her way, and she could see his mouth lift into an arrogant grin.

Another flash shot through her, one so powerful it nearly knocked her off the steel bleachers she was sitting on. Slides of pictures flew past her mind, of another place, another time.

Of Christian.

The trumpeter's horn pulled her back to the present. She put a hand to her forehead, feeling dizzy. As she watched Christian flip his visor and charge his opponent, another wash of . . . something, crept over her.

She knew she'd seen him do the exact same thing before.

Again, she shook it off.

"Dear, are you all right?"

Emma turned to Lady Follywolle. The bird on her head looked as if it were ready to peck out her eyes. She smiled. "I'm fine. Just . . . feeling a little strange, is all."

Lady Beauchamp leaned forward to peer around her ghostly companion. Seawater dripped from her sopping-wet gown. It seemed to drip from her eyes, as well. "Oh, Millicent," she said, sounding as though she were about to weep, "I can barely take it much longer. My heart is breaking!"

"Shh!" Lady Follywolle said quietly, patting her friend's knee. Then she turned to Emma. "She hates the tournament so. Too much blood and guts. Come, Lady Beauchamp. Let's take a walk, shall we?"

With that they disappeared.

On the other side sat Gabe and Allie. Gabe leaned forward. "You do look a bit pale, lass. Are you feeling ill?"

"No," said Emma, smiling. "I'm fine."

Just then, Christian made one more pass. Muscles in his shoulders bunched as they held the lance, and he tore off down the lane. He defeated his opponent, and everyone for Team Arrick cheered. She stood and waved as he looked in her direction.

Then he pulled his mount to a halt, squeezed his knees, and made the horse rear.

Everyone cheered louder.

And *then* he flipped up his visor, threw down his lance, and slung his right leg over the horse's neck and leaped down. As he walked toward her, he removed his helmet and clamped it under one arm. His hair poked out in several directions, and with his free hand he raked it out of his face. He tossed her a big, wide grin.

Helm still under his arm, he cupped his hands and hollered, "For you, Emma, love!"

Everyone for Team Arrick cheered, and Emma waved at him.

He turned and walked away.

Emma stared at his retreating back, taking in the chain mail, the swords, the hair in disarray, the arrogant swagger. He glanced over his shoulder and threw her another grin.

"I've seen him do that before, too," she muttered. "But that's impossible."

"What's that?" said Gabe. He leaned forward, ducked his head, and looked at her. "Emma? You're lookin' funny again, lass."

Emma turned to him then, meeting his worried gaze. "I'm fine, I . . . just have a headache," she said. "I'll go lie down and it'll be fine in no time."

"Do you want me to walk back with you?" asked Gabe.

Emma smiled and stood. "No, you guys enjoy the tournament. I'll be back in a bit."

She felt Gabe and Allie's eyes on her as she climbed down the bleachers, and she tossed them a wave before she turned and headed across the bailey. As she grew closer to the main keep, she hurried more, although she really didn't know what she was hurrying for. Everything seemed hazy, unclear, strange.

As soon as she stepped into the great hall's main entrance, it hit her.

It hit her *hard*.

Thank God, no one was around.

Just as she made it to the staircase, a surge of nausea hit as déjà vu washed over her again and again. Emma took several deep breaths, then bent over at the waist and drew several more, to keep from losing what little she had in her stomach. She grabbed the banister and held on tight as memories, fast and furious as though she were watching a movie in fast motion, washed over her. *So many, so very fast.*

The last one made her lose her breath, and she sank to the bottom step and sat.

Remembering.

Emma grabbed her head, willing it to stop spinning. She couldn't keep the barrage of memories at bay. There were too many to make much sense out of them. But one constant figure popped up repeatedly, every so often.

It barely surprised her.

Christian.

"Oh, God," she half whispered, half sobbed.

"Young lady, may I help you?"

Emma jumped at the voice, and focused on the man before her. Distinguished and elderly he was, with a pristine suit and a clipped British accent. She paused. She hadn't met him before. "I'm . . . fine. Just a headache."

One gray brow lifted. "Of course. A headache." He gave her a slight nod. "I'm Jameson, from the Dreadmoor lot. I only just arrived. Can I get you an aspirin, perhaps, or a pot of tea?"

She rose and gave him a smile. It felt weak, and it probably looked weak, too. "No, that's okay, really. I'm going to lie down for a bit. But thank you, anyway."

He looked at her, then gave one more nod. "Nicklesby is babysitting those dreadful Conwyk twins, so if you should need anything, I shall be around."

"Thank you," she said, and started up the steps.

She felt Jameson's eyes on her as she jogged up the stairs.

Finally, she reached the third floor, and relief washed over her to find it completely empty. Tears were streaming down her face now, and she felt a scream building in her throat. Temptation to let it rip ran through her, and she felt positive Christian would hear. Instead, she swallowed the scream.

At her door, she let herself in, threw it shut, and flung herself onto the bed. The tears came harder now, faster, turning into uncontrolled sobs that made her feel ashamed. Grabbing the pillow from behind her head, she covered her face to drown out the moans.

She'd been responsible for Christian's eternal life as a ghost.

She clearly recalled the day, so many hundreds of years before, when she had discovered an old Welsh conjuring book and decided to take fate into her own hands.

It had been a frightful mistake.

She'd screwed it up. Whether not reading the verse correctly, or mispronouncing the ancient Welsh words—either way, she'd screwed up. Not only had she cursed Christian, she'd cursed herself.

It was all too overwhelming.

She'd been born in another century. She'd lived multiple lives ever since. No wonder she'd had flashbacks while visiting the UK, though she hadn't understood them at the time. She'd been here before. Loads of times. "*Fi forever arhosa 'ch , 'm cara Cristion*," she whispered.

She knew Welsh. Of course she knew Welsh.

"I forever await you, my love Christian," she said out loud.

And no wonder she'd never been able to find true love. She already had it.

And those specific flashbacks of Christian? It all made complete sense now. Of course she'd seen him do those things before. She'd lived in another time with him, long, long ago. Many times over. She recalled every single time she fell in love with him all over again—every seventy-two years, thanks to her botched-up spell.

Pain and joy washed over her in cycles, and finally, when there were no more tears, she heaved a heavy sigh. The very last time she saw him alive swept through her mind like a tidal wave, and tears ran down her face as she remembered ...

"Please, Chris! I beg you, dunna leave me!" Emma cried. She dragged her hand across her teary eyes. "I fear I shall never see you again." Pain stabbed her in the gut, and her heart ached as though someone squeezed it in their fist.

Christian swung a leg over his horse's neck and jumped to the ground. In two strides he was at Emma's side. He cradled her face with his hands and met her gaze. With his thumbs, he wiped away the wetness from her cheeks. "I have to go, love. But I will return to you." He pressed his lips to hers, kissed each of her eyes, then pulled away. "I vow it, Emm. Wait for me."

Emma nodded. More tears leaked out. "I will wait forever," she whispered.

Then as she watched through tears that would not cease, her love leaped upon the back of his mount, and without another glance in her direction, heeled the horse's sides and sped off. She watched as Christian's form grew smaller and smaller, until he was no more than a mere spot in the distance.

"I will wait forever, my love," she whispered aloud again. "Come back to me ..."

As she considered her past lives, the past twelve chances she'd had with Christian of Arrick-by-the-Sea, she realized one thing in particular, and it struck her like a lightning bolt.

This time was different. This thirteenth chance was not like the other chances. Her parents were alive, and she was thriving. And ... she only just now recalled her past. It *had* to mean something. And by God, she couldn't let Christian know she knew. She'd have to keep it a complete secret. Something had to change this time. Something had to give.

For now, anyway . . .

Emma threw a small prayer heavenward. She hoped she had the strength to pull it off.

Chapter 32

Keeping a secret of such magnitude proved to be Emma's greatest challenge to date. Every time she looked at Christian, thought of Christian, or worse—*he* looked at *her*—she wanted to scream at the top of her lungs, *I remember! I love you!*

Zoë would be proud that she'd kept a secret such as this one.

Emma had been born in the twelfth century . . .

It was still so overwhelming, she could barely think about the memories that continuously assaulted her without her head spinning out of control. She recalled exactly what she was wearing the first time she met Christian de Gaultiers. A long, woolen gown the color of cream and stitched around the collar in emerald green, with a wide leather belt and garnet cloak. Leather boots. Not to mention the long woolen hose. She shook her head and fought a smile. Lord, how those things had itched!

She remembered her nurse's uniform and cap from her last life. Starched and pressed and pristine white, with heavy hose that had a solid seam on the back of her legs, and the prettiest pumps with the highest of heels. Funny. A nurse with heels. Nowadays, it was scrubs and sneakers. She recalled sitting with him in the Ballasters' parlor, listening to Cole Porter in front of a roaring fire.

She remembered how he used to watch her, take his calloused finger and trace the line of her jaw, her lips. Not really touching, yet scorching her just the same. God, how she loved him . . .

Emma had to really concentrate on not letting her secret out, because so many of her old selves started pounding away at her insides. Same soul, thirteen different lives.

She'd encountered Christian twelve times.

This was the thirteenth. And thirteen times, she'd fallen helplessly in love with him.

Now she knew why.

He was her Intended. Her soul mate. *For eternity* . . .

And she couldn't let him know *she knew*.

For almost two full days, she'd put on a façade. She didn't like it, but her gut told her she'd need to do things differently this time. Before, she'd thrown herself at Christian, so overwhelmed was she by love and joy at remembering. Soon after, an accident would happen. She never remembered anything after the accident, but she could only surmise that she'd died.

Emma crossed the room to the window seat and lowered herself onto the soft cushion. She pressed her cheek to the icy pane of glass and squeezed her eyes tightly shut. Grief washed over her, and her throat constricted, making it difficult to swallow. This time, it was grief for what Christian must have endured. Every seventy-two years he'd encounter a brand-new Emma, yet he knew she was the same soul. He'd wait on her, patiently. And each time they'd meet, he'd make her fall in love with him all over again. She'd gain her memory of him and their lives together, and they'd rejoice, she as a mortal, he as a spirit. But for such a short time. That stupid curse would force her to leave him, and God, he'd suffered. She knew he had, because never had a man been so loving and caring as Christian de Gaultiers of Arrick-by-the-Sea. When he loved, he loved with his whole self. His entire being. And she'd been given that love thirteen times . . .

Tears flooded her eyes, and she allowed the sobs to rack her body. God, how she'd missed him . . .

Finally, she jumped up, found a tissue, and patted her eyes dry. She stared at herself in the mirror, eyes red. Slowly, she let out a long breath.

It would not happen again.

This time, she wasn't going to allow it.

So for the remainder of the tournament, Emma would simply remain Emma—the Emma born in 1981. But she hadn't had to face Christian yet—not up close, anyway.

She would in about forty minutes, at the awards ceremony and banquet, when the warriors had finally finished and could mingle with their maids again.

She prayed Christian wouldn't see straight through her.

A light knock sounded at her door, and Emma pulled away from the mirror, patted her eyes, took a deep breath, and strode to the door. When she opened it, she found Ellie standing there, grinning. Her gaze studied Emma, and she gave an approving nod.

"That looks way better on you than it does on me," Ellie said. "It matches your hair perfectly." She narrowed her gaze. "Why are your eyes so red?"

Emma's face turned warm, and she shrugged. "It's nothing, honest. Just having a girl moment." She smoothed the front of her borrowed, cinnamon-colored cocktail dress and smiled. "But thanks, and you look gorgeous. That black dress is lovely." She poked her foot out and studied the black strappy heels. "And double thanks for the use of these. I didn't even bring one nice pair of shoes with me."

Ellie continued to study her, and then grinned. "They look great, but I think Christian would have adored you even in your Converses." She inclined her head. "Ready?"

Emma nodded, relieved her host was letting it go. "Let me grab my camera equipment." She did and then met Ellie back at the door. "Okay, ready."

She hoped she was, anyway.

As she and Ellie walked to the great hall, Emma thought how odd it felt to be at Grimm. She'd never been to Castle Grimm, but she remembered everyone, save the wives. They'd all come along since Emma's last return. Gawan was Christian's best friend since childhood. She'd even met him before he'd left for the Crusades. But she'd met him at Arrick. Yet Grimm *felt* familiar. She didn't understand.

"You seem to have a lot on your mind these past few days," commented Ellie. "Everything okay?"

Emma gave her an easy smile. And it was, in fact easy. Ellie was a nice, funny person—a very effortless sort of friend. "Everything's fine. I really want to thank you for such a great time." She shook her head. "Certainly a first for me."

"You've been a pleasure to have," she said. "And lucky us, no cooking or washing dishes! The whole thing's catered. Gawan's idea. Good thing, too, because I was just going to make an enormous cauldron of Hamburger Helper."

"Umm, I love that stuff," Emma said.

They both laughed.

As they entered the great hall, Emma set her camera equipment on a small table beneath an enormous mirror, just at the foot of the stairs, kept the camera itself, checked the settings, and followed Ellie.

Nicklesby was there, running after the twins, and the wives all had the children corralled, and they all looked fabulous doing it. Amelia had a head full of springy blond curls that looked glorious against the blue dress she wore. Andi had on a pink gauzy dress with the cutest matching strappy heels, and Allie's amber strapless dress made her wide eyes stand out. All extraordinary women.

All married to extraordinary men.

Emma wasted no time taking photos. The girls with their little ones, Nicklesby running after the Conwyk twins, and that guy Jameson looking all serious and so . . . *butlerish*. She captured them all.

And it kept her mind off things to come.

Just then, the trumpeter's blast sounded through the great hall. Ellie grabbed Emma's arm and pulled her to the side as the doors flew open.

A double line of warriors piled in and walked to the front of the hall, before the hearth. A long table had been set up, and several silver goblets of various sizes had been placed in rows. Jameson stood behind the table, nose in the air. He flicked something from his sleeve, glanced casually at his watch, and cast a bored look out at the approaching crowd of men.

Emma covered a smile with her hand.

Then, she saw Christian.

Her heart stopped beating.

He entered the great hall, just behind Gawan, and as soon as he did, his eyes searched for her. He found her. And his expression changed immediately.

It was an expression she hadn't seen before. *Ever*.

Dressed in head-to-toe battle regalia, including a long, black tunic with a silver cross over the left side of his chest, and those lethal double swords secured over each shoulder, Christian carried his helmet under one arm and stared at her as he passed. His eyes assessed her, and Emma thought she'd never been so fully weighed by another person in her entire life. Or, lives.

It was positively sensual, the way he looked at her. And just before he completely passed her, their eyes met. Hunger flamed in the depths of the blue—a hunger Emma hadn't seen so prominently before. She slowly sucked in a gasp. The corner of his sexy mouth lifted; then he passed by. Then the warriors lined up as Jameson handed out the goblets. Cheers went up for each winner. Tristan, of course, won first place in the mortal joust.

She'd counted on that one.

Gawan had taken first place in the broadsword, and Ethan had taken first place in hand-to-hand combat.

Not so surprisingly, Jason had come in second in all three events.

Christian had taken first place in all events for the ghostly team, much to the mumbled chagrin of Team Donovan. Second and third place winners across time and place accepted their awards. The ghosts who couldn't physically take the goblet left it to be displayed in Grimm's armory.

She took as many photos as possible.

Once Jameson had exclaimed, in the drollest voice Emma had ever heard, the tournament's closing, the warriors all hurried to their maids. The crowd was so thick with mortals and ghosts alike, Emma simply stood, staring through the bodies, waiting for one in particular.

Finally, the throng thinned, and in the center of the hall stood Christian. Slowly, he walked toward her.

She momentarily forgot that she'd known him for centuries.

She'd never known him like *this*.

As he walked, his eyes remained locked on to hers. Emma's mouth went dry, and she felt her skin flush warm. Finally, Christian stopped, no more than a foot away. He stood there, staring, his eyes raking over her from strappy-shoe toe to the top of her head.

"*Crist, ach fel 'n arddun,*" he said in a quiet voice.

"What does that mean?" Emma asked, although she already knew.

"Christ," he said, his eyes boring into hers, "you are so beautiful."

Christian had to remind himself that he didn't actually need bloody air to breathe.

Yet he could hardly draw a decent breath.

If possible, Emma was more beautiful now, this very night, than he'd ever seen in almost nine hundred years.

Her heart raced. He could hear it.

"Oh," she said quietly. "Thank you."

"Aye," he returned. He couldn't help but continue to stare. "Come," he said, inclining his head to the hearth. "I want to show you something."

She gave him a dazzling smile. "Okay."

They started across the great hall, but didn't make it far before Jason stopped them. The youngest Dragonhawk had an appreciative gleam in his eye that Christian fought hard not to punch out.

"My lady Emma," he said, taking her by the hand and twirling her in a slow circle. "You are the most beautiful creature in here, I'd warrant."

Emma blushed furiously. "Thanks, Jason."

"Jason," said Christian.

"Aye, Lord Arrick?" he answered.

"Go find your own maid."

And with that, Christian inclined his head in the direction they'd been going, Emma shrugged and patted Jason on the shoulder, and they continued on their way to the hearth.

He glanced over his shoulder.

Jason grinned from ear to ear.

When they reached the grand table with the silver goblet awards, Christian gave Jameson, who still stood vigilant behind it, a single nod. "Jameson."

"Yes, my lord," Jameson answered. Then he moved

his hand to the left and hefted the large, first place goblet and held it out to Emma. He blinked.

Emma smiled at Christian. "What's this?"

"Read it."

Emma turned back to the goblet and peered at the old-fashioned scroll work. GRIMM TOURNAMENT, FIRST PLACE IN JOUST, HAND-TO-HAND COMBAT, AND SWORD. FOR EMMA, YOUR CHAMPION ALWAYS, CHRISTIAN OF ARRICK-BY-THE-SEA.

"Oh," she whispered, reading the words. She looked at him. "For me? You knew you'd win, huh?"

"Aye, for a certainty," Christian said. "Now, take it from Jameson before he throws it." He grinned. "I wish I could carry it for you."

Emma reached over and hefted the big silver goblet from Jameson. "Thank you," she said.

Jameson gave a single nod. "My pleasure, lady."

She leaned toward Christian. "I can keep it?"

He grinned. "Aye, it would be an honor." He cleared his throat. "You can, err, take it home with you. A souvenir of your time here." He shrugged. "So you won't forget me."

Emma's eyes grew wide. She hastily looked away, and cleared her throat. "As if I could ever forget you."

Christian smiled. "I am quite memorable, aye?"

His heart sank as he said the words.

"Oh, you certainly are," she said.

"Are you ready to eat?" he asked.

"Always," she answered.

He fully believed it.

Christian sat across from Emma during the banquet. It was the first time in centuries he didn't actually miss consuming food. He was so busy watching her that he nearly forgot everything else around him.

Tonight, after the banquet, he noticed something

strikingly different about Emma. He couldn't put a finger on it.

He thought about it all night while he watched Emma in slumber. He'd hoped to catch her talking out loud again, but she slept like a baby all night. And he hadn't minded watching every single second.

By the next morning, it was finally time to leave Castle Grimm, and for once, Christian wasn't too unhappy about it. He was tired of sharing Emma with everyone, ghosts and mortals alike. He wanted her to himself.

He didn't know how much longer he had to enjoy her.

Good-byes and womanly hugs were passed all around in the great hall, then again at the helicopter pad. Christian rather liked how well Emma had taken to the other wives. They shared something, those maids. A special bond of sorts, he imagined.

Tristan and Gawan had both taken turns pulling Emma into a fierce hug and kissing her cheeks. Ethan had been a bit gentler, but not much. Gabe had kissed her knuckles. Christian had wanted to flatten them all.

Jason, the arrogant pup, had insisted on riding to Arrick, in order to aid Emma with her luggage and such, he'd claimed. The lad had talked her bloody ears off the whole way home, and once they'd landed, Christian had to remind him that he *was* in fact returning to Grimm. Or Dreadmoor. As long as it wasn't Arrick.

Jason had laughed, kissed Emma heartily on the mouth, and jumped back into the helicopter. With a wave, he lifted off.

As Christian and Emma stood together in the bailey of Arrick-by-the-Sea, he stared down at her, and she stared back. A grin slowly pulled at Christian's mouth, and he drew closer to Emma, who held his winning goblet fiercely under one arm.

"We're home," he said, and her smile rocked him to the bone.

Chapter 33

Emma had it completely and utterly figured out. She'd thought about nothing else for nearly two weeks since returning from Castle Grimm—a hard thing to do, in her mind, seeing as how Christian of Arrick-by-the-Sea was such a sexy distraction.

They'd spent nearly every moment together.

It still wasn't enough.

They'd hiked the hills, walked the beaches, and climbed the cliffs. They'd even ferried out to Puffin Island, and taken a tour of Beaumaris Castle. Stark and foreboding, it made for striking black-and-white photos. All in all, a perfect sightseeing trip with the most absolutely perfect sightseeing guide. One of her favorites had been their walk through the Ballasters' maze. Christian had chased her, she'd hidden from him, and they'd sat for hours, tucked in a secluded grotto of ivy, simply ... talking. Talking and looking at one another. When Christian stared at her, it was the single most sensual thing she could ever remember experiencing.

"Here you go, love," said Willoughby, bustling into the breakfast room. "A nice pot of tea to warm your toes this fine chilly morn." She set the white porcelain pot on the table beside Emma. She grinned, batting her red lashes that matched her red hair.

She'd felt the sisters were up to something from the

time she'd returned to Arrick. She just couldn't decide *what*.

"Thanks, Willoughby," she said, deciding that it really didn't matter what they were up to. *She*, Emma Calhoun, had a plan. And by God, it would work.

Nearly everything was in place.

Emma had one call to make, and she'd make it while Christian was in the bailey training with Justin Catesby. *As planned.*

She'd be eternally grateful to Justin for his cooperation. Emma had all but begged the young, handsome Scottish pirate to help distract Christian for an hour or two. She'd told Justin minimal information—enough that he knew exactly what was going on. Well, almost, anyway. She couldn't let him know everything. Though fond were her memories of Justin, she also recalled him being painfully faithful to Christian. If Justin thought she was doing anything dangerous, he'd rat her out to Christian in a heartbeat.

It was her last *please* that did him in. Apparently, Captain Justin Catesby had an affliction to saying no to beseeching women. Thank goodness. She'd be sure to beseech more often.

Finishing her breakfast with haste, Emma excused herself from the sisters' company, grabbed the cordless, and ran upstairs to her room.

She quickly dialed Castle Grimm.

Nicklesby answered. "Conwyk residence."

"Hi, Nicklesby. This is Emma. May I speak to Gawan?"

"Aye," he said. "He's just in from training. Just a moment."

Emma waited for several minutes, then Gawan's deep, accented voice came on the line. "Aye? Emma? Is all well?"

Emma sighed. "Well, I hope this time it will be."

Gawan was silent for several seconds; then he let out a heavy breath. "You remember."

Emma's heart jumped. "Yes. I remember. And I need your help."

Quickly, she told Gawan her plan.

"Nay, Emma, 'tisn't safe at all. You *know* what has happened to you in the past."

"Yes," whispered Emma, glancing out the window to make sure Justin still kept Christian busy. "I do. And I'm telling you, Gawan, this time is different. Something's changed. I can *feel* it."

He sighed. "You know 'tis only legend, Emma. A handful of ancient old men made it up. You could get hurt."

"Fate, Gawan. Remember fate? You should. Now, please. I'm begging you. Do this thing for me. *Please.* As an old friend?"

Several more seconds passed as Gawan decided. "Okay, girl. I'll do it. I cannot say I fully believe in it, but I shall do it. For the sake of you and Chris."

"Thank you," she whispered furtively. "I owe you big-time."

"You owe me nothing, save keeping your hardheaded self alive," he answered with a grumble. "If Chris were to lose you again, I'm not sure he'd survive. He loves you fiercely, you know. Now go. I'll send someone right away."

With a smile, her heart in her throat, Emma hung up. And *waited*.

Yeah, she knew Christian loved her fiercely.

But not nearly as fiercely as she loved him back.

"He needs you, lad," said Godfrey. "He said to tell you he wouldn't ask it of you, knowing you've . . . company." He glanced at Emma. "But it seems there are several spirits who are causing quite the ruckus and have decided not to leave Grimm. Lady Ellie is most upset, you see."

Christian rubbed the bridge of his nose. "Aye, I see. Fine, fine." Christian turned to Emma. "I have to go."

She smiled. "Time to flex your ghostly muscles, huh?" she asked.

"Aye," he replied. "For no one else, save Gawan and Ellie, would I do this." He looked at her gravely. "The last thing I want to do is leave you."

Emma met his gaze. She prayed fervently it wasn't the last time she saw him. Pasting on a big grin, which she hoped looked sincere, she sighed. "Don't worry, Chris. I'll be waiting for you."

He blinked. "What did you say?"

She cocked her head. "I'll . . . be waiting for you?"

Christian shook his head. "Very well. I shall return as soon as I can settle those feisty souls at Grimm." He stepped closer, and ducked his head. "Godfrey? If you don't mind?" he said, not taking his eyes off Emma.

"Err, right," said Godfrey, turning his head.

Christian slid his mouth close to Emma's, until that familiar tingling joined their essence together. He moved his lips to her ear. "I'll be right back."

Her heart skipped a few beats. "Okay," she said, breathless. "Be careful."

Christian pulled back, lifted an eyebrow, and grinned.

Then promptly disappeared.

Emma wasted no time. She took off for the manor house. Inside, she found Willoughby, who was baking something absolutely delicious smelling. She could almost taste a hint of apricot in the air.

"Willoughby, I have a huge favor to ask of you," Emma said.

"Anything, dear," said the older woman. She glanced at her sisters, then back to Emma. "What is it?"

Emma squirmed. "Can I borrow your truck? I promise to drive really slow and careful. And I'll fill it up with fuel before I return."

The sisters glanced at one another again. Willoughby smiled. "Och, of course you can, girl. Where are you off to?"

Emma's heart leaped. "It's a surprise for Christian."

"Well then," said Willoughby, beaming, "you run right along."

"Um, if he returns, don't tell him, okay?" Emma asked.

Willoughby beamed. "And ruin the surprise? I wouldn't dream of it!"

With that, she pulled the truck keys off the peg on the wall and tossed them to Emma. Emma caught them and grinned. "Thanks!"

"Don't forget our All Hallows' Eve banquet tomorrow night," called Willoughby. " 'Tis quite the event here in Arrick."

"I won't!" said Emma. Quickly, she ran upstairs, freshened up, grabbed her bag and jacket, and flew back down.

Willoughby was waiting at the foot of the stairs for her. She smiled and reached her hand out. "I wanted to give you this, love. 'Tis a gift. From my sisters and me."

Emma grasped a small, thin circle of . . . something from Willoughby's hands. She held it up and inspected it. "It's . . . beautiful. What is it?"

" 'Tis a thread of braided rowan bark," Willoughby said. "Just an old Welsh legend that it brings safety and good luck to the wearer." She smiled. "So wear it."

Emma smiled, slipped it over her wrist, and hugged her host. "Thank you. I love it."

"Now shoo," said Willoughby. "And behave yourself!"

She hadn't gone five miles when she reached into her bag and pulled out the map she'd hand-drawn—with the help of a ninth-century Pict warrior. Just as she unfolded it, and looked ahead at the next road sign, a voice scattered her thoughts.

And nearly made her run off the road.

"An' just where are you goin', lass?"

Emma screamed and gripped the wheel. "Justin! Oh, you! I nearly wrecked!" She glanced at him, sitting smugly in the passenger side of the Ballasters' truck. "What are you doing here?" She kept her eyes on the narrow road ahead of her, and waited.

"I might have a soft spot for beseechin' lasses, lass, but I'm no' daft. I knew you were up to somethin'. Now. Where are you goin'?" he said.

Emma glared at him, then directed her eyes back to the road. A light sprinkle had started. She turned on the windshield wipers. "St. Beuno's Well," she muttered. She knew it'd do no good to fib to the sea captain.

Justin said several things she didn't understand. Swear words, in Gaelic she supposed. She'd heard Ethan mutter a few, as well. They sounded very naughty.

Justin turned to her when he'd finished. "Why are you goin' there, girl? Are ye daft? 'Tisna for real, Beuno's. 'Tis nothin' more than a myth. Me own granddaddy used to tell me tales of its magical water when I was a wee lad." He shook his head. "Daft girl. Chris will be powerfully angry when he finds out."

"You had *better* not tell him, Justin Catesby," growled Emma. "I mean it. Promise me." She glanced at him. "Please?"

A frown pulled Justin's dark brows down. He glared at Emma. "Not playin' fair, Emma." He studied her, said a few more Gaelic swears, then sighed. "Only if I stay wi' you. I'll no' have you goin' off alone and gettin' yourself hurt. Chris would have my hide."

Emma glared right back. "Fine. Just stop trying to talk me out of it. A reliably good source told me St. Beuno's is a true place, and it isn't a legend only."

Justin snorted. "Who? That untamed, painted heathen from the tournament? Aye, I saw you talkin' to him."

Justin shook his dark head. "He's crazy, you know. Been hangin' round for centuries tellin' that tale." He glanced at Emma. "Just be safe. Dunna do anythin' stupid."

Emma growled and sped up. She ignored him for several miles.

"Come on, Emma, I'm sorry," he finally said. "Dunna be mad."

She glanced at him.

He gave her that roguish grin he was so famous for.

"Fine," she mumbled. Then she smiled, because he'd leaned back against the seat and crossed his arms smugly over his chest.

It was nearly two hours later when Emma saw the road leading to the cliffs the Pict had directed her to. She slowed, pulled the truck as far into the dirt lane as she could, then stopped. She put the truck in park, set the emergency brake, grabbed her bag, and hopped out.

Just as it started to rain harder.

The wind coming off the Irish Sea whipped furiously, blowing icy cold air laced with brine all over Emma. She pulled her hoodie up and tucked her hair back.

"You're as crazy as the Pict, lass," Justin muttered. "Think about this, Emma," he said, following her up the dirt lane. "You've only been to Arrick in the past a handful o' times at best. You dunno know the area, save that wee silly map drawn with a crayon."

"Jake lent it to me and it was the only thing I had," she commented, walking faster. "And yes, I do remember the area. Somewhat. Now stop pestering me, Justin. You promised."

"Och, fine, fine," he said. "At least you wore your boots instead of those girlie sneakers you wear. Those flat rubbery soles would have landed you square on your arse."

Emma glared up at him and kept on walking. She wished now that she'd asked the big Pict to accompany her. Dumb, dumb, dumb.

At the end of the incline stood a flat, grassy mini-meadow. No bigger than half an acre, perhaps, it stretched all the way to the edge of a fifty-foot drop-off to the ocean. The roar of the sea crashing against the base was so deafening, that had Justin not had the capability of talking right into her head, she'd not be able to hear him at all.

Which might have been a good thing. He was awfully naggy.

Emma pulled out the map and studied it. The Pict had urged her to make marks with her red crayon, little marks that crossed the minimeadow and all the way to the edge. He'd then done a little loop with his finger, and it'd taken her several times to figure out just what he was asking her to draw. All this, mind you, in the space of a handful of minutes. She'd drawn it while Christian had been busy talking to Tristan about the joust.

She crossed the field, but when she neared the edge, Justin stopped her.

"Nay, lass. No farther. 'Tis dangerous."

"Justin," she hollered against the wind and rain, "I know what I'm doing. *Trust me.*"

Emma gave him one last stare, then tossed her bag down and knelt on the spongy grass. She pulled out her empty makeup remover container and shoved it into her pocket, along with a length of rope she'd snitched from the sisters' garden house. Close to the edge of the cliff was a rowan bush—just as the Pict had told her there would be. She quickly tied off the rope, then looped it around her waist.

"Oh, no. Oh *hell*, no!" hollered Justin. "Emma Calhoun, you cannot do this!"

With fierce determination, Emma met Justin's fearful, angry gaze. "Watch me."

And with not as much fear as she'd expected, she eased herself over the edge.

Chapter 34

Emma's heart was in her throat. For all her false courage, that was exactly what it was. False.

She was scared out of her gourd.

But she was more scared of losing Christian, so this attempt to change their fate was *nothing* compared to a lifetime without him.

Besides, she tried to console herself, *you are a master dangler, don't forget.*

She took a long, deep, calming breath. "Okay. You are oh-kay."

"Emma?"

Slowly, she looked up. Justin's head peered over the edge at her. His face was wrought with worry, then relief. "Christ, woman, if I were no' already dead, you'd be killin' me about now." He looked below her. "Are you tryin' to tell me Beuno's Well is in the *cliff side*?"

Emma smiled. "So says that crazy Pict. Now," she said, looking below herself to the sea and rocks, "I'm a bit busy dangling here, Justin, and I have to admit, it's not the *coziest* of places. Can you let me find what I'm looking for and then interrogate me?"

Justin frowned. "Just hurry. You're makin' me bloody nervous."

"Well, you're making me bloody nervous by talking so much. Now shush," Emma continued, feeling the rock face with her boot toe. The Pict had indicated she'd feel a foothold, and once she did, she'd have to kick it—*hard*. It took several minutes, and by the time her toe found *something*, she was drenched. Her lips chattered, but she didn't care.

Justin's face hovered over the edge.

"I think this is *it*!" she hollered, kicking the place with all her might. She felt it give, and she reared her foot back and kicked it again. Three times later and she felt the hard-packed earth give way. Rock and dirt tumbled to the sea below. She felt a *whoosh* of air escape the hole she'd just created. It was just big enough for her to shimmy inside. She shoved first her feet inside, then her bottom.

The rope prevented her from going farther.

"Oh, crapola," she growled, and untied the rope from her waist. She let it dangle there, and scooted inside a hole in the cliff she was positive no one had seen the inside of in centuries.

"Are you okay, lass?" hollered Justin. "I'm coming in there wi' you."

"Yes! I'm fine, and no—if you came in here with me, we'd merge. It's too tight a fit," she said, turning and inching slowly down on her belly, feet first.

Suddenly, she heard a cracking noise, slow at first, then faster, louder. The earth beneath her shifted, and in the next second, the surface gave way. Emma yelped in surprise, then screamed as her body flailed, and she spiraled down, down . . .

"Chris, you've got to come *now*," said Justin.

Christian turned from the group of warriors hell-bent on setting up home and hearth directly in the great hall. He didn't like the urgency in his friend's voice. "What is it?"

"Emma."

"Och, *Crist*," said Gawan under his breath.

Christian turned to Gawan and stared. "What *is* it?" he said, louder this time.

"No time to explain," said Justin. "Christian, you follow me. Gawan, take your helicopter to the cliff known to be the area of St. Beuno's. You know the one?"

"Aye, I do."

Christian simply stared at both of them. "Are you two mad? What is going on?" he thundered.

"Chris, now," urged Justin, and disappeared.

Christian glared at Gawan, then followed his friend, as only ghosts do.

They emerged at the cliff together. Rain poured, and the wind whipped ferociously. Christian glared at Justin. "Please tell me she did not come here," he bellowed. Then, he spied a length of rope, tied off to the rowan next to the edge.

"Christ's blood!" he roared, and hurried to the edge. He whirled on Justin. *"Where is she?"*

"Down below," Justin yelled. "Over the edge and into the cliff itself."

Christian didn't wait for an answer, or an explanation. He leaned over the edge and willed himself into the same mortal space Emma was presently in. No sooner had his mind envisioned it than he was there, beside her.

"Oh, Christ, Emm," he breathed, taking in her form. "Emma?" he said, and when she didn't respond, he leaned his head to her ear. "Emma? Can you hear me?"

It was then Christian realized just where they were. A small cave—a cavern, really, no bigger round than a large cistern. A natural cistern, not man-made. The light from the hole Emma had created shot through, casting a dim glow over the grotto.

And in the center, where Emma lay and where he now knelt, was a very, very small body of shimmering, crystal clear water.

Emma groaned, and his eyes were immediately on her. "Emma?" he called again. "Hold on, love. Help's coming."

Emma's eyes fluttered open, and she glanced around. "Oops," she said softly.

Christian stared down at her. "Oops is right," he said. "Are you hurt?"

"I'm not sure," she said, then held out her hand.

He hadn't noticed she was clutching something. It was a vial, or a bottle.

"Here." She slowly reached up with her other hand and unscrewed the small blue lid.

"What is this?" he asked.

She coughed, and a pained look came across her face. "It's St. Beuno's mystical healing water, Chris," she said softly. She gently shook the vial. "For you."

Christian fought back anger. "Why, love? Nothing can be done for me. I've already *died*."

She looked at him, and the pleading in her eyes all but cracked his heart in half. "Please?" she begged, and that nearly undid him. "Humor me," she said. "Love."

His heart jumped to his throat at her word of endearment. Neither had confessed their love to the other yet, and for good reason.

Every time in the past they'd done so, disaster had soon followed.

"Chris?" said Justin. "There's no room for me in there. Is she all right?"

"Aye," Christian said, knowing he was probably lying. "Watch for Gawan."

"Don't be mad at them," Emma said. "I beseeched them both."

Christian gave her a forced smile. "So you did."

She held the vial up again. "Please. Just . . . try it? Even if it splashes right through you, try drinking it. Bring your head closer and open your mouth."

"Only because I cannot refuse you," Christian said, and he lowered his head and parted his lips.

Weakly, she lifted the vial and poured the mystical water in.

It, of course, leaked right out.

Her face fell. "I'm so . . . sorry . . ."

"Emma," he breathed.

Her eyes closed, and she drew in a long, ragged breath. Her arm dropped, her hand fell open, her fingers barely grasping the vial of water.

"Emma!" he yelled.

Then, his body jerked. Pain shot through his limbs, his vessels—as if someone had the end of one of his nerves and was yanking fiercely on it. He doubled over, grasping his stomach. "What—*Emma*!" He looked at her, unmoving, still as death. "No! I will not lose you! Not again! *Not this time!*"

Amidst the writhing spasms of pain, Justin's shouting, and the whirring of Gawan's helicopter blades above St. Beuno's, Christian willed his hand to reach toward Emma's, and somehow, curled his fingers around the vial she so desperately held on to. His hand turned to fire at the strength in which he conjured to heft the small container to Emma's lips. Breathing hard, he tipped the remaining contents into her parted lips. When the last drop seeped out, he dropped the vial.

And then he covered Emma's mouth with his, and whispered the words he prayed she'd hear. She'd already heard them once. He now said them a final time.

"*Cara 'ch hwchwaneg awron na 'r 'n flaen amsera Adfeiliasis i mewn cara chennych,*" he whispered for her ears only. "*Fi would braidd cerdd 'n dragwyddol, fel bwci at 'ch ochra, na heboch o gwbl.*"

"I love you more now than the first time I fell in love with you," he whispered in English. "And I would rather walk eternally, as a ghost by your side, than without you at all."

As pitch-blackness forced its way behind his eyes, and shards of glass pricked his skin, he slowly, slowly slipped farther away. "Live, Emma," he whispered. "Christ, please."

And then a wall of darkness crashed over him . . .

"Emma? Lass, open your eyes."

Emma heard Gawan's voice. Far away at first, it became annoyingly loud. Difficult, since he had such a cute voice to begin with.

Just then, she forced her eyes to open. She blinked several times, and looked around.

She was in her rented bedroom, at Arrick.

"Christian?" she said, looking around. She blinked several more times to clear her blurry vision. "Chris?"

"Emma, lie still," said Gawan, moving to sit beside her on the bed. "How do you feel?"

"What happened?" she asked, ignoring his question. She tried to push herself up on her elbows, but his big hands held her back.

Suddenly, Jason was on her other side.

"Sit back, Emma," the young knight said. "Stop trying to move so."

"Will everyone stop trying to tell me not to move," she grumbled. "Where is Christian?"

Just then, Jason wrapped his big, warm hands around hers and threaded their fingers together. He stared at her, his light green eyes boring into hers gravely. "He saved you, lady," he said, his voice cracking. "Somehow, he mustered the mortal strength and saved your life. I am ever so glad."

Emma frowned. "Saved *my* life?" She turned to Gawan. "No, that's not right. I saved *his* life. I made him drink the vial of mystical water." She glanced around the room. Justin stood against the wall, a somber look upon his face. Godfrey was there, as were all four Ballaster sisters.

Emma looked first at Jason, then at Gawan. "I ... found the well. It's real," she insisted. "And Christian drank the water I'd collected."

"Aye," said Gawan quietly. "And in doing so you gave him just enough mortal strength to heft that same vial from your hands and pour the rest of the water into your mouth." He brushed a strand of hair from her eyes. "The fall killed you, Emma. You ... died." He bent his head down to her ear, for words meant for her alone. "He gave you his newly acquired life force, Emma. He gave it back to you, so you could live."

Emma's throat constricted, so much that she couldn't swallow or breathe. She pushed herself up, against Gawan's restrictive hand. "You mean ... he's *gone*?" Her voice cracked.

The look on Gawan's face spoke the truth.

Waves of pain crashed over Emma, her breath sharp and catching in her throat. "No," she said quietly. "Please, no."

"I'm so verra sorry, girl," said Gawan, brushing her cheek with his knuckles. " 'Tis a mighty love he had for you." He grasped her hand with his and moved it over her heart. "He will always be here, Emma."

Jason grasped her hand tighter.

And Emma closed her eyes tightly as the ache of losing Christian engulfed her.

Sometime later, Emma woke up. She didn't want to, really, but her body had said, *Enough*. Slowly, she opened her eyes.

Long shadows stretched across the bed and floorboards, and a lone shaft of waning light lit the person's face that still ferociously held on to her hand.

"You're awake," Jason said, his smooth, accented voice somewhat soothing her.

"I guess so," she said. "How long have I been sleeping?"

Jason shifted in his chair to face her. "A score of hours." He brushed her hair from her eyes. "I'm sorry, Emma."

Emma fought back another wash of tears. She'd cried herself to sleep, and thought she'd cried out her last one. Apparently, she'd built up a new store of them. "I know," she said. "Thank you for staying. You didn't have to."

"Of course I did," he said. "Christian would have boxed my ears otherwise."

She gave a wan smile. "You're right."

They were quiet for a spell; then Jason spoke. "St. Beuno's water really is mystical," he said. "You believed."

"Christian did, too," she answered.

"Will you leave?" he said quietly.

With a heavy sigh, she gave a single nod. "Yes."

"When?" he said, his voice cracking.

"As soon as possible." She didn't know how much longer she could be at Arrick without Christian by her side.

"Stay at least through tomorrow," Jason said. "He would have wanted you to attend the All Hallows' Eve banquet. And the sisters are so looking forward to your presence, as well. Go with me. Please?"

Emma looked into his eyes, and she knew right away she couldn't refuse him. "Okay," she said. "I couldn't say no to you if I tried."

He smiled. "One of my better qualities." He grinned. "Thank you."

Emma prayed she could manage one more day at Arrick-by-the-Sea.

Chapter 35

"He would have liked this, you know," said Willoughby. Then she blew her nose into a white handkerchief. "Oh, Emma! We're so sorry!"

Emma fought back another round of tears and patted Willoughby's back as she hugged her. "I know, and I wouldn't dream of missing the occasion—especially if it was something Christian would have wanted."

Can you grieve someone's passing if they'd died more than eight hundred years in the past?

Answer: *Yes*. And it hurt twice as much.

"Your bracelet looks exquisite on you," commented Willoughby.

Emma glanced down at it. It was so lightweight, she'd forgotten she even had it on. "Thank you. It was a very nice thing for you to do."

"Emma, you look lovely," said Jason, walking into the sitting room. "As always." He moved toward her, kissed her cheek, and held out his arm. "Shall we?"

Emma slipped her hand into the crook of Jason's leather-jacket-clad muscular arm and forced a smile on her lips. "Yes, and thank you."

How he thought she looked lovely, she hadn't a clue. She wore her same old comfy jeans, and a big bulky brown sweater. Her eyes were swollen despite the cold wash and makeup.

"Sort of funny, having a banquet at midnight," she commented. She glanced at Willoughby and her sisters, who were accompanying them. "This is an annual thing, huh?"

Willoughby's eyes sparkled. "Oh, aye. 'Tis, indeed."

They left the manor together, she and Jason in the lead.

"Will you take me to the airport tomorrow?" asked Emma. She hated good-byes, and she knew she'd really hate one to Jason. A little more time with one of Christian's pals comforted her, somehow.

"Aye, I wouldn't think of allowing anyone else the task," he said. He leaned his head to hers. "I shall miss you, Emma Calhoun," he whispered. "Think you I could come for a visit sometime?"

She smiled at him. "I'd be mad if you didn't."

Minutes later, surprisingly, they were packed into Jason's Rover and the Ballasters' truck, and headed to the banquet. When they pulled onto an inclining dirt lane, Emma was surprised to find the gathering at the site of an ancient circle of standing stones. A breeze wafted through the copse of trees, and dead leaves flitted to the ground. Somewhere close by, a field of dried corn crackled as the brisk autumn wind slipped between the stalks. Above, a harvest moon, large, full, and bright, shone through the canopy of birch and oak, bathing everything it touched in glowing silver. Several bonfires flickered with orange flame. Tables were set out with covered dishes of food.

"You know," whispered Jason in her ear, " 'tis said that if a wish is made here at the stones, on the stroke of the bewitching hour, it might just come true."

His eyes sparkled with mischief.

Emma forced a smile. "I don't think my wish could come true."

He lifted a brow. "And here I thought you were fearless, Ms. Calhoun."

Emma stared at Jason for a long moment, then glanced about at the people gathered. She'd not really noticed before, but most were women. No, *all* were women. Funny, she thought. She wondered if the Ballasters belonged to a women's club of sorts.

Then, somewhere close by, a big *gong* echoed through the night air.

And so many things happened at once, Emma found it difficult to keep all of the events in order.

Out of nowhere, four large, cloaked figures emerged from the shadows. They surrounded Jason on both sides and before either he or Emma knew what was happening, they were pulling Jason away from her. Jason pulled viciously against them. He swore, and even at the tournament, Emma had never seen him look so furious. "Damn you, let me go! Emma!"

Emma looked around. "What's going on? Jason— hey!"

The figures stopped, but didn't release the young Dragonhawk knight. Emma surmised that they had to be men. No female—even four of them—could have held that fury restrained.

All at once, the banquet full of women moved toward her. The Ballasters were in the lead. Emma gaped, wondering what the seemingly innocent sisters and their cohorts could be up to.

She found out soon enough.

"Bring her to the Stone o' Gwynneldh," said Willoughby in her singsong voice. Then a chant began from the whole group. Emma could now easily distinguish that it was Welsh. First, it was only as a hum, and so low, Emma couldn't make out the words. Just as quickly, the wind kicked up, blowing leaves in crazy swirls—almost like miniature twisters—all over the banquet area. The chanting grew louder—so loud Emma could now only vaguely hear Jason's curses—and the leafy twisters danced around her. Willoughby, Maven, Millicent, and Agatha surrounded her as they drew close to the stone. All the while, that infuriating *gong* noise kept echoing through the trees. Maven gently pushed her back to the stone. Cold dampness seeped through her coat and clung to her skin. The pungent bite of brine settled on her tongue.

Willoughby stepped close and met her gaze. A copper pot she'd been carrying, tucked beneath her arm, emerged now, and she set it at Emma's feet. "As Jason said, you must make your wish, Emma Calhoun. You must make it and make it hastily! Make it as many times for as many chances!" she hollered over the increasing wind.

Confused, but feeling in her gut that the Ballasters wouldn't hurt her, she fought back tears. "What do you mean? What do I wish for? What could help now?" she yelled back.

"Only you know what lies in your heart, gel," said Willoughby. "Do it. Now!"

"Hurry," Jason yelled. He'd stopped fighting his restrainers. "Now, before the last stroke of the bewitching hour!"

Willoughby smiled. "Believe, child. You must believe."

For as many chances? Emma stared hard at Willoughby, drew a deep breath, then slowly let it out. She closed her eyes. She understood.

And she wished thirteen times in a row.

As her senses opened, the wind and leaves and darkness surrounded her, and the sea battered the cliffs, the frosty air clung like small flakes of ice to her skin. And while she repeated her wish over and over, the Ballasters grasped hands and began a new chant, all their own.

No, not a chant. More like a *spell*.

"Chan awron a throughout byth , Ddiddyma 'r bus-tachedig felltithia chan hoedlau yn ôl. Begone! Erioed adfer! Ad hyn 'n ddau eneidiau dangnefedd a hundeb!"

When the last stroke sounded, Emma opened her eyes. The chant ended. The wind ceased. The leaves flittered to the ground and lay still.

Everyone's eyes were on *her*.

And just that fast, every ounce of strength in Emma's body escaped, and her knees crumpled beneath her. The sisters all grasped her, and held her steady. Then Jason was there, holding her up. He pulled her close, her face pressed against the warmth of his chest. The scent of his leather jacket filled her lungs as she breathed deeply.

"I can't move," she muttered.

" 'Tis fine, girl," he said against her hair. "I shall hold you until you're able."

Jason held her as promised. His presence comforted her. Just knowing he was a friend of Christian's made her feel close to her love.

Just then, the four cloaked figures moved toward them. They reached up and pulled down their cowls. She felt Jason's body tense as Gawan, Tristan, Ethan, and Aiden stared back at them. The Ballasters crowded around. No one said anything for several moments.

Finally, Emma found the strength to speak. "I . . . don't understand."

Willoughby patted her cheek. "These were the only lads I knew who could hold young Jason here back long enough to get the finality of the spell in motion, love." She glanced at Gawan. "And I didn't think it would hurt overmuch to have a once-earthbound angel in our presence." She smiled at Emma. "We couldn't have Jason interfere. 'Twas no time left, and everything had to happen at exactly the precise moment. We couldn't speak of it to him, or anyone, beforehand. Especially to you. 'Twas forbidden. Even our young warrior Christian didn't know."

Emma stared long and hard at the older woman. "Who are you?"

Willoughby grasped her sisters' hands. They met one another's looks with a smile. "Let's just say we've been working on getting rid of that discombobulated curse of yours for quite some time now."

"Witches," muttered Aiden.

Emma's eyes widened. "Really?"

Willoughby shrugged.

"Does this mean . . . ," Emma began. She swallowed hard. "Christian will come back to me?"

A somber expression settled onto Willoughby's weathered features. She reached out and grasped Emma's hand in hers. "I'm so verra sorry, dear. Our intentions have always been to rescue you from that fatal curse you constructed so many centuries ago." She flashed a look at the others, then back to Emma. "We had no idea the turn of events would occur at St. Beuno's. 'Twas something no spell can reverse, I fear."

Emma's eyes filled with tears. "Why not?"

Gawan stepped forward and brushed her cheek with his knuckle. "Fate, lass."

Emma's insides hurt. A pain began in the pit of her stomach. A physical pain, as though someone had punched her in the gut. "Oh."

Gawan lifted her chin, forcing her to meet his gaze. "Whilst my friend is now gone, thanks to the Ballasters, Christian's soul and yours will one day reunite." He gave her a mournful smile. "Forever."

She nearly thought it would be better to at least see him every seventy-two years.

Tristan stepped forward and kissed her cheek. His sapphire eyes blazed in the moonlight. "I vow, 'twill be fine, girl. And we are all your family here, whenever you need us. Just as we always have been."

Emma gave a slight smile. At least she'd retain her memory of all the people from her past. From Christian's past. She met the gazes of Gawan, Tristan, Ethan, and Aiden. "Thank you," she whispered. She gripped Willoughby's hand. "I couldn't ask for a better family." She loved her parents, and her best friend, but these unbelievable people were her link to the man she'd loved for centuries, and whom she would love forever . . .

Jason hugged her tightly. "What did the sisters' spell mean?" he whispered in her ear.

Emma smiled at him and translated. "From now and throughout eternity, I annul the bungled curse from lifetimes ago. Begone! Never return! Allow these two souls peace and unity!"

Jason studied her, then smiled. "They're all right, you know. Everything will be fine. I can feel it. Now, come on, lass," he said, and chucked her under the chin with a knuckle. "Let's eat. I hear your tummy growling."

As Emma accompanied Jason, the knights, and the Ballasters in the feast, her heart sank again. She picked at her food, but for once in her life, hunger had taken a backseat.

She'd believed so hard in the water from St. Beuno's Well, and by God, it had worked. She hadn't counted on Christian believing in it, too. It was a relief to know that one day, she'd be reunited with her Intended. But for now, she ached for him so much, it pained her to breathe. She briefly wondered, no matter where Christian was, whether his heart would survive losing her again . . .

Suddenly she wanted to go home.

Forevermore Photography
Savannah, Georgia
Two months later . . .

"Emma, these are fantastic!" said Zoë, stretching on tiptoe and peering at one of Emma's newly framed photographs. "I can't believe you went to a real-life medieval jousting tournament." She turned and gave Emma a sly look. "I bet there were some hot guys there, huh?"

Emma smiled. "Yeah, there sure were."

And her heart still ached for one of them.

"God, who *are* these guys?" Zoë asked, pointing to one of Emma's favorites of Tristan and Gawan, in the sword-fighting arena.

"You wouldn't believe me if I told you," Emma muttered. She glanced at her palm, the one she'd cut on that small piece of glass. A slight line remained, and although it didn't hurt, she thought of it each time she flexed her fingers. And then she'd think of how Christian was so mad at her for even picking the stupid thing up. He'd stayed right by her side the whole time . . .

"You haven't been the same since you came home," Zoë said. "I thought I'd be the one down in the dumps, having my wedding postponed." She took in a deep breath. "But once Jay finishes this last tour in Afghanistan, he's done."

Emma smiled at her. "And I'll be all set to shoot your wedding."

Zoë walked over and stood before Emma, who was idly cleaning her lens. "It's closing time. Wanna go grab something to eat?"

Emma hadn't been able to tell Zoë or her parents about her heartbreak. Who would believe it? Who, in their right mind, would believe she'd fallen crazy in love with a ghost in the matter of a few weeks? And then lost that love?

Well, that actually wasn't correct.

She'd loved Christian of Arrick-by-the-Sea for centuries.

Another thing she couldn't share with anyone.

Thank God she'd made friends in the UK.

Ellie called frequently, as did the other wives. Jason? On a regular basis, as did Gawan and Justin Catesby, as well. And Godfrey had popped in on her several times. She finally had to shoo him away. Seeing him somehow made it hurt *worse*.

Still . . . life just wasn't the same . . .

"Emm, how 'bout it?"

Emma looked up at her friend. Zoë was running ninety-to-nothing lately, and she was glad. She didn't want her miserable. She gave her friend a weak smile. "I honestly don't feel like it, Zoë. You go ahead."

Zoë pulled her into a fierce hug. "If my stomach weren't screaming at me, I wouldn't dare go without you." She looked at her. "Want me to bring you something back?"

Emma smiled. "Yeah, sure."

"Okay." Zoë trotted down the creaky wooden steps, to the first floor. "See ya in a bit."

The downstairs door to the studio jingled as Zoë skipped out.

Leaving Emma alone.

Briefly, she glanced up at the photos on her walls. She'd taken so many great pictures at Castle Grimm, of the families, the kids, at the tournament—memories that brought Christian a little closer to her. She had to keep Christian's winning goblet safe at home. She wasn't sure she could explain the endearment to Zoë. Besides, she'd take what she could get.

It was all she had left of him. Besides centuries of memories. Thank God she'd been left those.

Just then, the door downstairs jingled again. "Delivery."

"Do I have to sign for it?" she called down.

No answer.

Hmm.

Pushing from her chair, Emma set aside her lens and cleaning cloth and trotted down the steps to the main hall of the studio. She scanned the room, but the FedEx guy must have just opened the door, set the package inside, and left. She spotted it, across the room, propped by the front door.

Walking to it, she hefted the box, approximately eleven by fourteen in diameter. She fished in her pocket for her knife to open it, then realized she'd left the knife upstairs. She couldn't imagine what was in the box. The last things she'd ordered were tiny little parts.

Quickly, she hastened upstairs. The waning afternoon light streamed through the window, and she couldn't help but think about the twinkling gloaming hour at Arrick. The light made her upstairs studio look surreal.

From the worktable, she lifted the knife and cut along the edge of the package.

Just as the bell on the door downstairs jingled. Again.

"Just a minute," she called out.

She pulled back the brown packing paper, revealing a load of Bubble Wrap.

Slowly, she slipped her knife along the tape and removed that, too.

A frame. A framed photograph.

A note ...

Nothing registered at once, yet everything washed over her at the same time. The photograph was of Christian, on the wall at Arrick, in full battle regalia, smiling from ear to ear. In the picture he held a single white rose, almost as if offering it to the viewer of the photo. How on earth had Christian's image been captured in a photograph?

Across the bottom of the frame, a note. All in big letters. A man's bold scrawl.

At the same time she read it, she *heard* it.

"Fyddi 'm gwraig achos byth?"

Will you be my wife for eternity?

Emma nearly dropped the frame as her head snapped up at the unmistakable, deep, strangely accented voice suddenly in her upstairs studio. They'd said the same ancient Welsh words she'd just read out loud.

Slowly, her mind registered the body as it climbed the last stair and stepped into view.

Her hands began to shake, and her breath lodged in her throat. Her heart slammed so hard against her chest, she gasped. It almost ached. Tears filled her eyes.

She looked. She blinked. She made her mouth work. "You can't be real . . ."

But striding across her two-hundred-year-old wood-planked floors was eight-hundred-plus-year-old Christian of Arrick-by-the-Sea. Same crazy hair, but pulled back at the nape, she imagined, with that sexy silver clasp. A white, long-sleeved cotton buttoned-up shirt, a pair of worn jeans, and boots. His face held one emotion.

Determination.

So stunned that his ghostly spirit had somehow made it back to her, she couldn't form a single solitary word. She just stood there, her hand gripping the frame, staring at his fast-approaching form.

"Christian?" she finally said softly.

When he reached her, just short of passing through her, he stopped. The scent of soap and freshly washed clothes wafted from him, and that ever-present, weighty stare bore into her, nearly causing her skin to catch on fire.

A scent wafted from him. That was a new one . . .

Then slowly, he reached out with one hand, and relieved her of the knife she still grasped so tightly.

Her jaw slacked open.

Then, he reached out with his other hand and relieved her of the frame she held on to for dear life.

She lost her breath.

And without the first word spoken, Christian, none too gently, wrapped his arms around Emma and pulled her so tightly against him, she all but lost her breath.

She'd gladly lose it a thousand more times.

She could *feel* him!

At first, he held her still. So still, she could barely move an inch. He buried his face in her hair, then her shoulder, inhaling, breathing.

Then his hands were everywhere, grasping her jaw, touching her ears, dragging a thumb across her lips. His eyes bore into hers with absolute wonder, and the most starved desire she'd ever in her life seen.

Oh, God—he was alive!

Still, without the first word being spoken, he grasped her head with his hands, used his thumbs to wipe the tears she'd cried, angled her just so, then slowly lowered his mouth to hers.

Just before his lips caressed hers, he whispered against them. "Christ, I love you, Emma Calhoun."

As soon as their mouths touched, heat collected in every ounce of Emma's body. Christian kissed her, not softly at all, but hungrily, uncontrolled, and he left nothing untasted. Fire pooled in her stomach as his tongue grazed hers, and his teeth pulled at her lower lip. Finally, when they were both out of breath, he pulled back, not too far, and stared into her eyes.

"You waited for me," he said, his voice near to cracking.

Emma tested her own voice. "I told you I would." Her head swam. She couldn't believe she was in his arms . . .

"So what's your answer? Aye or nay?"

Joy roared through every blood vessel in Emma's

body. So happy, she felt light-headed, as though she'd spiral to the floor if Christian weren't holding her upright.

Christian was holding her upright!

"If you don't answer me now, I shall shake the answer from you, woman."

With a laugh, Emma grabbed him by the hair and pulled him to her mouth. She kissed him, softly—softer than his feral-hunger kiss—murmuring against his soft lips with each kiss. "I love you, I love you, I love you . . ."

She'd get back to that later.

For now, she needed *this* kiss.

"Aye," she said, laughing out loud. "Definitely, aye!"

And it was there, in the waning afternoon light of Forevermore Studio, that an eight-hundred-plus-year-old warrior betrothed his equally eight-hundred-plus-year-old beloved Intended.

Emma had been in love with him forever.

They'd been given thirteen chances.

And finally, after thirteen tries, they'd *made* it.

She'd find out later the how of it all. Right now, she couldn't care less. All she wanted to do was remain in the tight, warm embrace of the other half of her heart.

And as the light faded from the studio, Christian held Emma in his arms and continued to kiss her breathless.

Epilogue

Arrick-by-the-Sea
Eveningish
Early spring . . .

"Holy ho-ho, I'm nervous!" cried Emma. She turned to her bridal party and smoothed the front of her gown. "How do I look?"

She sorely wished she could wear her Converses.

"Spectacular," breathed Zoë. "It's hard to believe. You—getting married!"

Emma exchanged a glance with her matrons.

They knew *just* how hard to believe it truly was.

"You're the most beautiful bride I've ever seen," whispered Emma's mom. She sniffed. "I'm so happy for you, dear."

Emma gave her mom a tight hug and kissed her on her cheek. "Thanks, Mom."

Emma stared at herself in the floor-length mirror in the Ballasters' manor. She'd chosen a simple, cream satin shift, sleeveless, with the smallest of pearls beaded at the scooping neckline.

The back scooped way lower.

They'd told her Christian would approve.

Form-fitting clear to her knees, the dress did feel . . . nice. More than nice. It felt . . . *right*.

Her party had given her the greatest traditional bridal gifts.

Her mom, something old: her grandmother's cameo. She'd pinned it to her left shoulder.

Andi, something new: a beautiful set of teardrop pearl earrings.

Amelia, something borrowed: a lovely pearl bracelet that matched Andi's gift perfectly.

Zoë, something blue: a small sapphire pin to wear in her hair.

Allie gave her a silver sixpence to wear in her shoe. She'd told Emma Gabe's mother had passed down one just like it for generations. Now Emma had one of her own.

She thought it was a lovely tradition.

Finally, her mom adjusted Emma's veil, which hung to her jaw in the front, and to her waist at the back.

A knock sounded at the door. It was Emma's dad. "Ready in there?"

Emma let out a long sigh. "Absolutely."

They all filed out.

As the bridal party walked ahead, Emma held tightly to her father's arm. He glanced down at her.

"Are you happy?"

Emma beamed. "You can't imagine how happy, Dad."

As they stepped outside, the crispest of late-evening April breezes lifted her veil.

"And you absolutely want to live here?" he asked.

Emma nodded. "Definitely."

He leaned down and kissed her through her veil. "You've always known what you've wanted in life, haven't you?"

She supposed she certainly had.

He waited for her by the Dangling Steps in Arrick's bailey.

As they walked along the lantern-lit lane, they chatted, Emma and her dad, and a peace fell over her as they passed through the gatehouse. Everything that had happened still seemed so surreal.

Sneaky Ballasters, they'd apparently worked for seventy-two years—twice—to get an aged spell reversed. It had worked, but it was only meant to work for one soul.

Hers.

Emma still couldn't believe the crazy things they'd done to produce their magic on her. Including feeding her a bunch of cinnamon-laced potions, crazy Welsh concoctions brewed with her hair, and eek!—some of her blood—as well as some ingredients she'd rather not think of, to keep her from gaining her memory too soon. Little devils.

Rather, little *witches*.

She'd love them for it always.

Little had the Ballasters realized that the spell-that-could-not-be-spoken-aloud would not work by itself. True, they'd performed superb White Witch magic in order to keep Emma's memory from returning too early. And the final spell in which they chanted at the aged stone on All Hallows' Eve had played a significant part, as well. Had they not performed each step precisely, nothing would have turned out the way it had.

When Emma's memory had returned, she had indeed changed her mind-set. She'd been determined to set her love free of roaming.

She'd followed her heart's belief to St. Beuno's, where she'd rescued Christian's soul, as well. Then, he'd rescued hers. Both of their sacrifices had reversed Christian's own vow to await his love for eternity, as well as set into motion the ending of Emma's own discombobulated spell. It had set them both free.

Now their souls would be together. Forever.

Funny, though. When Christian had disappeared, he'd regained his earthly body in the last place he'd lost it, during the Second Crusade. Just inside the boundaries of Jerusalem, a family had taken a lost and wandering Christian to a local infirmary. Once he'd been released, that same family had taken him in. Finally, his memory returned, and he'd managed a call to Gawan. The Lord of Grimm had immediately gone after Christian.

And then he'd returned to Emma.

Emma would be eternally grateful to the Abdeil family.

Just as they entered the bailey, Emma gasped. She'd not been allowed to see it since the decorating. The decision made on a twilight wedding, tiny candles had been lit all over the walls, in every crevice that would hold a candle. Lovely satin-covered chairs to match her dress were set in rows, from the Dangling Steps all the way back to the gatehouse. A narrow aisle lay between the sides, dusted with rose petals.

In those chairs sat the largest group of medieval men she'd ever seen.

The Munros, the Dreadmoors, the Conwyks, and the MacGowans, not to mention the ghostly folk she'd come to love so much, filled each seat. As a harp in the corner played the absolute loveliest of melodies, her father walked her . . . straight to Christian.

Emma could barely take her eyes from his.

Dressed in new battle regalia, with a polished suit of chain mail and covered with a long black cloak and double swords, minus the helmet, he stole her breath.

Christian's eyes locked on to hers, and followed her every step until she and her father reached the end of the aisle.

Then, Mr. Calhoun gave Emma to Christian.

Emma gladly accepted the exchange.

Jason gave her a wicked grin and a wink.

Gawan, Christian's best man, smiled at her from the other side of Christian.

"Do you, Christian de Gaultiers of Arrick-by-the-Sea, take this woman, Emma Calhoun, as your eternal beloved forever? Until death claims you both?"

Christian smiled as he slipped the most breathtaking platinum and diamond ring over her finger. "Aye, indeed I do."

"Do you, Emma Calhoun, take this man, Christian de Gaultiers of Arrick-by-the-Sea, as your eternal beloved forever? Until death claims you both?"

Emma's eyes burned with tears as she slipped a plain platinum band over his finger. "Aye."

A light chuckle ran through the crowd.

The priest said a short prayer in Welsh, then in English, and gave his blessing. "Please, kiss this bride, Christian."

He grinned. "Don't you worry," he whispered.

And he kissed her.

It was the craziest reception Emma had ever been to.

She loved every moment of it.

Presently, she was dancing with the handsomest medieval guy in the bailey.

Christian looked down at her with the absolute most starved look she'd ever seen. His eyes wandered from her chin, to her cheeks, to her ears, to her lips.

It made her skin turn hot.

"Mind if I cut in?"

The expression on Christian's face turned from ravenous to furious in a matter of seconds. It nearly made Emma burst out laughing.

Christian pulled his mouth close to Emma's ear. "I vow if one more idiot takes you from me, I shall strangle him."

Emma giggled.

Christian stood aside, and Justin stepped into his place.

"Wow," Emma said, smiling up at the rogue pirate. "This will be a trick to pull off, huh?"

Just grinned. "Not at all, lass. You just follow my lead."

And then Emma danced with the rest of the gorgeous medieval men, one by one, in the bailey. She'd known most of them for centuries.

After Tristan whirled her around the bailey so fast she thought she'd get dizzy, and Gawan elegantly danced a medieval step or two, and Ethan and Gabe took turns dancing versions of, strangely enough, the robot, followed by the waltz, Jason then took the lead.

"You know," he began, smiling down at her, "I must say you're the loveliest bride I've ever encountered." He twirled her about. "And I must confess, were it not for Sir Arrick, I would have tried my very best to woo you myself."

Emma smiled at the young knight. "Why, thank you. I do believe you would have been pretty hard to resist."

Ghosts from past centuries blended with men who'd lived in their time, as well as folks from the present. Somehow, to see a wild, blue-painted Pict warrior dancing with Zoë just seemed . . . right. Weird, but right. Her parents and best friend had had no choice but to accept the fact that there were unexplained things in the world—especially when said unexplained things had approached them, passed through them, and then had bowed and charmed the pants off them.

She'd thank that crazy Justin Catesby later for making her folks' transition a smooth one. Well, as smooth as could be expected. Especially when the Pict warrior had greeted her parents.

Emma and that same wild, blue-painted Pict warrior had shared a dance, too.

And Emma had indeed thanked him for his help with Beuno's Well.

Right through the blue war paint, he'd blushed.

Emma had decided to keep the fact that she'd been born several centuries before to herself. She didn't want to overload her parents.

The Ballasters beamed as they'd gathered around Emma, sharing hugs and squeals, and clapping hands. Willoughby pulled her close, squeezed her in a tight hug, and kissed her cheek. "We are so happy for you, young Emma. You and Christian are going to be so verra happy together." She smiled. "At last!"

"Aye," said Maven. "And the plans to rebuild Arrick are simply breathtaking."

Emma smiled and grabbed each of their hands. "Thank you all, so very much. None of this would be happening if you sisters hadn't taken on the case of Emma and Christian."

"We're so very glad we did," said Willoughby.

"And your plans to open your photography studio will continue, aye?" asked Millicent.

"Oh, indeed," said Agatha. "To have that view of the sea whilst you work? Spectacular!"

"Yes," Emma said. "It was all Christian's idea." She'd never have asked for it, and as much as she loved Arrick, she never would have asked to renovate the ruins. Her income as a photographer wasn't too bad, but it wasn't enough to support a castle renovation.

Christian's, though, was.

Gawan had retained every single penny the Crusader had ever made. All along, that devil Gawan had had an in with the higher-ups. He'd known, way back when Christian had first died, that things would eventually be turned around. Yet he'd had to keep it to himself—even from Christian. Although a modest amount of coin back in the twelfth century, the money Christian had made as a knight was an astoundingly enormous amount now.

He, for lack of a better term, was *loaded*. And he wanted to rebuild Arrick-by-the-Sea. Gawan had been remorseful that Christian had felt no desire to keep Arrick Castle up, and the ghost had refused to allow Gawan to do it himself. Luckily, though, Arrick had been strongly built. It wasn't in total disrepair. And Emma absolutely loved it.

"And Jason's going to build your photography chamber, isn't he?" asked Willoughby. "He did a marvelous job with Sir Tristan's and Sir Gawan's brooding chambers."

Emma glanced at Jason, who gave her a wicked grin. "Yes, he did. I can hardly wait to see what he does with my studio."

Emma took a second to glance around the bailey. In the light still cast by thousands of tiny candles and lanterns, she took in all the people she'd come to love— alive and not so alive. How very fortunate she was.

She'd been given a second chance.

Well, actually thirteen, she supposed.

And she'd not waste a second of it.

Christian hadn't been able to keep his eyes off her all night. Every time she looked, his eyes were on her.

It all but made her catch on fire.

"Thank God, we're finally alone," he whispered.

And they truly were. The Ballasters had taken up a grand offer to visit Castle Grimm, leaving Christian and Emma the manor to themselves.

Only they weren't in the manor.

She was wed to a medieval warrior, and medieval warriors liked the outdoors.

Christian, with the help of Gawan and Jason, had created a beautiful wedded grotto in the ruins. Behind a mountain of white gauze, they'd somehow managed to construct a wedding bed against the far bailey wall, complete with an enormous outdoor fireplace.

She wasn't sure she ever wanted to face whoever had helped her husband do that.

Oh, the humiliation.

" 'Tis the bewitching hour," whispered Christian, pulling her close.

Emma rested her head against his chest. "It's not even October."

"Doesn't matter."

She looked up at him. "Will the ghosts leave us alone?"

He grinned. "Justin has personally vowed to make it so."

Emma stared at him, her heart filled with joy. And something else.

"What's wrong?" Christian asked, never missing a thing.

She smiled. "I think I'm nervous."

He pulled her close then, and kissed her so softly she felt his lips shiver against hers. "Do you recall the first time I kissed you, Emm?"

Emma sighed against his mouth. "Good Lord, Chris. How could I ever forget that? You asked my permission. I thought there was nothing sexier."

Christian chuckled softly. He lifted her face to his. "I'm asking again, Emma. May I kiss you?"

Emma smiled. "Please."

Christian leaned toward her, settled his mouth over hers, and kissed her lightly.

Emma squirmed. "I'm still nervous."

I shall remedy that for you, Lady Arrick. I promise." He moved his lips to her ear. "Come with me." He lifted her hand, kissed the finger that now held her wedding ring, and smiled.

Emma shivered with anticipation.

And with the roar of the Irish Sea, Christian slipped his hand down her arm and linked their fingers together. Slowly, he pulled her to the grotto.

The fire blazed in the black iron hearth, and Christian stared down at her, his eyes starved, hungry. Without another word, he pushed her straps aside and placed his warm lips to her shoulder. His big, calloused hands moved over her exposed back, traced her spine, and eased around her waist, and Emma pushed her fingers through that crazy hair—which she'd forbidden him to cut—and pulled his mouth to hers.

From there, they created their own fire ...

Christian's mouth dragged against hers, tasting, suckling, and then he moved to her throat, pressed light kisses against her skin, and moved farther upward.

"I've waited so long to have you this way," he said in a low voice, against the shell of her ear. "Christ, I'm not sure how much longer I can stand it."

"Then don't," she said, and unbuttoned the shirt he'd worn beneath his mail.

It and her dress hit the floor.

Slowly, he lifted her in his arms, she in her slip, he in his wedding trousers, and kissed her as he walked her to the bed. He followed her down into the white softness, and with wonderment in his wide blue eyes, he kissed her everywhere he touched. His hands skimmed every surface of her body, and her heart raced out of control.

When Emma traced his back with her fingertip, and down his spine, he turned to her then, and without words, relieved her of the rest of her clothes. She did the same for him.

It was then she noticed one of the tattoos on his chest. She'd seen it before, had been curious about it. She traced her fingertips over it now. "What did you say this symbol meant?" she asked softly, in between kisses.

"He pulled back and stared into her eyes. " 'Tis your

name in Pict, love," he whispered. "I've always carried you with me."

And with that, with their bodies entwined, just like their hearts, they kissed, and moved, and became one. Emma's skin burned with every touch, every brush of Christian's hands, his lips. As they found their release together, he kissed her softly then, long, and deep, and pulled her to his chest.

"I would wait nine more centuries for you," he whispered, and buried his face in her neck. "I've loved you forever, Emma de Gaultiers."

Emma's heart soared with joy. She'd found the other half of her soul for the thirteenth time.

And this time, it was for keeps.

"I've loved you forever, too, Mr. Arrick." Then she whispered in his ear. "Thirteen really is a lucky number, aye?"

At that, her husband grinned. Then he kissed the breath from her.

And together, they became one again.

Acknowledgments

Once again, I send heartfelt thank-yous to the following for making *Thirteen Chances* such a special story for me.

To my agent, Jenny Bent, and my editor, Laura Cifelli. I appreciate all that you do! You both have made my writing so much better! I couldn't have been teamed up with a better pair of ladies. Thank you!

To my husband, Brian, and fantastic kids, Kyle and Tyler. Thanks for the inspiration and motivation! (And for leaving me blessedly *alone* when I'm on deadline!)

This time I won't mention all the crazy and silly stuff my friends get into (and coerce me to do too—wink wink!). This time, a true thank-you. I want Kim Lenox, Betsy Kane, Molly Hammond, Eveline Chapman, Allison Bunton, Valerie Morton, Karol Miles, and Rita-Marie Hester to know how very special they are. Their encouragement and enthusiasm throughout the writing of my books are as unforgettable and cherished as their friendships. A girl couldn't ask for a better group of pals. You will always have the dearest of places in my heart. And I mean it!

For my *whole* family. All of you: Mom, Dad, sisters, brothers, brothers-in-law, cousins, aunts, uncles—I love you all. You're the best!

For my sweet and crazy Denmark Sisterhood. I love you guys!

The fabulous band Linkin Park got me through hours and hours of writing. I love them! Thanks, guys!

A giant movie poster of Brendan Fraser and Alicia Silverstone, lip-locked in the sweetest kiss, from the film *Blast from the Past*, inspired me through the writing of Christian and Emma. If you've ever read my acknowledgments before, you know that Brendan is one of my favorites. Thanks, Brendan!

A final thank-you to my readers. Without you, none of this would be possible. Your e-mails and letters are the most rewarding of all, and I cherish each and every one of them.

Read on for a sneak peek at "A Christmas Spirit" from

CINDY MILES

DAWN
HALLIDAY

CINDY
MILES

SOPHIE
RENWICK

A Highlander Christmas

WRAPPED IN A KILT, HE'S
HER HOLIDAY WISH COME TRUE

Appearing in the upcoming anthology
A Highlander Christmas, along with novellas
by Dawn Halliday and Sophie Renwick
On sale November 3, 2009

Northwest Highlands
Somewhere near Inverness
December, present day

"Please don't die, please don't die, *puh-leeze* don't die," crooned Paige MacDonald. Gripping the steering wheel so tightly her knuckles turned white, she stared through the swirling snow ahead and held her breath. The little standard-shift rental car sputtered, lurched, but thankfully kept going.

A few minutes passed as Paige crept her way up the snowy lane, and then her heart soared. Up ahead a single light twinkled through the trees. A little farther and she'd be at the Gorloch Inn.

Suddenly the car coughed and pitched, and the engine died. With a heavy sigh, Paige shifted into neutral, coasted to the edge of the lane, and let the car roll to a stop. She yanked up the emergency brake and stared out into the blinding white downfall of snow. The wind whipped furiously, causing the rental car to sway. For as far as she could see, there was nothing but white. Unfolding the map she'd thrown on the passenger seat, she studied the small, threadlike marking that was supposed to be the road to her bed-and-breakfast. No signs, nothing—

not even a sign for Gorloch. She frowned. Lost *and* her car had officially bit the big one. *Great.*

Glancing at her watch, she silently said a naughty word, then leaned her head back and closed her eyes.

Perhaps a driving tour of the northwest Highlands in December hadn't been the most thought-through plan she'd ever had. But she'd been desperate to get out of the city, away from her job, her cramped apartment. So she was lost. And her car had croaked. And there was one heck of a storm outside.

At least she wasn't spending another Christmas home alone.

Grabbing her overnight pack, Paige tugged her hat down over her ears, tightened her scarf, and buttoned her wool coat. Pulling on her gloves, she gave a hefty sigh and uttered a bit of encouragement, then opened the door and jumped out into the cold.

The gray, wintry skies had begun to turn shadowy; before long, night would fall. She certainly didn't want to be stranded in the woods after dark. She began to move quickly.

Trudging up the snowy lane, Paige made her way to Gorloch's. With the biting cold and wall of snowflakes, it seemed to take forever. Not a sound in the air except the crunch of ice beneath her boots and the wind rushing through the branches. It felt dreamlike, yet calming at the same time. It looked like a true winter wonderland. The path wended around a copse of trees, and when it straightened, Paige stopped and gasped. Her breath slowly puffed out in front of her like white, billowy smoke.

The lone twinkling light hadn't come from a regular bed-and-breakfast or from a stone cottage or even from a Highland croft.

It came from a dark, looming castle.

Paige stood still, staring. An ancient stone fortress

rose from the frosty mist, uninviting and ominous. Apprehension gripped her, yet her lips were numb and snowflakes caked her eyelashes. She had no choice now but to continue on. Shifting her pack, Paige shoved her hands deep into her pockets and made for the castle doors.

As she neared the entrance, she noticed two things. One, the main castle tower was enormous. Two, unless there was a garage somewhere around back, it didn't look like a soul was home. With a deep breath, she took the remaining walk to the double doors, lifted her hand, grasped a large, tarnished brass ring, and knocked. She stepped back and waited.

No one answered.

Teeth chattering and her body shivering uncontrollably, Paige knocked again. Loudly. Seconds turned into minutes as she waited. *Oh, gosh—I'm going to freeze to death.*

"No vacancy. Go away."

Paige jumped at the sound of the deep voice and looked around. "Um, c-could I j-just use your phone to c-call a cab? My c-car's dead," she said, teeth chattering.

Moments passed, and Paige sighed and turned to leave.

"Come in, but be quick about it."

Paige looked about, but still saw no one. Should she go in? Why didn't he open the door himself? Her body quaked with uncontrolled shivers, and she stamped her feet and rubbed her arms vigorously.

"Come in before you bloody freeze to death."

With hesitancy Paige turned the handle, pushed open the massive door, and stepped inside. The wind caught the heavy oak, pulled it from her fingers, and slammed it shut behind her. She jumped, then looked around. She saw no one. A small table in the foyer contained an open ledger and a pen. A lamp burned low and cast shadows across the narrow space. Paige's gaze moved slowly and peered into the dim room beyond. "Hello?"

"Jus' sign in, lass, and sit. I'll be wi' you in a moment."

"So, you do have vacancy?" she asked, thinking she'd heard wrong the first time.

A moment passed, then that deep voice mumbled, "Aye." The throaty brogue was so thick that she barely understood the man.

"Er, great. Thanks," said Paige. Grasping the pen, she steadied her shaking hand and signed in.

In the great hall, Gabriel Munro shoved a hand through his hair and paced. He stopped, glanced at the girl, pushed his thumb and forefinger into his eye sockets, and cursed. Then he rested his hands on his hips and paced a bit more.

What, by the devil's cloven hooves, was he to do with *her*? Damn the Craigmires' arses for leaving him here alone. The old fool and his wife had sworn the weather would keep tourists away.

Gabriel glanced at the girl, who was still shivering in the foyer. Her gaze shifted first left, then right. Then she sat down.

The weather had kept all away, save *that one*. What was she doin' out in such a storm? And alone, as well?

He'd have let her leave, had she no' admitted to being stranded. He damn well couldna let her stay out in the snow and freeze. And freeze she surely would have, in such a wee, thin coat and scarf. Even the hat she had pulled nearly to her eyes looked paltry. 'Twas apparent she was no' from the Highlands. Her accent had been the proof o' that.

Now he was stuck wi' her. Alone.

Christ.

He had no choice but to handle things until the girl

left. With a final silent curse, Gabriel took a deep breath, readied himself, and stepped into the foyer.

The girl sprang to her feet the moment Gabriel appeared. Her eyes widened as she took in the sight of him, and he prayed mightily that he'd dressed appropriately. Still, she said nothing. She all but gaped.

"You're wantin' a room, aye?" said Gabriel.

She nodded, and her cheeks flushed. "I do."

He gave a curt nod toward the desk. "Chamber thirteen. Grab your key from yon drawer and follow me."

The girl's eyes darted to the desk, and with a gloved hand, she slowly pulled out the drawer. Finding the key, she picked it up, shouldered her pack, and looked at him. "Okay," she said quietly. Her voice, smooth and feminine, quivered just a bit. From fear or the chill, he didna know which.

Gabriel strode across the great hall toward the staircase. He'd settle her in for the night, then retreat to his own chamber. Hopefully by the morn, the weather would clear and she'd leave.

Just as the girl stepped into the great hall, every light in the room extinguished, leaving it pitch-black. She froze and waited several moments before she finally grew impatient, cleared her throat, and drew a deep breath. "Hello?" she called, and her voice cracked.

Gabriel stood mere yards from the girl. He could sense her urgency, yet he found himself unable to answer her calls. 'Twas as if his bloody tongue were tied. While she couldn't see in the darkness, he could, and verra clear. While the blackness covered him, he boldly studied the quiet American lass.

A wee thing, she came no higher than his chest. She'd pulled off her hat, and he could see hair the color of straw that was shorn at a sharp angle and swung at her jaw. Wide blue eyes stood in stark comparison to her fair skin and pixielike features. White, straight teeth worried her full bottom lip, and those large eyes shifted left, then right, trying to see in the dark. She wrapped her slender arms about herself, slowly spun in a circle, and heaved a sigh.

Then she stopped, faced him, and sucked in a startled breath. Her eyes, which appeared to be locked with his, widened to a frightening width, and she swore.

Only then did Gabriel realize the bloody lights had come back on.

She probably thought he was a lunatic.

Slowly she began to back away from him. Her eyes traveled the length of him, and then she glanced behind her, taking a few more hesitant steps.

Damnation, he hadn't meant for her to catch him looking at her so closely. He cocked his head as she continued to walk backward, seemingly toward the front entranceway.

"Why are you dressed like that?" she asked, her voice now barely above a whisper.

Gabriel frowned and glanced down at himself. The conjured image of his modern garb was gone, leaving him in his usual clothes: his plaid, boots, and sword.

He swore.

She turned and ran for the door.

Spirited Away
Cindy Miles

Knight Tristan de Barre and his men were murdered in 1292, their souls cursed to roam Dreadmoor Castle forever.

Forensic archaeologist Andi Monroe is excavating the site and studying the legend of a medieval knight who disappeared. But although she's usually rational, Andi could swear she's met the handsome knight's ghost. Until she finds a way to lift the curse, however, their love doesn't stand a ghost of a chance.

Also Available
MacGowan's Ghost
Into Thin Air